THE SELECTED POETRY OF

BROWNING

THE SELECTED POETRY OF
BROWNING

Edited and with an Introduction
by George M. Ridenour

A MERIDIAN BOOK

NEW AMERICAN LIBRARY

NEW YORK AND SCARBOROUGH, ONTARIO

Copyright © 1966 by George M. Ridenour

This book previously appeared in a Signet Classic edition
published by New American Library.

Library of Congress Cataloging in Publication Data: 84-61147

 MERIDIAN TRADEMARK REG. U.S. PAT. OFF. AND FOREIGN COUNTRIES
REG. TRADEMARK—MARCA REGISTRADA
HECHO EN FAIRFIELD, PA., U.S.A.

SIGNET, SIGNET CLASSIC, MENTOR, PLUME, MERIDIAN
and NAL BOOKS are published *in the United States*
by New American Library, 1633 Broadway, New York,
New York 10019, *in Canada* by The New American Library
of Canada Limited, 81 Mack Avenue, Scarborough,
Ontario M1L 1M8

First Meridian Printing, September, 1984

1 2 3 4 5 6 7 8 9

PRINTED IN THE UNITED STATES OF AMERICA

Table of Contents

CONTENTS

INTRODUCTION

I will tell
My state as though 'twere none of mine.
　　　　　　Browning, *Pauline*, lines 585–86.
I build on contrasts to discover, above those
contrasts, the harmony of the whole.
　　　　　　Hugo von Hofmannsthal to Richard
　　　　　　Strauss, June 15, 1911.[1]

Robert Browning was born in 1812 of modestly well-to-do parents in a pleasant suburb of London. The only other child was a younger sister, and Robert was easily the main object of attention in the family. He was a spoiled child, who never learned to take opposition with much grace. His father was a mild and bookish man, a clerk in the Bank of England. His mother was Scottish by birth and had been brought up in the Church of Scotland, as her husband had been in the Church of England. Both, however, left the established churches to become Dissenters, and Browning was baptized in an independent chapel, where he was also taken to service. Under the strong influence of his mother, who was very pious, Browning acquired that part of the "Dissenting conscience" that stresses the value of individual moral decision and of a personal and immediate relationship with God. The social aspects of this conscience were less highly developed in

1 *A Working Friendship: The Correspondence between Richard Strauss and Hugo von Hofmannsthal,* Trans. Hanns Hammelmann and Ewald Osers (New York: William Collins Sons & Co., Ltd., 1961), p. 90.

him. But Browning was always fiercely Protestant, even
when he was not especially Christian.

Browning grew up largely by himself, finding compan-
ions in his family, in pets, and in the great number of
books he read from his father's large library. His contacts
with school were brief and not very satisfactory, and his
formal education came largely from private tutors and,
perhaps, his father. A try at university life, in the newly
established University of London, was soon abandoned,
and Browning continued to live with his parents, sup-
ported by his father, until his marriage in 1846.

The circumstances of his bringing up were certainly in-
strumental in developing that "clear consciousness/Of
self, distinct from all its qualities" that the young man—
with perplexity, pride, and dismay—recognized as central
to his character. His problem was what to make of so
energetic an ego.

In his poem *Pauline* (published 1833), where he first
defined the problem as he understood it, Browning goes
on to consider two further "elements" of his character that
served as checks on his consuming selfhood. The first is
his power of imagination and the second his yearning
after God. His imagination is an "angel" to him that sus-
tains "a soul with such desire/Confined to clay." ("Clay"
is an obsessive word with Byron, and its use here reminds
us that Browning's early poems—destroyed by their au-
thor—were supposed to be in the manner of Byron, whom
Browning is recalling, along with Shelley, in *Pauline*.
There is strong influence of Byron's "Dream.") It enables
him to master his "dark past." But the imagination itself
poses problems of direction and control which are solved
by the premise of a divine Love which presents itself to
him as goal and as surrounding presence. The forces
united for the boy in the myths of ancient Greece, which
enabled his ego to exercise itself healthfully in imaginings
of godlike life, and these early experiences of integration
remain to some extent normative for him. It is experience
of this sort he wants to regain as he addresses himself in
Pauline to more radical representatives of imagination and
religion—Shelley and Christ. It is this he seeks also from

the woman Pauline, with her all-encompassing love, who is also the muse of the poem. (It was something very like this that he found in his love for his wife, a woman of deep piety and a poet.)

A similar view is presented sequentially in the speech of the dying Paracelsus, in Browning's drama of that name, defining a progression from the most primitive form of being to man, and from man to God. Two traditions have been traced by scholars here. There is that of man as the culmination of all lower forms, moving steadily toward God, and taking the whole creation with him into the divine life, which Browning might have been more likely to know in an occult version, though it is found in orthodoxy. And there is the more narrowly eighteenth-century tradition of plenitude and the chain of being that may, I suggest, have some obligation to James Thomson, author of *The Seasons*.

> By swift degrees the love of nature works,
> And warms the bosom; till at last, sublimed
> To rapture and enthusiastic heat,
> We feel the present Deity, and take
> The joy of God to see a happy world.
>
> (*Spring,* lines 899–903)
>
> God is ever present, ever felt,
> In the void waste as in the city full,
> And where he vital spreads there be joy.
>
> ("Hymn to the Seasons," lines 105–7) [2]

The two traditions unite in *Paracelsus* V, 641–47, where the hero claims to have known

> what God is, what we are,
> What life is—how God tastes an infinite joy
> In infinite ways—one everlasting bliss,
> From whom all being emanates, all power
> Proceeds; in whom is life for evermore,
> Yet whom existence in its lowest form
> Includes; where dwells enjoyment there is he.

[2] Browning remembers the last line of the "Hymn" in a letter to Kegan Paul, July 15, 1881.

Browning's combination of the two traditions presents a view that is in effect anticipatory of Teilhard de Chardin's vision of an unbroken progression from the geological to the biological to the mental, and on to the divine, each stage once manifest revealing its implicit presence in all preceding stages.

The vision of Paracelsus does not in itself, however, provide means for its implementation in other kinds of poem. It was only after years of attempts at writing a successful play for the stage that Browning fully developed the form of the dramatic monologue, brought to its maturity in the two volumes of *Men and Women* of 1855. Through this succession of self-preoccupied egoists, engaged in existential defense of the being each has made for himself, Browning, as J. Hillis Miller has pointed out, is able both to exercise his own ego and "get out of himself" by objectifying his drive to egoistic self-assertion in the creation of fictional characters. When we have noticed that in the course of their self-revelation they further reveal in their personal situation, directly or indirectly, the intensely Protestant version of the Incarnation that was Browning's governing myth, we can see how the monologues meet the demands of the earlier poems.

Browning's speakers in the monologues are apt to be persons of extremes in extreme situations. Even so winning a character as Lippo Lippi has something grotesque about him and displays an element of the pathologically self-dramatizing, in excess of what might be ascribed to the demands of the form. But like Dostoyevsky or the early Wordsworth, Browning uses his strange or abnormal types to dramatize what he regards as centrally human, which can be seen in these cases with especial clarity. In the following lines, for example, in which Fra Lippo lists the subjects of his first attempts as painter, he reveals not only his own personal situation but that of all men as Browning sees it:

> First, every sort of monk, the black and white,
> I drew them, fat and lean; then, folk at church,
> From good old gossips waiting to confess

Their cribs of barrel-droppings, candle-ends—
To the breathless fellow at the altar-foot,
Fresh from his murder, safe and sitting there
With the little children round him in a row
Of admiration, half for his beard and half
For that white anger of his victim's son
Shaking a fist at him with one fierce arm,
Signing himself with the other because of Christ
(Whose sad face on the cross sees only this
After the passion of a thousand years)
Till some poor girl, her apron o'er her head,
(Which the intense eyes looked through) came at eve
On tiptoe, said a word, dropped in a loaf,
Her pair of earrings and a bunch of flowers
(The brute took growling), prayed, and so was gone.

                                    (lines 145–62)

Here he elaborates the pictorial qualities implicit in the scene of the breathless murderer, the admiring children, the frustrated vindictiveness of the victim's son, and the girl's thankless devotion to the criminal—passions that arrange themselves by their inherent forces of attraction and repulsion into a satisfying composition. The picture is "placed" against another genre, that of the Man of Sorrows on the Cross. It is the world of the painting that Lippo is presented as gaining for art, but he himself sees it as under the judgment of the second, more traditional and more static mode. The exhibition of nonmoral human energies, however fine, asks the complement of the image of the dying God. The assimilation of the world of the painting into art has the effect of censuring it as life, but also, since the censor gains much of his authority by his presence to us in art, of encouraging us to enjoy the beauty produced by intense experience of any kind.

It must be confessed, however, that our main impression from the passage is less one of harmony than of competing claims that are hard to choose between, and the feeling grows that Browning's aim as a poet in the Romantic tradition is to devise forms in which the elements of reality as he experiences it may be contemplated as unified. (There seems to be at least a shift in emphasis in the development of Browning's poetry from problems of internal integration to those of perceiving reality itself as an integrated whole.) The list of attempted unions is imposing: power and love, love and knowledge, knowledge and power, imagination and reason, self and not-self, conscious and unconscious, spirit and matter, natural and supernatural, lyric and discursive, verse and prose. His attempts may usefully be broken down into at least four major types: the personal, the typical, the mythic, and the analytic. We may take "Fra Lippo Lippi" as representing the first, the vision of the dramatic monologues, where divisions are overcome in living, or which point toward harmony ironically through the dissonances of the speaker's life. The typical, mythic, and analytic modes, while not inherently more valuable, are in some ways harder to grasp, and it may be helpful to pay special attention to them. The modes will be examined by means of comment on poems drawn, like "Fra Lippo Lippi," from the great work of Browning's middle period, the *Men and Women* of 1855.

What I have called the typical mode may be seen most clearly in "Childe Roland to the Dark Tower Came." It is this typicality that causes our uneasiness in either calling the poem an allegory or in refraining from doing so. The knightly quest lends itself easily to allegorical treatment, because we are all of us looking for something all the time, in all our acts. The formality of the poem also encourages us to think of it as allegorical, even though it is not clear at once what it is allegorical of. This is especially striking since the allegorical mode invites simple and mechanical equation between the contents of the work and the world of values outside it. (This is true of even so refined a work as *The Faerie Queene,* as in the head-verses to the separate cantos. Though the poem is not limited to these crude equations, they influence our understanding of the dense and irreducible materials of the poem proper.) The allegory of "Childe Roland," in other words, is strangely self-contained, turning back on itself, so that the "allegoricalness" of the poem calls attention to itself as part of the meaning.

To shift the terms, allegory is apt to be strikingly rational and subrational, presenting a moral and conceptual organizing of the materials of fantasy; the moral will enters into close union with fierce unconscious drives. In Browning's poem the relations between the two elements are uncommonly problematic. This also tends to turn our attention into the poem in a manner unexpected in allegory, while we are still expecting the poem to fulfil its implied promise to be allegorical of something. One might be tempted to say, then, that the poem is an allegory of allegorizing (with Hawthorne's *Scarlet Letter* as partial analogy). But this would be too narrow, since the allegorical element is a metaphor of our attempts at directing our acts and at understanding them as purposive. It serves to represent the element of moral will in our acts and our understanding of those acts as directed by the moral will. It corresponds to our attempts, that is, at acting humanly for human goals—as "knights." The poem understood in this way becomes an allegory of what is involved in apparently purposeful human acts. It is "typical" of them.

Since the *geste* of Browning's knight is largely a trial by landscape, it may be useful to examine the handling of landscape in another poem, published in the same volume but apparently written later. In "Two in the Campagna" a woman speaks of her inability to love completely and constantly the man she addresses. She loves him only so much and for only so long. Her confession is placed against the reaches of the Roman Campagna, on a May morning.

> The champaign with its endless fleece
>   Of feathery grasses everywhere!
> Silence and passion, joy and peace,
>   An everlasting wash of air—
> Rome's ghost since her decease.
>
> Such life here, through such lengths of hours,
>   Such miracles performed in play,
> Such primal naked forms of flowers,
>   Such letting nature have her way
> While heaven looks from its towers.
>
> (lines 21–30)

The setting suggests, through its vast extent, vast ranges of possibility, and the impression is reinforced by the burgeoning life of early spring. At the same time, however, it suggests immedicable solitude and a tendency in the nature of things for life to squander itself, dispersedly, to no effect:

> Must I go
> Still like the thistle-ball, no bar,
> Onward, whenever light winds blow,
> Fixed by no friendly star?
>
> (lines 52–55)

Man's state and nature's correspond in their interplay of possibility and restriction, freedom and slavery: "Nor yours nor mine, nor slave nor free!" But the emphasis is on defeat.

These passages should recall the landscape of "Childe Roland":

> For mark! no sooner was I fairly found
> Pledged to the plain, after a pace or two,
> Than, pausing to throw backward a last view
> O'er the safe road, 'twas gone; gray plain all round;
> Nothing but plain to the horizon's bound.
> I might go on; naught else remained to do.
>
> (lines 49–54)

Here the extent of plain works similarly, with important differences. The possibilities are as great, the limitations more oppressive, and we get a feeling of stuffiness in a wide expanse. This reflects the mingled purposefulness and purposelessness, will and compulsion in the mind of the knight. But the effect is different from that of the landscape in "Two in the Campagna." The vast and monotonous spaces, as well as their painful contents, diminish, to be sure, the single human being who acts in them, but also "enlarge" him, extend his range, ennoble him. The impression is rather that of Burke's "sublime," with its vision of infinite possibility rising from experience of pain and monotony.[3] "Childe Roland" would seem, then, to celebrate the value of man's acts as he blunders doggedly toward goals which are both commonplace and unique:

> The round squat turret, blind as the fool's heart,
> Built of brown stone, without a counterpart
> In the whole world.
>
> (lines 182–84)

The mythic mode is in some ways similar to what I have called the typical, but the differences are important enough to make distinction worthwhile. The main difference is that the mythic mode attaches its action not merely to a central and recurring form of human experience, but to such a form as shaped and celebrated by the imagination of the race. A version of this is found in "The Heretic's Tragedy," which is presented as "a glimpse from the burning of Jacques du Bourg-Molay, at Paris, A.D. 1314; as distorted by the refraction from Flemish brain to brain, during the course of a couple of centuries." Jacques du Bourg-Molay had been grand master of the Order of the Knights Templar and was burned at the stake for reasons apparently more secular than religious. But he had been formally convicted of crimes against the faith, and was burned as a heretic.

The first thing to be noticed is Browning's emphasis on the fact that the event dealt with in the poem has been *distorted* as the account of it has passed down orally over a long period of time. It has been distorted by the un-Christian hatred of the pious Christians who cherished the tradition and handed it on, constantly sharpening in their account the hateful elements in it. By the time represented by the composition of the poem, the impiety of the victim has been made so grotesque as to be incredible. We re-

[3] The use of landscape in these poems looks back to Shelley's in "Julian and Maddalo" and forward to Swinburne's in "On the Downs." (Geoffrey Hartman, in his *Wordsworth's Poetry 1787–1814* [New Haven: Yale University Press, 1964], pp. 118–25, discusses the landscape of *Salisbury Plain* in similar terms. The influence of Burke—or of the tradition he represents—is surely present in Wordsworth's poem.)

spect Jacques du Bourg-Molay because he is hated so
violently by persons of so little moral perception.

But the effect of this malice is not merely to discredit
the speakers and to honor the victim. The distortion is also
clarifying. The corrosive hatred of the generations of faith-
ful has burned away the accidents of the situation, leaving
only an archetype which condemns them still more radi-
cally. What one sees in the situation of the master of the
Temple, as simplified by hate, suggests typically the state
of charity, burning in the flames of love (cf. John of the
Cross's *Burning Flame of Love*), and mythically the suf-
fering Master on the cross, exalted by the hatred of his
executioners. The imagination will tell the truth, it seems,
whatever the intent of the imaginer, even as the imagina-
tions of Lippo Lippi, Childe Roland, and the singers of
"The Heretic's Tragedy" reveal not merely themselves but
permanent forms of truth as the imagination knows them.

The analytic mode, as its name suggests, breaks down
experience into its separate elements and examines possi-
bilities of interrelationship. All of the poems so far exam-
ined have done this to some extent, but there are poems
that set about doing just this. The classical analytic work,
in this sense, would be Cervantes' *Don Quixote,* read from
a perspectivist viewpoint (i.e., as acting out relationships
between the opposed but complementary world views ex-
pressed in the figures of Don Quixote and Sancho Panza).
Closer to Browning in some ways would be Euripides, his
favorite Greek dramatist, who gives many examples of
"scenes where a situation is realized first in its lyric, then
in its iambic aspect—that is to say, first emotionally, then
in its reasoned form."[4] There is a good example in the
Alcestis, which Browning himself translated, in which
Alcestis, dying, celebrates her death and its meaning in
song, and then argues it out argumentatively. Euripides
"has simply juxtaposed these two aspects of Alcestis'
parting from life, rather than leave either incomplete."[5]
And though Browning, as A. M. Dale points out, tries to

---

[4] A. M. Dale, in the commentary to her edition of Euripides' *Alcestis*
(N.Y.: Oxford University Press, 1954), p. 74.
[5] Dale, pp. 74–75.

ground the argument psychologically in his rendering of the scene, the comparison is still useful.

There is a still closer resemblance, however, to works by the modern German poet and dramatist Hugo von Hofmannsthal, especially in texts for operas by Richard Strauss. This is especially striking in *Ariadne auf Naxos,* in which the oppositions of kinds of love and views of life —generally, tragic (in Ariadne) and comic (in Zerbinetta)—are united both ironically (as Hofmannsthal partly understood) and actually (as he apparently did not grasp) through qualities inherent in all love, and through the "harmony" of Strauss's score. The two points of view expose their weaknesses and strengths, their kinds of opposition and union, within the reconciling medium of music.[6]

It is this last, the use of music to define oppositions which are at the same time harmonized, that reminds one most vividly of Browning, whose poems on music attempt something very similar. If you are worried, as Browning often was, about the relation between fact and value, mind and heart, reason and imagination—summed up generally as an opposition between fact and fancy—music can be very helpful. A musical statement can be more abstract than anything in language and still more sensuous than language can ever be. This may give it a unique closeness to reality and at the same time a quality of remoteness, spirituality, fancifulness. Furthermore, it helps us see the two terms as interchangeable: the abstract pole may suggest both reason and unreality, the sensuous both concrete fact and imaginative sentiment. In more formal terms, either pole may suggest comedy or tragedy, poetry or prose.

Browning's finest achievement in this mode is probably "A Toccata of Galuppi's." Among the oppositions to

---

6 Browning's drama *Colombe's Birthday* suggests a Hofmannsthal libretto in the manner of *Rosenkavalier,* anticipating some of Hofmannsthal's favorite themes. The opposition of moods or types of personality is found also in the Eusebius-Florestan contrast in Schumann, e.g., the "Papillons" (as also in Handel's setting of Milton's "L'Allegro-Il Penseroso"). It appears in another form, based on Jean Paul's *Flegeljahre,* in Schumann's "Carnival," which Browning cites in *Fifine at the Fair,* one of his virtuoso works in the analytic mode.

be worked with here is that between eighteenth-century Italy and nineteenth-century England, as well as that between the "scientist" who speaks and the composer who answers. But it is the scientist who is inclined to put stress on value and the composer whose view is cold and analytic, chilling to the inhabitant of a century that is more humane and less elegant. The scientist's union of fancy and fact is unstable, and Galuppi has denied fancy in the name of fact, though his analysis is carried on in a mode that is itself an expression of fancy—i.e., through art. The main agent of union is the composer's clavichord piece, which both includes and is included by the speech of the scientist.

Within the culture that produced the musical form there are grave differences of caste and point of view, brought out by the relations between Galuppi and his audience. They are aristocrats and he a superior servant; their preoccupation with sexual conquest is the object of his rationalistic contempt. But both rationalism and sensuality are part of the period style, as formalized in its music, and the aristocratic audience is not wholly deceived in enjoying it. Furthermore, they find in Galuppi's art a compassion and solace the composer surely did not intend, but which is built into the formal qualities of the music, since it is in support of human purposes that all art inherently subsists.[7] The music, accordingly, in its expression of the central qualities of its period, is not limited by the points of view of artist or audience. The style at the same time separates and unites within its own period as well as between periods. It is in doing the first that it is able to do the second.

The identification of mode is largely on the basis of relative emphasis. It is useful to notice that a particular poem is engaged in a certain kind of activity with special concentration, but that does not mean that it is not doing other things too. "Fra Lippo Lippi" is primarily an expression of a personal state; both problems and ways of

[7] See my account of "Flute Music: with an Accompaniment" in "Browning's Music Poems: Fancy and Fact," *PMLA*, LXXVIII (1963), 369–377, pp. 372–73.

handling them are developed in terms of a vividly realized individual personality. But there are strong elements of other modes. The poem is analytic in its reduction of the problem to a competition between opposed areas of value, typical in that the state is seen as that of all men. In the same way, "Childe Roland" has a strong mythic side, as well as displaying analytic and personal aspects, and "The Heretic's Tragedy" reveals an important typical strain, as was noted in the analysis of the poem. "Galuppi" alone of the poems examined seems to be overwhelmingly in one mode, though even here there are elements of the personal and perhaps the typical.

None of this lessens the value of noticing, however, that all of these strains are united with especial force and clarity in Browning's longest and most ambitious work. *The Ring and the Book* is in this as in other ways the climax of Browning's career. *The Ring and the Book* makes a great point of the claim that it is true, and it is largely in terms of the modes I have defined that this claim is substantiated. (From the point of view of literary history, there are two main traditions of works that claim to be true and build this claim into themselves as part of their meaning.[8] There is the analytic tradition of which *Don Quixote* is exemplary, as we have seen. Works in this tradition often claim to be "true to nature." The other tradition is the mythic, represented by *Paradise Lost,* which claims to be true because the myth it enacts is true. These traditions meet in *The Ring and the Book.*)

In exploring possible relationships between the antitheses it includes, a work in the analytic mode might discover that the opposed elements fit without reduction into mythic form. This is what happens in *The Ring and the Book,* which attempts a sweeping transformation of brutal fact into ideal fancy. In terms of the four modes, *The Ring and the Book* is typical both ironically and unironi-

8 This is to leave out of account such relatively simple forms as the philosophic-didactic and satiric modes, the usually less problematic modes of reportorial realism and of "sincerity," as well as the complex but more limited "epistemological" mode, in which an act of knowing is enacted in such a way as to be, presumably, self-verifying (e.g., Shelley's "Mont Blanc").

cally. Ironically, it is a typical story of intrigue, adultery, revenge, enacting a recurrent pattern in human affairs. But the irony stems from the fact that it is unironically typical in very different terms, as a type of the action of divine love. Mythically, it reenacts the scandal of a manifestation of the divine in the sordid story of a Jewish wife who bore a child not conceived by her husband, as told by Luke. Analytically, it sees in the unlikely materials of the murder story both a clear opposition between the competing claims of fancy and fact and possibilities of overcoming the division. And both oppositions and possibilities of union are developed in terms of real human beings we are made to care about.

The general outlines of the story are clear enough, and I give it in Browning's own normative account, in the first book, since all of the other accounts given in the course of the poem are to be understood as modulations of this:

> Count Guido Franceschini the Aretine,
> Descended of an ancient house, though poor,
> A beak-nosed bushy-bearded black-haired lord,
> Lean, pallid, low of stature yet robust,
> Fifty years old—having four years ago
> Married Pompilia Comparini, young,
> Good, beautiful, at Rome, where she was born,
> And brought her to Arezzo, where they lived
> Unhappy lives, whatever curse the cause—
> This husband, taking four accomplices,
> Followed this wife to Rome, where she was fled
> From their Arezzo to find peace again,
> In convoy, eight months earlier, of a priest,
> Aretine also, of still nobler birth,
> Giuseppe Caponsacchi—caught her there
> Quiet in a villa on a Christmas night,
> With only Pietro and Violante by,
> Both her putative parents;[9] killed the three,
> Aged, they, seventy each, and she, seventeen
> And, two weeks since, the mother of his babe

9 The parents are described as "putative" because Violante claimed that she had bought the child from a prostitute, unknown to Paolo.

Firstborn and heir to what the style was worth
O' the Guido who determined, dared and did
This deed just as he purposed point by point.

In this first account, Browning is careful to label Pom-
pilia explicitly as good and to make it pretty clear that
for reasons as yet not understood, she was right in what
she did and that Guido was wrong. He points up the
pathos of the ages of the victims and of the fact that Pom-
pilia was a mother of two weeks. It is less that he is unsure
of the self-validating nature of truth or of his own ability
to present it adequately than that he does not trust us to
read correctly without help. He is conscious of the experi-
mental nature of his poem, and he is not sure that we will
be able to keep our bearings. The story of the murder will
be told again and again, from different points of view.
Some of these, such as the speeches of the "three halves"
of Rome, of the lawyers, and of Guido, are exercises in
dramatic irony, in which the speaker betrays himself and
his own weaknesses, and in doing so makes clear the sense
in which, in his version, the truth is being distorted. This
is to help us see what then the truth is. In the case of
Caponsacchi and, especially, Pompilia, deductions for per-
sonal limitations are minimal. What distortion there is
tends to be a reflection of their own goodness. And the
Pope, it is clear, is presented as entirely authoritative. It
is in his vision, Browning would have it, that the truth
revealed in the other accounts is contemplated as such,
is defined and judged. For "the joke" is that the perplexed
circumstances and multiple accounts do not, as we might
expect, lead to relativism and an inability to make clear
moral judgments, but to a polarizing of the issues into
choices between radical good and radical evil, clearly rec-
ognizable as such.

It is in the speech of the Pope that all of the modes
defined in this introduction manifest themselves with spe-
cial clarity: typical in the enactment of the archetype of
moral judgment; analytic in the understanding of the rela-
tion between unlikely fact and fanciful actuality; mythic
in its integration of the life and death of Pompilia into

that of Christ; personal in its depiction of a rich human being to whom we respond, and in whose personality, as we experience it, the problems raised by the work are persuasively resolved. And it is finally on the personal level, no doubt, that the poem justifies itself, in the vitality of the human beings whose lives raise the issues and offer ways of dealing with them.

It may also be at this level that it is most vulnerable. There is a cold-blooded ferocity in the handling of Guido, for example, by both Caponsacchi and the Pope that has some of the effect of the hatred of the singers of "The Heretic's Tragedy," without, in this case, the excuse of intentional irony. We are to take it all at the speaker's evaluation, and admire the speaker all the more for it. For many readers this may be hard to do. The tone is that of Browning himself at his most viciously self-righteous. It reflects a failing rather common in Browning, who had great faith in the poetic value of his own sentiments.

This weakness is increasingly evident in the volumes that follow *The Ring and the Book,* which tend to impress one as exercises in perversity or as lazy thinking in casual verse. There is nothing comparable to the rich harmonies attained by works of the middle period. Only rarely, as in "La Saisiaz," is he able to integrate argument into an imagined whole, and his success here is precarious. There are brilliant individual pieces in these later books, such as the stunning "Thamuris Marching," or some lyrics of surprising sharpness, but they must be sought out. This makes the success of his final volume, *Asolando,* all the more remarkable and gratifying. While it does not suggest the mellow old age of a Titian or Verdi—it is too thin for that —it is charming and in its way impressive. Browning takes up again his lifetime's preoccupation with "Fancies and Facts" (the subtitle of the volume), and announces his choice in the Prologue of "The naked very thing." But a world so seen is more magical, and not less, in that it points to a transcendent reality beyond itself (in the last lines of the Prologue) and that as our vision of fact becomes clearer, the more clearly we see it encompass the values of fancy (in "Flute Music," or "Development").

The tone of the book is one of delighted acceptance, the manner engagingly playful. It is a fitting *vivace*-finale to Browning's life's work.

The contents of the anthology reflect the belief that while Browning was at his best in works of some length, the sheer mass of his production can blunt the impact of his finest poems. I have chosen therefore to present fewer poems than might be expected in a collection of this length, and to give preference to longer poems of high quality. The old favorites are well represented, but the emphasis is on the Browning that seems to be taking shape for us at present.

GEORGE M. RIDENOUR
University of New Mexico

A GENERAL NOTE
ON THE TEXT

The overall textual policy for the Signet Classic Poetry series attempts to strike a balance between the convenience and dependability of total modernization, on the one hand, and the authenticity of an established text on the other. Starting with the Restoration and Augustan poets, the General Editor has set up the following guidelines for the individual editors:

Modern American spelling will be used, although punctuation may be adjusted by the editor of each volume when he finds it advisable. In any case, syllabic final "ed" will be rendered with grave accent to distinguish it from the silent one, which is written out without apostrophe (e.g., "to gild refinèd gold," but "asked" rather than "ask'd"). Archaic words and forms are to be kept, naturally, whenever the meter or the sense may require it.

In the case of poets from earlier periods, the text is more clearly a matter of the individual editor's choice, and the type and degree of modernization has been left to his decision. But, in any event, archaic typographical conventions ("i," "j," "u," "v," etc.) have all been normalized in the modern way.

JOHN HOLLANDER

A NOTE ON THIS EDITION

The poems are arranged in the order of their appearance in the volume in which they were first collected. The text is that prepared by the poet shortly before his death, which appeared in seventeen volumes in 1888–89. The spelling has been made to conform generally to modern American practice. Little attempt has been made to correct the pointing of Browning's text, which is often rhetorically effective, though the careful reader may suspect that a few passages are incorrectly punctuated.

GEORGE M. RIDENOUR

CHRONOLOGY

1812	May 7. Robert Browning born in Camberwell, a London suburb.
ca. 1820–1826	At boarding school near his home, where he spent weekends.
ca. 1824	His parents try unsuccessfully to find a publisher for his first collection of poems, called *Incondita* (i.e., irregular or confused pieces), presumably imitations, especially of Byron. The volume was destroyed by its author, and only two poems have been preserved.
ca. 1826	First reading of Shelley.
1828	Enrolls in newly opened University of London, but does not complete the first year.
1833	March. *Pauline,* paid for by his aunt. No copies sold.
1835	August. *Paracelsus,* paid for by his father.
1836	May. William Macready, the actor, asks Browning to write him a tragedy, stimulating Browning's attempt of ten years at writing a successful drama for the stage.
1837	May. *Strafford,* an historical drama. Four performances.
1838	Short visit to Italy.
1840	March. *Sordello.*
1841	April. *Pippa Passes.* This is the first of eight pamphlets that make up the series Browning called *Bells and Pomegranates.* They were paid for by his father. (Browning published

six other dramas in this series which will not
be taken note of here.)

1842   November. *Dramatic Lyrics,* in which he de-
velops the form of the dramatic monologue.
(*Bells and Pomegranates,* No. III.)

1844   Fall. Leisurely tour of Italy.
Publication of *Poems* by Elizabeth Barrett.

1845   January 10. "I love your verses with all my
heart," he writes to Miss Barrett, adding
later, "and I love you too." But Miss Barrett
was an invalid watched over by a father who
had determined that none of his children
should marry.
November. *Dramatic Romances and Lyrics*
(*Bells and Pomegranates,* No. VII).

1846   September 12. Marries Elizabeth Barrett
without her father's knowledge. The next
week they elope to the continent, stopping
in Pisa.

1847   April. Settle in Florence, in Casa Guidi, their
home during the rest of their life together.

1849   March. Birth of son, Robert Wiedemann Bar-
rett Browning, followed shortly afterwards
by the death of Browning's mother.

1850   April. *Christmas Eve and Easter Day.*

1855   November. *Men and Women.*

1860   June. Discovers the "Old Yellow Book," from
which *The Ring and the Book* is to develop,
in a bookstall in Florence.

1861   June 29. Death of Mrs. Browning.
October. With his son in London, where he
takes a house.

1864   May. *Dramatis Personae.*

1868–   *The Ring and the Book.* Published in four
1869   separate volumes in separate months.

1871–   *Balaustion's Adventure, Prince Hohenstiel-*
1876   *Schwangau, Fifine at the Fair, Red Cotton
Nightcap Country, Aristophanes' Apology,
The Inn Album, Pacchiarotto and How he
Worked in Distemper.*

1878	First visit to Italy after his wife's death.
	May. *La Saisiaz: The Two Poets of Croisic* (one volume).
1879	April. First series of *Dramatic Idyls*.
1880	June. Second series of *Dramatic Idyls*.
1883– 1887	*Jocoseria, Ferishtah's Fancies, Parleyings with Certain People of Importance in their Day.*
1889	December 12. *Asolando* published. Browning dies in Venice the evening of the same day, after hearing news of its success.
	December 31. Burial in Poet's Corner, Westminster Abbey.

SELECTED BIBLIOGRAPHY

Editions of the Works:

The Complete Works of Robert Browning ("Florentine Edition"), 12 vols., eds. Charlotte Porter and Helen A. Clarke (New York: 1898).

The Works of Robert Browning ("Centenary Edition"), 10 vols., ed. F. G. Kenyon (London: Smith, Elder & Co., 1912).

Letters:

The Letters of Robert Browning and Elizabeth Barrett Browning, 1845–46. 2 vols. (London: 1899).

Letters of Robert Browning, collected by Thomas J. Wise; ed. Thurman L. Hood (New Haven, Conn.: Yale University Press, 1933).

New Letters of Robert Browning, eds. William Clyde DeVane and Kenneth Leslie Knickerbocker (New Haven: Yale University Press, 1950).

Dearest Isa: Robert Browning's Letters to Isabella Blagden, ed. Edward C. McAleer (Austin: University of Texas Press, 1951).

Biographies:

Griffin, W. H. and Minchin, H. C., *The Life of Robert Browning,* third (revised) edition (London: Methuen & Co., Ltd., 1938).

Spiro, Betty Bergson (Mrs. Emanuel Miller), *Robert Browning: A Portrait* (New York: Charles Scribner's Sons, 1953).

Books of Reference:

Cook, A. K., *A Commentary Upon Browning's "The Ring and the Book"* (New York: Oxford University Press, 1920).

DeVane, William C., *A Browning Handbook,* revised ed. (New York: Appleton-Century-Crofts, Inc., 1955).

Criticism:

Cadbury, William, "Lyric and Anti-Lyric Forms: A Method for Judging Browning," *University of Toronto Quarterly,* XXXIV (1964), 49–67.

Charlton, H. B., series of essays in the *Bulletin of the John Rylands Library,* vols. XXII (1938), XXIII (1939), XXVII (1942–43), XXVIII (1944), XXXV (1952–53).

Crowell, Norton B., *The Triple Soul: Browning's Theory of Knowledge* (Albuquerque: University of New Mexico, 1963).

DeVane, William C., "The Virgin and the Dragon," *Yale Review,* XXXVII (1947), 33–46.

Duncan, Joseph E., "The Intellectual Kinship of John Donne and Robert Browning," *Studies in Philology,* L (1953), 81–100.

Hartle, Robert W., "Gide's Interpretation of Browning," *University of Texas Studies in English,* XXVIII (1949), 244–56.

Honan, Park, *Browning's Characters: A Study in Poetic Technique* (New Haven, Conn.: Yale University Press, 1961).

Johnson, E. D. H., *The Alien Vision of Victorian Poetry* (Princeton, New Jersey: Princeton University Press, 1952), pp. 71–143.

——————, "The Pluralistic Universe of Robert Browning," *University of Toronto Quarterly,* XXXI (1961), 20–41.

King, Roma A., *The Bow and the Lyre: The Art of Robert Browning* (Ann Arbor, Mich.: University of Michigan, 1957).

Langbaum, Robert, *The Poetry of Experience: The Dramatic Monologue in Modern Literary Tradition* (London: Chatto & Windus, Ltd., 1957).

Miller, J. Hillis, *The Disappearance of God: Five Nineteenth-Century Writers* (Cambridge, Mass.: Harvard University Press, 1963), pp. 81–156.

Preyer, Robert, "Robert Browning: A Reading of the Early Narratives," *Journal of English Literary History,* XXVI (1959), 531–48.

Raymond, William O., *The Infinite Moment and Other Essays on Robert Browning,* 2nd enlarged ed. (Toronto: University of Toronto Press, 1965).

Ridenour, George M., "Browning's Music Poems: Fancy and Fact," *PMLA,* LXXVIII (1963), 369–77.

Sypher, Wylie, Introduction to edition of *The Ring and the Book* (New York: W. W. Norton & Co., Inc., 1961).

Tracy, C. R., "Browning's Heresies," *Studies in Philology,* XXXIII (1936), 610–25.

Whitla, William, *The Central Truth: The Incarnation in Robert Browning's Poetry* (Toronto: University of Toronto Press, 1963).

PAULINE°

(1883)

PAULINE, mine own, bend o'er me—thy soft breast
Shall pant to mine—bend o'er me—thy sweet eyes,
And loosened hair and breathing lips, and arms
Drawing me to thee—these build up a screen
To shut me in with thee, and from all fear;   5
So that I might unlock the sleepless brood
Of fancies from my soul, their lurking-place,
Nor doubt that each would pass, ne'er to return
To one so watched, so loved and so secured.
But what can guard thee but thy naked love?   10
Ah dearest, whoso sucks a poisoned wound
Envenoms his own veins! Thou art so good,
So calm—if thou shouldst wear a brow less light
For some wild thought which, but for me, were kept
From out thy soul as from a sacred star!   15
Yet till I have unlocked them it were vain
To hope to sing; some woe would light on me;
Nature would point at one whose quivering lip
Was bathed in her enchantments, whose brow burned
Beneath the crown to which her secrets knelt,   20
Who learned the spell which can call up the dead,
And then departed smiling like a fiend

Pauline prefatory mottoes have been omitted.

1 The degree sign (°) indicates a footnote, which is keyed to the
text by line number. Text references are printed in **bold** type; the
annotation follows in roman type.

Who has deceived God—if such one should seek
Again her altars and stand robed and crowned
25 Amid the faithful! Sad confession first,
Remorse and pardon and old claims renewed,
Ere I can be—as I shall be no more.

I had been spared this shame if I had sat
By thee forever from the first, in place
30 Of my wild dreams of beauty and of good,
Or with them, as an earnest of their truth:
No thought nor hope having been shut from thee,
No vague wish unexplained, no wandering aim
Sent back to bind on fancy's wings and seek
35 Some strange fair world where it might be a law;
But, doubting nothing, had been led by thee,
Through youth, and saved, as one at length awaked
Who has slept through a peril. Ah vain, vain!

Thou lovest me; the past is in its grave
40 Though its ghost haunts us; still this much is ours,
To cast away restraint, lest a worse thing
Wait for us in the dark. Thou lovest me;
And thou art to receive not love but faith,
For which thou wilt be mine, and smile and take
45 All shapes and shames, and veil without a fear
That form which music follows like a slave:
And I look to thee and I trust in thee,
As in a Northern night one looks alway
Unto the East for morn and spring and joy.
50 Thou seest then my aimless, hopeless state,
And, resting on some few old feelings won
Back by thy beauty, wouldst that I essay
The task which was to me what now thou art:
And why should I conceal one weakness more?

55 Thou wilt remember one warm morn when winter
Crept aged from the earth, and spring's first breath
Blew soft from the moist hills; the blackthorn boughs,
So dark in the bare wood, when glistening
In the sunshine were white with coming buds,

Like the bright side of a sorrow, and the banks   60
Had violets opening from sleep like eyes.
I walked with thee who knew'st not a deep shame
Lurked beneath smiles and careless words which
    sought
To hide it till they wandered and were mute,
As we stood listening on a sunny mound   65
To the wind murmuring in the damp copse,
Like heavy breathings of some hidden thing
Betrayed by sleep; until the feeling rushed
That I was low indeed, yet not so low
As to endure the calmness of thine eyes.   70
And so I told thee all, while the cool breast
I leaned on altered not its quiet beating:
And long ere words like a hurt bird's complaint
Bade me look up and be what I had been,
I felt despair could never live by thee: 75
Thou wilt remember. Thou art not more dear
Than song was once to me; and I ne'er sung
But as one entering bright halls where all
Will rise and shout for him: sure I must own
That I am fallen, having chosen gifts   80
Distinct from theirs—that I am sad and fain
Would give up all to be but where I was,
Not high as I had been if faithful found,
But low and weak yet full of hope, and sure
Of goodness as of life—that I would lose   85
All this gay mastery of mind, to sit
Once more with them, trusting in truth and love
And with an aim—not being what I am.

Oh Pauline, I am ruined who believed
That though my soul had floated from its sphere   90
Of wild dominion into the dim orb
Of self—that it was strong and free as ever!
It has conformed itself to that dim orb,
Reflecting all its shades and shapes, and now
Must stay where it alone can be adored.   95
I have felt this in dreams—in dreams in which
I seemed the fate from which I fled; I felt

A strange delight in causing my decay.
I was a fiend in darkness chained forever
100 Within some ocean-cave; and ages rolled,
Till through the cleft rock, like a moonbeam, came
A white swan to remain with me; and ages
Rolled, yet I tired not of my first free joy
In gazing on the peace of its pure wings:
105 And then I said "It is most fair to me,
Yet its soft wings must sure have suffered change
From the thick darkness, sure its eyes are dim,
Its silver pinions must be cramped and numbed
With sleeping ages here; it cannot leave me,
110 For it would seem, in light beside its kind,
Withered, though here to me most beautiful."
And then I was a young witch whose blue eyes,
As she stood naked by the river springs,
Drew down a god: I watched his radiant form
115 Growing less radiant, and it gladdened me;
Till one morn, as he sat in the sunshine
Upon my knees, singing to me of Heaven,
He turned to look at me, ere I could lose
The grin with which I viewed his perishing:
120 And he shrieked and departed and sat long
By his deserted throne, but sunk at last
Murmuring, as I kissed his lips and curled
Around him, "I am still a god—to thee."

Still I can lay my soul bare in its fall,
125 Since all the wandering and all the weakness
Will be a saddest comment on the song:
And if, that done, I can be young again,
I will give up all gained, as willingly
As one gives up a charm which shuts him out
130 From hope or part or care in human kind.
As life wanes, all its care and strife and toil
Seem strangely valueless, while the old trees
Which grew by our youth's home, the waving mass
Of climbing plants heavy with bloom and dew,
135 The morning swallows with their songs like words,
All these seem clear and only worth our thoughts:

So, aught connected with my early life,
My rude songs or my wild imaginings,
How I look on them—most distinct amid
The fever and the stir of after years!   *140*

I ne'er had ventured e'en to hope for this,
Had not the glow I felt at His award,°
Assured me all was not extinct within:
His whom all honor, whose renown springs up
Like sunlight which will visit all the world,   *145*
So that e'en they who sneered at him at first,
Come out to it, as some dark spider crawls
From his foul nets which some lit torch invades,
Yet spinning still new films for his retreat.
Thou didst smile, poet, but can we forgive?   *150*

Sun-treader, life and light be thine forever!
Thou art gone from us; years go by and spring
Gladdens and the young earth is beautiful,
Yet thy songs come not, other bards arise,
But none like thee: they stand, thy majesties,   *155*
Like mighty works which tell some spirit there
Hath sat regardless of neglect and scorn,
Till, its long task completed, it hath risen
And left us, never to return, and all
Rush in to peer and praise when all in vain.   *160*
The air seems bright with thy past presence yet,
But thou art still for me as thou hast been
When I have stood with thee as on a throne
With all thy dim creations gathered round
Like mountains, and I felt of mold like them,   *165*
And with them creatures of my own were mixed,
Like things half-lived, catching and giving life.
But thou art still for me who have adored
Though single, panting but to hear thy name
Which I believed a spell to me alone,   *170*
Scarce deeming thou wast as a star to men!
As one should worship long a sacred spring

142 **His award** Shelley's (**Sun-treader** of 151).

Scarce worth a moth's flitting, which long grasses cross,
And one small tree embowers droopingly—
175 Joying to see some wandering insect won
To live in its few rushes, or some locust
To pasture on its boughs, or some wild bird
Stoop for its freshness from the trackless air:
And then should find it but the fountainhead,
180 Long lost, of some great river washing towns
And towers, and seeing old woods which will live
But by its banks untrod of human foot,
Which, when the great sun sinks, lie quivering
In light as some thing lieth half of life
185 Before God's foot, waiting a wondrous change;
Then girt with rocks which seek to turn or stay
Its course in vain, for it does ever spread
Like a sea's arm as it goes rolling on,
Being the pulse of some great country—so
190 Wast thou to me, and art thou to the world!
And I, perchance, half feel a strange regret
That I am not what I have been to thee:
Like a girl one has silently loved long
In her first loneliness in some retreat,
195 When, late emerged, all gaze and glow to view
Her fresh eyes and soft hair and lips which bloom
Like a mountain berry: doubtless it is sweet
To see her thus adored, but there have been
Moments when all the world was in our praise,
200 Sweeter than any pride of after hours.
Yet, sun-treader, all hail! From my heart's heart
I bid thee hail! E'en in my wildest dreams,
I proudly feel I would have thrown to dust
The wreaths of fame which seemed o'erhanging me,
205 To see thee for a moment as thou art.

And if thou livest, if thou lovest, spirit!
Remember me who set this final seal
To wandering thought—that one so pure as thou
Could never die. Remember me who flung
210 All honor from my soul, yet paused and said
"There is one spark of love remaining yet,

For I have nought in common with him, shapes
Which followed him avoid me, and foul forms
Seek me, which ne'er could fasten on his mind;
And though I feel how low I am to him,   215
Yet I aim not even to catch a tone
Of harmonies he called profusely up;
So, one gleam still remains, although the last."
Remember me who praise thee e'en with tears,
For never more shall I walk calm with thee;   220
Thy sweet imaginings are as an air,
A melody some wondrous singer sings,
Which, though it haunt men oft in the still eve,
They dream not to essay; yet it no less
But more is honored. I was thine in shame,   225
And now when all thy proud renown is out,
I am a watcher whose eyes have grown dim
With looking for some star which breaks on him
Altered and worn and weak and full of tears.

Autumn has come like spring returned to us,   230
Won from her girlishness; like one returned
A friend that was a lover, nor forgets
The first warm love, but full of sober thoughts
Of fading years; whose soft mouth quivers yet
With the old smile, but yet so changed and still!   235
And here am I the scoffer, who have probed
Life's vanity, won by a word again
Into my own life—by one little word
Of this sweet friend who lives in loving me,
Lives strangely on my thoughts and looks and words,   240
As fathoms down some nameless ocean thing
Its silent course of quietness and joy.
O dearest, if indeed I tell the past,
May'st thou forget it as a sad sick dream!
Or if it linger—my lost soul too soon   245
Sinks to itself and whispers we shall be
But closer linked, two creatures whom the earth
Bears singly, with strange feelings unrevealed
Save to each other; or two lonely things
Created by some power whose reign is done,   250

Having no part in God or his bright world.
I am to sing whilst ebbing day dies soft,
As a lean scholar dies worn o'er his book,
And in the heaven stars steal out one by one
255 As hunted men steal to their mountain watch.
I must not think, lest this new impulse die
In which I trust; I have no confidence:
So, I will sing on fast as fancies come;
Rudely, the verse being as the mood it paints.

260 I strip my mind bare, whose first elements
I shall unveil—not as they struggled forth
In infancy, nor as they now exist,
When I am grown above them and can rule
But in that middle stage when they were full
265 Yet ere I had disposed them to my will;
And then I shall show how these elements
Produced my present state, and what it is.
I am made up of an intensest life,
Of a most clear idea of consciousness
270 Of self, distinct from all its qualities,
From all affections, passions, feelings, powers;
And thus far it exists, if tracked, in all:
But linked, in me, to self-supremacy,
Existing as a center to all things,
275 Most potent to create and rule and call
Upon all things to minister to it;
And to a principle of restlessness
Which would be all, have, see, know, taste, feel, all—
This is myself; and I should thus have been
280 Though gifted lower than the meanest soul.

And of my powers, one springs up to save
From utter death a soul with such desire
Confined to clay—of powers the only one
Which marks me—an imagination which
285 Has been a very angel, coming not
In fitful visions but beside me ever
And never failing me; so, though my mind
Forgets not, not a shred of life forgets,

Yet I can take a secret pride in calling
The dark past up to quell it regally.   *290*

A mind like this must dissipate itself.
But I have always had one lodestar; now,
As I look back, I see that I have halted
Or hastened as I looked towards that star—
A need, a trust, a yearning after God: *295*
A feeling I have analyzed but late,
But it existed, and was reconciled
With a neglect of all I deemed his laws,
Which yet, when seen in others, I abhorred.
I felt as one beloved, and so shut in   *300*
From fear: and thence I date my trust in signs
And omens, for I saw God everywhere;
And I can only lay it to the fruit
Of a sad after-time that I could doubt
Even his being—e'en the while I felt   *305*
His presence, never acted from myself,
Still trusted in a hand to lead me through
All danger; and this feeling ever fought
Against my weakest reason and resolve.

And I can love nothing—and this dull truth   *310*
Has come the last: but sense supplies a love
Encircling me and mingling with my life.

These make myself: I have long sought in vain
To trace how they were formed by circumstance,
Yet ever found them mold my wildest youth   *315*
Where they alone displayed themselves, converted
All objects to their use: now see their course!

They came to me in my first dawn of life
Which passed alone with wisest ancient books
All halo-girt with fancies of my own;   *320*
And I myself went with the tale—a god
Wandering after beauty, or a giant
Standing vast in the sunset—an old hunter
Talking with gods, or a high-crested chief

325 Sailing with troops of friends to Tenedos.°
I tell you, nought has ever been so clear
As the place, the time, the fashion of those lives:
I had not seen a work of lofty art,
Nor woman's beauty nor sweet nature's face,
330 Yet, I say, never morn broke clear as those
On the dim clustered isles in the blue sea,
The deep groves and white temples and wet caves:
And nothing ever will surprise me now—
Who stood beside the naked Swift-footed,
335 Who bound my forehead with Proserpine's hair.°

And strange it is that I who could so dream
Should e'er have stooped to aim at aught beneath—
Aught low or painful; but I never doubted:
So, as I grew, I rudely shaped my life
340 To my immediate wants; yet strong beneath
Was a vague sense of power though folded up—
A sense that, though those shades and times were past,
Their spirit dwelt in me, with them should rule.

Then came a pause, and long restraint chained down
345 My soul till it was changed. I lost myself,
And were it not that I so loathe that loss,
I could recall how first I learned to turn
My mind against itself; and the effects
In deeds for which remorse were vain as for
350 The wanderings of delirious dream; yet thence
Came cunning, envy, falsehood, all world's wrong
That spotted me: at length I cleansed my soul.
Yet long world's influence remained; and nought
But the still life I led, apart once more,
355 Which left me free to seek soul's old delights,
Could e'er have brought me thus far back to peace.

321–25 **a god . . . Tenedos** rather general allusions to Greek myth.
The *god* is perhaps Apollo. The *giant* is Atlas. Some of the Greek
chiefs stopped at *Tenedos* on their return from Troy.   334–35 **the
naked Swift-footed . . . Proserpine's hair** the god Hermes had winged
feet. He led the souls of the dead to *Proserpine,* queen of the dead.

As peace returned, I sought out some pursuit;
And song rose, no new impulse but the one
With which all others best could be combined.
My life has not been that of those whose heaven   *360*
Was lampless save where poesy shone out;
But as a clime where glittering mountain-tops
And glancing sea and forests steeped in light
Give back reflected the far-flashing sun;
For music (which is earnest of a heaven,   *365*
Seeing we know emotions strange by it,
Not else to be revealed), is like a voice,
A low voice calling fancy, as a friend,
To the green woods in the gay summer time:
And she fills all the way with dancing shapes   *370*
Which have made painters pale, and they go on
Till stars look at them and winds call to them
As they leave life's path for the twilight world
Where the dead gather. This was not at first,
For I scarce knew what I would do. I had   *375*
An impulse but no yearning—only sang.

And first I sang as I in dream have seen
Music wait on a lyrist for some thought,
Yet singing to herself until it came.
I turned to those old times and scenes where all   *380*
That's beautiful had birth for me, and made
Rude verses on them all; and then I paused—
I had done nothing, so I sought to know
What other minds achieved. No fear outbroke
As on the works of mighty bards I gazed,   *385*
In the first joy at finding my own thoughts
Recorded, my own fancies justified,
And their aspirings but my very own.
With them I first explored passion and mind—
All to begin afresh! I rather sought   *390*
To rival what I wondered at than form
Creations of my own; if much was light
Lent by the others, much was yet my own.

I paused again: a change was coming—came:

395 I was no more a boy, the past was breaking
     Before the future and like fever worked.
     I thought on my new self, and all my powers
     Burst out. I dreamed not of restraint, but gazed
     On all things: schemes and systems went and came,
400 And I was proud (being vainest of the weak)
     In wandering o'er thought's world to seek some one
     To be my prize, as if you wandered o'er
     The White Way for a star.

                              And my choice fell
     Not so much on a system as a man—°
405 On one, whom praise of mine shall not offend,
     Who was as calm as beauty, being such
     Unto mankind as thou to me, Pauline—
     Believing in them and devoting all
     His soul's strength to their winning back to peace;
410 Who sent forth hopes and longings for their sake,
     Clothed in all passion's melodies: such first
     Caught me and set me, slave of a sweet task,
     To disentangle, gather sense from song:
     Since, song-inwoven, lurked there words which seemed
415 A key to a new world, the muttering
     Of angels, something yet unguessed by man.
     How my heart leapt as still I sought and found
     Much there, I felt my own soul had conceived,
     But there living and burning! Soon the orb
420 Of his conceptions dawned on me; its praise
     Lives in the tongues of men, men's brows are high
     When his name means a triumph and a pride,
     So, my weak voice may well forbear to shame
     What seemed decreed my fate: I threw myself
425 To meet it, I was vowed to liberty,
     Men were to be as gods and earth as heaven,
     And I—ah, what a life was mine to prove!
     My whole soul rose to meet it. Now, Pauline,
     I shall go mad, if I recall that time!

404 **a man** no doubt Shelley.

Oh let me look back ere I leave forever   430
The time which was an hour one fondly waits
For 'a fair girl that comes a withered hag!
And I was lonely, far from woods and fields,
And amid dullest sights, who should be loose
As a stag; yet I was full of bliss, who lived   435
With Plato and who had the key to life;
And I had dimly shaped my first attempt,
And many a thought did I build up on thought,
As the wild bee hangs cell to cell; in vain,
For I must still advance, no rest for mind.   440

'Twas in my plan to look on real life,
The life all new to me; my theories
Were firm, so them I left, to look and learn
Mankind, its cares, hopes, fears, its woes and joys;
And, as I pondered on their ways, I sought   445
How best life's end might be attained—an end
Comprising every joy. I deeply mused.

And suddenly without heart-wreck I awoke
As from a dream: I said " 'Twas beautiful,
Yet but a dream, and so adieu to it!"   450
As some world-wanderer sees in a far meadow
Strange towers and high-walled gardens thick with
    trees,
Where song takes shelter and delicious mirth
From laughing fairy creatures peeping over,
And on the morrow when he comes to lie   455
Forever 'neath those garden-trees fruit-flushed
Sung round by fairies, all his search is vain.
First went my hopes of perfecting mankind,
Next—faith in them, and then in freedom's self
And virtue's self, then my own motives, ends   460
And aims and loves, and human love went last.
I felt this no decay, because new powers
Rose as old feelings left—wit, mockery,
Light-heartedness; for I had oft been sad,
Mistrusting my resolves, but now I cast   465

Hope joyously away: I laughed and said
"No more of this!" I must not think: at length
I looked again to see if all went well.

My powers were greater: as some temple seemed
470 My soul, where nought is changed and incense rolls
Around the altar, only God is gone
And some dark spirit sitteth in his seat.
So, I passed through the temple and to me
Knelt troops of shadows, and they cried "Hail, king!
475 We serve thee now and thou shalt serve no more!
Call on us, prove us, let us worship thee!"
And I said "Are ye strong? Let fancy bear me
Far from the past!" And I was borne away,
As Arab birds float sleeping in the wind,
480 O'er deserts, towers and forests, I being calm.
And I said "I have nursed up energies,
They will prey on me." And a band knelt low
And cried "Lord, we are here and we will make
Safe way for thee in thine appointed life!
485 But look on us!" And I said "Ye will worship
Me; should my heart not worship too?" They shouted
"Thyself, thou art our king!" So, I stood there
Smiling—oh, vanity of vanities!
For buoyant and rejoicing was the spirit
490 With which I looked out how to end my course;
I felt once more myself, my powers—all mine;
I knew while youth and health so lifted me
That, spite of all life's nothingness, no grief
Came nigh me, I must ever be light-hearted;
495 And that this knowledge was the only veil
Betwixt joy and despair: so, if age came,
I should be left—a wreck linked to a soul
Yet fluttering, or mind-broken and aware
Of my decay. So a long summer morn
500 Found me; and ere noon came, I had resolved
No age should come on me ere youth was spent,
For I would wear myself out, like that morn
Which wasted not a sunbeam; every hour
I would make mine, and die.

And thus I sought

To chain my spirit down which erst I freed   505
For flights to fame: I said "The troubled life
Of genius, seen so gay when working forth
Some trusted end, grows sad when all proves vain—
How sad when men have parted with truth's peace
For falsest fancy's sake, which waited first   510
As an obedient spirit when delight
Came without fancy's call: but alters soon,
Comes darkened, seldom, hastens to depart,
Leaving a heavy darkness and warm tears.
But I shall never lose her; she will live   515
Dearer for such seclusion. I but catch
A hue, a glance of what I sing: so, pain
Is linked with pleasure, for I ne'er may tell
Half the bright sights which dazzle me; but now
Mine shall be all the radiance: let them fade   520
Untold—others shall rise as fair, as fast!
And when all's done, the few dim gleams trans-
      ferred,"—
(For a new thought sprang up how well it were,
Discarding shadowy hope, to weave such lays
As straight encircle men with praise and love,   525
So, I should not die utterly—should bring
One branch from the gold forest, like the knight
Of old tales, witnessing I had been there)—
"And when all's done, how vain seems e'en success—
The vaunted influence poets have o'er men!   530
'Tis a fine thing that one weak as myself
Should sit in his lone room, knowing the words
He utters in his solitude shall move
Men like a swift wind—that though dead and gone,
New eyes shall glisten when his beauteous dreams   535
Of love come true in happier frames than his.
Ay, the still night brings thoughts like these, but morn
Comes and the mockery again laughs out
At hollow praises, smiles allied to sneers;
And my soul's idol ever whispers me   540
To dwell with him and his unhonored song:
And I foreknow my spirit, that would press

First in the struggle, fail again to make
All bow enslaved, and I again should sink."

545 "And then know that this curse will come on us,
To see our idols perish; we may wither,
No marvel, we are clay, but our low fate
Should not extend to those whom trustingly
We sent before into time's yawning gulf
550 To face what dread may lurk in darkness there.
To find the painter's glory pass, and feel
Music can move us not as once, or, worst,
To weep decaying wits ere the frail body
Decays! Nought makes me trust some love is true,
555 But the delight of the contented lowness
With which I gaze on him I keep forever
Above me; I to rise and rival him?
Feed his fame rather from my heart's best blood,
Wither unseen that he may flourish still."
560 Pauline, my soul's friend, thou dost pity yet
How this mood swayed me when that soul found thine,
When I had set myself to live this life,
Defying all past glory. Ere thou camest
I seemed defiant, sweet, for old delights
565 Had flocked like birds again; music, my life,
Nourished me more than ever; then the lore
Loved for itself and all it shows—that king°
Treading the purple calmly to his death,
While round him, like the clouds of eve, all dusk,
570 The giant shades of fate, silently flitting,
Pile the dim outline of the coming doom;
And him° sitting alone in blood while friends
Are hunting far in the sunshine; and the boy°
With his white breast and brow and clustering curls
575 Streaked with his mother's blood, but striving hard

567 **that king** Agamemnon, who on his return from Troy walked on
a purple carpet as he entered his palace, where he was killed by his
queen, Clytemnestra.   572 **him** perhaps Actaeon. While hunting he
came on the goddess Artemis at her bath. The goddess had him
torn apart by his dogs.   573 **the boy** Orestes, son of Agamemnon
and Clytemnestra, who killed his mother to avenge his father's
death and was driven mad by the furies.

To tell his story ere his reason goes.
And when I loved thee as love seemed so oft,
Thou lovedst me indeed: I wondering searched
My heart to find some feeling like such love,
Believing I was still much I had been.   *580*
Too soon I found all faith had gone from me,
And the late glow of life, like change on clouds,
Proved not the morn-blush widening into day,
But eve faint-colored by the dying sun
While darkness hastens quickly. I will tell   *585*
My state as though 'twere none of mine—despair
Cannot come near us—this it is, my state.

Souls alter not, and mine must still advance;
Strange that I knew not, when I flung away
My youth's chief aims, their loss might lead to loss   *590*
Of what few I retained, and no resource
Be left me: for behold how changed is all!
I cannot chain my soul: it will not rest
In its clay prison, this most narrow sphere:
It has strange impulse, tendency, desire,   *595*
Which nowise I account for nor explain,
But cannot stifle, being bound to trust
All feelings equally, to hear all sides:
How can my life indulge them? yet they live,
Referring to some state of life unknown.   *600*

My selfishness is satiated not,
It wears me like a flame; my hunger for
All pleasure, howsoe'er minute, grows pain;
I envy—how I envy him whose soul
Turns its whole energies to some one end,   *605*
To elevate an aim, pursue success
However mean! So, my still baffled hope
Seeks out abstractions; I would have one joy,
But one in life, so it were wholly mine,
One rapture all my soul could fill: and this   *610*
Wild feeling places me in dream afar
In some vast country where the eye can see
No end to the far hills and dales bestrewn

With shining towers and towns, till I grow mad
615 Well-nigh, to know not one abode but holds
Some pleasure, while my soul could grasp the world,
But must remain this vile form's slave. I look
With hope to age at last, which quenching much,
May let me concentrate what sparks it spares.

620 This restlessness of passion meets in me
A craving after knowledge: the sole proof
Of yet commanding will is in that power
Repressed; for I beheld it in its dawn,
The sleepless harpy with just-budding wings,
625 And I considered whether to forego
All happy ignorant hopes and fears, to live,
Finding a recompense in its wild eyes.
And when I found that I should perish so,
I bade its wild eyes close from me forever,
630 And I am left alone with old delights;
See! it lies in me a chained thing, still prompt
To serve me if I loose its slightest bond:
I cannot but be proud of my bright slave.

How should this earth's life prove my only sphere?
635 Can I so narrow sense but that in life
Soul still exceeds it? In their elements
My love outsoars my reason; but since love
Perforce receives its object from this earth
While reason wanders chainless, the few truths
640 Caught from its wanderings have sufficed to quell
Love chained below; then what were love, set free,
Which, with the object it demands, would pass
Reason companioning the seraphim?
No, what I feel may pass all human love
645 Yet fall far short of what my love should be.
And yet I seem more warped in this than aught,
Myself stands out more hideously: of old
I could forget myself in friendship, fame,
Liberty, nay, in love of mightier souls;
650 But I begin to know what thing hate is—
To sicken and to quiver and grow white—

And I myself have furnished its first prey.
Hate of the weak and ever-wavering will,
The selfishness, the still-decaying frame . . .
But I must never grieve whom wing can waft   655
Far from such thoughts—as now. Andromeda!°
And she is with me: years roll, I shall change,
But change can touch her not—so beautiful
With her fixed eyes, earnest and still, and hair
Lifted and spread by the salt-sweeping breeze,   660
And one red beam, all the storm leaves in heaven,
Resting upon her eyes and hair, such hair,
As she awaits the snake on the wet beach
By the dark rock and the white wave just breaking
At her feet; quite naked and alone; a thing   665
I doubt not, nor fear for, secure some god
To save will come in thunder from the stars.
Let it pass! Soul requires another change.
I will be gifted with a wondrous mind,
Yet sunk by error to men's sympathy,   670
And in the wane of life, yet only so
As to call up their fears; and there shall come
A time requiring youth's best energies;
And lo, I fling age, sorrow, sickness off,
And rise triumphant, triumph through decay.   675

And thus it is that I supply the chasm
'Twixt what I am and all I fain would be:
But then to know nothing, to hope for nothing,
To seize on life's dull joys from a strange fear
Lest, losing them, all's lost and nought remains!   680

There's some vile juggle with my reason here;
I feel I but explain to my own loss
These impulses: they live no less the same.
Liberty! what though I despair? my blood
Rose never at a slave's name proud as now.   685
Oh sympathies, obscured by sophistries!—

656 **Andromeda** tied naked to a rock to be sacrificed to a sea mon-
ster, she was rescued by the hero Perseus. Browning is recalling a
print he owned of a painting on the subject.

Why else have I sought refuge in myself,
But from the woes I saw and could not stay?
Love! is not this to love thee, my Pauline?
690 I cherish prejudice, lest I be left
Utterly loveless? witness my belief
In poets, though sad change has come there too;
No more I leave myself to follow them—
Unconsciously I measure me by them—
695 Let me forget it: and I cherish most
My love of England—how her name, a word
Of hers in a strange tongue makes my heart beat!

Pauline, could I but break the spell! Not now—
All's fever—but when calm shall come again,
700 I am prepared: I have made life my own.
I would not be content with all the change
One frame should feel, but I have gone in thought
Through all conjuncture, I have lived all life
When it is most alive, where strangest fate
705 New-shapes it past surmise—the throes of men
Bit by some curse or in the grasps of doom
Half-visible and still-increasing round,
Or crowning their wide being's general aim.
These are wild fancies, but I feel, sweet friend,
710 As one breathing his weakness to the ear
Of pitying angel—dear as a winter flower,
A slight flower growing alone, and offering
Its frail cup of three leaves to the cold sun,
Yet joyous and confiding like the triumph
715 Of a child: and why am I not worthy thee?
I can live all the life of plants, and gaze
Drowsily on the bees that flit and play,
Or bare my breast for sunbeams which will kill,
Or open in the night of sounds, to look
720 For the dim stars; I can mount with the bird
Leaping airily his pyramid of leaves
And twisted boughs of some tall mountain tree,
Or rise cheerfully springing to the heavens;
Or like a fish breathe deep the morning air
725 In the misty sun-warm water; or with flower

And tree can smile in light at the sinking sun
Just as the storm comes, as a girl would look
On a departing lover—most serene.

Pauline, come with me, see how I could build
A home for us, out of the world, in thought!   730
I am uplifted: fly with me, Pauline!

Night, and one single ridge of narrow path
Between the sullen river and the woods
Waving and muttering, for the moonless night
Has shaped them into images of life,   735
Like the uprising of the giant-ghosts,
Looking on earth to know how their sons fare:
Thou art so close by me, the roughest swell
Of wind in the treetops hides not the panting
Of thy soft breasts. No, we will pass to morning—   740
Morning, the rocks and valleys and old woods.
How the sun brightens in the mist, and here,
Half in the air, like creatures of the place,
Trusting the element, living on high boughs
That swing in the wind—look at the silver spray   745
Flung from the foam-sheet of the cataract
Amid the broken rocks! Shall we stay here
With the wild hawks? No, ere the hot noon come,
Dive we down—safe! See this our new retreat
Walled in with a sloped mound of matted shrubs,   750
Dark, tangled, old and green, still sloping down
To a small pool whose waters lie asleep
Amid the trailing boughs turned water-plants:
And tall trees overarch to keep us in,
Breaking the sunbeams into emerald shafts,   755
And in the dreamy water one small group
Of two or three strange trees are got together
Wondering at all around, as strange beasts herd
Together far from their own land: all wildness,
No turf nor moss, for boughs and plants pave all,   760
And tongues of bank go shelving in the lymph,°

761 **lymph** water.

Where the pale-throated snake reclines his head,
And old gray stones lie making eddies there,
765 The wild-mice cross them dry-shod. Deeper in!
Shut thy soft eyes—now look—still deeper in!
This is the very heart of the woods all round
Mountain-like heaped above us; yet even here
One pond of water gleams; far off the river
Sweeps like a sea, barred out from land; but one—
770 One thin clear sheet has overleaped and wound
Into this silent depth, which gained, it lies
Still, as but let by sufferance; the trees bend
O'er it as wild men watch a sleeping girl,
And through their roots long creeping plants outstretch
775 Their twined hair, steeped and sparkling; farther on,
Tall rushes and thick flag-knots have combined
To narrow it; so, at length, a silver thread,
It winds, all noiselessly through the deep wood
Till through a cleft-way, through the moss and stone,
780 It joins its parent-river with a shout.

Up for the glowing day, leave the old woods!
See, they part, like a ruined arch: the sky!
Nothing but sky appears, so close the roots
And grass of the hilltop level with the air—
785 Blue sunny air, where a great cloud floats laden
With light, like a dead whale that white birds pick,
Floating away in the sun in some north sea.
Air, air, fresh life-blood, thin and searching air,
The clear, dear breath of God that loveth us,
790 Where small birds reel and winds take their delight!
Water is beautiful, but not like air:
See, where the solid azure waters lie
Made as of thickened air, and down below,
The fern-ranks like a forest spread themselves
795 As though each pore could feel the element;
Where the quick glancing serpent winds his way,
Float with me there, Pauline!—but not like air.

Down the hill! Stop—a clump of trees, see, set
On a heap of rock, which look o'er the far plain:

So, envious climbing shrubs would mount to rest   *800*
And peer from their spread boughs; wide they wave,
   looking
At the muleteers who whistle on their way,
To the merry chime of morning bells, past all
The little smoking cots, mid fields and banks
And copses bright in the sun. My spirit wanders: *805*
Hedgerows for me—those living hedgerows where
The bushes close and clasp above and keep
Thought in—I am concentrated—I feel;
But my soul saddens when it looks beyond:
I cannot be immortal, taste all joy.   *810*

O God, where do they tend—these struggling aims?°
What would I have? What is this "sleep" which seems
To bound all? can there be a "waking" point
Of crowning life? The soul would never rule;
It would be first in all things, it would have   *815*
Its utmost pleasure filled, but, that complete,
Commanding, for commanding, sickens it.
The last point I can trace is—rest beneath
Some better essence than itself, in weakness;
This is "myself," not what I think should be: *820*
And what is that I hunger for but God?

My God, my God, let me for once look on thee
As though nought else existed, we alone!
And as creation crumbles, my soul's spark
Expands till I can say—Even from myself   *825*
I need thee and I feel thee and I love thee.
I do not plead my rapture in thy works
For love of thee, nor that I feel as one
Who cannot die: but there is that in me
Which turns to thee, which loves or which should love.   *830*

Why have I girt myself with this hell-dress?
Why have I labored to put out my life?
Is it not in my nature to adore,

811 **O God . . . aims?** a long note in French by "Pauline" has been
omitted.

And e'en for all my reason do I not
835 Feel him, and thank him, and pray to him—now?
Can I forego the trust that he loves me?
Do I not feel a love which only ONE . . .
O thou pale form, so dimly seen, deep-eyed!
I have denied thee calmly—do I not
840 Pant when I read of thy consummate power,
And burn to see thy calm pure truths outflash
The brightest gleams of earth's philosophy?
Do I not shake to hear aught question thee?
If I am erring save me, madden me,
845 Take from me powers and pleasures, let me die
Ages, so I see thee! I am knit round
As with a charm by sin and lust and pride,
Yet though my wandering dreams have seen all shapes
Of strange delight, oft have I stood by thee—
850 Have I been keeping lonely watch with thee
In the damp night by weeping Olivet,°
Or leaning on thy bosom, proudly less,
Or dying with thee on the lonely cross,
Or witnessing thine outburst from the tomb.

855 A mortal, sin's familiar friend, doth here
Avow that he will give all earth's reward,
But to believe and humbly teach the faith,
In suffering and poverty and shame,
Only believing he is not unloved.

860 And now, my Pauline, I am thine forever!
I feel the spirit which has buoyed me up
Desert me, and old shades are gathering fast;
Yet while the last light waits, I would say much,
This chiefly, it is gain that I have said
865 Somewhat of love I ever felt for thee
But seldom told; our hearts so beat together
That speech seemed mockery; but when dark hours
    come,
And joy departs, and thou, sweet, deem'st it strange

851 **Olivet** the Mount of Olives, called "weeping" because of Jesus'
agony there before his betrayal by Judas. Luke 22:39 ff.

A sorrow moves me, thou canst not remove,
Look on this lay I dedicate to thee,   870
Which through thee I began, which thus I end,
Collecting the last gleams to strive to tell
How I am thine, and more than ever now
That I sink fast: yet though I deeplier sink,
No less song proves one word has brought me bliss,   875
Another still may win bliss surely back.
Thou knowest, dear, I could not think all calm,
For fancies followed thought and bore me off,
And left all indistinct; ere one was caught
Another glanced; so, dazzled by my wealth,   880
I knew not which to leave nor which to choose,
For all so floated, nought was fixed and firm.
And then thou said'st a perfect bard was one
Who chronicled the stages of all life,
And so thou bad'st me shadow this first stage.   885
'Tis done, and even now I recognize
The shift, the change from last to past—discern
Faintly how life is truth and truth is good.
And why thou must be mine is, that e'en now
In the dim hush of night, that I have done,   890
Despite the sad forebodings, love looks through—
Whispers—E'en at the last I have her still,
With her delicious eyes as clear as heaven
When rain in a quick shower has beat down mist,
And clouds float white above like broods of swans.   895
How the blood lies upon her cheek, outspread
As thinned by kisses! only in her lips
It wells and pulses like a living thing,
And her neck looks like marble misted o'er
With love-breath—a Pauline from heights above,   900
Stooping beneath me, looking up—one look
As I might kill her and be loved the more.

So, love me—me, Pauline, and nought but me,
Never leave loving! Words are wild and weak,
Believe them not, Pauline! I stained myself   905
But to behold thee purer by my side,
To show thou art my breath, my life, a last

Resource, an extreme want: never believe
Aught better could so look on thee; nor seek
910 Again the world of good thoughts left for mine!
There were bright troops of undiscovered suns,
Each equal in their radiant course; there were
Clusters of far fair isles which ocean kept
For his own joy, and his waves broke on them
915 Without a choice; and there was a dim crowd
Of visions, each a part of some grand whole:
And one star left his peers and came with peace
Upon a storm, and all eyes pined for him;
And one isle harbored a sea-beaten ship,
920 And the crew wandered in its bowers and plucked
Its fruits and gave up all their hopes of home;
And one dream came to a pale poet's sleep,
And he said, "I am singled out by God,
No sin must touch me." Words are wild and weak,
925 But what they would express is—Leave me not,
Still sit by me with beating breast and hair
Loosened, be watching earnest by my side,
Turning my books or kissing me when I
Look up—like summer wind! Be still to me
930 A help to music's mystery which mind fails
To fathom, its solution, no mere clue!
O reason's pedantry, life's rule prescribed!
I hopeless, I the loveless, hope and love.
Wiser and better, know me now, not when
935 You loved me as I was. Smile not! I have
Much yet to dawn on you, to gladden you.
No more of the past! I'll look within no more.
I have too trusted my own lawless wants,
Too trusted my vain self, vague intuition—
940 Draining soul's wine alone in the still night,
And seeing how, as gathering films arose,
As by an inspiration life seemed bare
And grinning in its vanity, while ends
Foul to be dreamed of, smiled at me as fixed
945 And fair, while others changed from fair to foul
As a young witch turns an old hag at night.
No more of this! We will go hand in hand,

I with thee, even as a child—love's slave,
Looking no farther than his liege commands.

And thou hast chosen where this life shall be: *950*
The land which gave me thee shall be our home,
Where nature lies all wild amid her lakes
And snow-swathed mountains and vast pines begirt
With ropes of snow—where nature lies all bare,
Suffering none to view her but a race   *955*
Or stinted or deformed,° like the mute dwarfs
Which wait upon a naked Indian queen.
And there (the time being when the heavens are thick
With storm) I'll sit with thee while thou dost sing
Thy native songs, gay as a desert bird   *960*
Which crieth as it flies for perfect joy,
Or telling me old stories of dead knights;
Or I will read great lays to thee—how she,
The fair pale sister,° went to her chill grave
With power to love and to be loved and live: *965*
Or we will go together, like twin gods
Of the infernal world, with scented lamp
Over the dead, to call and to awake,
Over the unshaped images which lie
Within my mind's cave: only leaving all,   *970*
That tells of the past doubt. So, when spring comes
With sunshine back again like an old smile,
And the fresh waters and awakened birds
And budding woods await us, I shall be
Prepared, and we will question life once more,   *975*
Till its old sense shall come renewed by change,
Like some clear thought which harsh words veiled
    before;
Feeling God loves us, and that all which errs
Is but a dream which death will dissipate.
And then what need of longer exile? Seek   *980*
My England, and, again there, calm approach
All I once fled from, calmly look on those

951–56 **The land . . . deformed** Switzerland.   964 **fair pale sister**
presumably Antigone. In Sophocles' tragedy she rejoices at joining
her family in the community of death.

The works of my past weakness, as one views
Some scene where danger met him long before.
985 Ah that such pleasant life should be but dreamed!

But whate'er come of it, and though it fade,
And though ere the cold morning all be gone,
As it may be—though music wait to wile,
And strange eyes and bright wine lure, laugh like sin
990 Which steals back softly on a soul half saved,
And I the first deny, decry, despise,
With this avowal, these intents so fair—
Still be it all my own, this moment's pride!
No less I make an end in perfect joy.
995 E'en in my brightest time, a lurking fear
Possessed me: I well knew my weak resolves,
I felt the witchery that makes mind sleep
Over its treasure, as one half afraid
To make his riches definite: but now
1000 These feelings shall not utterly be lost,
I shall not know again that nameless care
Lest, leaving all undone in youth, some new
And undreamed end reveal itself too late:
For this song shall remain to tell forever
1005 That when I lost all hope of such a change,
Suddenly beauty rose on me again.
No less I make an end in perfect joy,
For I, who thus again was visited,
Shall doubt not many another bliss awaits,
1010 And, though this weak soul sink and darkness whelm,
Some little word shall light it, raise aloft,
To where I clearlier see and better love,
As I again go o'er the tracts of thought
Like one who has a right, and I shall live
1015 With poets, calmer, purer still each time,
And beauteous shapes will come for me to seize,
And unknown secrets will be trusted me
Which were denied the waverer once; but now
I shall be priest and prophet as of old.

1020 Sun-treader, I believe in God and truth

SOLILOQUY OF THE SPANISH CLOISTER

I

GR-R-R—there go, my heart's abhorrence!
　　Water your damned flower-pots, do!
If hate killed men, Brother Lawrence,
　　God's blood, would not mine kill you!
What? your myrtle-bush wants trimming?   *5*
　　Oh, that rose has prior claims—
Needs its leaden vase filled brimming?
　　Hell dry you up with its flames!

II

At the meal we sit together:
　　Salve tibi!° I must hear   *10*
Wise talk of the kind of weather,
　　Sort of season, time of year:
Not a plenteous cork-crop: scarcely
　　Dare we hope oak-galls, I doubt:
What's the Latin name for "parsley"?   *15.*
　　What's the Greek name for Swine's Snout?

III

Whew! We'll have our platter burnished,
　　Laid with care on our own shelf!
With a fire-new spoon we're furnished,
　　And a goblet for ourself,   *20*
Rinsed like something sacrificial
　　Ere 'tis fit to touch our chaps—

10 **Salve tibi!** hail to thee!

Marked with L. for our initial!
　　(He-he! There his lily snaps!)

IV

25　*Saint,* forsooth! While brown Dolores
　　　Squats outside the Convent bank
With Sanchicha, telling stories,
　　　Steeping tresses in the tank,
Blue-black, lustrous, thick like horsehairs,
30　　—Can't I see his dead eye glow,
Bright as 'twere a Barbary corsair's?°
　　　(That is, if he'd let it show!)

V

When he finishes refection,
　　　Knife and fork he never lays
35　Crosswise, to my recollection,
　　　As do I, in Jesu's praise.
I the Trinity illustrate,
　　　Drinking watered orange-pulp—
In three sips the Arian° frustrate;
40　　While he drains his at one gulp.

VI

Oh, those melons? If he's able
　　We're to have a feast! so nice!
One goes to the Abbot's table,
　　All of us get each a slice.
45　How go on your flowers? None double?
　　Not one fruit-sort can you spy?
Strange!—And I, too, at such trouble,
　　Keep them close-nipped on the sly!

---

31 **Barbary corsair** pirate from North Africa.　39 **Arian** the Arian
heresy denied the divinity of Christ, and hence the orthodox doctrine
of the Trinity.

VII

There's a great text in Galatians,°
  One you trip on it, entails   *50*
Twenty-nine distinct damnations,
  Once you trip on it, entails
If I trip him just a-dying,
  Sure of Heaven as sure can be,
Spin him round and send him flying   *55*
  Off to hell, a Manichee?°

VIII

Or, my scrofulous French novel
  On gray paper with blunt type!
Simply glance at it, you grovel
  Hand and foot in Belial's gripe: *60*
If I double down its pages
  At the woeful sixteenth print,
When he gathers his greengages,
  Ope a sieve and slip it in't?

IX

Or, there's Satan!——one might venture   *65*
  Pledge one's soul to him, yet leave
Such a flaw in the indenture
  As he'd miss till, past retrieve,
Blasted lay that rose-acacia
  We're so proud of! *Hy, Zy, Hine*° . . .   *70*
'St, there's Vespers! *Plena gratiâ
Ave, Virgo!*° Gr-r-r—you swine!

---

49 a great text in Galatians Galatians 5:19–21. The brother is re-
membering hazily. (We may be expected to think of Galatians 6:7:
"whatsoever a man soweth, that shall he also reap." The irony
would anticipate that of "The Heretic's Tragedy.") **56 Manichee**
here used generally for heretic. **70 Hy, Zy, Hine** apparently begin-
ning of a curse. **71-72 Plena . . . Virgo!** hail Virgin, full of grace.
Version of the prayer "Hail Mary" (Ave Maria).

RUDEL TO THE LADY OF TRIPOLI°

I

I KNOW a Mount, the gracious Sun perceives
First, when he visits, last, too, when he leaves
The world; and, vainly favored, it repays
The day-long glory of his steadfast gaze
5   By no change of its large calm front of snow.
And underneath the Mount, a Flower I know,
He cannot have perceived, that changes ever
At his approach; and, in the lost endeavor
To live his life, has parted, one by one,
10   With all a flower's true graces, for the grace
Of being but a foolish mimic sun,
With ray-like florets round a disk-like face.
Men nobly call by many a name the Mount
As over many a land of theirs its large
15   Calm front of snow like a triumphal targe°
Is reared, and still with old names, fresh names vie,
Each to its proper praise and own account:
Men call the Flower the Sunflower, sportively.

II

Oh, Angel of the East, one, one gold look
20   Across the waters to this twilight nook,
—The far sad waters, Angel, to this nook!

III

Dear Pilgrim, art thou for the East indeed?

Rudel . . . Tripoli Geoffrey Rudel was a troubadour of the twelfth
century. He fell in love with a Countess of Tripoli, whom he knew
only by report. There is a legend that he went to Tripoli and died in
his lady's arms.　15 **targe** shield.

Go!—saying ever as thou dost proceed,
That I, French Rudel, choose for my device
A sunflower outspread like a sacrifice   25
Before its idol. See! These inexpert
And hurried fingers could not fail to hurt
The woven picture; 'tis a woman's skill
Indeed; but nothing baffled me, so, ill
Or well, the work is finished. Say, men feed   30
On songs I sing, and therefore bask the bees
On my flower's breast as on a platform broad:
But, as the flower's concern is not for these
But solely for the sun, so men applaud
In vain this Rudel, he not looking here   35
But to the East—the East! Go, say this, Pilgrim dear!

JOHANNES AGRICOLA° IN MEDITATION

THERE'S heaven above, and night by night
    I look right through its gorgeous roof;
No suns and moons though e'er so bright
    Avail to stop me; splendor-proof
    I keep the broods of stars aloof: 5
For I intend to get to God,
    For 'tis to God I speed so fast,
For in God's breast, my own abode,
    Those shoals of dazzling glory, passed,
    I lay my spirit down at last.   10
I lie where I have always lain,

Johannes Agricola taught that the moral law did not apply to persons saved by God's grace. This and the following poem were first published together under the title of "Madhouse Cells."

God smiles as he has always smiled;
Ere suns and moons could wax and wane,
　Ere stars were thundergirt, or piled
15　The heavens, God thought on me his child;
Ordained a life for me, arrayed
　Its circumstances every one
To the minutest; ay, God said
　This head this hand should rest upon
20　Thus, ere he fashioned star or sun.
And having thus created me,
　Thus rooted me, he bade me grow,
Guiltless forever, like a tree
　That buds and blooms, nor seeks to know
25　The law by which it prospers so:
But sure that thought and word and deed
　All go to swell his love for me,
Me, made because that love had need
　Of something irreversibly
30　Pledged solely its content to be.
Yes, yes, a tree which must ascend,
　No poison-gourd foredoomed to stoop.
I have God's warrant, could I blend
　All hideous sins, as in a cup,
35　To drink the mingled venoms up;
Secure my nature will convert
　The draught to blossoming gladness fast:
While sweet dews turn to the gourd's hurt,
　And bloat, and while they bloat it, blast,
40　As from the first its lot was cast.
For as I lie, smiled on, full-fed
　By unexhausted power to bless,
I gaze below on hell's fierce bed,
　And those its waves of flame oppress,
45　Swarming in ghastly wretchedness;
Whose life on earth aspired to be
　One altar-smoke, so pure!—to win
If not love like God's love for me,
　At least to keep his anger in;
50　And all their striving turned to sin.
Priest, doctor, hermit, monk grown white

With prayer, the broken-hearted nun,
The martyr, the wan acolyte,
   The incense-swinging child—undone
   Before God fashioned star or sun! *55*
God, whom I praise; how could I praise,
   If such as I might understand,
Make out and reckon on his ways,
   And bargain for his love, and stand,
   Paying a price, at his right hand? *60*

PORPHYRIA'S LOVER

THE rain set early in tonight,
   The sullen wind was soon awake,
It tore the elm-tops down for spite,
   And did its worst to vex the lake:
   I listened with heart fit to break. *5*
When glided in Porphyria; straight
   She shut the cold out and the storm,
And kneeled and made the cheerless grate
   Blaze up, and all the cottage warm;
   Which done, she rose, and from her form *10*
Withdrew the dripping cloak and shawl,
   And laid her soiled gloves by, untied
Her hat and let the damp hair fall,
   And, last, she sat down by my side
   And called me. When no voice replied, *15*
She put my arm about her waist,
   And made her smooth white shoulder bare,
And all her yellow hair displaced,
   And, stooping, made my cheek lie there,
   And spread, o'er all, her yellow hair, *20*

Murmuring how she loved me—she
　　Too weak, for all her heart's endeavor,
To set its struggling passion free
　　From pride, and vainer ties dissever,
25　　And give herself to me forever.
But passion sometimes would prevail,
　　Nor could tonight's gay feast restrain
A sudden thought of one so pale
　　For love of her, and all in vain:
30　　So, she was come through wind and rain.
Be sure I looked up at her eyes
　　Happy and proud; at last I knew
Porphyria worshipped me; surprise
　　Made my heart swell, and still it grew
35　　While I debated what to do.
That moment she was mine, mine, fair,
　　Perfectly pure and good: I found
A thing to do, and all her hair
　　In one long yellow string I wound
40　　Three times her little throat around,
And strangled her. No pain felt she;
　　I am quite sure she felt no pain.
As a shut bud that holds a bee,
　　I warily oped her lids: again
45　　Laughed the blue eyes without a stain.
And I untightened next the tress
　　About her neck; her cheek once more
Blushed bright beneath my burning kiss:
　　I propped her head up as before,
50　　Only, this time my shoulder bore
Her head, which droops upon it still:
　　The smiling rosy little head,
So glad it has its utmost will,
　　That all it scorned at once is fled,
55　　And I, its love, am gained instead!
Porphyria's love: she guessed not how
　　Her darling one wish would be heard.
And thus we sit together now,
　　And all night long we have not stirred,
60　　And yet God has not said a word!

COLOMBE'S BIRTHDAY

A PLAY

(1844)

IVY and violet, what do ye here
With blossom and shoot in the warm spring-weather,
Hiding the arms of Monchenci and Vere?—HANMER.

PERSONS

COLOMBE OF RAVESTEIN, Duchess of Juliers and
    Cleves°
SABYNE, ADOLF, *her attendants*
GUIBERT, GAUCELME, MAUFROY, CLUGNET, *courtiers*
VALENCE, *advocate of Cleves*
PRINCE BERTHOLD, *claimant of the Duchy*
MELCHIOR, *his confidant*

PLACE—*The Palace at Juliers*
TIME, 16—

Juliers and Cleves on the northern Rhine.

ACT I

MORNING

Scene—*A corridor leading to the Audience-chamber*

Gaucelme, Clugnet, Maufroy *and other* Courtiers,
round Guibert, *who is silently reading a paper:
as he drops it at the end*—

Guibert. That this should be her birthday; and the day
    We all invested her, twelve months ago,
    As the late Duke's true heiress and our liege;
    And that this also must become the day . . .
    Oh, miserable lady!

5   1*st Courtier.*   Ay, indeed?

2nd Courtier. Well, Guibert?

3rd Courtier. But your news, my friend, your news!
    The sooner, friend, one learns Prince Berthold's
      pleasure,
    The better for us all: how writes the Prince?
    Give me! I'll read it for the common good.

10 *Guibert.* In time, sir—but till time comes, pardon me!
    Our old Duke just disclosed his child's retreat,
    Declared her true succession to his rule,
    And died: this birthday was the day, last year,
    We convoyed her from Castle Ravestein—
15   That sleeps out trustfully its extreme age
    On the Meuse' quiet bank, where she lived queen
    Over the water-buds—to Juliers' court
    With joy and bustle. Here again we stand;
    Sir Gaucelme's buckle's constant to his cap:
20   Today's much such another sunny day!

Gaucelme. Come, Guibert, this outgrows a jest, I
    think!

You're hardly such a novice as to need
The lesson, you pretend.

Guibert.   What lesson, sir?
That everybody, if he'd thrive at court,
Should, first and last of all, look to himself?   25
Why, no: and therefore with your good example,
(—Ho, Master Adolf!)—to myself I'll look.

Enter ADOLF.

Guibert. The Prince's letter; why, of all men else,
Comes it to me?

Adolf.   By virtue of your place,
Sir Guibert! 'Twas the Prince's express charge,   30
His envoy told us, that the missive there
Should only reach our lady by the hand
Of whosoever held your place.

Guibert.   Enough: [ADOLF *retires.*]
Then, gentles, who'll accept a certain poor
Indifferently honorable place,   35
My friends, I make no doubt, have gnashed their
    teeth
At leisure minutes these half-dozen years,
To find me never in the mood to quit?
Who asks may have it, with my blessing, and—
This to present our lady. Who'll accept?   40
You—you—you? There it lies, and may, for me!

Maufroy [*a youth, picking up the paper, reads aloud*].
"Prince Berthold, proved by titles following
Undoubted Lord of Juliers, comes this day
To claim his own, with license from the Pope,
The Emperor, the Kings of Spain and France" . . .   45

Gaucelme. Sufficient "titles following," I judge!
Don't read another! Well—"to claim his own"?

Maufroy. "—And take possession of the Duchy held
Since twelve months, to the true heir's prejudice,
By" . . . Colombe, Juliers' mistress, so she thinks,   50
And Ravestein's mere lady, as we find.

Who wants the place and paper? Guibert's right.
I hope to climb a little in the world—
I'd push my fortunes—but, no more than he,
55   Could tell her on this happy day of days,
That, save the nosegay in her hand, perhaps,
There's nothing left to call her own. Sir Clugnet,
You famish for promotion; what say you?

Clugnet [an old man]. To give this letter were a sort,
     I take it,
60   Of service: services ask recompense:
What kind of corner may be Ravestein?

Guibert. The castle? Oh, you'd share her fortunes?
     Good!
Three walls stand upright, full as good as four,
With no such bad remainder of a roof.

Clugnet. Oh—but the town?

65   *Guibert.*   Five houses, fifteen huts;
A church whereto was once a spire, 'tis judged;
And half a dike, except in time of thaw.

Clugnet. Still, there's some revenue?

Guibert.   Else Heaven forfend!
You hang a beacon out, should fogs increase;
70   So, when the autumn floats of pinewood steer
Safe 'mid the white confusion, thanks to you,
Their grateful raftsman flings a guilder° in;
—That's if he mean to pass your way next time.

Clugnet. If not?

Guibert.   Hang guilders, then! He blesses you.

Clugnet. What man do you suppose me? Keep your
75   paper!
And, let me say, it shows no handsome spirit
To dally with misfortune: keep your place!

Gaucelme. Someone must tell her.

----

72 guilder Dutch coin.

Guibert.   Someone may: you may!

Gaucelme. Sir Guibert, 'tis no trifle turns me sick
  Of court-hypocrisy at years like mine,   80
  But this goes near it. Where's there news at all?
  Who'll have the face, for instance, to affirm
  He never heard, e'en while we crowned the girl,
  That Juliers' tenure was by Salic law;°
  That one, confessed her father's cousin's child,   85
  And, she away, indisputable heir,
  Against our choice protesting and the Duke's,
  Claimed Juliers?—nor, as he preferred his claim,
  That first this, then another potentate,
  Inclined to its allowance?—I or you,   90
  Or any one except the lady's self?
  Oh, it had been the direst cruelty
  To break the business to her! Things might change:
  At all events, we'd see next masque at end,
  Next mummery over first: and so the edge   95
  Was taken off sharp tidings as they came,
  Till here's the Prince upon us, and there's she
  —Wreathing her hair, a song between her lips,
  With just the faintest notion possible
  That some such claimant earns a livelihood   100
  About the world, by feigning grievances—
  Few pay the story of, but grudge its price,
  And fewer listen to, a second time.
  Your method proves a failure; now try mine!
  And, since this must be carried . . .

Guibert [*snatching the paper from him*]. By your
     leave!   105
  Your zeal transports you! 'Twill not serve the Prince
  So much as you expect, this course you'd take.
  If she leaves quietly her palace—well;
  But if she died upon its threshold—no:
  He'd have the trouble of removing her.   110
  Come, gentles, we're all—what the devil knows!
  You, Gaucelme, won't lose character, beside:

84 **Salic law** forbidding inheritance by women.

You broke your father's heart superiorly
To gather his succession—never blush!
115 You're from my province, and, be comforted,
They tell of it with wonder to this day.
You can afford to let your talent sleep.
We'll take the very worst supposed, as true:
There, the old Duke knew, when he hid his child
120 Among the river-flowers at Ravestein,
With whom the right lay! Call the Prince our Duke!
There, she's no Duchess, she's no anything
More than a young maid with the bluest eyes:
And now, sirs, we'll not break this young maid's
   heart
125 Coolly as Gaucelme could and would! No haste!
His talent's full-blown, ours but in the bud:
We'll not advance to his perfection yet—
Will we, Sir Maufroy? See, I've ruined Maufroy
Forever as a courtier!

Gaucelme.   Here's a coil!°
130 And, count us, will you? Count its residue,
This boasted convoy, this day last year's crowd!
A birthday, too, a gratulation day!
I'm dumb: bid that keep silence!

Maufroy and others.   Eh, Sir Guibert?
He's right: that does say something: that's bare
   truth.
135 Ten—twelve, I make: a perilous dropping off!

Guibert. Pooh—is it audience hour? The vestibule
Swarms too, I wager, with the common sort
That want our privilege of entry here.

Gaucelme. Adolf! [*Reenter* ADOLF.] Who's outside?

Guibert.   Oh, your looks suffice!
Nobody waiting?

Maufroy [*looking through the door-folds*]. Scarce our
   number!

---

129 **coil** disturbance.

Guibert.   'Sdeath!   *140*
   Nothing to beg for, to complain about?
   It can't be! Ill news spreads, but not so fast
   As thus to frighten all the world!

Gaucelme.   The world
   Lives out of doors, sir—not with you and me
   By presence-chamber porches, stateroom stairs,   *145*
   Wherever warmth's perpetual: outside's free
   To every wind from every compass point,
   And who may get nipped needs be weather-wise.
   The Prince comes and the lady's People go;
   The snow-goose settles down, the swallows flee—   *150*
   Why should they wait for winter-time? 'Tis instinct.
   Don't you feel somewhat chilly?

Guibert.   That's their craft?
   And last year's crowders-round and criers-forth
   That strewed the garlands, overarched the roads,
   Lighted the bonfires, sang the loyal songs!   *155*
   Well 'tis my comfort, you could never call me
   The People's Friend! The People keep their word—
   I keep my place: don't doubt I'll entertain
   The People when the Prince comes, and the People
   Are talked of! Then, their speeches—no one tongue   *160*
   Found respite, not a pen had holiday
   —For they wrote, too, as well as spoke, these
      knaves!
   Now see: we tax and tithe them, pill and poll,°
   They wince and fret enough, but pay they must
   —We manage that—so, pay with a good grace   *165*
   They might as well, it costs so little more.
   But when we've done with taxes, meet folk next
   Outside the tollbooth and the rating-place,
   In public—there they have us if they will,
   We're at their mercy after that, you see!   *170*
   For one tax not ten devils could extort—
   Over and above necessity, a grace;
   This prompt disbosoming of love, to wit—

163 **pill and poll** peel and shear.

Their vine-leaf wrappage of our tribute penny,
175   And crowning attestation, all works well.
Yet this precisely do they thrust on us!
These cappings quick, these crook-and-cringings
low,
Hand to the heart, and forehead to the knee,
With grin that shuts the eyes and opes the mouth—
180   So tender they their love; and, tender made,
Go home to curse us, the first doit we ask.
As if their souls were any longer theirs!
As if they had not given ample warrant
To who should clap a collar on their neck,
185   Rings in their nose, a goad to either flank,
And take them for the brute they boast themselves!
Stay—there's a bustle at the outer door—
And somebody entreating . . . that's my name!
Adolf—I heard my name!

Adolf.   'Twas probably
The suitor.

Guibert. Oh, there is one?

190 *Adolf.*   With a suit
He'd fain enforce in person.

Guibert.   The good heart
—And the great fool! Just ope the mid-door's fold!
Is that a lappet of his cloak, I see?

Adolf. If it bear plenteous sign of travel . . . ay,
The very cloak my comrades tore!

195 *Guibert.*   Why tore?

Adolf. He seeks the Duchess' presence in that trim:
Since daybreak, was he posted hereabouts
Lest he should miss the moment.

Guibert.   Where's he now?

Adolf. Gone for a minute possibly, not more:
200   They have ado enough to thrust him back.

Guibert. Ay—but my name, I caught?

Adolf.   Oh, sir—he said
  —What was it?—You had known him formerly,
  And, he believed, would help him did you guess
  He waited now; you promised him as much:
  The old plea! 'Faith, he's back—renews the charge!   205

[*Speaking at the door.*] So long as the man parleys,
        peace outside—
  Nor be too ready with your halberts,° there!

Gaucelme. My horse bespattered, as he blocked the
        path
  A thin sour man, not unlike somebody.

Adolf. He holds a paper in his breast, whereon   210
  He glances when his cheeks flush and his brow
  At each repulse—

Gaucelme.   I noticed he'd a brow.

Adolf. So glancing, he grows calmer, leans awhile
  Over the balustrade, adjusts his dress,
  And presently turns round, quiet again,   215
  With some new pretext for admittance.— Back!
  [*To* GUIBERT.]—Sir, he has seen you! Now cross
        halberts! Ha—
  Pascal is prostrate—there lies Fabian too!
  No passage! Whither would the madman press?
  Close the doors quick on me!

Guibert.   Too late! He's here.   220

Enter, hastily and with discomposed dress, VALENCE.

Valence. Sir Guibert, will you help me?—me, that
        come
  Charged by your townsmen, all who starve at
        Cleves,
  To represent their heights and depths of woe
  Before our Duchess and obtain relief!
  Such errands barricade such doors, it seems: 225
  But not a common hindrance drives me back
  On all the sad yet hopeful faces, lit

207 **halberts** weapons.

With hope for the first time, which sent me forth.
Cleves, speak for me! Cleves' men and women, speak!

230   Who followed me—your strongest—many a mile
That I might go the fresher from their ranks,
—Who sit—your weakest—by the city gates,
To take me fuller of what news I bring
As I return—for I must needs return!

235   —Can I? 'Twere hard, no listener for their wrongs,
To turn them back upon the old despair—
Harder, Sir Guibert, than imploring thus—
So, I do—any way you please—implore!
If you . . . but how should you remember Cleves?

240   Yet they of Cleves remember you so well!
Ay, comment on each trait of you they keep,
Your words and deeds caught up at second hand,—
Proud, I believe, at bottom of their hearts,
O' the very levity and recklessness

245   Which only prove that you forget their wrongs.
Cleves, the grand town, whose men and women starve,
Is Cleves forgotten? Then, remember me!
You promised me that you would help me once,
For other purpose: will you keep your word?

Guibert. And who may you be, friend?

250   *Valence.*   Valence of Cleves.

Guibert. Valence of . . . not the advocate of Cleves,
I owed my whole estate to, three years back?
Ay, well may you keep silence! Why, my lords,
You've heard, I'm sure, how, Pentecost three years,

255   I was so nearly ousted of my land
By some knave's pretext—(eh? when you refused me
Your ugly daughter, Clugnet!)—and you've heard
How I recovered it by miracle
—(When I refused her!) Here's the very friend,

260   —Valence of Cleves, all parties have to thank!
Nay, Valence, this procedure's vile in you!
I'm no more grateful than a courtier should,

But politic am I—I bear a brain,
Can cast about a little, might require
Your services a second time. I tried 265
To tempt you with advancement here to court
—"No!"—well, for curiosity at least
To view our life here—"No!"—our Duchess, then—
A pretty woman's worth some pains to see,
Nor is she spoiled, I take it, if a crown 270
Complete the forehead pale and tresses pure . . .

Valence. Our city trusted me its miseries,
And I am come.

Guibert.   So much for taste! But "come,"—
So may you be, for anything I know,
To beg the Pope's cross, or Sir Clugnet's daughter, 275
And with an equal chance you get all three.
If it was ever worth your while to come,
Was not the proper way worth finding too?

Valence. Straight to the palace-portal, sir, I came—

Guibert. —And said?—

Valence.   —That I had brought the miseries 280
Of a whole city to relieve.

Guibert.   —Which saying
Won your admittance? You saw me, indeed,
And here, no doubt, you stand: as certainly,
My intervention, I shall not dispute,
Procures you audience; which, if I procure— 285
That paper's closely written—by Saint Paul,
Here flock the Wrongs, follow the Remedies,
Chapter and verse, One, Two, A, B and C!
Perhaps you'd enter, make a reverence,
And launch these "miseries" from first to last? 290

Valence. How should they let me pause or turn aside?

Gaucelme [*to* VALENCE]. My worthy sir, one question!
    You've come straight
From Cleves, you tell us: heard you any talk
At Cleves about our lady?

Valence.   Much.

Gaucelme.   And what?

295 *Valence.* Her wish was to redress all wrongs she knew.

Gaucelme. That, you believed?

Valence.   You see me, sir!

Gaucelme.   —Nor stopped
Upon the road from Cleves to Juliers here,
For any—rumors you might find afloat?

Valence. I had my townsmen's wrongs to busy me.

300 *Gaucelme.* This is the lady's birthday, do you know?
—Her day of pleasure?

Valence.   —That the great, I know,
For pleasure born, should still be on the watch
To exclude pleasure when a duty offers:
Even as, for duty born, the lowly too
305   May ever snatch a pleasure if in reach:
Both will have plenty of their birthright, sir!

Gaucelme [*aside to* GUIBERT]. Sir Guibert, here's your
    man! No scruples now—
You'll never find his like! Time presses hard.
I've seen your drift and Adolf's too, this while,
310   But you can't keep the hour of audience back
Much longer, and at noon the Prince arrives.
[*Pointing to* VALENCE.] Entrust him with it—fool
    no chance away!

Guibert. Him?

Gaucelme.   —With the missive! What's the man to
    her?

Guibert. No bad thought! Yet, 'tis yours, who ever
    played
315   The tempting serpent: else 'twere no bad thought!
I should—and do—mistrust it for your sake,
Or else . . .

Enter an Official *who communicates with* ADOLF.

Adolf. The Duchess will receive the court.

Guibert. Give us a moment, Adolf! Valence, friend,
  I'll help you. We of the service, you're to mark,
  Have special entry, while the herd . . . the folk   *320*
  Outside, get access through our help alone;
  —Well, it is so, was so, and I suppose
  So ever will be: your natural lot is, therefore,
  To wait your turn and opportunity,
  And probably miss both. Now, I engage   *325*
  To set you, here and in a minute's space,
  Before the lady, with full leave to plead
  Chapter and verse, and A, and B, and C,
  To heart's content.

Valence.   I grieve that I must ask—
  This being, yourself admit, the custom here—   *330*
  To what the price of such a favor mounts?

Guibert. Just so! You're not without a courtier's tact.
  Little at court, as your quick instinct prompts,
  Do such as we without a recompense.

Valence. Yours is?—

Guibert.   A trifle: here's a document   *335*
  'Tis someone's duty to present her Grace—
  I say, not mine—these say, not theirs—such points
  Have weight at court. Will you relieve us all
  And take it? Just say, "I am bidden lay
  This paper at the Duchess' feet!"

Valence.   No more?   *340*
  I thank you, sir!

Adolf.   Her Grace receives the court,

Guibert [*aside*]. Now, *sursum corda,*° quoth the mass
  priest! Do—

---

342 **sursum corda** lift up your hearts (beginning of the most solemn
part of the Mass).

Whoever's my kind saint, do let alone
These pushings to and fro, and pullings back;
345 Peaceably let me hang o' the devil's arm
The downward path, if you can't pluck me off
Completely! Let me live quite his, or yours!
    [*The* Courtiers *begin to range themselves, and
      move toward the door.*]
After me, Valence! So, our famous Cleves
Lacks bread? Yet don't we gallants buy their lace?
350 And dear enough—it beggars me, I know,
To keep my very gloves fringed properly.
This, Valence, is our Great State Hall you cross;
Yon gray urn's veritable marcasite,
The Pope's gift: and those salvers testify
355 The Emperor. Presently you'll set your foot
. . . But you don't speak, friend Valence!

Valence.   I shall speak.

Gaucelme [*aside to* GUIBERT]. Guibert—it were no
    such ungraceful thing
If you and I, at first, seemed horror-struck
With the bad news. Look here, what you shall do.
360 Suppose you, first, clap hand to sword and cry
"Yield strangers our allegiance? First I'll perish
Beside your Grace!"—and so give me the cue
To . . .

Guibert. —Clap your hand to notebook and jot down
That to regale the Prince with? I conceive.
    [*To* VALENCE.] Do, Valence, speak, or I shall half
365   suspect
You're plotting to supplant us, me the first,
I' the lady's favor! Is't the grand harangue
You mean to make, that thus engrosses you?
—Which of her virtues you'll apostrophize?
370 Or is 't the fashion you aspire to start,
Of that close-curled, not unbecoming hair?
Or what else ponder you?

Valence.   My townsmen's wrongs.

ACT II

NOON

SCENE—*The Presence-chamber*

The DUCHESS *and* SABYNE.

The Duchess. Announce that I am ready for the court!

Sabyne. 'Tis scarcely audience-hour, I think; your
    Grace
  May best consult your own relief, no doubt,
  And shun the crowd: but few can have arrived.

The Duchess. Let those not yet arrived, then, keep
    away!   5
  'Twas me, this day last year at Ravestein,
  You hurried. It has been full time, beside,
  This half-hour. Do you hesitate?

Sabyne.   Forgive me!

The Duchess. Stay, Sabyne; let me hasten to make sure
  Of one true thanker: here with you begins   10
  My audience, claim you first its privilege!
  It is my birth's event they celebrate:
  You need not wish me more such happy days,
  But—ask some favor! Have you none to ask?
  Has Adolf none, then? this was far from least   15
  Of much I waited for impatiently,
  Assure yourself! It seemed so natural
  Your gift, beside this bunch of river-bells,
  Should be the power and leave of doing good
  To you, and greater pleasure to myself.   20
  You ask my leave today to marry Adolf?
  The rest is my concern.

Sabyne.   Your Grace is ever
Our lady of dear Ravestein,—but, for Adolf . . .

The Duchess. "But"? You have not, sure, changed in
     your regard
And purpose towards him?

Sabyne.   We change?

25 *The Duchess.*   Well then? Well?

Sabyne. How could we two be happy, and, most like,
     Leave Juliers, when—when . . . but 'tis audience-
     time!

The Duchess. "When, if you left me, I were left in-
     deed!"
Would you subjoin that?—Bid the court approach!
—Why should we play thus with each other,
30   Sabyne?
Do I not know, if courtiers prove remiss,
If friends detain me, and get blame for it,
There is a cause? Of last year's fervid throng
Scarce one half comes now.

Sabyne [*aside*].   One half? No, alas!

35 *The Duchess.* So can the mere suspicion of a cloud
Over my fortunes, strike each loyal heart.
They've heard of this Prince Berthold; and, forsooth,
Some foolish arrogant pretense he makes,
May grow more foolish and more arrogant,
40   They please to apprehend! I thank their love.
Admit them!

Sabyne [*aside*]. How much has she really learned?

The Duchess. Surely, whoever's absent, Tristan waits?
     —Or at least Romuald, whom my father raised
From nothing—come, he's faithful to me, come!
45   (Sabyne, I should but be the prouder—yes,
The fitter to comport myself aright)
Not Romuald? Xavier—what said he to that?
For Xavier hates a parasite, I know!
                        [SABYNE *goes out.*]

The Duchess. Well, sunshine's everywhere, and sum-
    mer too.
  Next year 'tis the old place again, perhaps—   *50*
  The water-breeze again, the birds again.
  —It cannot be! It is too late to be!
  What part had I, or choice in all of it?
  Hither they brought me; I had not to think
  Nor care, concern myself with doing good   *55*
  Or ill, my task was just—to live—to live,
  And, answering ends there was no need explain,
  To render Juliers happy—so they said.
  All could not have been falsehood: some was love,
  And wonder and obedience. I did all   *60*
  They looked for: why then cease to do it now?
  Yet this is to be calmly set aside,
  And—ere next birthday's dawn, for aught I know,
  Things change, a claimant may arrive, and I . . .
  It cannot nor it shall not be! His right?   *65*
  Well then, he has the right, and I have not,
  —But who bade all of you surround my life
  And close its growth up with your ducal crown
  Which, plucked off rudely, leaves me perishing?
  I could have been like one of you—loved, hoped,   *70*
  Feared, lived and died like one of you—but you
  Would take that life away and give me this,
  And I will keep this! I will face you! Come!

Enter the Courtiers *and* VALENCE.

The Courtiers. Many such happy mornings to your
    Grace!

The Duchess [*aside, as they pay their devoir°*]. The
    same words, the same faces—the same love!   *75*
  I have been overfearful. These are few;
  But these, at least, stand firmly: these are mine.
  As many come as may; and if no more,
  'Tis that these few suffice—they do suffice!
  What succor may not next year bring me? Plainly,   *80*

75 **devoir** homage.

I feared too soon. [*To the* Courtiers.] I thank you,
sirs: all thanks!

Valence [*aside, as the* DUCHESS *passes from one group
to another, conversing*].

'Tis she—the vision this day last year brought,
When, for a golden moment at our Cleves,
She tarried in her progress hither. Cleves
85 Chose me to speak its welcome, and I spoke
—Not that she could have noted the recluse
—Ungainly, old before his time—who gazed.
Well, Heaven's gifts are not wasted, and that gaze
Kept, and shall keep me to the end, her own!
90 She was above it—but so would not sink
My gaze to earth! The People caught it, hers—
Thenceforward, mine; but thus entirely mine,
Who shall affirm, had she not raised my soul
Ere she retired and left me—them? She turns—
95 There's all her wondrous face at once! The ground
Reels and . . . [*suddenly occupying himself with
his paper*]
These wrongs of theirs I have to plead!

The Duchess [*to the* Courtiers]. Nay, compliment
enough! and kindness' self
Should pause before it wish me more such years.
'Twas fortunate that thus, ere youth escaped,
100 I tasted life's pure pleasure—one such, pure,
Is worth a thousand, mixed—and youth's for pleas-
ure:
Mine is received; let my age pay for it.

Gaucelme. So, pay, and pleasure paid for, thinks your
Grace,
Should never go together?

Guibert. How, Sir Gaucelme?
105 Hurry one's feast down unenjoyingly
At the snatched breathing-intervals of work?
As good you saved it till the dull day's end

When, stiff and sleepy, appetite is gone.
Eat first, then work upon the strength of food!

The Duchess. True: you enable me to risk my future,   *110*
By giving me a past beyond recall.
I lived, a girl, one happy leisure year:
Let me endeavor to be the Duchess now!
And so—what news, Sir Guibert, spoke you of?
   [*As they advance a little, and* GUIBERT *speaks—*]
—That gentleman?

Valence [*aside*].   I feel her eyes on me.   *115*

Guibert [*to* VALENCE]. The Duchess, sir, inclines to
   hear your suit.
Advance! He is from Cleves.

Valence [*coming forward. Aside*]. Their wrongs—their
   wrongs!

The Duchess. And you, sir, are from Cleves? How
   fresh in mind,
The hour or two I passed at queenly Cleves!
She entertained me bravely, but the best   *120*
Of her good pageant seemed its standers-by
With insuppressive joy on every face!
What says my ancient famous happy Cleves?

Valence. Take the truth, lady—you are made for
   truth!
So think my friends: nor do they less deserve   *125*
The having you to take it, you shall think,
When you know all—nay, when you only know
How, on that day you recollect at Cleves,
When the poor acquiescing multitude
Who thrust themselves with all their woes apart   *130*
Into unnoticed corners, that the few,
Their means sufficed to muster trappings for,
Might fill the foreground, occupy your sight
With joyous faces fit to bear away
And boast of as a sample of all Cleves   *135*
—How, when to daylight these crept out once more,

Clutching, unconscious, each his empty rags
Whence the scant coin, which had not half bought
   bread,
That morn he shook forth, counted piece by piece,
140 And, well-advisedly, on perfumes spent them
To burn, or flowers to strew, before your path
—How, when the golden flood of music and bliss
Ebbed, as their moon retreated, and again
Left the sharp black-point rocks of misery bare
145 —Then I, their friend, had only to suggest
"Saw she the horror as she saw the pomp!"
And as one man they cried "He speaks the truth:
Show her the horror! Take from our own mouths
Our wrongs and show them, she will see them too!"
150 This they cried, lady! I have brought the wrongs.

The Duchess. Wrongs? Cleves has wrongs—apparent
   now and thus?
I thank you! In that paper? Give it me!

Valence. (There, Cleves!) In this! (What did I prom-
   ise, Cleves?)
Our weavers, clothiers, spinners are reduced
155 Since . . . Oh, I crave your pardon! I forget
I buy the privilege of this approach,
And promptly would discharge my debt. I lay
This paper humbly at the Duchess' feet.
            [*Presenting* GUIBERT'S *paper.*]

Guibert. Stay! for the present . . .

The Duchess.   Stay, sir? I take aught
160 That teaches me their wrongs with greater pride
Than this your ducal circlet. Thank you, sir!

     [*The* DUCHESS *reads hastily; then, turning*
        to the Courtiers—]

What have I done to you? Your deed or mine
Was it, this crowning me? I gave myself
No more a title to your homage, no,
Than church-flowers, born this season, wrote the
165   words

In the saint's-book that sanctified them first.
For such a flower, you plucked me; well, you erred—
Well, 'twas a weed; remove the eyesore quick!
But should you not remember it has lain
Steeped in the candles' glory, palely shrined,   *170*
Nearer God's Mother than most earthly things?
—That if't be faded 'tis with prayer's sole breath—
That the one day it boasted was God's day?
Still, I do thank you! Had you used respect,
Here might I dwindle to my last white leaf,   *175*
Here lose life's latest freshness, which even yet
May yield some wandering insect rest and food:
So, fling me forth, and—all is best for all!
[*After a pause.*] Prince Berthold, who art Juliers'
   Duke it seems—
The King's choice, and the Emperor's, and the
   Pope's—   *180*
Be mine, too! Take this People! Tell not me
Of rescripts, precedents, authorities,
—But take them, from a heart that yearns to give!
Find out their love—I could not; find their fear—
I would not; find their like—I never shall,   *185*
Among the flowers!   [*Taking off her coronet.*]
          Colombe of Ravestein
Thanks God she is no longer Duchess here!

Valence [*advancing to* GUIBERT]. Sir Guibert, knight,
   they call you—this of mine
Is the first step I ever set at court.
You dared make me your instrument, I find;   *190*
For that, so sure as you and I are men,
We reckon to the utmost presently:
But as you are a courtier and I none,
Your knowledge may instruct me. I, already,
Have too far outraged, by my ignorance   *195*
Of courtier-ways, this lady, to proceed
A second step and risk addressing her:
—I am degraded—you let me address!
Out of her presence, all is plain enough
What I shall do—but in her presence, too,   *200*

Surely there's something proper to be done.
[*To the others.*] You, gentles, tell me if I guess
    aright—
May I not strike this man to earth?

The Courtiers [*as* GUIBERT *springs forward, withhold-*
    ing him].   Let go!
—The clothiers' spokesman, Guibert? Grace a
    churl?

The Duchess [*to* VALENCE]. Oh, be acquainted with
205   your party, sir!
He's of the oldest lineage Juliers boasts;
A lion crests him for a cognizance;
"Scorning to waver"—that's his 'scutcheon's word;°
His office with the new Duke—probably
210   The same in honor as with me; or more,
By so much as this gallant turn deserves.
He's now, I dare say, of a thousand times
The rank and influence that remain with her
Whose part you take! So, lest for taking it
You suffer . . .

215 *Valence.*   I may strike him then to earth?

Guibert [*falling on his knee*]. Great and dear lady, par-
    don me! Hear once!
Believe me and be merciful—be just!
I could not bring myself to give that paper
Without a keener pang than I dared meet
220   —And so felt Clugnet here, and Maufroy here
—No one dared meet it. Protestation's cheap,—
But, if to die for you did any good,
[*To* GAUCELME.] Would not I die, sir? Say your
    worst of me!
But it does no good, that's the mournful truth.
225   And since the hint of a resistance, even,
Would just precipitate, on you the first,
A speedier ruin—I shall not deny,
Saving myself indubitable pain,

207–8 **lion . . . word** his "device" (heraldic insignia) bore a lion as
its crest; his coat of arms bore the motto given.

I thought to give you pleasure (who might say?)
By showing that your only subject found   *230*
To carry the sad notice, was the man
Precisely ignorant of its contents;
A nameless, mere provincial advocate;
One whom 'twas like you never saw before,
Never would see again. All has gone wrong;   *235*
But I meant right, God knows, and you, I trust!

The Duchess. A nameless advocate, this gentleman?
    —(I pardon you, Sir Guibert!)

Guibert [*rising, to* VALENCE]. Sir, and you?

Valence. —Rejoice that you are lightened of a load.
    Now, you have only me to reckon with.   *240*

The Duchess. One I have never seen, much less
    obliged?

Valence. Dare I speak, lady?

The Duchess.   Dare you! Heard you not
    I rule no longer?

Valence.   Lady, if your rule
Were based alone on such a ground as these
                   [*Pointing to the* Courtiers.]
Could furnish you,—abjure it! They have hidden   *245*
A source of true dominion from your sight.

The Duchess. You hear them—no such source is
    left . . .

Valence.   Hear Cleves!
Whose haggard craftsmen rose to starve this day,
Starve now, and will lie down at night to starve,
Sure of a like tomorrow—but as sure   *250*
Of a most unlike morrow-after-that,
Since end things must, end howsoe'er things may.
What curbs the brute-force instinct in its hour?
What makes—instead of rising, all as one,
And teaching fingers, so expert to wield   *255*
Their tool, the broadsword's play or carbine's trick,

—What makes that there's an easier help, they
     think,
For you, whose name so few of them can spell,
Whose face scarce one in every hundred saw—
260 You simply have to understand their wrongs,
And wrongs will vanish—so, still trades are plied,
And swords lie rusting, and myself stand here?
There is a vision in the heart of each
Of justice, mercy, wisdom, tenderness
265 To wrong and pain, and knowledge of its cure:
And these embodied in a woman's form
That best transmits them, pure as first received,
From God above her, to mankind below.
Will you derive your rule from such a ground,
270 Or rather hold it by the suffrage, say,
Of this man—this—and this?

   The Duchess [*after a pause*]. You come from Cleves:
     How many are at Cleves of such a mind?

   Valence [*from his paper*]. "We, all the manufacturers
     of Cleves—"

   The Duchess. Or stay, sir—lest I seem too covetous—
275 Are you my subject? such as you describe,
Am I to you, though to no other man?

   Valence [*from his paper*]. —"Valence, ordained your
     Advocate at Cleves"—

   The Duchess [*replacing the coronet*]. Then I remain
     Cleves' Duchess! Take you note,
While Cleves but yields one subject of this stamp,
280 I stand her lady till she waves me off!
For her sake, all the Prince claims I withhold;
Laugh at each menace; and, his power defying,
Return his missive with its due contempt!
                              [*Casting it away.*]

   Guibert [*picking it up*].—Which to the Prince I will
     deliver, lady,
285 (Note it down, Gaucelme)—with your message too!

The Duchess. I think the office is a subject's, sir!
  —Either . . . how style you him?—my special
    guarder
  The Marshal's—for who knows but violence
  May follow the delivery?—Or, perhaps,
  My Chancellor's—for law may be to urge   290
  On its receipt!—Or, even my Chamberlain's—
  For I may violate established form!
  [*To* VALENCE.] Sir—for the half-hour till this service
    ends,
  Will you become all these to me?

Valence [*falling on his knee*].   My liege!

The Duchess. Give me! [*The* Courtiers *present their
    badges of office.*] [*Putting them by.*] Whatever
    was their virtue once,   295
  They need new consecration. [*Raising* VALENCE.]
    Are you mine?
  I will be Duchess yet!   [*She retires.*]

The Courtiers.   Our Duchess yet!
  A glorious lady! Worthy love and dread!
  I'll stand by her—And I, whate'er betide!

Guibert [*to* VALENCE]. Well done, well done, sir! I
    care not who knows,   300
  You have done nobly and I envy you—
  Though I am but unfairly used, I think:
  For when one gets a place like this I hold,
  One gets too the remark that its mere wages,
  The pay and the preferment, make our prize.   305
  Talk about zeal and faith apart from these,
  We're laughed at—much would zeal and faith sub-
    sist
  Without these also! Yet, let these be stopped,
  Our wages discontinue—then, indeed,
  Our zeal and faith (we hear on every side),   310
  Are not released—having been pledged away
  I wonder, for what zeal and faith in turn?
  Hard money purchased me my place! No, no—

I'm right, sir—but your wrong is better still,
315   If I had time and skill to argue it.
Therefore, I say, I'll serve you, how you please—
If you like—fight you, as you seem to wish—
(The kinder of me that, in sober truth,
I never dreamed I did you any harm) . . .

Gaucelme. —Or, kinder still, you'll introduce, no
320   doubt,
His merits to the Prince who's just at hand,
And let no hint drop he's made Chancellor
And Chamberlain and Heaven knows what beside!

Clugnet [*to* VALENCE]. You stare, young sir, and
threaten! Let me say,
325   That at your age, when first I came to court,
I was not much above a gentleman;
While now . . .

Valence.   —You are Head-Lackey? With your
office
I have not yet been graced, sir!

Other Courtiers [*to* CLUGNET]. Let him talk!
Fidelity, disinterestedness,
330   Excuse so much! Men claim my worship ever
Who staunchly and steadfastly . . .

Enter ADOLF.

Adolf.   The Prince arrives.

Courtiers. Ha? How?

Adolf.   He leaves his guard a stage behind
At Aix, and enters almost by himself.

1st Courtier. The Prince! This foolish business puts all
out.

2nd Courtier. Let Gaucelme speak first!

335 *3rd Courtier.*   Better I began
About the state of Juliers: should one say
All's prosperous and inviting him?

4th Courtier.   —Or rather,
All's prostrate and imploring him?

5th Courtier.   That's best.
Where's the Cleves' paper, by the way?

4th Courtier [*to* VALENCE].   Sir—sir—
If you'll but lend that paper—trust it me,   340
I'll warrant . . .

5th Courtier.   Softly, sir—the Marshal's duty!

Clugnet. Has not the Chamberlain a hearing first
By virtue of his patent?

Gaucelme.   Patents?—Duties?
All that, my masters, must begin again!
One word composes the whole controversy: 345
We're simply now—the Prince's!

The Others.   Ay—the Prince's!

Enter SABYNE.

Sabyne. Adolf! Bid . . . Oh, no time for ceremony!
Where's whom our lady calls her only subject?
She needs him. Who is here the Duchess'?

Valence [*starting from his reverie*]. Most gratefully I
follow to her feet.   350

ACT III

SCENE—*The Vestibule*

Enter PRINCE BERTHOLD *and* MELCHIOR.

Berthold. A thriving little burgh this Juliers looks.
 [*Half apart*.] Keep Juliers, and as good you kept
  Cologne:
 Better try Aix, though!—

Melchior.   Please't your Highness speak?

Berthold [*as before*]. Aix, Cologne, Frankfort—Milan;
 —Rome!—

Melchior.   The Grave.
5 More weary seems your Highness, I remark,
 Than sundry conquerors whose path I've watched
 Through fire and blood to any prize they gain.
 I could well wish you, for your proper sake,
 Had met some shade of opposition here
10 —Found a blunt seneschal° refuse unlock,
 Or a scared usher lead your steps astray.
 You must not look for next achievement's palm
 So easily: this will hurt your conquering.

Berthold. My next? Ay, as you say, my next and next!
15 Well, I am tired, that's truth, and moody too,
 This quiet entrance-morning: listen why!
 Our little burgh, now, Juliers—'tis indeed
 One link, however insignificant,
 Of the great chain by which I reach my hope,
20 —A link I must secure; but otherwise,

10 **seneschal** steward.

106

You'd wonder I esteem it worth my grasp.
Just see what life is, with its shifts and turns!
It happens now—this very nook—to be
A place that once . . . not a long while since,
    neither—
When I lived an ambiguous hanger-on   *25*
Of foreign courts, and bore my claims about,
Discarded by one kinsman, and the other
A poor priest merely—then, I say, this place
Shone my ambition's object; to be Duke—
Seemed then, what to be Emperor seems now.   *30*
My rights were far from judged as plain and sure
In those days as of late, I promise you:
And 'twas my daydream, Lady Colombe here
Might e'en compound the matter, pity me,
Be struck, say, with my chivalry and grace   *35*
(I was a boy!)—bestow her hand at length,
And make me Duke, in her right if not mine.
Here am I, Duke confessed, at Juliers now.
Hearken: if ever I be Emperor,
Remind me what I felt and said today!   *40*

Melchior. All this consoles a bookish man like me.
    —And so will weariness cling to you. Wrong,
    Wrong! Had you sought the lady's court yourself—
    Faced the redoubtables composing it,
    Flattered this, threatened that man, bribed the
        other—   *45*
    Pleaded by writ and word and deed, your cause—
    Conquered a footing inch by painful inch—
    And, after long years' struggle, pounced at last
    On her for prize—the right life had been lived,
    And justice done to divers faculties   *50*
    Shut in that brow. Yourself were visible
    As you stood victor, then; whom now—(your par-
        don!)
    I am forced narrowly to search and see,
    So are you hid by helps—this Pope, your uncle—
    Your cousin, the other King! You are a mind—   *55*
    They, body: too much of mere legs-and-arms

Obstructs the mind so! Match these with their like:
Match mind with mind!

Berthold.   And where's your mind to match?
They show me legs-and-arms to cope withal!
60 I'd subjugate this city—where's its mind?
                    [*The* Courtiers *enter slowly.*]

Melchior. Got out of sight when you came troops and
   all!
And in its stead, here greets you flesh-and-blood:
A smug economy of both, this first!
                    [*As* CLUGNET *bows obsequiously.*]
Well done, gout, all considered!—I may go?

Berthold. Help me receive them!

65 *Melchior.*   Oh, they just will say
What yesterday at Aix their fellows said—
At Treves, the day before! Sir Prince, my friend,
Why do you let your life slip thus?—Meantime,
I have my little Juliers to achieve—
70 The understanding this tough Platonist,
Your holy uncle disinterred, Amelius:
Lend me a company of horse and foot,
To help me through his tractate—gain my Duchy!

Berthold. And Empire, after that is gained, will be—?

Melchior. To help me through your uncle's comment,
75 Prince!   [*Goes.*]

Berthold. Ah? Well: he o'er-refines—the scholar's
   fault!
How do I let my life slip? Say, this life,
I lead now, differs from the common life
Of other men in mere degree, not kind,
80 Of joys and griefs—still there is such degree
Mere largeness in a life is something, sure—
Enough to care about and struggle for,
In this world: for this world, the size of things;
The sort of things, for that to come, no doubt.
85 A great is better than a little aim:

And when I wooed Priscilla's rosy mouth
And failed so, under that gray convent-wall,
Was I more happy than I should be now
[*By this time, the* Courtiers *are ranged before him.*]
If failing of my Empire? Not a whit.
—Here comes the mind, it once had tasked me sore   *90*
To baffle, but for my advantages!
All's best as 'tis: these scholars talk and talk.
                              [*Seats himself.*]

The Courtiers. Welcome our Prince to Juliers!—to his
    heritage!
Our dutifullest service proffer we!

Clugnet. I, please your Highness, having exercised   *95*
The function of Grand Chamberlain at court,
With much acceptance, as men testify . . .

Berthold. I cannot greatly thank you, gentlemen!
The Pope declares my claim to the Duchy founded
On strictest justice—you concede it, therefore,   *100*
I do not wonder: and the kings my friends
Protest they mean to see such claim enforced—
You easily may offer to assist.
But there's a slight discretionary power
To serve me in the matter, you've had long,
Though late you use it. This is well to say—   *105*
But could you not have said it months ago?
I'm not denied my own Duke's truncheon, true—
'Tis flung me—I stoop down, and from the ground
Pick it, with all you placid standers-by:
And now I have it, gems and mire at once,   *110*
Grace go with it to my soiled hands, you say!

Guibert. (By Paul, the advocate our doughty friend
Cuts the best figure!)

Gaucelme.   If our ignorance
May have offended, sure our loyalty . . .   *115*

Berthold. Loyalty? Yours? Oh—of yourselves you
    speak!
I mean the Duchess all this time, I hope!

And since I have been forced repeat my claims
As if they never had been urged before,
120   As I began, so must I end, it seems.
The formal answer to the grave demand!
What says the lady?

Courtiers [*one to another*]. 1*st Courtier*. Marshal!
    2*nd Courtier*. Orator!

Guibert. A variation of our mistress' way!
    Wipe off his boots' dust, Clugnet!—that, he waits!

1*st Courtier*. Your place!

2*nd Courtier*. Just now it was your own!

125 *Guibert*.   The devil's!

Berthold [*to* GUIBERT]. Come forward, friend—you
    with the paper, there!
    Is Juliers the first city I've obtained?
    By this time, I may boast proficiency
    In each decorum of the circumstance.
130   Give it me as she gave it—the petition,
    Demand, you style it! What's required, in brief?
    What title's reservation, appanage's
    Allowance? I heard all at Treves, last week.

Gaucelme [*to* GUIBERT]. "Give it him as she gave it!"

Guibert.   And why not?
    [*To* BERTHOLD.] The lady crushed your summons
135   thus together,
    And bade me, with the very greatest scorn
    So fair a frame could hold, inform you . . .

Courtiers.   Stop—
    Idiot!

Guibert. —Inform you she denied your claim,
    Defied yourself! (I tread upon his heel,
    The blustering advocate!)

140 *Berthold*.   By heaven and earth!
    Dare you jest, sir?

Guibert.   Did they at Treves, last week?

Berthold [*starting up*]. Why then, I look much bolder
  than I knew,
And you prove better actors than I thought:
Since, as I live, I took you as you entered
For just so many dearest friends of mine,   145
Fled from the sinking to the rising power
—The sneaking'st crew, in short, I e'er despised!
Whereas, I am alone here for the moment,
With every soldier left behind at Aix!
Silence? That means the worst? I thought as much!   150
What follows next then?

Courtiers.   Gracious Prince, he raves!

Guibert. He asked the truth and why not get the
  truth?

Berthold. Am I a prisoner? Speak, will somebody?
—But why stand paltering with imbeciles?
Let me see her, or . . .

Guibert.   Her, without her leave,   155
Shall no one see: she's Duchess yet!

Courtiers [*footsteps without, as they are disputing*].
  Good chance!
She's here—the Lady Colombe's self!

Berthold.   'Tis well!
[*Aside.*] Array a handful thus against my world?
Not ill done, truly! Were not this a mind
To match one's mind with? Colombe! Let us wait!   160
I failed so, under that gray convent wall!
She comes.

Guibert. The Duchess! Strangers, range yourselves!

[*As the* DUCHESS *enters in conversation with*
  VALENCE, BERTHOLD *and the* Courtiers
  fall back a little.]

The Duchess. Presagefully it beats, presagefully,
My heart: the right is Berthold's and not mine.

165 *Valence.* Grant that he has the right, dare I mistrust
            Your power to acquiesce so patiently
            As you believe, in such a dream-like change
            Of fortune—change abrupt, profound, complete?

The Duchess. Ah, the first bitterness is over now!
170   Bitter I may have felt it to confront
            The truth, and ascertain those natures' value
            I had so counted on; that was a pang:
            But I did bear it, and the worst is over.
            Let the Prince take them!

Valence.   And take Juliers too?
175   —Your people without crosses, wands and chains—
            Only with hearts?

The Duchess.   There I feel guilty, sir!
            I cannot give up what I never had:
            For I ruled these, not them—these stood between.
            Shall I confess, sir? I have heard by stealth
180   Of Berthold from the first; more news and more:
            Closer and closer swam the thundercloud,
            But I was safely housed with these, I knew.
            At times when to the casement I would turn,
            At a bird's passage or a flower-trail's play,
185   I caught the storm's red glimpses on its edge—
            Yet I was sure some one of all these friends
            Would interpose: I followed the bird's flight
            Or plucked the flower: someone would interpose!

Valence. Not one thought on the People—and Cleves
            there!

The Duchess. Now, sadly conscious my real sway was
190   missed,
            Its shadow goes without so much regret:
            Else could I not again thus calmly bid you,
            Answer Prince Berthold!

Valence.   Then you acquiesce?

The Duchess. Remember over whom it was I ruled!

Guibert [*stepping forward*]. Prince Berthold, yonder,
    craves an audience, lady!   195

The Duchess [*to* VALENCE]. I only have to turn, and I
    shall face
    Prince Berthold! Oh, my very heart is sick!
    It is the daughter of a line of dukes
    This scornful insolent adventurer
    Will bid depart from my dead father's halls!   200
    I shall not answer him—dispute with him—
    But, as he bids, depart! Prevent it, sir!
    Sir—but a mere day's respite! Urge for me
    —What I shall call to mind I should have urged
    When time's gone by: 'twill all be mine, you urge!   205
    A day—an hour—that I myself may lay
    My rule down! 'Tis too sudden—must not be!
    The world's to hear of it! Once done—forever!
    How will it read, sir? How be sung about?
    Prevent it!

Berthold [*approaching*]. Your frank indignation, lady,   210
    Cannot escape me. Overbold I seem;
    But somewhat should be pardoned my surprise
    At this reception—this defiance, rather.
    And if, for their and your sake, I rejoice
    Your virtues could inspire a trusty few   215
    To make such gallant stand in your behalf,
    I cannot but be sorry, for my own,
    Your friends should force me to retrace my steps:
    Since I no longer am permitted speak
    After the pleasant peaceful course prescribed   220
    No less by courtesy than relationship—
    Which I remember, if you once forgot.
    But never must attack pass unrepelled.
    Suffer that, through you, I demand of these,
    Who controverts my claim to Juliers?

The Duchess.   —Me   225
    You say, you do not speak to—

Berthold.   Of your subjects

I ask, then: whom do you accredit? Where
Stand those should answer?

Valence [*advancing*].   The lady is alone.

Berthold. Alone, and thus? So weak and yet so bold?

Valence. I said she was alone—

230 *Berthold.*   And weak, I said.

Valence. When is man strong until he feels alone?
  It was some lonely strength at first, be sure,
  Created organs, such as those you seek,
  By which to give its varied purpose shape:
235 And, naming the selected ministrants,
  Took sword, and shield, and scepter—each, a man!
  That strength performed its work and passed its
       way:
  You see our lady: there, the old shapes stand!
  —A Marshal, Chamberlain, and Chancellor—
240 "Be helped their way, into their death put life
  And find advantage!"—so you counsel us.
  But let strength feel alone, seek help itself—
  And, as the inland-hatched sea-creature hunts
  The sea's breast out—as, littered 'mid the waves
245 The desert-brute makes for the desert's joy—
  So turns our lady to her true resource,
  Passing o'er hollow fictions, worn-out types,
  —And I am first her instinct fastens on.
  And prompt I say, as clear as heart can speak,
250 The People will not have you; nor shall have!
  It is not merely I shall go bring Cleves
  And fight you to the last—though that does much,
  And men and children—ay, and women too,
  Fighting for home, are rather to be feared
255 Than mercenaries fighting for their pay—
  But, say you beat us, since such things have been,
  And, where this Juliers laughed, you set your foot
  Upon a steaming bloody plash—what then?
  Stand you the more our lord that there you stand?
260 Lord it o'er troops whose force you concentrate,

A pillared flame whereto all ardors tend—
Lord it 'mid priests whose schemes you amplify,
A cloud of smoke 'neath which all shadows brood—
But never, in this gentle spot of earth,
Can you become our Colombe, our play-queen,   *265*
For whom, to furnish lilies for her hair,
We'd pour our veins forth to enrich the soil.
—Our conqueror? Yes!—Our despot? Yes!—Our
    Duke?
Know yourself, know us!

Berthold [*who has been in thought*]. Know your lady,
    also!
[*Very deferentially.*]—To whom I needs must excul-
    pate myself   *270*
For having made a rash demand, at least.
Wherefore to you, sir, who appear to be
Her chief adviser, I submit my claims,
                [*Giving papers.*]
But, this step taken, take no further step,
Until the Duchess shall pronounce their worth.   *275*
Here be our meeting-place; at night, its time:
Till when I humbly take the lady's leave!

    [*He withdraws. As the* DUCHESS *turns to*
    VALENCE, *the* Courtiers *interchange*
    glances and come forward a little.]

1st Courtier. So, this was their device!

2nd Courtier. No bad device!

3rd Courtier. You'd say they love each other, Gui-
    bert's friend
From Cleves, and she, the Duchess!

4th Courtier.   —And moreover,   *280*
That all Prince Berthold comes for, is to help
Their loves!

5th Courtier. Pray, Guibert, what is next to do?

Guibert [*advancing*]. I laid my office at the Duchess'
    foot—

Others. And I—and I—and I!

The Duchess.   I took them, sirs.

Guibert [*apart to* VALENCE]. And now, sir, I am sim-
285   ple knight again—
       Guibert, of the great ancient house, as yet
       That never bore affront; whate'er your birth—
       As things stand now, I recognize yourself
       (If you'll accept experience of some date)
290   As like to be the leading man o' the time,
       Therefore as much above me now, as I
       Seemed above you this morning. Then, I offered
       To fight you: will you be as generous
       And now fight me?

Valence.   Ask when my life is mine!

Guibert. ('Tis hers now!)

Clugnet [*apart to* VALENCE, *as* GUIBERT *turns from*
295   *him*].   You, sir, have insulted me
       Grossly—will grant me, too, the selfsame favor
       You've granted him, just now, I make no question?

Valence. I promise you, as him, sir.

Clugnet.   Do you so?
       Handsomely said! I hold you to it, sir.
300   You'll get me reinstated in my office
       As you will Guibert!

The Duchess.   I would be alone!

       [*They begin to retire slowly; as* VALENCE
              is about to follow—]

       Alone, sir—only with my heart: you stay!

Gaucelme. You hear that? Ah, light breaks upon me!
       Cleves—
       It was at Cleves some man harangued us all—
305   With great effect—so those who listened said,
       My thoughts being busy elsewhere: was this he?
       Guibert—your strange, disinterested man!

Your uncorrupted, if uncourtly friend!
The modest worth you mean to patronize!
He cares about no Duchesses, not he— 310
His sole concern is with the wrongs of Cleves!
What, Guibert? What, it breaks on you at last?

Guibert. Would this hall's floor were a mine's roof!
    I'd back
And in her very face . . .

Gaucelme.   Apply the match
    That fired the train—and where would you be,
    pray? 315

Guibert. With him!

Gaucelme.   Stand, rather, safe outside with me!
    The mine's charged: shall I furnish you the match
    And place you properly? To the antechamber!

Guibert. Can you?

Gaucelme.   Try me! Your friend's in fortune!

Guibert.   Quick— 320
    To the antechamber! He is pale with bliss!

Gaucelme. No wonder! Mark her eyes!

Guibert.   To the antechamber!
    [*The* Courtiers *retire.*]

The Duchess. Sir, could you know all you have done
    for me
You were content! You spoke, and I am saved.

Valence. Be not too sanguine, lady! Ere you dream, 325
    That transient flush of generosity
Fades off, perchance. The man, beside, is gone—
Him we might bend; but see, the papers here—
Inalterably his requirement stays,
And cold hard words have we to deal with now. 330
In that large eye there seemed a latent pride,
To self-denial not incompetent,
But very like to hold itself dispensed

From such a grace: however, let us hope!
335 He is a noble spirit in noble form.
I wish he less had bent that brow to smile
As with the fancy how he could subject
Himself upon occasion to—himself!
From rudeness, violence, you rest secure;
340 But do not think your Duchy rescued yet!

The Duchess. You—who have opened a new world
     to me,
Will never take the faded language up
Of that I leave? My Duchy—keeping it,
Or losing it—is that my sole world now?

345 *Valence.* Ill have I spoken if you thence despise
Juliers; although the lowest, on true grounds,
Be worth more than the highest rule, on false:
Aspire to rule, on the true grounds!

The Duchess.   Nay, hear—
False, I will never—rash, I would not be!
350 This is indeed my birthday—soul and body,
Its hours have done on me the work of years.
You hold the requisition: ponder it!
If I have right, my duty's plain: if he—
Say so, nor ever change a tone of voice!
355 At night you meet the Prince; meet me at eve!
Till when, farewell! This discomposes you?
Believe in your own nature, and its force
Of renovating mine! I take my stand
Only as under me the earth is firm:
360 So, prove the first step stable, all will prove.
That first, I choose: [*Laying her hand on his.*]—the
next to take, choose you!   [*She withdraws.*]

Valence [*after a pause*]. What drew down this on me?
     —on me, dead once,
She thus bids live—since all I hitherto
Thought dead in me, youth's ardors and emprise,
365 Burst into life before her, as she bids
Who needs them. Whither will this reach, where
     end?

Her hand's print burns on mine. . . . Yet she's
   above—
So very far above me! All's too plain:
I served her when the others sank away,
And she rewards me as such souls reward—   *370*
The changed voice, the suffusion of the cheek,
The eye's acceptance, the expressive hand,
  —Reward, that's little, in her generous thought,
Though all to me . . .
            I cannot so disclaim
Heaven's gift, nor call it other than it is!   *375*
She loves me!
[*Looking at the* Prince's *papers.*]—Which love,
  these, perchance, forbid.
Can I decide against myself—pronounce
She is the Duchess and no mate for me?
—Cleves, help me! Teach me—every haggard
  face—
To sorrow and endure! I will do right   *380*
Whatever be the issue. Help me, Cleves!

ACT IV

EVENING

SCENE—*An Antechamber*

Enter the Courtiers.

Maufroy. Now, then, that we may speak—how spring
  this mine?

Gaucelme. Is Guibert ready for its match? He cools!
  Not so friend Valence with the Duchess there!
  "Stay, Valence! Are not you my better self?"
  And her cheek mantled—

5 *Guibert.*   Well, she loves him, sir:
     And more—since you will have it I grow cool—
     She's right: he's worth it.

   Gaucelme.   For his deeds today?
     Say so!

   Guibert. What should I say beside?

   Gaucelme.   Not this—
     For friendship's sake leave this for me to say—
10   That we're the dupes of an egregious cheat!
     This plain unpracticed suitor, who found way
     To the Duchess through the merest die's turn-up
     A year ago, had seen her and been seen,
     Loved and been loved.

   Guibert.   Impossible!

   Gaucelme.   —Nor say,
15   How sly and exquisite a trick, moreover,
     Was this which—taking not their stand on facts
     Boldly, for that had been endurable,
     But worming on their way by craft, they choose
     Resort to, rather—and which you and we,
20   Sheep-like, assist them in the playing-off!
     The Duchess thus parades him as preferred,
     Not on the honest ground of preference,
     Seeing first, liking more, and there an end—
     But as we all had started equally,
25   And at the close of a fair race he proved
     The only valiant, sage and loyal man.
     Herself, too, with the pretty fits and starts—
     The careless, winning, candid ignorance
     Of what the Prince might challenge or forego—
30   She had a hero in reserve! What risk
     Ran she? This deferential easy Prince
     Who brings his claims for her to ratify
     —He's just her puppet for the nonce! You'll see—
     Valence pronounces, as is equitable,
35   Against him: off goes the confederate:
     As equitably, Valence takes her hand!

The Chancellor. You run too fast: her hand, no sub-
    ject takes.
    Do not our archives hold her father's will?
    That will provides against such accident,
    And gives next heir, Prince Berthold, the reversion   *40*
    Of Juliers, which she forfeits, wedding so.

Gaucelme. I know that, well as you—but does the
    Prince?
    Knows Berthold, think you, that this plan, he helps,
    For Valence's ennoblement—would end,
    If crowned with the success which seems its due,   *45*
    In making him the very thing he plays,
    The actual Duke of Juliers? All agree
    That Colombe's title waived or set aside,
    He is next heir.

The Chancellor. Incontrovertibly.

Gaucelme. Guibert, your match, now, to the train!

Guibert.   Enough!   *50*
    I'm with you: selfishness is best again.
    I thought of turning honest—what a dream!
    Let's wake now!

Gaucelme.   Selfish, friend, you never were:
    'Twas but a series of revenges taken
    On your unselfishness for prospering ill.   *55*
    But now that you're grown wiser, what's our course?

Guibert. —Wait, I suppose, till Valence weds our
    lady,
    And then, if we must needs revenge ourselves,
    Apprise the Prince.

Gaucelme.   —The Prince, ere then dismissed   *60*
    With thanks for playing his mock part so well?
    Tell the Prince now, sir! Ay, this very night,
    Ere he accepts his dole and goes his way,
    Explain how such a marriage makes him Duke,
    Then trust his gratitude for the surprise!

Guibert. —Our lady wedding Valence all the same   *65*

As if the penalty were undisclosed?
Good! If she loves, she'll not disown her love,
Throw Valence up. I wonder you see that.

Gaucelme. The shame of it—the suddenness and
shame!
70 Within her, the inclining heart—without,
A terrible array of witnesses—
And Valence by, to keep her to her word,
With Berthold's indignation or disgust!
We'll try it!—Not that we can venture much.
75 Her confidence we've lost forever: Berthold's
Is all to gain.

Guibert.   Tonight, then, venture we!
Yet—if lost confidence might be renewed?

Gaucelme. Never in noble natures! With the base
ones—
Twist off the crab's claw, wait a smarting-while,
80 And something grows and grows and gets to be
A mimic of the lost joint, just so like
As keeps in mind it never, never will
Replace its predecessor! Crabs do that:
But lop the lion's foot—and . . .

Guibert.   To the Prince!

Gaucelme [*aside*]. And come what will to the lion's
85 foot, I pay you,
My cat's-paw, as I long have yearned to pay.
[*Aloud.*] Footsteps! Himself! 'Tis Valence breaks
on us,
Exulting that their scheme succeeds. We'll hence—
And perfect ours! Consult the archives, first—
90 Then, fortified with knowledge, seek the Hall!

Clugnet [*to* GAUCELME *as they retire*]. You have not
smiled so since your father died!

As they retire, enter VALENCE *with papers.*

Valence. So must it be! I have examined these
With scarce a palpitating heart—so calm,

Keeping her image almost wholly off,
Setting upon myself determined watch,   *95*
Repelling to the uttermost his claims:
And the result is—all men would pronounce
And not I, only, the result to be—
Berthold is heir; she has no shade of right
To the distinction which divided us,   *100*
But, suffered to rule first, I know not why,
Her rule connived at by those Kings and Popes,
To serve some devil's purpose—now 'tis gained,
Whate'er it was, the rule expires as well.
—Valence, this rapture . . . selfish can it be?   *105*
Eject it from your heart, her home!—It stays!
Ah, the brave world that opens on us both!
—Do my poor townsmen so esteem it? Cleves—
I need not your pale faces! This, reward
For service done to you? Too horrible!   *110*
I never served you: 'twas myself I served—
Nay, served not—rather saved from punishment
Which, had I failed you then, would plague me now.
My life continues yours, and your life, mine.
But if, to take God's gift, I swerve no step—   *115*
Cleves! If I breathe no prayer for it—if she,
                              [*Footsteps without.*]
Colombe, that comes now, freely gives herself—
Will Cleves require, that, turning thus to her,
I . . .

Enter Prince BERTHOLD.

          Pardon, sir! I did not look for you
Till night, i' the Hall; nor have as yet declared   *120*
My judgment to the lady.

Berthold.   So I hoped.

Valence. And yet I scarcely know why that should check
     The frank disclosure of it first to you—
What her right seems, and what, in consequence,
She will decide on.

125 *Berthold.*   That I need not ask.

Valence. You need not: I have proved the lady's
    mind:
And, justice being to do, dare act for her.

Berthold. Doubtless she has a very noble mind.

Valence. Oh, never fear but she'll in each conjuncture
130   Bear herself bravely! She no whit depends
On circumstance; as she adorns a throne,
She had adorned . . .

Berthold.   A cottage—in what book
Have I read that, of every queen that lived?
A throne! You have not been instructed, sure,
To forestall my request?

135 *Valence.*   'Tis granted, sir!
My heart instructs me. I have scrutinized
Your claims . . .

Berthold.   Ah—claims, you mean, at first pre-
    ferred?
I come, before the hour appointed me,
To pray you let those claims at present rest,
140   In favor of a new and stronger one.

Valence. You shall not need a stronger: on the part
O' the lady, all you offer I accept,
Since one clear right suffices: yours is clear.
Propose!

Berthold. I offer her my hand.

Valence.   Your hand?

145 *Berthold.* A Duke's, yourself say; and, at no far time,
Something here whispers me—an Emperor's.
The lady's mind is noble: which induced
This seizure of occasion ere my claims
Were—settled, let us amicably say!

Valence. Your hand!

150 *Berthold.*   (He will fall down and kiss it next!)

Sir, this astonishment's too flattering,
Nor must you hold your mistress' worth so cheap.
Enhance it, rather—urge that blood is blood—
The daughter of the Burgraves, Landgraves, Mark-
    graves,
Remains their daughter! I shall scarce gainsay.   *155*
Elsewhere or here, the lady needs must rule:
Like the imperial crown's great chrysoprase,
They talk of—somewhat out of keeping there,
And yet no jewel for a meaner cap.

Valence. You wed the Duchess?

Berthold.   Cry you mercy, friend!   *160*
Will the match also influence fortunes here?
A natural solicitude enough.
Be certain, no bad chance it proves for you!
However high you take your present stand,
There's prospect of a higher still remove—   *165*
For Juliers will not be my resting-place,
And, when I have to choose a substitute
To rule the little burgh, I'll think of you
Who need not give your mates a character.
And yet I doubt your fitness to supplant   *170*
The gray smooth Chamberlain: he'd hesitate
A doubt his lady could demean herself
So low as to accept me. Courage, sir!
I like your method better: feeling's play
Is franker much, and flatters me beside.   *175*

Valence. I am to say, you love her?

Berthold.   Say that too!
Love has no great concernment, thinks the world,
With a duke's marriage. How go precedents
In Juliers' story—how use Juliers' dukes?
I see you have them here in goodly row;   *180*
Yon must be Luitpold—ay, a stalwart sire!
Say, I have been arrested suddenly
In my ambition's course, its rocky course,
By this sweet flower: I fain would gather it
And then proceed: so say and speedily   *185*

—(Nor stand there like Duke Luitpold's brazen
 self!)
Enough, sir: you possess my mind, I think.
This is my claim, the others being withdrawn,
And to this be it that, i' the Hall tonight,
190 Your lady's answer comes; till when, farewell!
           [*He retires.*]

Valence [*after a pause*]. The heavens and earth stay
 as they were; my heart
Beats as it beat: the truth remains the truth.
What falls away, then, if not faith in her?
Was it my faith, that she could estimate
195 Love's value, and, such faith still guiding me,
Dare I now test her? Or grew faith so strong
Solely because no power of test was mine?

     Enter the DUCHESS.

The Duchess. My fate, sir! Ah, you turn away. All's
 over.
But you are sorry for me? Be not so!
200 What I might have become, and never was,
Regret with me! What I have merely been,
Rejoice I am no longer! What I seem
Beginning now, in my new state, to be,
Hope that I am!—for, once my rights proved void,
205 This heavy roof seems easy to exchange
For the blue sky outside—my lot henceforth.

Valence. And what a lot is Berthold's!

The Duchess.   How of him?

Valence. He gathers earth's whole good into his arms;
Standing, as man now, stately, strong and wise,
210 Marching to fortune, not surprised by her.
One great aim, like a guiding-star, above—
Which tasks strength, wisdom, stateliness, to lift
His manhood to the height that takes the prize;
A prize not near—lest overlooking earth
215 He rashly spring to seize it—nor remote,
So that he rest upon his path content:

But day by day, while shimmering grows shine,
And the faint circlet prophesies the orb,
He sees so much as, just evolving these,
The stateliness, the wisdom and the strength,   220
To due completion, will suffice this life,
And lead him at his grandest to the grave.
After this star, out of a night he springs;
A beggar's cradle for the throne of thrones
He quits; so, mounting, feels each step he mounts,   225
Nor, as from each to each exultingly
He passes, overleaps one grade of joy.
This, for his own good:—with the world, each gift
Of God and man—reality, tradition,
Fancy and fact—so well environ him,   230
That as a mystic panoply they serve—
Of force, untenanted, to awe mankind,
And work his purpose out with half the world,
While he, their master, dexterously slipped
From such encumbrance, is meantime employed   235
With his own prowess on the other half.
Thus shall he prosper, every day's success
Adding, to what is he, a solid strength—
An aery might to what encircles him,
Till at the last, so life's routine lends help,   240
That as the Emperor only breathes and moves,
His shadow shall be watched, his step or stalk
Become a comfort or a portent, how
He trails his ermine take significance—
Till even his power shall cease to be most power,   245
And men shall dread his weakness more, nor dare
Peril their earth its bravest, first and best,
Its typified invincibility.
Thus shall he go on, greatening, till he ends—
The man of men, the spirit of all flesh,   250
The fiery center of an earthly world!

The Duchess. Some such a fortune I had dreamed
    should rise
  Out of my own—that is, above my power
  Seemed other, greater potencies to stretch—

Valence. For you?

255 *The Duchess.*   It was not I moved there, I think:
But one I could—though constantly beside,
And aye approaching—still keep distant from,
And so adore. 'Twas a man moved there.

Valence.   Who?

The Duchess. I felt the spirit, never saw the face.

260 *Valence.* See it! 'Tis Berthold's! He enables you
To realize your vision.

The Duchess.   Berthold?

Valence.   Duke—
Emperor to be: he proffers you his hand.

The Duchess. Generous and princely!

Valence.   He is all of this.

The Duchess. Thanks, Berthold, for my father's sake!
No hand
Degrades me.

265 *Valence.*   You accept the proffered hand?

The Duchess. That he should love me!

Valence.   "Loved" I did not say.
Had that been—love might so incline the Prince
To the world's good, the world that's at his foot—
I do not know, this moment, I should dare
270 Desire that you refused the world—and Cleves—
The sacrifice he asks.

The Duchess.   Not love me, sir?

Valence. He scarce affirmed it.

The Duchess.   May not deeds affirm?

Valence. What does he? . . . Yes, yes, very much he
does!
All the shame saved, he thinks, and sorrow saved—

Immitigable sorrow, so he thinks— 275
Sorrow that's deeper than we dream, perchance.

The Duchess. Is not this love?

Valence. So very much he does!
For look, you can descend now gracefully:
All doubts are banished, that the world might have,
Or worst, the doubts yourself, in after-time, 280
May call up of your heart's sincereness now.
To such, reply, "I could have kept my rule—
Increased it to the utmost of my dreams—
Yet I abjured it." This, he does for you:
It is munificently much.

The Duchess. Still "much!" 285
But why is it not love, sir? Answer me!

Valence. Because not one of Berthold's words and
looks
Had gone with love's presentment of a flower
To the beloved: because bold confidence,
Open superiority, free pride— 290
Love owns not, yet were all that Berthold owned:
Because where reason, even, finds no flaw,
Unerringly a lover's instinct may.

The Duchess. You reason, then, and doubt?

Valence. I love, and know.

The Duchess. You love? How strange! I never cast a
thought 295
On that. Just see our selfishness! You seemed
So much my own . . . I had no ground—and yet,
I never dreamed another might divide
My power with you, much less exceed it.

Valence. Lady,
I am yours wholly.

The Duchess. Oh, no, no, not mine! 300
'Tis not the same now, never more can be.

—Your first love, doubtless. Well, what's gone from
   me?
What have I lost in you?

Valence.   My heart replies—
No loss there! So, to Berthold back again:
305 This offer of his hand, he bids me make—
Its obvious magnitude is well to weigh.

The Duchess. She's . . . yes, she must be very fair for
   you!

Valence. I am a simple advocate of Cleves.

The Duchess. You! With the heart and brain that so
   helped me,
310 I fancied them exclusively my own,
Yet find are subject to a stronger sway!
She must be . . . tell me, is she very fair?

Valence. Most fair, beyond conception or belief.

The Duchess. Black eyes?—no matter! Colombe, the
   world leads
315 Its life without you, whom your friends professed
The only woman: see how true they spoke!
One lived this while, who never saw your face,
Nor heard your voice—unless. . . . Is she from
   Cleves?

Valence. Cleves knows her well.

The Duchess.   Ah—just a fancy, now!
When you poured forth the wrongs of Cleves—I
320 said,
—Thought, that is, afterward . . .

Valence.   You thought of me?

The Duchess. Of whom else? Only such great cause,
   I thought,
For such effect: see what true love can do!
Cleves is his love. I almost fear to ask
325 . . . And will not. This is idling: to our work!
Admit before the Prince, without reserve,

My claims misgrounded; then may follow better
. . . . When you poured out Cleves' wrongs im-
   petuously,
Was she in your mind?

Valence.   All done was done for her
—To humble me!

The Duchess.   She will be proud at least.   *330*

Valence. She?

The Duchess. When you tell her.

Valence.   That will never be.

The Duchess. How——are there sweeter things you
   hope to tell?
No, sir! You counseled me——I counsel you
In the one point I——any woman——can.
Your worth, the first thing; let her own come next—— *335*
Say what you did through her, and she through
   you——
The praises of her beauty afterward!
Will you?

Valence. I dare not.

The Duchess.   Dare not?

Valence.   She I love
Suspects not such a love in me.

The Duchess.   You jest.

Valence. The lady is above me and away.   *340*
Not only the brave form, and the bright mind,
And the great heart, combine to press me low——
But all the world calls rank divides us.

The Duchess.   Rank!
Now grant me patience! Here's a man declares
Oracularly in another's case——   *345*
Sees the true value and the false, for them——
Nay, bids them see it, and they straight do see.
You called my court's love worthless——so it turned:

    I threw away as dross my heap of wealth,
350 And here you stickle for a piece or two!
    First—has she seen you?

Valence.   Yes.

The Duchess.   She loves you, then.

Valence. One flash of hope burst; then succeeded
    night:
    And all's at darkest now. Impossible!

The Duchess. We'll try: you are—so to speak—my
    subject yet?

Valence. As ever—to the death.

355 *The Duchess.*   Obey me, then!

Valence. I must.

The Duchess. Approach her, and . . . no! first of all
    Get more assurance. "My instructress," say,
    "Was great, descended from a line of kings,
    And even fair"—(wait why I say this folly)—
360 "She said, of all men, none for eloquence,
    Courage, and (what cast even these to shade)
    The heart they sprung from—none deserved like
     him
    Who saved her at her need: if she said this,
    What should not one I love, say?"

Valence.   Heaven—this hope—
365 Oh, lady, you are filling me with fire!

The Duchess. Say this!—nor think I bid you cast aside
    One touch of all the awe and reverence;
    Nay, make her proud for once to heart's content
    That all this wealth of heart and soul's her own!
370 Think you are all of this—and, thinking it,
    . . . (Obey!)

Valence. I cannot choose.

The Duchess.   Then, kneel to her!
        [VALENCE *sinks on his knee.*]
  I dream!

Valence. Have mercy! Yours, unto the death—
    I have obeyed. Despise, and let me die!

The Duchess. Alas, sir, is it to be ever thus?
    Even with you as with the world? I know   *375*
    This morning's service was no vulgar deed
    Whose motive, once it dares avow itself,
    Explains all done and infinitely more,
    So, takes the shelter of a nobler cause.
    Your service named its true source—loyalty!   *380*
    The rest's unsaid again. The Duchess bids you,
    Rise, sir! The Prince's words were in debate.

Valence [*rising*]. Rise? Truth, as ever, lady, comes
    from you!
    I should rise—I who spoke for Cleves, can speak
    For Man—yet tremble now, who stood firm then.   *385*
    I laughed—for 'twas past tears—that Cleves should
        starve
    With all hearts beating loud the infamy,
    And no tongue daring trust as much to air:
    Yet here, where all hearts speak, shall I be mute?
    Oh, lady, for your own sake look on me!   *390*
    On all I am, and have, and do—heart, brain,
    Body and soul—this Valence and his gifts!
    I was proud once: I saw you, and they sank,
    So that each, magnified a thousand times,
    Were nothing to you—but such nothingness,   *395*
    Would a crown gild it, or a scepter prop,
    A treasure speed, a laurel-wreath enhance?
    What is my own desert? But should your love
    Have . . . there's no language helps here . . . singled
        me—
    Then—oh, that wild word "then!"—be just to love,   *400*
    In generosity its attribute!
    Love, since you pleased to love! All's cleared—a
        stage
    For trial of the question kept so long:
    Judge you—Is love or vanity the best?
    You, solve it for the world's sake—you, speak first   *405*
    What all will shout one day—you, vindicate
    Our earth and be its angel! All is said.

Lady, I offer nothing—I am yours:
But, for the cause' sake, look on me and him,
And speak!

410 *The Duchess.* I have received the Prince's message:
Say, I prepare my answer!

Valence.   Take me, Cleves!
                                   [*He withdraws.*]

The Duchess. Mournful—that nothing's what it calls
itself!
Devotion, zeal, faith, loyalty—mere love!
And, love in question, what may Berthold's be?
415 I did ill to mistrust the world so soon:
Already was this Berthold at my side.
The valley-level has its hawks no doubt:
May not the rock-top have its eagles, too?
Yet Valence . . . let me see his rival then!

ACT V

NIGHT

SCENE—*The Hall*

Enter BERTHOLD *and* MELCHIOR.

Melchior. And here you wait the matter's issue?

Berthold.   Here.

Melchior. I don't regret I shut Amelius, then.
But tell me, on this grand disclosure—how
Behaved our spokesman with the forehead?

Berthold.   Oh,
5 Turned out no better than the foreheadless—

Was dazzled not so very soon, that's all!
For my part, this is scarce the hasty showy
Chivalrous measure you give me credit of.
Perhaps I had a fancy—but 'tis gone.
—Let her commence the unfriended, innocent   10
And carry wrongs about from court to court?
No, truly! The least shake of fortune's sand,
—My uncle-Pope chokes in a coughing fit,
King-cousin takes a fancy to blue eyes—
And wondrously her claims would brighten up;   15
Forth comes a new gloss on the ancient law,
O'er-looked provisos, o'er-past premises,
Follow in plenty. No: 'tis the safe step.
The hour beneath the convent-wall is lost:
Juliers and she, once mine, are ever mine.   20

Melchior. Which is to say, you, losing heart already,
   Elude the adventure.

Berthold.   Not so—or, if so—
Why not confess at once that I advise
None of our kingly craft and guild just now
To lay, one moment, down their privilege   25
With the notion they can any time at pleasure
Retake it: that may turn out hazardous.
We seem, in Europe, pretty well at end
O' the night, with our great masque:° those favored
   few
Who keep the chamber's top, and honor's chance   30
Of the early evening, may retain their place
And figure as they list till out of breath.
But it is growing late: and I observe
A dim grim kind of tipstaves° at the doorway
Not only bar newcomers entering now,   35
But caution those who left, for any cause,
And would return, that morning draws too near;
The ball must die off, shut itself up. We—
I think, may dance lights out and sunshine in,
And sleep off headache on our frippery: 40

---

29 **masque** elaborate court drama.   34 **tipstaves** constables.

But friend the other, who cunningly stole out,
And, after breathing the fresh air outside,
Means to reenter with a new costume,
Will be advised go back to bed, I fear.
45   I stick to privilege, on second thoughts.

Melchior. Yes—you evade the adventure: and, beside,
Give yourself out for colder than you are.
King Philip, only, notes the lady's eyes?
Don't they come in for somewhat of the motive
With you too?

50   *Berthold.*   Yes—no: I am past that now.
Gone 'tis: I cannot shut my soul to fact.
Of course, I might by forethought and contrivance
Reason myself into a rapture. Gone:
And something better come instead, no doubt.

55   *Melchior.* So be it! Yet, all the same, proceed my way,
Though to your ends; so shall you prosper best!
The lady—to be won for selfish ends—
Will be won easier my unselfish . . . call it,
Romantic way.

Berthold.   Won easier?

Melchior.   Will not she?

60   *Berthold.* There I profess humility without bound:
Ill cannot speed—not I—the Emperor.

Melchior. And I should think the Emperor best
     waived,
From your description of her mood and way.
You could look, if it pleased you, into hearts;
65   But are too indolent and fond of watching
Your own—you know that, for you study it.

Berthold. Had you but seen the orator her friend,
So bold and voluble an hour before,
Abashed to earth at aspect of the change!
70   Make her an Empress? Ah, that changed the case!
Oh, I read hearts! 'Tis for my own behoof,
I court her with my true worth: wait the event!

I learned my final lesson on that head
When years ago—my first and last essay—
Before the priest my uncle could by help   *75*
Of his superior, raise me from the dirt—
Priscilla left me for a Brabant lord
Whose cheek was like the topaz on his thumb.
I am past illusion on that score.

Melchior.   Here comes
The lady—

Berthold. —And there you go. But do not! Give me   *80*
Another chance to please you! Hear me plead!

Melchior. You'll keep, then, to the lover, to the man?

Enter the DUCHESS—*followed by* ADOLF *and* SABYNE
and, after an interval, by the COURTIERS.

Berthold. Good auspice to our meeting!

The Duchess   May it prove!
—And you, sir, will be Emperor one day?

Berthold. (Ay, that's the point!) I may be Emperor.   *85*

The Duchess. 'Tis not for my sake only, I am proud
Of this you offer: I am prouder far
That from the highest state should duly spring
The highest, since most generous, of deeds.

Berthold. (Generous—still that!) You underrate your-
self.   *90*
You are, what I, to be complete, must gain—
Find now, and may not find, another time.
While I career on all the world for stage,
There needs at home my representative.

The Duchess. —Such, rather, would some warrior-
woman be—   *95*
One dowered with lands and gold, or rich in
friends—
One like yourself.

Berthold.   Lady, I am myself,

And have all these: I want what's not myself,
Nor has all these. Why give one hand two swords?
100   Here's one already: be a friend's next gift
A silk glove, if you will—I have a sword.

The Duchess. You love me, then?

Berthold.   Your lineage I revere,
Honor your virtue, in your truth believe,
Do homage to your intellect, and bow
Before your peerless beauty.

105   *The Duchess.*   But, for love—

Berthold. A further love I do not understand.
Our best course is to say these hideous truths,
And see them, once said, grow endurable:
Like waters shuddering from their central bed,
110   Black with the midnight bowels of the earth,
That, once upspouted by an earthquake's throe,
A portent and a terror—soon subside,
Freshen apace, take gold and rainbow hues
In sunshine, sleep in shadow, and at last
115   Grow common to the earth as hills or trees—
Accepted by all things they came to scare.

The Duchess. You cannot love, then?

Berthold.   —Charlemagne,° perhaps!
Are you not over-curious in love-lore?

The Duchess. I have become so, very recently.
120   It seems, then, I shall best deserve esteem,
Respect, and all your candor promises,
By putting on a calculating mood—
Asking the terms of my becoming yours?

Berthold. Let me not do myself injustice, neither.
125   Because I will not condescend to fictions
That promise what my soul can ne'er acquit,
It does not follow that my guarded phrase
May not include far more of what you seek,

117 **Charlemagne** emperor of the Franks.

Than wide profession of less scrupulous men.
You will be Empress, once for all: with me   *130*
The Pope disputes supremacy—you stand,
And none gainsays, the earth's first woman.

The Duchess.   That—
Or simple Lady of Ravestein again?

Berthold. The matter's not in my arbitrament:
Now I have made my claims—which I regret—   *135*
Cede one, cede all.

The Duchess.   This claim then, you enforce?

Berthold. The world looks on.

The Duchess.   And when must I decide?

Berthold. When, lady? Have I said thus much so
     promptly
For nothing?—Poured out, with such pains, at once
What I might else have suffered to ooze forth   *140*
Droplet by droplet in a lifetime long—
For aught less than as prompt an answer, too?
All's fairly told now: who can teach you more?

The Duchess. I do not see him.

Berthold.   I shall ne'er deceive.
This offer should be made befittingly   *145*
Did time allow the better setting forth
The good of it, with what is not so good,
Advantage, and disparagement as well:
But as it is, the sum of both must serve.
I am already weary of this place;   *150*
My thoughts are next stage on to Rome. Decide!
The Empire—or—not even Juliers now!
Hail to the Empress—farewell to the Duchess!

[*The* Courtiers, *who have been drawing nearer
          and nearer, interpose.*]

Gaucelme. —"Farewell," Prince? when we break in
     at our risk—

155 *Clugnet.* Almost upon court-license trespassing—

Gaucelme. —To point out how your claims are valid
    yet!
You know not, by the Duke her father's will,
The lady, if she weds beneath her rank,
Forfeits her Duchy in the next heir's favor—
160 So 'tis expressly stipulate. And if
It can be shown 'tis her intent to wed
A subject, then yourself, next heir, by right
Succeed to Juliers.

Berthold.   What insanity?—

Guibert. Sir, there's one Valence, the pale fiery man
You saw and heard this morning—thought, no
165   doubt,
Was of considerable standing here:
I put it to your penetration, Prince,
If aught save love, the truest love for her
Could make him serve the lady as he did!
170 He's simply a poor advocate of Cleves
—Creeps here with difficulty, finds a place
With danger, gets in by a miracle,
And for the first time meets the lady's face—
So runs the story: is that credible?
175 For, first—no sooner in, than he's apprised
Fortunes have changed; you are all-powerful here,
The lady as powerless: he stands fast by her!

The Duchess [*aside*]. And do such deeds spring up
    from love alone?

Guibert. But here occurs the question, does the lady
180 Love him again? I say, how else can she?
Can she forget hcw he stood singly forth
In her defense, dared outrage all of us,
Insult yourself—for what, save love's reward?

The Duchess [*aside*]. And is love then the sole reward
    of love?

185 *Guibert.* But, love him as she may and must—you ask,

Means she to wed him? "Yes," both natures answer!
Both, in their pride, point out the sole result;
Naught less would he accept nor she propose.
For each conjecture was she great enough
—Will be, for this.

Clugnet.   Though, now that this is known, *190*
Policy, doubtless, urges she deny . . .

The Duchess. —What, sir, and wherefore?—since I
    am not sure
That all is any other than you say!
You take this Valence, hold him close to me,
Him with his actions: can I choose but look? *195*
I am not sure, love trulier shows itself
Than in this man, you hate and would degrade,
Yet, with your worst abatement, show me thus.
Nor am I—(thus made look within myself,
Ere I had dared)—now that the look is dared— *200*
Sure that I do not love him!

Guibert.   Hear you, Prince?

Berthold. And what, sirs, please you, may this prattle
    mean
Unless to prove with what alacrity
You give your lady's secrets to the world?
How much indebted, for discovering *205*
That quality, you make me, will be found
When there's a keeper for my own to seek.

Courtiers. "Our lady?"

Berthold.   —She assuredly remains.

The Duchess. Ah, Prince—and you too can be gen-
    erous?
You could renounce your power, if this were so, *210*
And let me, as these phrase it, wed my love
Yet keep my Duchy? You perhaps exceed
Him, even, in disinterestedness!

Berthold. How, lady, should all this affect my purpose?
Your will and choice are still as ever, free. *215*

Say, you have known a worthier than myself
In mind and heart, of happier form and face—
Others must have their birthright: I have gifts.
To balance theirs, not blot them out of sight.
220 Against a hundred alien qualities,
I lay the prize I offer. I am nothing:
Wed you the Empire?

The Duchess.   And my heart away?

Berthold. When have I made pretension to your
       heart?
I give none. I shall keep your honor safe;
225 With mine I trust you, as the sculptor trusts
Yon marble woman with the marble rose,
Loose on her hand, she never will let fall,
In graceful, slight, silent security.
You will be proud of my worldwide career,
230 And I content in you the fair and good.
What were the use of planting a few seeds
The thankless climate never would mature—
Affections all repelled by circumstance?
Enough: to these no credit I attach—
235 To what you own, find nothing to object.
Write simply on my requisition's face
What shall content my friends—that you admit,
As Colombe of Ravestein, the claims therein,
Or never need admit them, as my wife—
And either way, all's ended!

240 *The Duchess.*   Let all end!

Berthold. The requisition!

Guibert.   —Valence holds, of course!

Berthold. Desire his presence!   [ADOLF *goes out.*]

Courtiers [*to each other*]. Out it all comes yet;
He'll have his word against the bargain yet;
He's not the man to tamely acquiesce.
245 One passionate appeal—upbraiding even,
May turn the tide again. Despair not yet!
                     [*They retire a little.*]

Berthold [*to* MELCHIOR]. The Empire has its old suc-
cess, my friend!

Melchior. You've had your way: before the spokes-
man speaks,
Let me, but this once, work a problem out,
And ever more be dumb! The Empire wins?   250
To better purpose have I read my books!

Enter VALENCE.

Melchior [*to the* Courtiers]. Apart, my masters!
[*To* VALENCE.] Sir, one word with you!
I am a poor dependent of the Prince's—
Pitched on to speak, as of slight consequence.
You are no higher, I find: in other words,   255
We two, as probably the wisest here,
Need not hold diplomatic talk like fools.
Suppose I speak, divesting the plain fact
Of all their tortuous phrases, fit for them?
Do you reply so, and what trouble saved!   260
The Prince, then—an embroiled strange heap of
news
This moment reaches him—if true or false,
All dignity forbids he should inquire
In person, or by worthier deputy;
Yet somehow must inquire, lest slander come: 265
And so, 'tis I am pitched on. You have heard
His offer to your lady?

Valence.   Yes.

Melchior.   —Conceive
Her joy thereat?

Valence.   I cannot.

Melchior.   No one can.
All draws to a conclusion, therefore.

Valence [*aside*].   So!
No after-judgment—no first thought revised—   270
Her first and last decision!—me, she leaves,
Takes him; a simple heart is flung aside,

The ermine o'er a heartless breast embraced.
Oh Heaven, this mockery has been played too oft!
275   Once, to surprise the angels—twice, that fiends
Recording, might be proud they chose not so—
Thrice, many thousand times, to teach the world
All men should pause, misdoubt their strength, since men
Can have such chance yet fail so signally,
280   —But ever, ever this farewell to Heaven,
Welcome to earth—this taking death for life—
This spurning love and kneeling to the world—
Oh Heaven, it is too often and too old!

Melchior. Well, on this point, what but an absurd rumor
285   Arises—these, its source—its subject, you!
Your faith and loyalty misconstruing,
They say, your service claims the lady's hand!
Of course, nor Prince nor lady can respond:
Yet something must be said: for, were it true
You made such claim, the Prince would . . .

290   *Valence.*   Well, sir—would?

Melchior. —Not only probably withdraw his suit,
But, very like, the lady might be forced
Accept your own. Oh, there are reasons why!
But you'll excuse at present all save one—
295   I think so. What we want is, your own witness,
For, or against—her good, or yours: decide!

Valence [*aside*]. Be it her good if she accounts it so!
[*After a contest.*] For what am I but hers, to choose as she?
Who knows how far, beside, the light from her
300   May reach, and dwell with, what she looks upon?

Melchior [*to the* Prince]. Now to him, you!

Berthold [*to* VALENCE]. My friend acquaints you, sir,
The noise runs . . .

Valence.   —Prince, how fortunate are you,

Wedding her as you will, in spite of noise,
To show belief in love! Let her but love you,
All else you disregard! What else can be?   *305*
You know how love is incompatible
With falsehood—purifies, assimilates
All other passions to itself.

Melchior.   Ay, sir:
But softly! Where, in the object we select,
Such love is, perchance, wanting?

Valence.   Then indeed,   *310*
What is it you can take?

Melchior.   Nay, ask the world!
Youth, beauty, virtue, an illustrious name,
An influence o'er mankind.

Valence.   When man perceives . . .
—Ah, I can only speak as for myself!

The Duchess. Speak for yourself!

Valence.   May I?—no, I have spoken,   *315*
And time's gone by. Had I seen such an one,
As I loved her—weighing thoroughly that word—
So should my task be to evolve her love:
If for myself!—if for another—well.

Berthold. Heroic truly! And your sole reward—   *320*
The secret pride in yielding up love's right?

Valence. Who thought upon reward? And yet how
     much
Comes after—oh, what amplest recompense!
Is the knowledge of her, naught? the memory,
     naught?
—Lady, should such an one have looked on you,   *325*
Ne'er wrong yourself so far as quote the world
And say, love can go unrequited here!
You will have blessed him to his whole life's end—
Low passions hindered, baser cares kept back,
All goodness cherished where you dwelled—and   *330*
     dwell.

What would he have? He holds you—you, both
    form
And mind, in his—where self-love makes such
    room
For love of you, he would not serve you now
The vulgar way—repulse your enemies,
335 Win you new realms, or best, to save the old
Die blissfully—that's past so long ago!
He wishes you no need, thought, care of him—
Your good, by any means, himself unseen,
Away, forgotten!—He gives that life's task up,
340 As it were . . . but this charge which I return—
       [*Offers the requisition, which she takes.*]
Wishing your good.

The Duchess [*having subscribed it*]. And opportunely,
    sir—
Since at a birthday's close, like this of mine,
Good wishes gentle deeds reciprocate.
Most on a wedding-day, as mine is too,
Should gifts be thought of: yours comes first by
345   right.
Ask of me!

Berthold. He shall have whate'er he asks,
For your sake and his own.

Valence [*aside*].   If I should ask—
The withered bunch of flowers she wears—perhaps,
One last touch of her hand, I never more
Shall see!
    [*After a pause, presenting his paper to the* Prince.]
350   Cleves' Prince, redress the wrongs of Cleves!

Berthold. I will, sir!

The Duchess [*as* VALENCE *prepares to retire*]. —Nay,
    do out your duty, first!
You bore this paper; I have registered
My answer to it: read it and have done!
              [VALENCE *reads it.*]
I take him—give up Juliers and the world.
This is my Birthday.

Melchior.   Berthold, my one hero   *355*
    Of the world she gives up, one friend worth my
      books,
    Sole man I think it pays the pains to watch—
    Speak, for I know you through your Popes and
      Kings!

Berthold [after a pause]. Lady, well rewarded! Sir,
    as well deserved!
    I could not imitate—I hardly envy—   *360*
    I do admire you. All is for the best.
    Too costly a flower were this, I see it now,
    To pluck and set upon my barren helm
    To wither—any garish plume will do.
    I'll not insult you and refuse your Duchy—   *365*
    You can so well afford to yield it me,
    And I were left, without it, sadly lorn.
    As it is—for me—if that will flatter you,
    A somewhat wearier life seems to remain
    Than I thought possible where . . . 'faith, their life *370*
    Begins already! They're too occupied
    To listen: and few words content me best.
    [*Abruptly to the* Courtiers.] I am your Duke, though!
      Who obey me here?

The Duchess. Adolf and Sabyne follow us—

Guibert [starting from the Courtiers]. —And I?
    Do I not follow them, if I mayn't you?   *375*
    Shall not I get some little duties up
    At Ravestein and emulate the rest?
    God save you, Gaucelme! 'Tis my Birthday, too!

Berthold. You happy handful that remain with me
    . . . That is, with Dietrich the black Barnabite°   *380*
    I shall leave over you—will earn your wages
    Or Dietrich has forgot to ply his trade!
    Meantime—go copy me the precedents
    Of every installation, proper styles
    And pedigrees of all your Juliers' dukes—   *385*

380 **Barnabite** monk.

While I prepare to plod on my old way,
And somewhat wearily, I must confess!

The Duchess [*with a light joyous laugh as she turns
from them*]. Come, Valence, to our friends, God's
earth . . .

Valence [*as she falls into his arms*].—And thee!

from DRAMATIC ROMANCES AND LYRICS

(1845)

GARDEN FANCIES

I. THE FLOWER'S NAME

I

Here's the garden she walked across,
　　Arm in my arm, such a short while since:
Hark, now I push its wicket, the moss
　　Hinders the hinges and makes them wince!
She must have reached this shrub ere she turned,　　*5*
　　As back with that murmur the wicket swung;
For she laid the poor snail, my chance foot spurned,
　　To feed and forget it the leaves among.

II

Down this side of the gravel-walk
　　She went while her robe's edge brushed the box:　　*10*
And here she paused in her gracious talk
　　To point me a moth on the milk-white phlox.
Roses, ranged in valiant row,
　　I will never think that she passed you by!
She loves you noble roses, I know;　　*15*
　　But yonder, see, where the rock-plants lie!

149

III

This flower she stopped at, finger on lip,
   Stooped over, in doubt, as settling its claim;
Till she gave me, with pride to make no slip,
20   Its soft meandering Spanish name:
What a name! Was it love or praise?
   Speech half-asleep or song half-awake?
I must learn Spanish, one of these days,
   Only for that slow sweet name's sake.

IV

25 Roses, if I live and do well,
   I may bring her, one of these days,
To fix you fast with as fine a spell,
   Fit you each with his Spanish phrase;
But do not detain me now; for she lingers
30   There, like sunshine over the ground,
And ever I see her soft white fingers
   Searching after the bud she found.

V

Flower, you Spaniard, look that you grow not,
   Stay as you are and be loved forever!
35 Bud, if I kiss you 'tis that you blow not:
   Mind, the shut pink mouth opens never!
For while it pouts, her fingers wrestle,
   Twinkling the audacious leaves between,
Till round they turn and down they nestle—
40   Is not the dear mark still to be seen?

VI

Where I find her not, beauties vanish;
   Whither I follow her, beauties flee;
Is there no method to tell her in Spanish
   June's twice June since she breathed it with me?

Come, bud, show me the least of her traces,
  Treasure my lady's lightest footfall!
—Ah, you may flout and turn up your faces—
  Roses, you are not so fair after all!   *45*

II. SIBRANDUS SCHAFNABURGENSIS°

I

Plague take all your pedants, say I!
  He who wrote what I hold in my hand,
Centuries back was so good as to die,
  Leaving this rubbish to cumber the land;
This, that was a book in its time,   *5*
  Printed on paper and bound in leather,
Last month in the white of a matin-prime
  Just when the birds sang all together.

II

Into the garden I brought it to read,
  And under the arbute and laurustine   *10*
Read it, so help me grace in my need,
  From title page to closing line.
Chapter on chapter did I count,
  As a curious traveler counts Stonehenge;
Added up the mortal amount;   *15*
  And then proceeded to my revenge.

III

Yonder's a plum-tree with a crevice
  An owl would build in, were he but sage;

Sibrandus Schafnaburgensis name of the "pedant" who wrote the
book.

For a lap of moss, like a fine pont-levis°
20   In a castle of the Middle Age,
Joins to a lip of gum, pure amber;
     When he'd be private, there might he spend
Hours alone in his lady's chamber:
     Into this crevice I dropped our friend.

IV

25   Splash, went he, as under he ducked,
     —At the bottom, I knew, rain-drippings stagnate:
Next, a handful of blossoms I plucked
     To bury him with, my bookshelf's magnate;
Then I went indoors, brought out a loaf,
30   Half a cheese, and a bottle of Chablis;
Lay on the grass and forgot the oaf
     Over a jolly chapter of Rabelais.°

V

Now, this morning, betwixt the moss
     And gum that locked our friend in limbo,
35   A spider had spun his web across,
     And sat in the midst with arms akimbo:
So, I took pity, for learning's sake,
     And, *de profundis, accentibus lætis,*
Cantate!° quoth I, as I got a rake;
40   And up I fished his delectable treatise.

VI

Here you have it, dry in the sun,
     With all the binding all of a blister,
And great blue spots where the ink has run,
     And reddish streaks that wink and glister
45   O'er the page so beautifully yellow:
     Oh, well have the droppings played their tricks!

19 **pont-levis** drawbridge. 32 **Rabelais** lusty humorist. 38–39 **de
profundis . . . Cantate!** sing joyfully from the depths!

Did he guess how toadstools grow, this fellow?
   Here's one stuck in his chapter six!

VII

How did he like it when the live creatures
   Tickled and toused and browsed him all over,   *50*
And worm, slug, eft, with serious features,
   Came in, each one, for his right of trover?°
—When the water-beetle with great blind deaf face
   Made of her eggs the stately deposit,
And the newt borrowed just so much of the preface   *55*
   As tiled in the top of his black wife's closet?

VIII

All that life and fun and romping,
   All that frisking and twisting and coupling,
While slowly our poor friend's leaves were swamping
   And clasps were cracking and covers suppling!   *60*
As if you had carried sour John Knox°
   To the playhouse at Paris, Vienna or Munich,
Fastened him into a front-row box,
   And danced off the ballet with trousers and tunic.

IX

Come, old martyr! What, torment enough is it?   *65*
   Back to my room shall you take your sweet self.
Good-bye, mother-beetle; husband-eft, *sufficit!*°
   See the snug niche I have made on my shelf!
A.'s book shall prop you up, B.'s shall cover you,
   Here's C. to be grave with, or D. to be gay,   *70*
And with E. on each side, and F. right over you,
   Dry-rot at ease till the Judgment Day!

---

52 **trover** finder.   61 **John Knox** Calvinist preacher and theologian.
67 **sufficit!** enough!

from MEN AND WOMEN

(1855)

A WOMAN'S LAST WORD

I

LET'S contend no more, Love,
   Strive nor weep:
All be as before, Love,
   —Only sleep!

II

What so wild as words are?
   I and thou
In debate, as birds are,
   Hawk on bough!

III

See the creature stalking
   While we speak!
Hush and hide the talking,
   Cheek on cheek!

IV

What so false as truth is,
    False to thee?
Where the serpent's tooth is   *15*
    Shun the tree—

V

Where the apple reddens
    Never pry—
Lest we lose our Edens,
    Eve and I.   *20*

VI

Be a god and hold me
    With a charm!
Be a man and fold me
    With thine arm!

VII

Teach me, only teach, Love!   *25*
    As I ought
I will speak thy speech, Love,
    Think thy thought—

VIII

Meet, if thou require it,
    Both demands,   *30*
Laying flesh and spirit
    In thy hands.

IX

That shall be tomorrow
    Not tonight:

35   I must bury sorrow
       Out of sight:

           X

    —Must a little weep, Love,
       (Foolish me!)
    And so fall asleep, Love,
40   Loved by thee.

FRA LIPPO LIPPI°

I AM poor brother Lippo, by your leave!
You need not clap your torches to my face.
Zooks,° what's to blame? you think you see a monk!
What, 'tis past midnight, and you go the rounds,
5   And here you catch me at an alley's end
Where sportive ladies leave their doors ajar?
The Carmine's my cloister: hunt it up,
Do—harry out, if you must show your zeal,
Whatever rat, there, haps on his wrong hole,
10 And nip each softling of a wee white mouse,
Weke, weke, that's crept to keep him company!
Aha, you know your betters! Then, you'll take
Your hand away that's fiddling on my throat,
And please to know me likewise. Who am I?
15 Why, one, sir, who is lodging with a friend
Three streets off—he's a certain . . . how d'ye call?
Master—a . . . Cosimo of the Medici,°

Fra Lippo Lippi Florentine painter of the Renaissance. **3 Zooks**
mild oath. **17 Cosimo of the Medici** banker, statesman, patron of
art. A man of great wealth and power.

I' the house that caps the corner. Boh! you were best!
Remember and tell me, the day you're hanged,
How you affected such a gullet's-gripe!   20
But you, sir, it concerns you that your knaves
Pick up a manner nor discredit you:
Zooks, are we pilchards,° that they sweep the streets
And count fair prize what comes into their net?
He's Judas to a tittle, that man is!   25
Just such a face! Why, sir, you make amends.
Lord, I'm not angry! Bid your hangdogs go
Drink out this quarter-florin to the health
Of the munificent House that harbors me
(And many more beside, lads! more beside!)   30
And all's come square again. I'd like his face—
His, elbowing on his comrade in the door
With the pike and lantern—for the slave that holds
John Baptist's head a-dangle by the hair
With one hand ("Look you, now," as who should say)   35
And his weapon in the other, yet unwiped!
It's not your chance to have a bit of chalk,
A wood-coal or the like? or you should see!
Yes, I'm the painter, since you style me so.
What, brother Lippo's doings, up and down,   40
You know them and they take you? like enough!
I saw the proper twinkle in your eye—
'Tell you, I liked your looks at very first.
Let's sit and set things straight now, hip to haunch.
Here's spring come, and the nights one makes up
        bands   45
To roam the town and sing out carnival,
And I've been three weeks shut within my mew,
A-painting for the great man, saints and saints
And saints again. I could not paint all night—
Ouf! I leaned out of window for fresh air.   50
There came a hurry of feet and little feet,
A sweep of lute-strings, laughs, and whiffs of song—
Flower o' the broom,
Take away love, and our earth is a tomb!

23 **pilchards** sardines.

55   *Flower o' the quince,*
    I let Lisa go, and what good in life since?
    Flower o' the thyme—and so on. Round they went.
    Scarce had they turned the corner when a titter
    Like the skipping of rabbits by moonlight—three slim
        shapes,
    And a face that looked up . . . zooks, sir, flesh and
60   blood,
    That's all I'm made of! Into shreds it went,
    Curtain and counterpane and coverlet,
    All the bed-furniture—a dozen knots,
    There was a ladder! Down I let myself,
65   Hands and feet, scrambling somehow, and so dropped,
    And after them. I came up with the fun
    Hard by Saint Lawrence, hail fellow, well met—
    Flower o' the rose,
    If I've been merry, what matter who knows?
70   And so as I was stealing back again
    To get to bed and have a bit of sleep
    Ere I rise up tomorrow and go work
    On Jerome° knocking at his poor old breast
    With his great round stone to subdue the flesh,
75   You snap me of the sudden. Ah, I see!
    Though your eye twinkles still, you shake your head—
    Mine's shaved—a monk, you say—the sting's in that!
    If Master Cosimo announced himself,
    Mum's the word naturally; but a monk!
80   Come, what am I a beast for? tell us, now!
    I was a baby when my mother died
    And father died and left me in the street.
    I starved there, God knows how, a year or two
    On fig-skins, melon-parings, rinds and shucks,
85   Refuse and rubbish. One fine frosty day,
    My stomach being empty as your hat,
    The wind doubled me up and down I went.
    Old Aunt Lapaccia trussed me with one hand,
    (Its fellow was a stinger as I knew)
90   And so along the wall, over the bridge,

73 Jerome the saint.

By the straight cut to the convent. Six words there,
While I stood munching my first bread that month:
"So, boy, you're minded," quoth the good fat father
Wiping his own mouth, 'twas refection-time—
"To quit this very miserable world? 95
Will you renounce" . . . "the mouthful of bread?"
    thought I;
By no means! Brief, they made a monk of me;
I did renounce the world, its pride and greed,
Palace, farm, villa, shop and banking-house,
Trash, such as these poor devils of Medici 100
Have given their hearts to—all at eight years old.
Well, sir, I found in time, you may be sure,
'Twas not for nothing—the good bellyful,
The warm serge and the rope that goes all round,
And day-long blessed idleness beside! 105
"Let's see what the urchin's fit for"—that came next.
Not overmuch their way, I must confess.
Such a to-do! They tried me with their books:
Lord, they'd have taught me Latin in pure waste!
Flower o' the clove, 110
All the Latin I construe is, "amo" I love!
But, mind you, when a boy starves in the streets
Eight years together, as my fortune was,
Watching folk's faces to know who will fling
The bit of half-stripped grape-bunch he desires, 115
And who will curse or kick him for his pains—
Which gentleman processional and fine,
Holding a candle to the Sacrament,
Will wink and let him lift a plate and catch
The droppings of the wax to sell again, 120
Or holla for the Eight° and have him whipped—
How say I?—nay, which dog bites, which lets drop
His bone from the heap of offal in the street—
Why, soul and sense of him grow sharp alike,
He learns the look of things, and none the less 125
For admonition from the hunger-pinch.
I had a store of such remarks, be sure,

121 **the Eight** magistrates of Florence.

Which, after I found leisure, turned to use.
I drew men's faces on my copy-books,
130 Scrawled them within the antiphonary's° marge,
Joined legs and arms to the long music-notes,
Found eyes and nose and chin for A's and B's,
And made a string of pictures of the world
Betwixt the ins and outs of verb and noun,
On the wall, the bench, the door. The monks looked
135   black.
"Nay," quoth the Prior, "turn him out, d'ye say?
In no wise. Lose a crow and catch a lark.
What if at last we get our man of parts,
We Carmelites, like those Camaldolese
140 And Preaching Friars,° to do our church up fine
And put the front on it that ought to be!"
And hereupon he bade me daub away.
Thank you! my head being crammed, the walls a
    blank,
Never was such prompt disemburdening.
145 First, every sort of monk, the black and white,
I drew them, fat and lean: then, folk at church,
From good old gossips waiting to confess
Their cribs of barrel-droppings, candle-ends—
To the breathless fellow at the altar-foot,
150 Fresh from his murder, safe and sitting there
With the little children round him in a row
Of admiration, half for his beard and half
For that white anger of his victim's son
Shaking a fist at him with one fierce arm,
155 Signing himself with the other because of Christ
(Whose sad face on the cross sees only this
After the passion of a thousand years)
Till some poor girl, her apron o'er her head,
(Which the intense eyes look through) came at eve
160 On tiptoe, said a word, dropped in a loaf,
Her pair of earrings and a bunch of flowers
(The brute took growling), prayed, and so was gone.
I painted all, then cried " 'Tis ask and have;

130 **antiphonary** choir book.   139–140 **Carmelites . . . Friars** mon-
astic orders.

Choose, for more's ready!"—laid the ladder flat,
And showed my covered bit of cloister-wall.   *165*
The monks closed in a circle and praised loud
Till checked, taught what to see and not to see,
Being simple bodies—"That's the very man!
Look at the boy who stoops to pat the dog!
That woman's like the Prior's niece who comes   *170*
To care about his asthma: it's the life!"
But there my triumph's straw-fire flared and funked;
Their betters took their turn to see and say:
The Prior and the learned pulled a face
And stopped all that in no time. "How? what's here?   *175*
Quite from the mark of painting, bless us all!
Faces, arms, legs and bodies like the true
As much as pea and pea! it's devil's-game!
Your business is not to catch men with show,
With homage to the perishable clay,   *180*
But lift them over it, ignore it all,
Make them forget there's such a thing as flesh.
Your business is to paint the souls of men—
Man's soul, and it's a fire, smoke . . . no, it's not . . .
It's vapor done up like a newborn babe—   *185*
(In that shape when you die it leaves your mouth)
It's . . . well, what matters talking, it's the soul!
Give us no more of body than shows soul!
Here's Giotto,° with his Saint a-praising God,
That sets us praising—why not stop with him?   *190*
Why put all thoughts of praise out of our head
With wonder at lines, colors, and what not?
Paint the soul, never mind the legs and arms!
Rub all out, try at it a second time.
Oh, that white smallish female with the breasts,   *195*
She's just my niece . . . Herodias,° I would say—
Who went and danced and got men's heads cut off!
Have it all out!" Now, is this sense, I ask?
A fine way to paint soul, by painting body
So ill, the eye can't stop there, must go further   *200*
And can't fare worse! Thus, yellow does for white

189 **Giotto** Florentine painter (1276–1337).   196 **Herodias** Matthew
14:6–11.

When what you put for yellow's simply black,
And any sort of meaning looks intense
When all beside itself means and looks naught.
205 Why can't a painter lift each foot in turn,
Left foot and right foot, go a double step,
Make his flesh liker and his soul more like,
Both in their order? Take the prettiest face,
The Prior's niece . . . patron-saint—is it so pretty
210 You can't discover if it means hope, fear,
Sorrow or joy? won't beauty go with these?
Suppose I've made her eyes all right and blue,
Can't I take breath and try to add life's flash,
And then add soul and heighten them threefold?
215 Or say there's beauty with no soul at all—
(I never saw it—put the case the same—)
If you get simple beauty and naught else,
You get about the best thing God invents:
That's somewhat: and you'll find the soul you have
    missed,
220 Within yourself, when you return him thanks.
"Rub all out!" Well, well, there's my life, in short,
And so the thing has gone on ever since.
I'm grown a man no doubt, I've broken bounds:
You should not take a fellow eight years old
225 And make him swear to never kiss the girls.
I'm my own master, paint now as I please—
Having a friend, you see, in the Corner-house!
Lord, it's fast holding by the rings in front—
Those great rings serve more purposes than just
230 To plant a flag in, or tie up a horse!
And yet the old schooling sticks, the old grave eyes
Are peeping o'er my shoulder as I work,
The heads shake still—"It's art's decline, my son!
You're not of the true painters, great and old;
235 Brother Angelico's the man, you'll find;
Brother Lorenzo° stands his single peer;
Fag on at flesh, you'll never make the third!"

235–36 **Brother Angelico . . . Brother Lorenzo** Fra Angelico and
Lorenzo Monaco, monastic painters of great piety.

Flower o' the pine,
You keep your mistr . . . manners, and I'll stick to
   mine!
I'm not the third, then: bless us, they must know!   240
Don't you think they're the likeliest to know,
They with their Latin? So, I swallow my rage,
Clench my teeth, suck my lips in tight, and paint
To please them—sometimes do and sometimes don't;
For, doing most, there's pretty sure to come   245
A turn, some warm eve finds me at my saints—
A laugh, a cry, the business of the world—
(*Flower o' the peach,*
Death for us all, and his own life for each!)
And my whole soul revolves, the cup runs over,   250
The world and life's too big to pass for a dream,
And I do these wild things in sheer despite,
And play the fooleries you catch me at,
In pure rage! The old mill-horse, out at grass
After hard years, throws up his stiff heels so,   255
Although the miller does not preach to him
The only good of grass is to make chaff.
What would men have? Do they like grass or no—
May they or mayn't they? all I want's the thing
Settled forever one way. As it is,   260
You tell too many lies and hurt yourself:
You don't like what you only like too much,
You do like what, if given you at your word,
You find abundantly detestable.
For me, I think I speak as I was taught;   265
I always see the garden and God there
A-making man's wife: and, my lesson learned,
The value and significance of flesh,
I can't unlearn ten minutes afterwards,

   You understand me: I'm a beast, I know.   270
But see, now—why, I see as certainly
As that the morning-star's about to shine,
What will hap some day. We've a youngster here
Comes to our convent, studies what I do,

275 Slouches and stares and lets no atom drop:
His name is Guidi°—he'll not mind the monks—
They call him Hulking Tom, he lets them talk—
He picks my practice up—he'll paint apace,
I hope so—though I never live so long,
280 I know what's sure to follow. You be judge!
You speak no Latin more than I, belike;
However, you're my man, you've seen the world
—The beauty and the wonder and the power,
The shapes of things, their colors, lights and shades,
285 Changes, surprises—and God made it all!
—For what? Do you feel thankful, ay or no,
For this fair town's face, yonder river's line,
The mountain round it and the sky above,
Much more the figures of man, woman, child,
290 These are the frame to? What's it all about?
To be passed over, despised? or dwelled upon,
Wondered at? oh, this last of course!—you say.
But why not do as well as say—paint these
Just as they are, careless what comes of it?
295 God's works—paint anyone, and count it crime
To let a truth slip. Don't object, "His works
Are here already; nature is complete:
Suppose you reproduce her—(which you can't)
There's no advantage! you must beat her, then."
300 For, don't you mark? we're made so that we love
First when we see them painted, things we have passed
Perhaps a hundred times nor cared to see;
And so they are better, painted—better to us,
Which is the same thing. Art was given for that;
305 God uses us to help each other so,
Lending our minds out. Have you noticed, now,
Your cullion's° hanging face? A bit of chalk,
And trust me but you should, though! How much
  more,
If I drew higher things with the same truth!
310 That were to take the Prior's pulpit-place,

276 **Guidi** Browning thought Tommaso Guidi (Masaccio) was
Lippo Lippi's pupil. He actually was his predecessor. 307 **cullion**
rascal (i.e. the guard who had collared him earlier).

Interpret God to all of you! Oh, oh,
It makes me mad to see what men shall do
And we in our graves! This world's no blot for us,
Nor blank; it means intensely, and means good:
To find its meaning is my meat and drink. 315
"Ay, but you don't so instigate to prayer!"
Strikes in the Prior: "when your meaning's plain
It does not say to folk—remember matins,
Or, mind you fast next Friday!" Why, for this
What need of art at all? A skull and bones, 320
Two bits of stick nailed crosswise, or, what's best,
A bell to chime the hour with, does as well.
I painted a Saint Lawrence six months since
At Prato, splashed the fresco in fine style:
"How looks my painting, now the scaffold's down?" 325
I ask a brother: "Hugely," he returns—
"Already not one phiz of your three slaves
Who turn the Deacon off his toasted side,
But's scratched and prodded to our heart's content,
The pious people have so eased their own 330
With coming to say prayers there in a rage:
We get on fast to see the bricks beneath.
Expect another job this time next year,
For pity and religion grow i' the crowd—
Your painting serves its purpose!" Hang the fools! 335

—That is—you'll not mistake an idle word
Spoke in a huff by a poor monk, Got wot,
Tasting the air this spicy night which turns
The unaccustomed head like Chianti wine!
Oh, the church knows! don't misreport me, now! 340
It's natural a poor monk out of bounds
Should have his apt word to excuse himself:
And hearken how I plot to make amends.
I have bethought me: I shall paint a piece
. . . There's for you! Give me six months, then go, see 345
Something in Sant' Ambrogio's! Bless the nuns!
They want a cast o' my office. I shall paint
God in the midst, Madonna and her babe,
Ringed by a bowery flowery angel-brood,

350 Lilies and vestments and white faces, sweet
As puff on puff of grated orris-root°
When ladies crowd to church at midsummer.
And then i' the front, of course a saint or two—
Saint John, because he saves the Florentines,
355 Saint Ambrose, who puts down in black and white
The convent's friends and gives them a long day,
And Job, I must have him there past mistake,
The man of Uz (and Us without the z,
Painters who need his patience). Well, all these
360 Secured at their devotion, up shall come
Out of a corner when you least expect,
As one by a dark stair into a great light,
Music and talking, who but Lippo! I!—
Mazed, motionless and moonstruck—I'm the man!
365 Back I shrink—what is this I see and hear?
I, caught up with my monk's-things by mistake,
My old serge gown and rope that goes all round,
I, in this presence, this pure company!
Where's a hole, where's a corner for escape?
370 Then steps a sweet angelic slip of a thing
Forward, puts out a soft palm—"Not so fast!"
—Addresses the celestial presence, "nay—
He made you and devised you, after all,
Though he's none of you! Could Saint John there
    draw—
375 His camel-hair° make up a painting-brush?
We come to brother Lippo for all that,
Iste perfecit opus!"° So, all smile—
I shuffle sideways with my blushing face
Under the cover of a hundred wings
380 Thrown like a spread of kirtles° when you're gay
And play hot cockles, all the doors being shut,
Till, wholly unexpected, in there pops

---

351 **grated orris-root** root of the orris plant, used pulverized as perfume.   375 **camel-hair** John the Baptist wore a garment of camel's hair.   377 **"Iste perfecit opus!"** Browning understood these words, painted in the lower right-hand corner of Lippo Lippi's "Coronation of the Virgin," to mean "This is the maker of the work," and to call attention to a portrait of the painter himself.   380 **kirtles** skirts.

The hothead husband! Thus I scuttle off
To some safe bench behind, not letting go
The palm of her, the little lily thing   *385*
That spoke the good word for me in the nick,
Like the Prior's niece . . . Saint Lucy, I would say.
And so all's saved for me, and for the church
A pretty picture gained. Go, six months hence!
Your hand, sir, and good-bye: no lights, no lights!   *390*
The street's hushed, and I know my own way back,
Don't fear me! There's the gray beginning. Zooks!

A TOCCATA OF GALUPPI'S°

I

Oh Galuppi, Baldassaro, this is very sad to find!
I can hardly misconceive you; it would prove me deaf
  and blind;
But although I take your meaning, 'tis with such a
  heavy mind!

II

Here you come with your old music, and here's all the
  good it brings.
What, they lived once thus at Venice where the mer-
  chants were the kings,   *5*
Where Saint Mark's is, where the Doges used to wed
  the sea with rings?

A Toccata of Galuppi's a toccata is a rapid piece for keyboard in
which the instrument is "touched" only lightly, nothing dwelt upon.
Here it suggests the light and inconclusive nature of the poem.
Baldassare Galuppi was a Venetian composer of the eighteenth
century.

III

Ay, because the sea's the street there; and 'tis arched
     by . . . what you call
. . . Shylock's bridge with houses on it, where they
     kept the carnival:
I was never out of England—it's as if I saw it all.

IV

Did young people take their pleasure when the sea
10   was warm in May?
Balls and masks begun at midnight, burning ever to
     midday,
When they made up fresh adventures for the morrow,
     do you say?

V

Was a lady such a lady, cheeks so round and lips so
     red—
On her neck the small face buoyant, like a bellflower
     on its bed,
O'er the breast's superb abundance where a man
15   might base his head?

VI

Well, and it was graceful of them—they'd break talk
     off and afford
—She, to bite her mask's black velvet—he, to finger
     on his sword,
While you sat and played toccatas, stately at the clavi-
     chord?

VII

What? Those lesser thirds so plaintive, sixths dimin-
     ished, sigh on sigh,

Told them something? Those suspensions, those solu-
    tions—"Must we die?"   *20*
Those commiserating sevenths—"Life might last! we
    can but try!"

VIII

"Were you happy?"—"Yes."—"And are you still as
    happy?"—"Yes. And you?"
—"Then, more kisses!"—"Did *I* stop them, when a
    million seemed so few?"
Hark, the dominant's persistence till it must be an-
    swered to!

IX

So, an octave struck the answer. Oh, they praised you,
    I dare say!   *25*
"Brave Galuppi! that was music! good alike at grave
    and gay!
I can always leave off talking when I hear a master
    play!"

X

Then they left you for their pleasure: till in due time,
    one by one,
Some with lives that came to nothing, some with deeds
    as well undone,
Death stepped tacitly and took them where they never
    see the sun.   *30*

XI

But when I sit down to reason, think to take my stand
    nor swerve,
While I triumph o'er a secret wrung from nature's
    close reserve,
In you come with your cold music till I creep through
    every nerve.

XII

Yes, you, like a ghostly cricket, creaking where a
     house was burned:
"Dust and ashes, dead and done with, Venice spent
35   what Venice earned.
The soul, doubtless, is immortal—where a soul can be
     discerned.

XIII

"Yours for instance: you know physics, something of
     geology,
Mathematics are your pastime; souls shall rise in their
     degree;
Butterflies may dread extinction—you'll not die, it
     cannot be!

XIV

"As for Venice and her people, merely born to bloom
40   and drop,
Here on earth they bore their fruitage, mirth and folly
     were the crop:
What of soul was left, I wonder, when the kissing had
     to stop?

XV

"Dust and ashes!" So you creak it, and I want the
     heart to scold.
Dear dead women, with such hair, too—what's be-
     come of all the gold
Used to hang and brush their bosoms? I feel chilly
45   and grown old.

BY THE FIRESIDE

I

HOW well I know what I mean to do
   When the long dark autumn-evenings come.
And where, my soul, is thy pleasant hue?
   With the music of all thy voices, dumb
In life's November too!   *5*

II

I shall be found by the fire, suppose,
   O'er a great wise book as beseemeth age,
While the shutters flap as the crosswind blows
   And I turn the page, and I turn the page,
Not verse now, only prose!   *10*

III

Till the young ones whisper, finger on lip,
   "There he is at it, deep in Greek:
Now then, or never, out we slip
   To cut from the hazels by the creek
A mainmast for our ship!"   *15*

IV

I shall be at it indeed, my friends:
   Greek puts already on either side
Such a branch-work forth as soon extends
   To a vista opening far and wide,
And I pass out where it ends.   *20*

V

The outside-frame, like your hazel-trees:
    But the inside-archway widens fast,
And a rarer sort succeeds to these,
    And we slope to Italy at last
25 And youth, by green degrees.

VI

I follow wherever I am led,
    Knowing so well the leader's hand:
Oh woman-country, wooed not wed,
    Loved all the more by earth's male-lands,
30 Laid to their hearts instead!

VII

Look at the ruined chapel again
    Halfway up in the Alpine gorge!
Is that a tower, I point you plain,
    Or is it a mill, or an iron-forge
35 Breaks solitude in vain?

VIII

A turn, and we stand in the heart of things;
    The woods are round us, heaped and dim;
From slab to slab how it slips and springs,
    The thread of water single and slim,
40 Through the ravage some torrent brings!

IX

Does it feed the little lake below?
    That speck of white just on its marge
Is Pella; see, in the evening-glow,
    How sharp the silver spearheads charge
45 When Alp meets heaven in snow!

X

On our other side is the straight-up rock;
   And a path is kept 'twixt the gorge and it
By boulder-stones where lichens mock
   The marks on a moth, and small ferns fit
Their teeth to the polished block.   *50*

XI

Oh the sense of the yellow mountain-flowers,
   And thorny balls, each three in one,
The chestnuts throw on our path in showers!
   For the drop of the woodland fruit's begun,
These early November hours,   *55*

XII

That crimson the creeper's leaf across
   Like a splash of blood, intense, abrupt,
O'er a shield else gold from rim to boss,
   And lay it for show on the fairy-cupped
Elf-needled mat of moss,   *60*

XIII

By the rose-flesh mushrooms, undivulged
   Last evening—nay, in today's first dew
Yon sudden coral nipple bulged,
   Where a freaked fawn-colored flaky crew
Of toadstools peep indulged.   *65*

XIV

And yonder, at foot of the fronting ridge
   That takes the turn to a range beyond,
Is the chapel reached by the one-arched bridge
   Where the water is stopped in a stagnant pond
Danced over by the midge.   *70*

XV

The chapel and bridge are of stone alike,
    Blackish-gray and mostly wet;
Cut hemp-stalks steep in the narrow dyke.
    See here again, how the lichens fret
75 And the roots of the ivy strike!

XVI

Poor little place, where its one priest comes
    On a festa-day, if he comes at all,
To the dozen folk from their scattered homes,
    Gathered within that precinct small
80 By the dozen ways one roams—

XVII

To drop from the charcoal-burners' huts,
    Or climb from the hemp-dressers' low shed,
Leave the grange where the woodman stores his
        nuts,
    Or the wattled cote where the fowlers spread
85 Their gear on the rock's bare juts.

XVIII

It has some pretension too, this front,
    With its bit of fresco half-moon-wise
Set over the porch, art's early wont:
    'Tis John in the Desert, I surmise,
90 But has borne the weather's brunt—

XIX

Not from the fault of the builder, though,
    For a penthouse properly projects
Where three carved beams make a certain show,
    Dating—good thought of our architect's—
95 'Five, six, nine, he lets you know.

XX

And all day long a bird sings there,
   And a stray sheep drinks at the pond at times;
The place is silent and aware;
   It has had its scenes, its joys and crimes,
But that is its own affair.   *100*

XXI

My perfect wife, my Leonor,
   Oh heart, my own, oh eyes, mine too,
Whom else could I dare look backward for,
   With whom beside should I dare pursue
The path gray heads abhor?   *105*

XXII

For it leads to a crag's sheer edge with them;
   Youth, flowery all the way, there stops—
Not they; age threatens and they contemn,
   Till they reach the gulf wherein youth drops,
One inch from life's safe hem!   *110*

XXIII

With me, youth led . . . I will speak now,
   No longer watch you as you sit
Reading by firelight, that great brow
   And the spirit-small hand propping it,
Mutely, my heart knows how—   *115*

XXIV

When, if I think but deep enough,
   You are wont to answer, prompt as rhyme;
And you, too, find without rebuff
   Response your soul seeks many a time
Piercing its fine flesh-stuff.   *120*

XXV

My own, confirm me! If I tread
  This path back, is it not in pride
To think how little I dreamed it led
  To an age so blessed that, by its side,
125 Youth seems the waste instead?

XXVI

My own, see where the years conduct!
  At first, 'twas something our two souls
Should mix as mists do; each is sucked
  In each now: on, the new stream rolls,
130 Whatever rocks obstruct.

XXVII

Think, when our one soul understands
  The great Word which makes all things new,°
When earth breaks up and heaven expands,
  How will the change strike me and you
135 In the house not made with hands?

XXVIII

Oh I must feel your brain prompt mine,
  Your heart anticipate my heart,
You must be just before, in fine,
  See and make me see, for your part,
140 New depths of the divine!

XXIX

But who could have expected this
  When we two drew together first
Just for the obvious human bliss,
  To satisfy life's daily thirst
145 With a thing men seldom miss?

132 **Word . . . new** Revelation 21:5.

XXX

Come back with me to the first of all,
   Let us lean and love it over again,
Let us now forget and now recall,
   Break the rosary in a pearly rain,
And gather what we let fall!   *150*

XXXI

What did I say?—that a small bird sings
   All day long, save when a brown pair
Of hawks from the wood float with wide wings
   Strained to a bell: 'gainst noonday glare
You count the streaks and rings.   *155*

XXXII

But at afternoon or almost eve
   'Tis better; then the silence grows
To that degree, you half believe
   It must get rid of what it knows,
Its bosom does so heave.   *160*

XXXIII

Hither we walked then, side by side,
   Arm in arm and cheek to cheek,
And still I questioned or replied,
   While my heart, convulsed to really speak,
Lay choking in its pride.   *165*

XXXIV

Silent the crumbling bridge we cross,
   And pity and praise the chapel sweet,
And care about the fresco's loss,
   And wish for our souls a like retreat,
And wonder at the moss.   *170*

XXXV

Stoop and kneel on the settle under,
　　Look through the window's grated square:
Nothing to see! For fear of plunder,
　　The cross is down and the altar bare,
175　As if thieves don't fear thunder.

XXXVI

We stoop and look in through the grate,
　　See the little porch and rustic door,
Read duly the dead builder's date;
　　Then cross the bridge that we crossed before,
180　Take the path again—but wait!

XXXVII

Oh moment, one and infinite!
　　The water slips o'er stock and stone;
The West is tender, hardly bright:
　　How gray at once is the evening grown—
185　One star, its chrysolite!°

XXXVIII

We two stood there with never a third,
　　But each by each, as each knew well:
The sights we saw and the sounds we heard,
　　The lights and the shades made up a spell
190　Till the trouble grew and stirred.

XXXIX

Oh, the little more, and how much it is!
　　And the little less, and what worlds away!
How a sound shall quicken content to bliss,
　　Or a breath suspend the blood's best play,
195　And life be a proof of this!

185 **chrysolite** semiprecious stone. "Jewel."

XL

Had she willed it, still had stood the screen
  So slight, so sure, 'twixt my love and her:
I could fix her face with a guard between,
  And find her soul as when friends confer,
Friends—lovers that might have been.   200

XLI

For my heart had a touch of the woodland-time,
  Wanting to sleep now over its best.
Shake the whole tree in the summer-prime,
  But bring to the last leaf no such test!
"Hold the last fast!" runs the rhyme.   205

XLII

For a chance to make your little much,
  To gain a lover and lose a friend,
Venture the tree and a myriad such,
  When nothing you mar but the year can mend:
But a last leaf—fear to touch!   210

XLIII

Yet should it unfasten itself and fall
  Eddying down till it find your face
At some slight wind—best chance of all!
  Be your heart henceforth its dwelling-place
You trembled to forestall!   215

XLIV

Worth how well, those dark gray eyes,
  That hair so dark and dear, how worth
That a man should strive and agonize,
  And taste a veriest hell on earth
For the hope of such a prize!   220

XLV

You might have turned and tried a man,
   Set him a space to weary and wear,
And prove which suited more your plan,
   His best of hope or his worst despair,
225 Yet end as he began.

XLVI

But you spared me this, like the heart you are,
   And filled my empty heart at a word.
If two lives join, there is oft a scar,
   They are one and one, with a shadowy third;
230 One near one is too far.

XLVII

A moment after, and hands unseen
   Were hanging the night around us fast;
But we knew that a bar was broken between
   Life and life: we were mixed at last
235 In spite of the mortal screen.

XLVIII

The forests had done it; there they stood;
   We caught for a moment the powers at play:
They had mingled us so, for once and good,
   Their work was done—we might go or stay,
240 They relapsed to their ancient mood.

XLIX

How the world is made for each of us!
   How all we perceive and know in it
Tends to some moment's product thus,
   When a soul declares itself—to wit,
245 By its fruit, the thing it does!

L

Be hate that fruit or love that fruit,
   It forwards the general deed of man,
And each of the many helps to recruit
   The life of the race by a general plan;
Each living his own, to boot.   *250*

LI

I am named and known by that moment's feat;
   There took my station and degree;
So grew my own small life complete,
   As nature obtained her best of me—
One born to love you, sweet!   *255*

LII

And to watch you sink by the fireside now
   Back again, as you mutely sit
Musing by firelight, that great brow
   And the spirit-small hand propping it,
Yonder, my heart knows how!   *260*

LIII

So, earth has gained by one man the more,
   And the gain of earth must be heaven's gain too;
And the whole is well worth thinking o'er
   When autumn comes: which I mean to do
One day, as I said before.   *265*

"CHILDE ROLAND TO THE DARK TOWER CAME"

(See Edgar's song in *Lear*°)

I

My first thought was, he lied in every word,
  That hoary cripple, with malicious eye
  Askance to watch the working of his lie
On mine, and mouth scarce able to afford
5 Suppression of the glee, that pursed and scored
  Its edge, at one more victim gained thereby.

II

What else should he be set for, with his staff?
  What, save to waylay with his lies, ensnare
  All travelers who might find him posted there,
10 And ask the road? I guessed what skull-like laugh
Would break, what crutch 'gin write my epitaph
  For pastime in the dusty thoroughfare,

III

If at his counsel I should turn aside
  Into that ominous tract which, all agree,
15 Hides the Dark Tower. Yet acquiescingly
I did turn as he pointed: neither pride
Nor hope rekindling at the end descried,
  So much as gladness that some end might be.

IV

For, what with my whole worldwide wandering,

Edgar's song in King Lear III.iv.

182

What with my search drawn out through years, my
    hope   20
Dwindled into a ghost not fit to cope
With that obstreperous joy success would bring—
I hardly tried now to rebuke the spring
    My heart made, finding failure in its scope.

V

As when a sick man very near to death   25
    Seems dead indeed, and feels begin and end
    The tears and takes the farewell of each friend,
And hears one bid the other go, draw breath
Freelier outside ("since all is o'er," he saith,
    "And the blow fallen no grieving can amend;")   30

VI

While some discuss if near the other graves
    Be room enough for this, and when a day
    Suits best for carrying the corpse away,
With care about the banners, scarves and staves:
And still the man hears all, and only craves   35
    He may not shame such tender love and stay.

VII

Thus, I had so long suffered in this quest,
    Heard failure prophesied so oft, been writ
    So many times among "The Band"—to wit,
The knights who to the Dark Tower's search
    addressed   40
Their steps—that just to fail as they, seemed best,
    And all the doubt was now—should I be fit?

VIII

So, quiet as despair, I turned from him,
    That hateful cripple, out of his highway
    Into the path he pointed. All the day   45

Had been a dreary one at best, and dim
  Was settling to its close, yet shot one grim
    Red leer to see the plain catch its estray.°

IX

For mark! no sooner was I fairly found
50   Pledged to the plain, after a pace or two,
    Than, pausing to throw backward a last view
O'er the safe road, 'twas gone; gray plain all round:
Nothing but plain to the horizon's bound.
    I might go on; naught else remained to do.

X

55 So, on I went. I think I never saw
    Such starved ignoble nature; nothing throve:
    For flowers—as well expect a cedar grove!
But cockle, spurge, according to their law
Might propagate their kind, with none to awe,
60   You'd think; a burr had been a treasure-trove.

XI

No! penury, inertness and grimace,
    In some strange sort, were the land's portion. "See
    Or shut your eyes," said Nature peevishly,
"It nothing skills: I cannot help my case:
65 'Tis is the Last Judgment's fire must cure this place,
    Calcine its clods and set my prisoners free."

XII

If there pushed any ragged thistle-stalk
    Above its mates, the head was chopped; the bents°
    Were jealous else. What made those holes and
      rents
70 In the dock's harsh swarth leaves, bruised as to balk

48 **estray** strayed animal.   68 **bents** rough grass.

All hope of greenness; 'tis a brute must walk
   Pashing their life out, with a brute's intents.

XIII

As for the grass, it grew as scant as hair
   In leprosy; thin dry blades pricked the mud
   Which underneath looked kneaded up with blood. *75*
One stiff blind horse, his every bone a-stare,
Stood stupefied, however he came there:
   Thrust out past service from the devil's stud!

XIV

Alive? he might be dead for aught I know,
   With that red gaunt and colloped° neck a-strain, *80*
   And shut eyes underneath the rusty mane;
Seldom went such grotesqueness with such woe;
I never saw a brute I hated so;
   He must be wicked to deserve such pain.

XV

I shut my eyes and turned them on my heart. *85*
   As a man calls for wine before he fights,
   I asked one draught of earlier, happier sights,
Ere fitly I could hope to play my part.
Think first, fight afterwards—the soldier's art:
   One taste of the old time sets all to rights. *90*

XVI

Not it! I fancied Cuthbert's reddening face
   Beneath its garniture of curly gold,
   Dear fellow, till I almost felt him fold
An arm in mine to fix me to the place,
That way he used. Alas, one night's disgrace! *95*
   Out went my heart's new fire and left it cold.

80 **colloped** ridged.

XVII

Giles then, the soul of honor—there he stands
    Frank as ten years ago when knighted first.
    What honest man should dare (he said) he durst.
Good—but the scene shifts—faugh! what hangman-
100   hands
    Pin to his breast a parchment? His own bands
    Read it. Poor traitor, spit upon and cursed!

XVIII

Better this present than a past like that;
    Back therefore to my darkening path again!
105   No sound, no sight as far as eye could strain.
Will the night send a howlet or a bat?
I asked: when something on the dismal flat
    Came to arrest my thoughts and change their train.

XIX

A sudden little river crossed my path
110   As unexpected as a serpent comes.
    No sluggish tide congenial to the glooms;
This, as it frothed by, might have been a bath
For the fiend's glowing hoof—to see the wrath
    Of its black eddy bespate with flakes and spumes.

XX

115 So petty yet so spiteful! All along,
    Low scrubby alders kneeled down over it;
    Drenched willows flung them headlong in a fit
Of mute despair, a suicidal throng:
The river which had done them all the wrong,
120   Whate'er that was, rolled by, deterred no whit.

XXI

Which, while I forded—good saints, how I feared

To set my foot upon a dead man's cheek,
  Each step, or feel the spear I thrust to seek
For hollows tangled in his hair or beard!
—It may have been a water-rat I speared,   *125*
  But, ugh! it sounded like a baby's shriek.

XXII

Glad was I when I reached the other bank.
  Now for a better country. Vain presage!
  Who were the strugglers, what war did they wage,
Whose savage trample thus could pad the dank   *130*
Soil to a plash? Toads in a poisoned tank,
  Or wild cats in a red-hot iron cage—

XXIII

The fight must so have seemed in that fell cirque.
  What penned them there, with all the plain to
    choose?
  No footprint leading to that horrid mews,°   *135*
None out of it. Mad brewage set to work
Their brains, no doubt, like galley-slaves the Turk
  Pits for his pastime, Christians against Jews.

XXIV

And more than that—a furlong on—why, there!
  What bad use was that engine for, that wheel,   *140*
  Or brake, not wheel—that harrow fit to reel
Men's bodies out like silk? with all the air
Of Tophet's° tool, on earth left unaware,
  Or brought to sharpen its rusty teeth of steel.

XXV

Then came a bit of stubbed ground, once a wood,   *145*
  Next a marsh, it would seem, and now mere earth

135 **mews** place of confinement. 143 **Tophet** hell.

Desperate and done with; (so a fool finds mirth,
Makes a thing and then mars it, till his mood
Changes and off he goes!) within a rood—
150   Bog, clay and rubble, sand and stark black dearth.

XXVI

Now blotches rankling, colored gay and grim,
Now patches where some leanness of the soil's
Broke into moss or substances like boils;
Then came some palsied oak, a cleft in him
155 Like a distorted mouth that splits its rim
Gaping at death, and dies while it recoils.

XXVII

And just as far as ever from the end!
Naught in the distance but the evening, naught
To point my footstep further! At the thought,
160 A great black bird, Apollyon's° bosom-friend,
Sailed past, nor beat his wide wing dragon-penned°
That brushed my cap—perchance the guide I
sought.

XXVIII

For, looking up. aware I somehow grew,
'Spite of the dusk, the plain had given place
165 All round to mountains—with such name to grace
Mere ugly heights and heaps now stolen in view.
How thus they had surprised me—solve it, you!
How to get from them was no clearer case.

XXIX

Yet half I seemed to recognize some trick
170 Of mischief happened to me, God knows when—
In a bad dream perhaps. Here ended, then,

160 **Apollyon** the devil. 161 **dragon-penned** with dragon feathers.

Progress this way. When, in the very nick
Of giving up, one time more, came a click
   As when a trap shuts—you're inside the den!

XXX

Burningly it came on me all at once,   *175*
   This was the place! those two hills on the right,
   Crouched like two bulls locked horn in horn in
      fight;
While to the left, a tall scalped mountain . . . Dunce,
Dotard, a-dozing at the very nonce,
   After a life spent training for the sight!   *180*

XXXI

What in the midst lay but the Tower itself?
   The round squat turret, blind as the fool's heart,
   Built of brown stone, without a counterpart
In the whole world. The tempest's mocking elf
Points to the shipman thus the unseen shelf   *185*
   He strikes on, only when the timbers start.

XXXII

Not see? because of night perhaps?—why, day
   Came back again for that! before it left,
   The dying sunset kindled through a cleft:
The hills, like giants at a hunting, lay,   *190*
Chin upon hand, to see the game at bay—
   "Now stab and end the creature—to the heft!"

XXXIII

Not hear? when noise was everywhere! it tolled
   Increasing like a bell. Names in my ears
   Of all the lost adventurers my peers—   *195*
How such a one was strong, and such was bold,
And such was fortunate, yet each of old
   Lost, lost! one moment knelled the woe of years.

XXXIV

> There they stood, ranged along the hillsides, met
> 200   To view the last of me, a living frame
>   For one more picture! in a sheet of flame
> I saw them and I knew them all. And yet
> Dauntless the slug-horn° to my lips I set,
>   And blew. *"Childe Roland to the Dark Tower
>   came."*

MASTER HUGUES OF SAXE-GOTHA°

I

> HIST, but a word, fair and soft!
>   Forth and be judged, Master Hugues!
> Answer the question I've put you so oft:
>   What do you mean by your mountainous fugues?°
> 5 See, we're alone in the loft—

II

> I, the poor organist here,
>   Hugues, the composer of note,
> Dead though, and done with, this many a year:
>   Let's have a colloquy, something to quote,
> 10 Make the world prick up its ear!

203 **slug-horn** (incorrect archaism).
Master Hugues of Saxe-Gotha Hugues is an imaginary composer from the former German duchy of Saxe-Coburg-Gotha. 4 **fugues** the fugue is a musical form in which a melody is taken up by successive voices, each entering before the previous voice has completed the melody (as in a round). After further development the piece may end in the original key.

III

See, the church empties apace:
   Fast they extinguish the lights.
Hallo there, sacristan! Five minutes' grace!
   Here's a crank pedal wants setting to rights,
Balks one of holding the base.   15

IV

See, our huge house of the sounds,
   Hushing its hundreds at once,
Bids the last loiterer back to his bounds!
   —O you may challenge them, not a response
Get the church-saints on their rounds!   20

V

(Saints go their rounds, who shall doubt?
   —March, with the moon to admire,
Up nave, down chancel, turn transept about,
   Supervise all betwixt pavement and spire,
Put rats and mice to the rout—   25

VI

Aloys and Jurien and Just—
   Order things back to their place,
Have a sharp eye lest the candlesticks rust,
   Rub the church-plate, darn the sacrament-lace,
Clear the desk-velvet of dust.)   30

VII

Here's your book, younger folks shelve!
   Played I not offhand and runningly,
Just now, your masterpiece, hard number twelve?
   Here's what should strike, could one handle it
      cunningly:
Help the ax, give it a helve!   35

VIII

Page after page as I played,
   Every bar's rest, where one wipes
Sweat from one's brow, I looked up and surveyed,
   O'er my three claviers,° yon forest of pipes
40 Whence you still peeped in the shade.

IX

Sure you were wishful to speak?
   You, with brow ruled like a score,
Yes, and eyes buried in pits on each cheek,
   Like two great breves,° as they wrote them of yore,
45 Each side that bar, your straight beak!

X

Sure you said—"Good, the mere notes!
   Still, couldst thou take my intent,
Know what procured me our Company's votes—
   A master were lauded and sciolists shent,
50 Parted the sheep from the goats!"

XI

Well then, speak up, never flinch!
   Quick, ere my candle's a snuff
—burned, do you see? to its uttermost inch—
   I believe in you, but that's not enough:
55 Give my conviction a clinch!

XII

First you deliver your phrase
   —Nothing propound, that I see,
Fit in itself for much blame or much praise—
   Answered no less, where no answer needs be:
60 Off start the Two on their ways.

39 claviers keyboards. **44 breves** marks of musical notation,
formerly square.

XIII

Straight must a Third interpose,
  Volunteer needlessly help;
In strikes a Fourth, a Fifth thrusts in his nose,
  So the cry's open, the kennel's a-yelp,
Argument's hot to the close.   *65*

XIV

One dissertates, he is candid;
  Two must discept°—has distinguished;
Three helps the couple, if ever yet man did;
  Four protests; Five makes a dart at the thing
    wished:
Back to One, goes the case bandied.   *70*

XV

One says his say with a difference;
  More of expounding, explaining!
All now is wrangle, abuse, and vociferance;
  Now there's a truce, all's subdued, self-restraining,
Five, though, stands out all the stiffer hence.   *75*

XVI

One is incisive, corrosive;
  Two retorts, nettled, curt, crepitant;
Three makes rejoinder, expansive, explosive;
  Four overbears them all, strident and strepitant:
Five . . . O Danaides,° O Sieve!   *80*

XVII

Now, they ply axes and crowbars;
  Now, they prick pins at a tissue

---

67 **discept** differ.   80 **Danaïdes** daughters of Danaus. Their punishment in Hades was to pour water through a seive forever.

Fine as a skein of the casuist Escobar's
  Worked on the bone of a lie. To what issue?
85 Where is our gain at the Two-bars?

XVIII

Est fuga, volvitur rota.°
  On we drift: where looms the dim port?
One, Two, Three, Four, Five, contribute their quota;
  Something is gained, if one caught but the import—
90 Show it us, Hugues of Saxe-Gotha!

XIX

·What with affirming, denying,
  Holding, risposting, subjoining,
All's like . . . it's like . . . for an instance I'm trying . . .
  There! See our roof, its gilt molding and groining
95 Under those spider webs lying!

XX

So your fugue broadens and thickens,
  Greatens and deepens and lengthens,
Till we exclaim—"But where's music, the dickens?
  Blot ye the gold, while your spider web strengthens
100 —Blacked to the stoutest of tickens?"°

XXI

I for man's effort am zealous:
  Prove me such censure unfounded!
Seems it surprising a lover grows jealous—
  Hopes 'twas for something, his organ-pipes sounded,
105 Tiring three boys at the bellows?

86 **Est fuga, volvitur rota** it is a flight [i.e. fugue], the wheel revolves.
100 **ticken** ticking is a heavy material used to cover pillows and
mattresses.

XXII

Is it your moral of Life?
　Such a web, simple and subtle,
Weave we on earth here in impotent strife,
　Backward and forward each throwing his shuttle,
Death ending all with a knife?   *110*

XXIII

Over our heads truth and nature—
　Still our life's zigzags and dodges,
Ins and outs, weaving a new legislature—
　God's gold just shining its last where that lodges,
Palled beneath man's usurpature.   *115*

XXIV

So we o'ershroud stars and roses,
　Cherub and trophy and garland;
Nothings grow something which quietly closes
　Heaven's earnest eye: not a glimpse of the far land
Gets through our comments and glozes.   *120*

XXV

Ah but traditions, inventions,
　(Say we and make up a visage)
So many men with such various intentions,
　Down the past ages, must know more than this age!
Leave we the web its dimensions!   *125*

XXVI

Who thinks Hugues wrote for the deaf,
　Proved a mere mountain in labor?
Better submit; try again; what's the clef?
　'Faith, 'tis no trifle for pipe and for tabor—
Four flats, the minor in F.   *130*

XXVII

Friend, your fugue taxes the finger:
   Learning it once, who would lose it?
Yet all the while a misgiving will linger,
   Truth's golden o'er us although we refuse it—
135 Nature, through cobwebs we string her.

XXVIII

Hugues! I advise *meâ poenâ*°
   (Counterpoint glares like a Gorgon)°
Bid One, Two, Three, Four, Five, clear the arena!
   Say the word, straight I unstop the full-organ,
140 Blare out the *mode Palestrina.*°

XXIX

While in the roof, if I'm right there,
   . . . Lo you, the wick in the socket!
Hallo, you sacristan, show us a light there!
   Down it dips, gone like a rocket.
145 What, you want, do you, to come unawares,
Sweeping the church up for first morning-prayers,
And find a poor devil has ended his cares
At the foot of your rotten-runged rat-riddled stairs?
   Do I carry the moon in my pocket?

136 meâ poenâ at my peril. **137 Gorgon** monster whose glance turned beholders to stone. **140 mode Palestrina** he threatens to abandon Hugues for something less pointlessly ingenious, in the manner of the composer Palestrina.

MEMORABILIA°

I

Ah, did you once see Shelley plain,
   And did he stop and speak to you
And did you speak to him again?
   How strange it seems and new!

II

But you were living before that,   *5*
   And also you are living after;
And the memory I started at—
   My starting moves your laughter.

III

I crossed a moor, with a name of its own
   And a certain use in the world no doubt,   *10*
Yet a hand's-breadth of it shines alone
   'Mid the blank miles round about:

IV

For there I picked up on the heather
   And there I put inside my breast
A molted feather, an eagle-feather!   *15*
   Well, I forget the rest.

Memorabilia things worth remembering.

ANDREA DEL SARTO°

(CALLED "THE FAULTLESS PAINTER")

BUT do not let us quarrel any more,
No, my Lucrezia; bear with me for once:
Sit down and all shall happen as you wish.
You turn your face, but does it bring your heart?
5   I'll work then for your friend's friend, never fear,
Treat his own subject after his own way,
Fix his own time, accept too his own price,
And shut the money into this small hand
When next it takes mine. Will it? tenderly?
10 Oh, I'll content him—but tomorrow, Love!
I often am much wearier than you think,
This evening more than usual, and it seems
As if—forgive now—should you let me sit
Here by the window with your hand in mine
15 And look a half hour forth on Fiesole,°
Both of one mind, as married people use,
Quietly, quietly the evening through,
I might get up tomorrow to my work
Cheerful and fresh as ever. Let us try.
20 Tomorrow, how you shall be glad for this!
Your soft hand is a woman of itself,
And mine the man's bared breast she curls inside.
Don't count the time lost, neither; you must serve
For each of the five pictures we require:
25 It saves a model. So! keep looking so—
My serpentining beauty, rounds on rounds!
—How could you ever prick those perfect ears,
Even to put the pearl there! oh, so sweet—

Andrea del Sarto Florentine painter of the sixteenth century.
15 Fiesole town on the hills above Florence.

198

My face, my moon, my everybody's moon,
Which everybody looks on and calls his,   *30*
And, I suppose, is looked on by in turn,
While she looks—no one's: very dear, no less.
You smile? why, there's my picture ready made,
There's what we painters call our harmony!
A common grayness silvers everything—   *35*
All in a twilight, you and I alike
—You, at the point of your first pride in me
(That's gone you know)—but I, at every point;
My youth, my hope, my art, being all toned down
To yonder sober pleasant Fiesole.   *40*
There's the bell clinking from the chapel-top;
That length of convent-wall across the way
Holds the trees safer, huddled more inside;
The last monk leaves the garden; days decrease,
And autumn grows, autumn in everything.   *45*
Eh? the whole seems to fall into a shape
As if I saw alike my work and self
And all that I was born to be and do,
A twilight-piece. Love, we are in God's hand.
How strange now, looks the life he makes us lead;   *50*
So free we seem, so fettered fast we are!
I feel he laid the fetter: let it lie!
This chamber for example—turn your head—
All that's behind us! You don't understand
Nor care to understand about my art,   *55*
But you can hear at least when people speak:
And that cartoon, the second from the door
—It is the thing, Love! so such things should be—
Behold Madonna!—I am bold to say.
I can do with my pencil what I know,   *60*
What I see, what at bottom of my heart
I wish for, if I ever wish so deep—
Do easily, too—when I say, perfectly,
I do not boast, perhaps: yourself are judge,
Who listened to the Legate's° talk last week,   *65*

65 **Legate** the Pope's representative.

And just as much they used to say in France.
At any rate 'tis easy, all of it!
No sketches first, no studies, that's long past:
I do what many dream of, all their lives,
70 —Dream? strive to do, and agonize to do,
And fail in doing. I could count twenty such
On twice your fingers, and not leave this town,
Who strive—you don't know how the others strive
To paint a little thing like that you smeared
75 Carelessly passing with your robes afloat—
Yet do much less, so much less, Someone says,
(I know his name, no matter)—so much less!
Well, less is more, Lucrezia: I am judged.
There burns a truer light of God in them,
80 In their vexed beating stuffed and stopped-up brain,
Heart, or whate'er else, than goes on to prompt
This low-pulsed forthright craftsman's hand of mine.
Their works drop groundward, but themselves, I know,
Reach many a time a Heaven that's shut to me,
85 Enter and take their place there sure enough,
Though they come back and cannot tell the world.
My works are nearer Heaven, but I sit here.
The sudden blood of these men! at a word—
Praise them, it boils, or blame them, it boils too.
90 I, painting from myself and to myself,
Know what I do, am unmoved by men's blame
Or their praise either. Somebody remarks
Morello's outline there is wrongly traced,
His hue mistaken; what of that? or else,
95 Rightly traced and well ordered; what of that?
Speak as they please, what does the mountain care?
Ah, but a man's reach should exceed his grasp,
Or what's a Heaven for? All is silver-gray
Placid and perfect with my art: the worse!
100 I know both what I want and what might gain,
And yet how profitless to know, to sigh
"Had I been two, another and myself,
Our head would have o'erlooked the world!" No
    doubt.
Yonder's a work now, of that famous youth

The Urbinate° who died five years ago.   *105*
('Tis copied, George Vasari sent it me.)
Well, I can fancy how he did it all,
Pouring his soul, with kings and popes to see,
Reaching, that heaven might so replenish him,
Above and through his art—for it gives way;   *110*
That arm is wrongly put—and there again—
A fault to pardon in the drawing's lines,
Its body, so to speak: its soul is right,
He means right—that, a child may understand.
Still, what an arm! and I could alter it: *115*
But all the play, the insight and the stretch—
Out of me, out of me! And wherefore out?
Had you enjoined them on me, given me soul,
We might have risen to Raphael, I and you!
Nay, Love, you did give all I asked, I think—   *120*
More than I merit, yes, by many times.
But had you—oh, with the same perfect brow,
And perfect eyes, and more than perfect mouth,
And the low voice my soul hears, as a bird
The fowler's pipe, and follows to the snare—   *125*
Had you, with these the same, but brought a mind!
Some women do so. Had the mouth there urged
"God and the glory! never care for gain.
The present by the future, what is that?
Live for fame, side by side with Agnolo!°   *130*
Raphael is waiting: up to God, all three!"
I might have done it for you. So it seems:
Perhaps not. All is as God overrules.
Beside, incentives come from the soul's self;
The rest avail not. Why do I need you?   *135*
What wife had Raphael, or has Agnolo?
In this world, who can do a thing, will not;
And who would do it, cannot, I perceive:
Yet the will's somewhat—somewhat, too, the power—
And thus we half-men struggle. At the end,   *140*
God, I conclude, compensates, punishes.
'Tis safer for me, if the award be strict,

105 **The Urbinate** the painter Raphael, born in Urbino. 130
Agnolo Michelangelo.

That I am something underrated here,
Poor this long while, despised, to speak the truth.
145 I dared not, do you know, leave home all day,
For fear of chancing on the Paris lords.°
The best is when they pass and look aside;
But they speak sometimes; I must bear it all.
Well may they speak! That Francis, that first time,
150 And that long festal year at Fontainebleau!
I surely then could sometimes leave the ground,
Put on the glory, Raphael's daily wear,
In that humane great monarch's golden look—
One finger in his beard or twisted curl
155 Over his mouth's good mark that made the smile,
One arm about my shoulder, round my neck,
The jingle of his gold chain in my ear,
I painting proudly with his breath on me,
All his court round him, seeing with his eyes,
160 Such frank French eyes, and such a fire of souls
Profuse, my hand kept plying by those hearts—
And, best of all, this, this, this face beyond,
This in the background, waiting on my work,
To crown the issue with a last reward!
165 A good time, was it not, my kingly days?
And had you not grown restless . . . but I know—
'Tis done and past; 'twas right, my instinct said;
Too live the life grew, golden and not gray,
And I'm the weak-eyed bat no sun should tempt
170 Out of the grange whose four walls make his world.
How could it end in any other way?
You called me, and I came home to your heart.
The triumph was—to reach and stay there; since
I reached it ere the triumph, what is lost?
175 Let my hands frame your face in your hair's gold,
You beautiful Lucrezia that are mine!
"Raphael did this, Andrea painted that;
The Roman's° is the better when you pray,

---

146 **the Paris lords** Andrea del Sarto had served Francis I of France
(149). He was said to have spent on his wife money Francis had
given him to buy works of art. 178 **The Roman** Raphael, who
worked in Rome.

But still the other's Virgin was his wife—"
Men will excuse me. I am glad to judge   *180*
Both pictures in your presence; clearer grows
My better fortune, I resolve to think.
For, do you know, Lucrezia, as God lives,
Said one day Agnolo, his very self,
To Raphael . . . I have known it all these years . . .   *185*
(When the young man was flaming out his thoughts
Upon a palace-wall for Rome to see,
Too lifted up in heart because of it)
"Friend, there's a certain sorry little scrub
Goes up and down our Florence, none cares how,   *190*
Who, were he set to plan and execute
As you are, pricked on by your popes and kings,
Would bring the sweat into that brow of yours!"
To Raphael's!—And indeed the arm is wrong.
I hardly dare . . . yet, only you to see,   *195*
Give the chalk here—quick, thus the line should go!
Ay, but the soul! he's Raphael! rub it out!
Still, all I care for, if he spoke the truth,
(What he? why, who but Michel Agnolo?
Do you forget already words like those?)   *200*
If really there was such a chance, so lost—
Is, whether you're—not grateful—but more pleased.
Well, let me think so. And you smile indeed!
This hour has been an hour! Another smile?
If you would sit thus by me every night   *205*
I should work better, do you comprehend?
I mean that I should earn more, give you more.
See, it is settled dusk now; there's a star;
Morello's gone, the watch-lights show the wall,
The cue-owls speak the name we call them by.   *210*
Come from the window, love—come in, at last,
Inside the melancholy little house
We built to be so gay with. God is just.
King Francis may forgive me: oft at nights
When I look up from painting, eyes tired out,   *215*
The walls become illumined, brick from brick
Distinct, instead of mortar, fierce bright gold,
That gold of his I did cement them with!

Let us but love each other. Must you go?
220 That Cousin here again? he waits outside?
Must see you—you, and not with me? Those loans?
More gaming debts to pay? you smiled for that?
Well, let smiles buy me! have you more to spend?
While hand and eye and something of a heart .
225 Are left me, work's my ware, and what's it worth?
I'll pay my fancy. Only let me sit
The gray remainder of the evening out,
Idle, you call it, and muse perfectly
How I could paint, were I but back in France,
230 One picture, just one more—the Virgin's face,
Not yours this time! I want you at my side
To hear them—that is, Michel Agnolo—
Judge all I do and tell you of its worth.
Will you? Tomorrow, satisfy your friend.
235 I take the subjects for his corridor,
Finish the portrait out of hand—there, there,
And throw him in another thing or two
If he demurs; the whole should prove enough
To pay for this same Cousin's freak. Beside,
240 What's better and what's all I care about,
Get you the thirteen scudi for the ruff!
Love, does that please you? Ah, but what does he,
The Cousin! what does he to please you more?

I am grown peaceful as old age tonight.
245 I regret little, I would change still less.
Since there my past life lies, why alter it?
The very wrong to Francis!—it is true
I took his coin, was tempted and complied,
And built this house and sinned, and all is said.
250 My father and my mother died of want.
Well, had I riches of my own? you see
How one gets rich! Let each one bear his lot.
They were born poor, lived poor, and poor they died:
And I have labored somewhat in my time
255 And not been paid profusely. Some good son
Paint my two hundred pictures—let him try!
No doubt, there's something strikes a balance. Yes,

You loved me quite enough, it seems tonight.
This must suffice me here. What would one have?
In Heaven, perhaps, new chances, one more chance— 260
Four great walls in the New Jerusalem,°
Meted on each side by the angel's reed,
For Leonard,° Raphael, Agnolo and me
To cover—the three first without a wife,
While I have mine! So—still they overcome 263
Because there's still Lucrezia—as I choose.

Again the cousin's whistle! Go, my Love.

WOMEN AND ROSES

I

I DREAM of a red-rose tree.
And which of its roses three
Is the dearest rose to me?

II

Round and round, like a dance of snow
In a dazzling drift, as its guardians, go 5
Floating the women faded for ages,
Sculptured in stone, on the poet's pages.
Then follow women fresh and gay,
Living and loving and loved today.
Last, in the rear, flee the multitude of maidens, 10

261 **New Jerusalem** Heaven.   263 **Leonard** Leonardo da Vinci.

Beauties yet unborn. And all, to one cadence,
They circle their rose on my rose tree.

III

Dear rose, thy term is reached,
Thy leaf hangs loose and bleached:
15 Bees pass it unimpeached.

IV

Stay then, stoop, since I cannot climb,
You, great shapes of the antique time!
How shall I fix you, fire you, freeze you,
Break my heart at your feet to please you?
20 Oh, to possess and be possessed!
Hearts that beat 'neath each pallid breast!
Once but of love, the poesy, the passion,
Drink but once and die!—In vain, the same fashion,
They circle their rose on my rose tree.

V

25 Dear rose, thy joy's undimmed,
Thy cup is ruby-rimmed,
Thy cup's heart nectar-brimmed.

VI

Deep, as drops from a statue's plinth°
The bee sucked in by the hyacinth,
30 So will I bury me while burning,
Quench like him at a plunge my yearning,
Eyes in your eyes, lips on your lips!
Fold me fast where the cincture slips,
Prison all my soul in eternities of pleasure,
35 Girdle me for once! But no—the old measure,
They circle their rose on my rose tree.

28 **plinth** base.

VII

Dear rose without a thorn,°
Thy bud's the babe unborn:
First streak of a new morn.

VIII

Wings, lend wings for the cold, the clear!   *40*
What is far conquers what is near.
Roses will bloom nor want beholders,
Sprung from the dust where our flesh molders.
What shall arrive with the cycle's change?
A novel grace and a beauty strange.   *45*
I will make an Eve, be the artist that began her,
Shaped her to his mind!—Alas! in like manner
They circle their rose on my rose tree.

37 **rose without a thorn** symbol of the Virgin Mary.

THE HERETIC'S TRAGEDY

A MIDDLE-AGE INTERLUDE°

ROSA MUNDI; SEU, FULCITE ME FLORIBUS. A CONCEIT OF
MASTER GYSBRECHT, CANON-REGULAR OF SAINT JODOCUS-
BY-THE-BAR, YPRES CITY. CANTUQUE, *Virgilius.* AND
HATH OFTEN BEEN SUNG AT HOCK-TIDE AND FESTIVALS.
GAVISUS ERAM, *Jessides.*°

(It would seem to be a glimpse from the burning of Jacques du
Bourg-Molay, at Paris, A.D. 1314; as distorted by the refraction
from Flemish brain to brain, during the course of a couple of
centuries. R. B.)

I

PREADMONISHETH THE ABBOT DEODAET

THE Lord, we look to once for all,
    Is the Lord we should look at, all at once:
He knows not to vary, saith Saint Paul,
    Nor the shadow of turning, for the nonce.
5 See him no other than as he is!
    Give both the infinitudes their due—
Infinite mercy, but, I wis,
        As infinite a justice too.

                    [*Organ: plagal-cadence.*°]

    As infinite a justice too.

Interlude a short play performed at banquets between acts of a
mystery play. ROSA MUNDI . . . **Jessides:** *Rosa mundi* rose of the
world. *Fulcite me floribus* support me with flowers (Song of Solomon
2:5). **Conceit** invention. **Cantuque, Virgilius** the music is by Virgil-
ius. **Gavisus eram, Jessides** I, a son of Jesse, rejoice in it. The author
is putting himself in the line of David, the Psalmist, who was the
son of Jesse. See "Introduction."   8 **Plagal-cadence** closing chords.
Pun.

II

ONE SINGETH

John, Master of the Temple of God,   *10*
  Falling to sin the Unknown Sin,
What he bought of Emperor Aldabrod,
  He sold it to Sultan Saladin:
Till, caught by Pope Clement, a-buzzing there,
  Hornet-prince of the mad wasps' hive,   *15*
And clipped of his wings in Paris square,
  They bring him now to be burned alive.
    [And wanteth there grace of lute or clavicithern,
      ye shall say to confirm him who singeth—]
  We bring John now to be burned alive.

III

In the midst is a goodly gallows built;
  'Twixt fork and fork, a stake is stuck;   *20*
But first they set divers tumbrils° atilt,
  Make a trench all round with the city muck;
Inside they pile log upon log, good store;
  Faggots no few, blocks great and small,
Reach a man's mid-thigh, no less, no more—   *25*
  For they mean he should roast in the sight of all.

CHORUS

We mean he should roast in the sight of all.

IV

Good sappy bavins that kindle forthwith;
  Billets that blaze substantial and slow;
Pine-stump split deftly, dry as pith;   *30*
  Larch-heart that chars to a chalk-white glow:
Then up they hoist me John in a chafe,
  Sling him fast like a hog to scorch,

21 **tumbril** cart.

Spit in his face, then leap back safe,
35   Sing "Laudes"° and bid clap-to the torch.

CHORUS

Laus Deo°—who bids clap-to the torch.

V

John of the Temple, whose fame so bragged,
        Is burning alive in Paris square!
How can he curse, if his mouth is gagged?
40   Or wriggle his neck, with a collar there?
Or heave his chest, which a band goes round?
        Or threat with his fist, since his arms are spliced?
Or kick with his feet, now his legs are bound?
        —Thinks John, I will call upon Jesus Christ.
                    [*Here one crosseth himself.*]

VI

45 Jesus Christ—John had bought and sold,
        Jesus Christ—John had eaten and drunk;
To him, the Flesh meant silver and gold.
        (*Salvâ reverentiâ.*)°
Now it was, "Savior, bountiful lamb,
50   "I have roasted thee Turks, though men roast me!
"See thy servant, the plight wherein I am!
        "Art thou a savior? Save thou me!"

CHORUS

'Tis John the mocker cries, "Save thou me!"

VII

Who maketh God's menace an idle word?

35 **"Laudes"** hymns of praise. 36 **Laus Deo** praise be to God.
48 **Salvâ reverentiâ** direction to make a reverence (bow or genu-
flection) to the Body of God (the "Flesh") in the Sacrament.

—Saith, it no more means what it proclaims,   *55*
Than a damsel's threat to her wanton bird?—
   For she too prattles of ugly names.
—Saith, he knoweth but one thing—what he knows?
   That God is good and the rest is breath;
Why else is the same styled Sharon's rose?°   *60*
   Once a rose, ever a rose, he saith.

CHORUS

O, John shall yet find a rose, he saith!

VIII

Alack, there be roses and roses, John!
   Some, honied of taste like your leman's° tongue:
Some, bitter; for why? (roast gaily on!)   *65*
   Their tree struck root in devil's-dung.
When Paul once reasoned of righteousness
   And of temperance and of judgment to come,
Good Felix trembled,° he could no less:
   John, snickering, crook'd his wicked thumb.   *70*

CHORUS

What cometh to John of the wicked thumb?

IX

Ha ha, John plucketh now at his rose
   To rid himself of a sorrow at heart!
Lo—petal on petal, fierce rays unclose;
   Anther on anther, sharp spikes outstart;   *75*
And with blood for dew, the bosom boils;
   And a gust of sulphur is all its smell;
And lo, he is horribly in the toils
   Of a coal-black giant flower of hell!

---

60 **Sharon's rose** Song of Solomon 2:1.   64 **leman** mistress.   67–69
Paul . . . trembled Acts 24:25.

CHORUS

80   What maketh Heaven, That maketh hell.

X

So, as John called now, through the fire amain,
    On the Name, he had cursed with, all his life—
To the Person, he bought and sold again—
    For the Face, with his daily buffets rife—
85 Feature by feature It took its place:
    And his voice, like a mad dog's choking bark,
At the steady whole of the Judge's face—
    Died. Forth John's soul flared into the dark.

SUBJOINETH THE ABBOT DEODAẸT

God help all poor souls lost in the dark!

TWO IN THE CAMPAGNA°

I

I WONDER do you feel today
    As I have felt since, hand in hand,
We sat down on the grass, to stray
    In spirit better through the land,
5 This morn of Rome and May?

Campagna the great plain (*champaign*, 21) surrounding the City of
Rome, sprinkled with ruins.

II

For me, I touched a thought, I know,
　Has tantalized me many times,
(Like turns of thread the spiders throw
　Mocking across our path) for rhymes
To catch at and let go. 　　　　　　　10

III

Help me to hold it! First it left
　The yellowing fennel, run to seed
There, branching from the brickwork's cleft,
　Some old tomb's ruin: yonder weed
Took up the floating weft, 　　　　　15

IV

Where one small orange cup amassed
　Five beetles—blind and green they grope
Among the honey-meal: and last,
　Everywhere on the grassy slope
I traced it. Hold it fast! 　　　　　20

V

The champaign with its endless fleece
　Of feathery grasses everywhere!
Silence and passion, joy and peace,
　An everlasting wash of air—
Rome's ghost since her decease. 　　25

VI

Such life here, through such lengths of hours,
　Such miracles performed in play,
Such primal naked forms of flowers,
　Such letting nature have her way
While heaven looks from its towers! 　　30

VII

How say you? Let us, O my dove,
　Let us be unashamed of soul,
As earth lies bare to heaven above!
　How is it under our control
35 To love or not to love?

VIII

I would that you were all to me,
　You that are just so much, no more.
Nor yours nor mine, nor slave nor free!
　Where does the fault lie? What the core
40 O' the wound, since wound must be?

IX

I would I could adopt your will,
　See with your eyes, and set my heart
Beating by yours, and drink my fill
　At your soul's springs—your part my part
45 In life, for good and ill.

X

No. I yearn upward, touch you close,
　Then stand away. I kiss your cheek,
Catch your soul's warmth—I pluck the rose
　And love it more than tongue can speak—
50 Then the good minute goes.

XI

Already how am I so far
　Out of that minute? Must I go
Still like the thistle-ball, no bar,
　Onward, whenever light winds blow,
55 Fixed by no friendly star?

XII

Just when I seemed about to learn!
    Where is the thread now? Off again!
The old trick! Only I discern—
    Infinite passion, and the pain
Of finite hearts that yearn.   *60*

from *DRAMATIS PERSONAE*

(1864)

ABT VOGLER°

(AFTER HE HAS BEEN EXTEMPORIZING UPON THE MUSICAL INSTRUMENT° OF HIS INVENTION)

I

WOULD that the structure brave, the manifold music I
    build,
    Bidding my organ obey, calling its keys to their
      work,
Claiming each slave of the sound, at a touch, as when
    Solomon willed
    Armies of angels that soar, legions of demons that
      lurk,
5 Man, brute, reptile, fly—alien of end and of aim,
    Adverse, each from the other heaven-high, hell-
      deep removed—
Should rush into sight at once as he named the in-
    effable Name,°
    And pile him a palace straight, to pleasure the prin-
      cess he loved!

Abt Vogler German musician of the eighteenth and early nine-
teenth centuries. **Musical Instrument** a small organ. 7 **the in-
effable Name** the name of God, not spoken by pious Jews, used in
magic.

II

Would it might tarry like his, the beautiful building of
    mine,
    This which my keys in a crowd pressed and impor-
       tuned to raise!   *10*
Ah, one and all, how they helped, would dispart now
    and now combine,
    Zealous to hasten the work, heighten their master
       his praise!
And one would bury his brow with a blind plunge
    down to hell,
    Burrow awhile and build, broad on the roots of
       things,
Then up again swim into sight, having based me my
    palace well,   *15*
    Founded it, fearless of flame, flat on the nether
       springs.

III

And another would mount and march, like the excellent
    minion° he was,
    Ay, another and yet another, one crowd but with
       many a crest,
Raising my rampired walls of gold as transparent as
    glass,
    Eager to do and die, yield each his place to the rest: *20*
For higher still and higher (as a runner tips with fire,
    When a great illumination surprises a festal night—
Outlining round and round Rome's dome from space
    to spire)
    Up, the pinnacled glory reached, and the pride of
       my soul was in sight.

IV

In sight? Not half! for it seemed, it was certain, to
    match man's birth,   *25*

17 **minion** servant.

Nature in turn conceived, obeying an impulse as I;
And the emulous heaven yearned down, made effort to
    reach the earth,
    As the earth had done her best, in my passion, to
    scale the sky:
Novel splendors burst forth, grew familiar and dwelled
    with mine,
    Not a point nor peak but found and fixed its wan-
30   dering star;
Meteor-moons, balls of blaze: and they did not pale
    nor pine,
    For earth had attained to heaven, there was no
    more near nor far.

V

Nay more; for there wanted not who walked in the
    glare and glow,
    Presences plain in the place; or, fresh from the
    Protoplast,°
Furnished for ages to come, when a kindlier wind
35   should blow,
    Lured now to begin and live, in a house to their
    liking at last;
Or else the wonderful dead who have passed through
    the body and gone,
    But were back once more to breathe in an old
    world worth their new:
What never had been, was now; what was, as it shall
    be anon;
    And what is—shall I say, matched both? for I was
40   made perfect too.

VI

All through my keys that gave their sounds to a wish
    of my soul,

34 **Protoplast** first fashioner or creator.

All through my soul that praised as its wish flowed
   visibly forth,
All through music and me! For think, had I painted
   the whole,
     Why, there it had stood, to see, nor the process so
     wonder-worth:
Had I written the same, made verse—still, effect pro-
   ceeds from cause,   *45*
     Ye know why the forms are fair, ye hear how the
     tale is told;
It is all triumphant art, but art in obedience to laws,
     Painter and poet are proud in the artist-list en-
     rolled:—

VII

But here is the finger of God, a flash of the will that
   can,
     Existent behind all laws, that made them and, lo,
     they are!   *50*
And I know not if, save in this, such gift be allowed
   to man,
     That out of three sounds he frame, not a fourth
     sound, but a star.
Consider it well: each tone of our scale in itself is
   naught;
     It is everywhere in the world—loud, soft, and all
     is said:
Give it to me to use! I mix it with two in my thought: *55*
     And, there! Ye have heard and seen: consider and
     bow the head!

VIII

Well!, it is gone at last, the palace of music I reared;
     Gone! and the good tears start, the praises that
     come too slow;
For one is assured at first, one scarce can say that he
   feared,

That he even gave it a thought, the gone thing was
60   to go.
Never to be again! But many more of the kind
    As good, nay, better perchance: is this your com-
      fort to me?
To me, who must be saved because I cling with my
    mind
    To the same, same self, same love, same God: ay,
      what was, shall be.

IX

Therefore to whom turn I but to thee, the ineffable
65   Name?
    Builder and maker, thou, of houses not made with
      hands!
What, have fear of change from thee who art ever the
    same?
    Doubt that thy power can fill the heart that thy
      power expands?
There shall never be one lost good! What was, shall
    live as before;
70   The evil is null, is naught, is silence implying sound;
What was good shall be good, with, for evil, so much
    good more;
    On the earth the broken arcs; in the Heaven, a per-
      fect round.

X

All we have willed or hoped or dreamed of good shall
    exist;
    Not its semblance, but itself; no beauty, nor good,
    nor power
Whose voice has gone forth, but each survives for
75   the melodist
    When eternity affirms the conception of an hour.
The high that proved too high, the heroic for earth
    too hard,

The passion that left the ground to lose itself in
  the sky,
Are music sent up to God by the lover and the bard;
  Enough that he heard it once: we shall hear it by-
  and-by.   *80*

XI

And what is our failure here but a triumph's evidence
  For the fullness of the days? Have we withered or
  agonized?
Why else was the pause prolonged but that singing
  might issue thence?
  Why rushed the discords in but that harmony
  should be prized?
Sorrow is hard to bear, and doubt is slow to clear,   *85*
  Each sufferer says his say, his scheme of the weal
  and woe:
But God has a few of us whom he whispers in the ear;
  The rest may reason and welcome: 'tis we
  musicians know.

XII

Well, it is earth with me; silence resumes her reign:
  I will be patient and proud, and soberly acquiesce.   *90*
Give me the keys. I feel for the common chord again,
  Sliding by semitones, till I sink to the minor—yes,
And I blunt it into a ninth, and I stand on alien
  ground,
  Surveying awhile the heights I rolled from into the
  deep;
Which, hark, I have dared and done, for my resting-
  place is found,   *95*
  The C Major of this life: so, now I will try to sleep.

CALIBAN UPON SETEBOS; OR, NATURAL THEOLOGY IN THE ISLAND°

"Thou thoughtest that I was altogether such a one as thyself."°

['WILL sprawl, now that the heat of day is best,
Flat on his belly in the pit's much mire,
With elbows wide, fists clenched to prop his chin.
And, while he kicks both feet in the cool slush,
5   And feels about his spine small eft-things° course,
Run in and out each arm, and make him laugh:
And while above his head a pompion-plant,
Coating the cave-top as a brow its eye,
Creeps down to touch and tickle hair and beard,
10   And now a flower drops with a bee inside,
And now a fruit to snap at, catch and crunch—
He looks out o'er yon sea which sunbeams cross
And recross till they weave a spider web
(Meshes of fire, some great fish breaks at times)
15   And talks to his own self, howe'er he please,
Touching that other, whom his dam° called God.
Because to talk about Him, vexes—ha,
Could He but know! and time to vex is now,
When talk is safer than in winter-time.
20   Moreover Prosper and Miranda° sleep
In confidence he drudges at their task,
And it is good to cheat the pair, and gibe,
Letting the rank tongue blossom into speech.]

Caliban . . . Island Caliban is the brute in Shakespeare's *The Tempest*. Setebos is his God. Natural theology claims to prove the existence of God and to define his nature apart from revelation by arguing from the created to the creator. **"Thou thoughtest . . . thyself"** Psalm 50:21. **5 eft-things** lizards, etc. **16 his dam** Caliban's mother worshipped Setebos. **20 Prosper and Miranda** Caliban's master and mistress.

Setebos, Setebos, and Setebos!
'Thinketh, He dwelleth i' the cold o' the moon.   25

'Thinketh He made it, with the sun to match,
But not the stars; the stars came otherwise;
Only made clouds, winds, meteors, such as that:
Also this isle, what lives and grows thereon,
And snaky sea which rounds and ends the same.   30

'Thinketh, it came of being ill at ease:
He hated that He cannot change His cold,
Nor cure its ache. 'Hath spied an icy fish
That longed to 'scape the rock-stream where she lived,
And thaw herself within the lukewarm brine   35
O' the lazy sea her stream thrusts far amid,
A crystal spike 'twixt two warm walls of wave;
Only, she ever sickened, found repulse
At the other kind of water, not her life,
(Green-dense and dim-delicious, bred o' the sun)   40
Flounced back from bliss she was not born to breathe,
And in her old bounds buried her despair,
Hating and loving warmth alike: so He.

'Thinketh, He made thereat the sun, this isle,
Trees and the fowls here, beast and creeping thing.   45
Yon otter, sleek-wet, black, lithe as a leech;
Yon auk, one fire-eye in a ball of foam,
That floats and feeds; a certain badger brown
He hath watched hunt with that slant white-wedge eye
By moonlight; and the pie with the long tongue   50
That pricks deep into oakwarts for a worm,
And says a plain word when she finds her prize,
But will not eat the ants; the ants themselves
That build a wall of seeds and settled stalks
About their hole—He made all these and more,   55
Made all we see, and us, in spite: how else?
He could not, Himself, make a second self
To be His mate; as well have made Himself:
He would not make what he mislikes or slights,
An eyesore to Him, or not worth His pains: 60

But did, in envy, listlessness or sport,
Make what Himself would fain, in a manner, be—
Weaker in most points, stronger in a few,
Worthy, and yet mere playthings all the while,
65 Things He admires and mocks too—that is it.
Because, so brave, so better though they be,
It nothing skills if He begin to plague.
Look now, I melt a gourd-fruit into mash,
Add honeycomb and pods, I have perceived,
70 Which bite like finches when they bill and kiss—
Then, when froth rises bladdery, drink up all,
Quick, quick, till maggots scamper through my brain;
Last, throw me on my back i' the seeded thyme,
And wanton, wishing I were born a bird.
75 Put case, unable to be what I wish,
I yet could make a live bird out of clay:
Would not I take clay, pinch my Caliban
Able to fly?—for, there, see, he hath wings,
And great comb like the hoopoe's to admire,
80 And there, a sting to do his foes offense,
There, and I will that he begin to live,
Fly to yon rock-top, nip me off the horns
Of grigs high up that make the merry din,
Saucy through their veined wings, and mind me not.
85 In which feat, if his leg snapped, brittle clay,
And he lay stupid-like—why, I should laugh;
And if he, spying me, should fall to weep,
Beseech me to be good, repair his wrong,
Bid his poor leg smart less or grow again—
90 Well, as the chance were, this might take or else
Not take my fancy: I might hear his cry,
And give the mankin three sound legs for one,
Or pluck the other off, leave him like an egg,
And lessoned he was mine and merely clay.
95 Were this no pleasure, lying in the thyme,
Drinking the mash, with brain become alive,
Making and marring clay at will? So He.

'Thinketh, such shows nor right nor wrong in Him,
Nor kind, nor cruel: He is strong and Lord.

'Am strong myself compared to yonder crabs   *100*
That march now from the mountain to the sea,
'Let twenty pass, and stone the twenty-first,
Loving not, hating not, just choosing so.
'Say, the first straggler that boasts purple spots
Shall join the file, one pincer twisted off;   *105*
'Say, this bruised fellow shall receive a worm,
And two worms he whose nippers end in red;
As it likes me each time, I do: so He.

Well then, 'supposeth He is good i' the main,
Placable if His mind and ways were guessed,   *110*
But rougher than His handiwork, be sure!
Oh, He hath made things worthier than Himself,
And envieth that, so helped, such things do more
Than He who made them! What consoles but this?
That they, unless through Him, do naught at all,   *115*
And must submit: what other use in things?
'Hath cut a pipe of pithless elder-joint
That, blown through, gives exact the scream o' the
          jay
When from her wing you twitch the feathers blue:
Sound this, and little birds that hate the jay   *120*
Flock within stone's throw, glad their foe is hurt:
Put case such pipe could prattle and boast forsooth
"I catch the birds, I am the crafty thing,
I make the cry my maker cannot make
With his great round mouth; he must blow through
          mine!"   *125*
Would not I smash it with my foot? So He.

But wherefore rough, why cold and ill at ease?
Aha, that is a question! Ask, for that,
What knows—the something over Setebos
That made Him, or He, may be, found and fought,   *130*
Worsted, drove off and did to nothing, perchance.
There may be something quiet o'er His head,
Out of His reach, that feels nor joy nor grief,
Since both derive from weakness in some way.
I joy because the quails come; would not joy   *135*

Could I bring quails here when I have a mind:
This Quiet, all it hath a mind to, doth.
'Esteemeth stars the outposts of its couch,
But never spends much thought nor care that way.
140 It may look up, work up—the worse for those
It works on! 'Careth but for Setebos
The many-handed as a cuttle-fish,
Who, making Himself feared through what He does,
Looks up, first, and perceives he cannot soar
145 To what is quiet and hath happy life;
Next looks down here, and out of very spite
Makes this a bauble-world to ape yon real,
These good things to match those as hips do grapes.
'Tis solace making baubles, ay, and sport.
150 Himself peeped late, eyed Prosper at his books
Careless and lofty, lord now of the isle:
Vexed, 'stitched a book of broad leaves, arrow-shaped,
Wrote thereon, he knows what, prodigious words;
Has peeled a wand and called it by a name;
155 Weareth at whiles for an enchanter's robe
The eyed skin of a supple oncelot;
And hath an ounce sleeker than youngling mole,
A four-legged serpent he makes cower and couch,
Now snarl, now hold its breath and mind his eye.
160 And saith she is Miranda and my wife:
'Keeps for his Ariel° a tall pouch-bill crane
He bids go wade for fish and straight disgorge;
Also a sea-beast, lumpish, which he snared,
Blinded the eyes of, and brought somewhat tame,
165 And split its toe-webs, and now pens the drudge
In a hole o' the rock and calls him Caliban;
A bitter heart that bides its time and bites.
'Plays thus at being Prosper in a way,
Taketh his mirth with make-believes: so He.

170 His dam held that the Quiet made all things
Which Setebos vexed only: 'holds not so.
Who made them weak, meant weakness He might vex.

161 **Ariel** Prospero's fairy servant.

Had He meant other, while His hand was in,
Why not make horny eyes no thorn could prick,
Or plate my scalp with bone against the snow,   *175*
Or overscale my flesh 'neath joint and joint,
Like an orc's armor? Ay—so spoil His sport!
He is the One now: only He doth all.

'Saith, He may like, perchance, what profits Him.
Ay, himself loves what does him good; but why?   *180*
'Gets good no otherwise. This blinded beast
Loves whoso places flesh-meat on his nose,
But, had he eyes, would want no help, but hate
Or love, just as it liked him: He hath eyes.
Also it pleaseth Setebos to work,   *185*
Use all His hands, and exercise much craft,
By no means for the love of what is worked.
'Tasteth, himself, no finer good i' the world
When all goes right, in this safe summertime,
And he wants little, hungers, aches not much,   *190*
Than trying what to do with wit and strength.
'Falls to make something: 'piled yon pile of turfs,
And squared and stuck there squares of soft white
      chalk,
And, with a fish-tooth, scratched a moon on each,
And set up endwise certain spikes of tree,   *195*
And crowned the whole with a sloth's skull atop,
Found dead i' the woods, too hard for one to kill.
No use at all i' the work, for work's sole sake;
'Shall some day knock it down again: so He.

'Saith He is terrible: watch His feats in proof!   *200*
One hurricane will spoil six good months' hope.
He hath a spite against me, that I know,
Just as He favors Prosper, who knows why?
So it is, all the same, as well I find.
'Wove wattles° half the winter, fenced them firm   *205*
With stone and stake to stop she-tortoises
Crawling to lay their eggs here: well, one wave,

205 **wattles** wattling is the interlacing of rods with twigs or the like
for making enclosures.

Feeling the foot of Him upon its neck,
Gaped as a snake does, lolled out its large tongue,
210 And licked the whole labor flat: so much for spite.
'Saw a ball flame down late (yonder it lies)
Where, half an hour before, I slept i' the shade:
Often they scatter sparkles: there is force!
'Dug up a newt He may have envied once
215 And turned to stone, shut up inside a stone.
Please Him and hinder this?—What Prosper does?
Aha, if He would tell me how! Not He!
There is the sport: discover how or die!
All need not die, for of the things o' the isle
220 Some flee afar, some dive, some run up trees;
Those at His mercy—why, they please Him most
When . . when . . well, never try the same way twice!
Repeat what act has pleased, He may grow wroth.
You must not know His ways, and play Him off,
225 Sure of the issue. 'Doth the like himself:
'Spareth a squirrel that it nothing fears
But steals the nut from underneath my thumb,
And when I threat, bites stoutly in defense:
'Spareth an urchin that contrariwise,
230 Curls up into a ball, pretending death
For fright at my approach: the two ways please.
But what would move my choler more than this,
That either creature counted on its life
Tomorrow and next day and all days to come,
235 Saying, forsooth, in the inmost of its heart,
"Because he did so yesterday with me,
And otherwise with such another brute,
So must he do henceforth and always."—Ay?
Would teach the reasoning couple what "must" means
240 'Doth as he likes, or wherefore Lord? So He.

'Conceiveth all things will continue thus,
And we shall have to live in fear of Him
So long as He lives, keeps His strength: no change,
If He have done His best, make no new world
245 To please Him more, so leave off watching this—
If He surprise not even the Quiet's self

Some strange day—or, suppose, grow into it
As grubs grow butterflies: else, here are we,
And there is He, and nowhere help at all.

'Believeth with the life, the pain shall stop. 250
His dam held different, that after death
He both plagued enemies and feasted friends:
Idly! He doth His worst in this our life,
Giving just respite lest we die through pain,
Saving last pain for worst—with which, an end. 255
Meanwhile, the best way to escape His ire
Is, not to seem too happy. 'Sees, himself,
Yonder two flies, with purple films and pink,
Bask on the pompion-bell above: kills both.
'Sees two black painful beetles roll their ball 260
On head and tail as if to save their lives:
Moves them the stick away they strive to clear.

Even so, 'would have Him misconceive, suppose
This Caliban strives hard and ails no less,
And always, above all else, envies Him; 265
Wherefore he mainly dances on dark nights,
Moans in the sun, gets under holes to laugh,
And never speaks his mind save housed as now:
Outside, 'groans, curses. If He caught me here,
O'erheard this speech, and asked "What chucklest at?" 270
'Would, to appease Him, cut a finger off,
Or of my three kid yearlings burn the best,
Or let the toothsome apples rot on tree,
Or push my tame beast for the orc to taste:
While myself lit a fire, and made a song 275
And sung it, *"What I hate, be consecrate*
To celebrate Thee and Thy state, no mate
For Thee; what see for envy in poor me?"
Hoping the while, since evils sometimes mend,
Warts rub away and sores are cured with slime, 280
That some strange day, will either the Quiet catch
And conquer Setebos, or likelier He
Decrepit may doze, doze, as good as die.
[What, what? A curtain o'er the world at once!

285 Crickets stop hissing; not a bird—or, yes,
There scuds His raven that has told Him all!
It was fool's play, this prattling! Ha! The wind
Shoulders the pillared dust, death's house o' the move,
And fast invading fires begin! White blaze—
A tree's head snaps—and there, there, there, there,
290   there,
His thunder follows! Fool to gibe at Him!
Lo! 'Lieth flat and loveth Setebos!
'Maketh his teeth meet through his upper lip,
Will let those quails fly, will not eat this month
295 One little mess of whelks, so he may 'scape!]

EPILOGUE

FIRST SPEAKER, *as David*

I

ON the first of the Feast of Feasts,
    The Dedication Day,°
When the Levites joined the Priests
    At the Altar in robed array,
5 Gave signal to sound and say—

II

When the thousands, rear and van,
    Swarming with one accord
Became as a single man
    (Look, gesture, thought and word)
10 In praising and thanking the Lord—

2 **Dedication Day** ceremonial dedication of the Temple in Jerusalem.

III

When the singers lift up their voice,
   And the trumpets made endeavor,
Sounding, "In God rejoice!"
   Saying, "In Him rejoice
Whose mercy endureth forever!"—   *15*

IV

Then the Temple filled with a cloud,
   Even the House of the Lord;
Porch bent and pillar bowed:
   For the presence of the Lord,
In the glory of His cloud,   *20*
   Had filled the House of the Lord.

SECOND SPEAKER, *as Renan*°

Gone now! All gone across the dark so far,
   Sharpening fast, shuddering ever, shutting still,
Dwindling into the distance, dies that star
   Which came, stood, opened once! We gazed our
      fill   *25*
With upturned faces on as real a Face
   That, stooping from grave music and mild fire,
Took in our homage, made a visible place
   Through many a depth of glory, gyre on gyre,°
For the dim human tribute. Was this true?   *30*
   Could man indeed avail, mere praise of his,
To help by rapture God's own rapture too,
   Thrill with a heart's red tinge that pure pale bliss?
Why did it end? Who failed to beat the breast,
   And shriek, and throw the arms protesting wide, *35*
When a first shadow showed the star addressed
   Itself to motion, and on either side
The rims contracted as the rays retired;
   The music, like a fountain's sickening pulse,

Renan Ernest Renan, author of a *Life of Jesus* (1863) that explained away the mysteries. **29 gyre** spiral.

40   Subsided on itself; awhile transpired
         Some vestige of a Face no pangs convulse,
     No prayers retard; then even this was gone,
         Lost in the night at last. We, lone and left
     Silent through centuries, ever and anon
45   Venture to probe again the vault bereft
     Of all now save the lesser lights, a mist
         Of multitudinous points, yet suns, men say—
     And this leaps ruby, this lurks amethyst,
         But where may hide what came and loved our clay?
50   How shall the sage detect in yon expanse
         The star which chose to stoop and stay for us?
     Unroll the records! Hailed ye such advance
         Indeed, and did your hope evanish thus?
     Watchers of twilight, is the worst averred?
55   We shall not look up, know ourselves are seen,
     Speak, and be sure that we again are heard,
         Acting or suffering, have the disk's serene
     Reflect our life, absorb an earthly flame,
         Nor doubt that, were mankind inert and numb,
60   Its core had never crimsoned all the same,
         Nor, missing ours, its music fallen dumb?
     Oh, dread succession to a dizzy post,
         Sad sway of scepter whose mere touch appalls,
     Ghastly dethronement, cursed by those the most
65   On whose repugnant brow the crown next falls!

THIRD SPEAKER

I

Witless alike of will and way divine,
How heaven's high with earth's low should intertwine!
Friends, I have seen through your eyes: now use mine!

II

Take the least man of all mankind, as I;

Look at his head and heart, find how and why 70
He differs from his fellows utterly:

III

Then, like me, watch when nature by degrees
Grows alive round him, as in Arctic seas
(They said of old) the instinctive water flees

IV

Toward some elected point of central rock, 75
As though, for its sake only, roamed the flock
Of waves about the waste: awhile they mock

V

With radiance caught for the occasion—hues
Of blackest hell now, now such reds and blues
As only heaven could fitly interfuse— 80

VI

The mimic monarch of the whirlpool, king
O' the current for a minute: then they wring
Up by the roots and oversweep the thing,

VII

And hasten off, to play again elsewhere
The same part, choose another peak as bare, 85
They find and flatter, feast and finish there.

VIII

When you see what I tell you—nature dance
About each man of us, retire, advance,
As though the pageant's end were to enhance

IX

90 His worth, and——once the life, his product, gained——
Roll away elsewhere, keep the strife sustained,
And show thus real, a thing the North but feigned——

X

When you acknowledge that one world could do
All the diverse work, old yet ever new,
95 Divide us, each from other, me from you——

XI

Why, where's the need of Temple, when the walls
O' the world are that? What use of swells and falls
From Levites' choir, Priests' cries, and trumpet-calls?

XII

That one Face, far from vanish, rather grows,
100 Or decomposes but to recompose,
Become my universe that feels and knows.

from THE RING AND THE BOOK

(1868–69)

O LYRIC LOVE°

O LYRIC Love, half angel and half bird
And all a wonder and a wild desire—
Boldest of hearts that ever braved the sun,
Took sanctuary within the holier blue,
And sang a kindred soul out to his face—   *5*
Yet human at the red-ripe of the heart—
When the first summons from the darkling earth
Reached thee amid thy chambers, blanched their blue,
And bared them of the glory—to drop down,
To toil for man, to suffer or to die—   *10*
This is the same voice: can thy soul know change?
Hail then, and hearken from the realms of help!
Never may I commence my song, my due
To God who best taught song by gift of thee,

O lyric Love conclusion of the first book of *The Ring and the Book*,
here renumbered. It is addressed to the poet's wife, now dead,
thought of as the muse of the poem. A ring given him by his wife
suggested the ring of the title, the circle of truth created by the
imagination out of the square of fact (literally the Old Yellow Book
Browning had found in a bookstall in Florence, a collection of
documents dealing with a seventeenth century Roman murder case;
See "Introduction").

15 Except with bent head and beseeching hand—
That still, despite the distance and the dark,
What was, again may be; some interchange
Of grace, some splendor once thy very thought,
Some benediction anciently thy smile:
20 —Never conclude, but raising hand and head
Thither where eyes, that cannot reach, yet yearn
For all hope, all sustainment, all reward,
Their utmost up and on—so blessing back
In those thy realms of help, that heaven thy home,
25 Some whiteness which, I judge, thy face makes proud,
Some wanness where, I think, thy foot may fall!

GIUSEPPE CAPONSACCHI°

ANSWER you, Sirs? Do I understand aright?
Have patience! In this sudden smoke from hell—
So things disguise themselves—I cannot see
My own hand held thus broad before my face
5 And know it again. Answer you? Then that means
Tell over twice what I, the first time, told
Six months ago: 'twas here, I do believe,
Fronting you same three in this very room,
I stood and told you: yet now no one laughs,
10 Who then . . . nay, dear my lords, but laugh you did,
As good as laugh, what in a judge we style
Laughter—no levity, nothing indecorous, lords!
Only—I think I apprehend the mood:

Giuseppe Caponsacchi the priest who accompanied Pompilia in her
flight from her husband, Guido. (Selections from *The Ring and the
Book* have been renumbered in accordance with usual practice.)

There was the blameless shrug, permissible smirk,
The pen's pretense at play with the pursed mouth,   15
The titter stifled in the hollow palm
Which rubbed the eyebrow and caressed the nose,
When I first told my tale: they meant, you know,
"The sly one, all this we are bound believe!
Well, he can say no other than what he says.   20
We have been young, too—come, there's greater
      guilt!
Let him but decently disembroil himself,
Scramble from out the scrape nor move the mud—
We solid ones may risk a finger-stretch!
And now you sit as grave, stare as aghast   25
As if I were a phantom: now 'tis—"Friend,
Collect yourself!"—no laughing matter more—
"Counsel the Court in this extremity,
Tell us again!"—tell that, for telling which,
I got the jocular piece of punishment,   30
Was sent to lounge a little in the place
Whence now of a sudden here you summon me
To take the intelligence from just—your lips!
You, Judge Tommati, who then tittered most—
That she I helped eight months since to escape   35
Her husband, was retaken by the same,
Three days ago, if I have seized your sense—
(I being disallowed to interfere,
Meddle or make in a matter none of mine,
For you and law were guardians quite enough   40
O' the innocent, without a pert priest's help)—
And that he has butchered her accordingly,
As she foretold and as myself believed—
And, so foretelling and believing so,
We were punished, both of us, the merry way: 45
Therefore, tell once again the tale! For what?
Pompilia is only dying while I speak!
Why does the mirth hang fire and miss the smile?
My masters, there's an old book, you should con
For strange adventures, applicable yet,   50
'Tis stuffed with. Do you know that there was once
This thing: a multitude of worthy folk

Took recreation, watched a certain group
Of soldiery intent upon a game--
55 How first they wrangled, but soon fell to play,
Threw dice—the best diversion in the world.
A word in your ear—they are now casting lots,
Ay, with that gesture quaint and cry uncouth,
For the coat of One murdered an hour ago!
60 I am a priest—talk of what I have learned.
Pompilia is bleeding out her life belike,
Gasping away the latest breath of all,
This minute, while I talk—not while you laugh?

Yet, being sobered now, what is it you ask
65 By way of explanation? There's the fact!
It seems to fill the universe with sight
And sound—from the four corners of this earth
Tells itself over, to my sense at least.
But you may want it lower set i' the scale—
70 Too vast, too close it clangs in the ear, perhaps;
You'd stand back just to comprehend it more.
Well then, let me, the hollow rock, condense
The voice o' the sea and wind, interpret you
The mystery of this murder. God above!
75 It is too paltry, such a transference
O' the storm's roar to the cranny of the stone!

This deed, you saw begin—why does its end
Surprise you? Why should the event enforce
The lesson, we ourselves learned, she and I,
80 From the first o' the fact, and taught you, all in vain?
This Guido from whose throat you took my grasp,
Was this man to be favored, now, or feared,
Let do his will, or have his will restrained,
In the relation with Pompilia? Say!
85 Did any other man need interpose
—Oh, though first comer, though as strange at the
        work
As fribble must be, coxcomb, fool that's near
To knave as, say, a priest who fears the world—
Was he bound brave the peril, save the doomed,

Or go on, sing his snatch and pluck his flower,   90
Keep the straight path and let the victim die?
I held so; you decided otherwise,
Saw no such peril, therefore no such need
To stop song, loosen flower, and leave path. Law,
Law was aware and watching, would suffice,   95
Wanted no priest's intrusion, palpably
Pretense, too manifest a subterfuge!
Whereupon I, priest, coxcomb, fribble and fool,
Ensconced me in my corner, thus rebuked,
A kind of culprit, overzealous hound   100
Kicked for his pains to kennel; I gave place
To you, and let the law reign paramount:
I left Pompilia to your watch and ward,
And now you point me—there and thus she lies!

Men, for the last time, what do you want with me?   105
Is it—you acknowledge, as it were, a use,
A profit in employing me?—at length
I may conceivably help the august law?
I am free to break the blow, next hawk that swoops
On next dove, nor miss much of good repute?   110
Or what if this your summons, after all,
Be but the form of mere release, no more,
Which turns the key and lets the captive go?
I have paid enough in person at Civita,
Am free—what more need I concern me with?   115
Thank you! I am rehabilitated then,
A very reputable priest. But she—
The glory of life, the beauty of the world,
The splendor of heaven . . . well, Sirs, does no one
    move?
Do I speak ambiguously? The glory, I say,   120
And the beauty, I say, and splendor, still say I,
Who, priest and trained to live my whole life long
On beauty and splendor, solely at their source,
God—have thus recognized my food in her,
You tell me, that's fast dying while we talk,   125
Pompilia! How does lenity to me,
Remit one deathbed pang to her? Come smile!

The proper wink at the hot-headed youth
Who lets his soul show, through transparent words,
130 The mundane love that's sin and scandal too!
You are all struck acquiescent now, it seems:
It seems the oldest, gravest signor here,
Even the redoubtable Tommati, sits
Chop-fallen—understands how law might take
135 Service like mine, of brain and heart and hand,
In good part. Better late than never, law
You understand of a sudden, gospel too
Has a claim here, may possibly pronounce
Consistent with my priesthood, worthy Christ,
That I endeavored to save Pompilia?

140   Then,
You were wrong, you see: that's well to see, though
     late:
That's all we may expect of man, this side
The grave: his good is—knowing he is bad:
Thus will it be with us when the books ope
145 And we stand at the bar on Judgment Day.
Well then, I have a mind to speak, see cause
To relume the quenched flax° by this dreadful light,
Burn my soul out in showing you the truth.
I heard, last time I stood here to be judged,
150 What is priest's-duty—labor to pluck tares
And weed the corn of Molinism;° let me
Make you hear, this time, how, in such a case,
Man, be he in the priesthood or at plough,
Mindful of Christ or marching step by step
155 With . . . what's his style, the other potentate
Who bids have courage and keep honor safe,
Nor let minuter admonition tease?—
How he is bound, better or worse, to act.
Earth will not end through this misjudgment, no!

147 **quenched flax** Isaiah 42:3.   151 **Molinism** Miguel de Molinos
was a Spanish writer on the spiritual life who minimized the im-
portance of the externals of religion. Browning thinks of him as a
kind of Protestant

For you and the others like you sure to come,   160
Fresh work is sure to follow—wickedness
That wants withstanding. Many a man of blood,
Many a man of guile will clamor yet,
Bid you redress his grievance—as he clutched
The prey, forsooth a stranger stepped between,   165
And there's the good gripe in pure waste! My part
Is done; i' the doing it, I pass away
Out of the world. I want no more with earth.
Let me, in Heaven's name, use the very snuff
O' the taper in one last spark shall show truth   170
For a moment, show Pompilia who was true!
Not for her sake, but yours: if she is dead,
Oh, Sirs, she can be loved by none of you
Most or least priestly! Saints, to do us good,
Must be in Heaven, I seem to understand: 175
We never find them saints before, at least.
Be her first prayer then presently for you—
She has done the good to me . . .
                                        What is all this?
There, I was born, have lived, shall die, a fool!
This is a foolish outset:—might with cause   180
Give color to the very lie o' the man,
The murderer—make as if I loved his wife,
In the way he called love. He is the fool there!
Why, had there been in me the touch of taint,
I had picked up so much of knaves'-policy   185
As hide it, keep one hand pressed on the place
Suspected of a spot would damn us both.
Or no, not her!—not even if any of you
Dares think that I, i' the face of death, her death
That's in my eyes and ears and brain and heart,   190
Lie—if he does, let him! I mean to say,
So he stop there, stay thought from smirching her
The snow-white soul that angels fear to take
Untenderly. But, all the same, I know
I too am taintless, and I bare my breast.   195
You can't think, men as you are, all of you,
But that, to hear thus suddenly such an end
Of such a wonderful white soul, that comes

Of a man and murderer calling the white black,
200 Must shake me, trouble and disadvantage. Sirs,
Only seventeen!

                     Why, good and wise you are!
You might at the beginning stop my mouth:
So, none would be to speak for her, that knew.
I talk impertinently, and you bear,
205 All the same. This it is to have to do
With honest hearts: they easily may err,
But in the main they wish well to the truth.
You are Christians; somehow, no one ever plucked
A rag, even, from the body of the Lord,
210 To wear and mock with, but, despite himself,
He looked the greater and was the better. Yes,
I shall go on now. Does she need or not
I keep calm? Calm I'll keep as monk that croons
Transcribing battle, earthquake, famine, plague,
215 From parchment to his cloister's chronicle.
Not one word more from the point now!

                             I begin.
Yes, I am one of your body and a priest.
Also I am a younger son o' the House
Oldest now, greatest once, in my birth-town
220 Arezzo, I recognize no equal there—
(I want all arguments, all sorts of arms
That seem to serve—use this for a reason, wait!)
Not therefore thrust into the Church, because
O' the piece of bread one gets there. We were first
225 Of Fiesole, that rings still with the fame
Of Capo-in-Sacco our progenitor:
When Florence ruined Fiesole, our folk
Migrated to the victor-city, and there
Flourished—our palace and our tower attest,
230 In the Old Mercato—this was years ago,
Four hundred, full—no, it wants fourteen just.
Our arms are those of Fiesole itself,
The shield quartered with white and red: a branch
Are the Salviati of us, nothing more.

That were good help to the Church? But better still— 235
Not simply for the advantage of my birth
I' the way of the world, was I proposed for priest;
But because there's an illustration, late
I' the day, that's loved and looked to as a saint
Still in Arezzo, he was bishop of,   240
Sixty years since: he spent to the last doit
His bishop's-revenue among the poor,
And used to tend the needy and the sick,
Barefoot, because of his humility.
He it was—when the Granduke Ferdinand   245
Swore he would raze our city, plough the place
And sow it with salt, because we Aretines
Had tied a rope about the neck, to hale
The statue of his father from its base
For hate's sake—he availed by prayers and tears 250
To pacify the Duke and save the town.
This was my father's father's brother. You see,
For his sake, how it was I had a right
To the selfsame office, bishop in the egg,
So, grew i' the garb and prattled in the school, 255
Was made expect, from infancy almost,
The proper mood o' the priest; till time ran by
And brought the day when I must read the vows,
Declare the world renounced and undertake
To become priest and leave probation—leap   260
Over the ledge into the other life,
Having gone trippingly hitherto up to the height
O'er the wan water. Just a vow to read!

I stopped short awestruck. "How shall holiest flesh
Engage to keep such vow inviolate,   265
How much less mine? I know myself too weak,
Unworthy! Choose a worthier stronger man!"
And the very Bishop smiled and stopped my mouth
In its mid-protestation. "Incapable?
Qualmish of conscience? Thou ingenuous boy!   270
Clear up the clouds and cast thy scruples far!
I satisfy thee there's an easier sense
Wherein to take such vow than suits the first

Rough rigid reading. Mark what makes all smooth,
275 Nay, has been even a solace to myself!
The Jews who needs must, in their synagogue,
Utter sometimes the holy name of God,
A thing their superstition boggles at,
Pronounce aloud the ineffable sacrosanct—
280 How does their shrewdness help them? In this wise;
Another set of sounds they substitute,
Jumble so consonants and vowels—how
Should I know?—that there grows from out the old
Quite a new word that means the very same—
285 And o'er the hard place slide they with a smile.
Giuseppe Maria Caponsacchi mine,
Nobody wants you in these latter days
To prop the Church by breaking your backbone—
As the necessary way was once, we know,
290 When Diocletian flourished and his like.
That building of the buttress-work was done
By martyrs and confessors: let it bide,
Add not a brick, but, where you see a chink,
Stick in a sprig of ivy or root a rose
295 Shall make amends and beautify the pile!
We profit as you were the painfullest
O' the martyrs, and you prove yourself a match
For the cruelest confessor ever was,
If you march boldly up and take your stand
300 Where their blood soaks, their bones yet strew the soil,
And cry 'Take notice, I the young and free
And well-to-do i' the world, thus leave the world,
Cast in my lot thus with no gay young world
But the grand old Church: she tempts me of the two!'
305 Renounce the world? Nay, keep and give it us!
Let us have you, and boast of what you bring.
We want the pick o' the earth to practice with,
Not its offscouring, halt and deaf and blind
In soul and body. There's a rubble-stone
310 Unfit for the front o' the building, stuff to stow
In a gap behind and keep us weather-tight;
There's porphyry for the prominent place. Good lack!
Saint Paul has had enough and to spare, I trow,

Of ragged runaway Onesimus:°
He wants the right-hand with the signet-ring   315
Of King Agrippa,° now, to shake and use.
I have a heavy scholar cloistered up,
Close under lock and key, kept at his task
Of letting Fénelon° know the fool he is,
In a book I promise Christendom next spring.   320
Why, if he covets so much meat, the clown,
As a lark's wing next Friday, or, any day,
Diversion beyond catching his own fleas,
He shall be properly swinged, I promise him.
But you, who are so quite another paste   325
Of a man—do you obey me? Cultivate
Assiduous that superior gift you have
Of making madrigals—(who told me? Ah!)
Get done a Marinesque Adoniad° straight
With a pulse o' the blood a-pricking, here and there,   330
That I may tell the lady 'And he's ours!' "

So I became a priest: those terms changed all,
I was good enough for that, nor cheated so;
I could live thus and still hold head erect.
Now you see why I may have been before   335
A fribble and coxcomb, yet, as priest, break word
Nowise, to make you disbelieve me now.
I need that you should know my truth. Well, then,
According to prescription did I live,
—Conformed myself, both read the breviary   340
And wrote the rhymes, was punctual to my place
I' the Pieve,° and as diligent at my post
Where beauty and fashion rule. I throve apace,
Subdeacon, canon, the authority
For delicate play at tarocs,° and arbiter   345
O' the magnitude of fan-mounts: all the while

314 **Onesimus** Philemon 10–18.   316 **Agrippa** Acts 25–26.   319
Fénelon French churchman and man of letters who taught Molinist
doctrines.   329 **Marinesque Adoniad** i.e. in the manner of the
Adone of Marino, a fashionable poet whose work is elaborately
artificial.   342 **Pieve** Caponsacchi was attached to the Church of
Santa Maria della Pieve.   345 **tarocs** card game.

Wanting no whit the advantage of a hint
Benignant to the promising pupil—thus:
"Enough attention to the Countess now,
350 The young one; 'tis her mother rules the roast,
We know where, and puts in a word: go pay
Devoir tomorrow morning after mass!
Break that rash promise to preach, Passion-week!
Has it escaped you the Archbishop grunts
355 And snuffles when one grieves to tell his Grace
No soul dares treat the subject of the day
Since his own masterly handling it (ha, ha!)
Five years ago—when somebody could help
And touch up an odd phrase in time of need,
360 (He, he!)—and somebody helps you, my son!
Therefore, don't prove so indispensable
At the Pieve, sit more loose i' the seat, nor grow
A fixture by attendance morn and eve!
Arezzo's just a haven midway Rome—
365 Rome's the eventual harbor—make for port,
Crowd sail, crack cordage! And your cargo be
A polished presence, a genteel manner, wit
At will, and tact at every pore of you!
I sent our lump of learning, Brother Clout,
370 And Father Slouch, our piece of piety,
To see Rome and try suit the Cardinal.
Thither they clump-clumped, beads and book in hand
And ever since 'tis meat for man and maid
How both flopped down, prayed blessing on bent pate
375 Bald many an inch beyond the tonsure's need,
Never once dreaming, the two moony dolts,
There's nothing moves his Eminence so much
As—far from all this awe at sanctitude—
Heads that wag, eyes that twinkle, modified mirth
380 At the closet-lectures on the Latin tongue
A lady learns so much by, we know where.
Why, body o' Bacchus, you should crave his rule
For pauses in the elegiac couplet, chasms
Permissible only to Catullus! There!
385 Now go to duty: brisk, break Priscian's head
By reading the day's office—there's no help.

You've Ovid° in your poke to plaster that;
Amen's at the end of all: then sup with me!"

  Well, after three or four years of this life,
In prosecution of my calling, I   *390*
Found myself at the theater one night
With a brother canon, in a mood and mind
Proper enough for the place, amused or no:
When I saw enter, stand, and seat herself
A lady, young, tall, beautiful, strange and sad.   *395*
It was as when, in our cathedral once,
As I got yawningly through matin-song,
I saw *facchini*° bear a burden up,
Base it on the high-altar, break away
A board or two, and leave the thing inside   *400*
Lofty and lone: and lo, when next I looked,
There was the Raphael! I was still one stare,
When—"Nay, I'll make her give you back your gaze"—
Said Canon Conti; and at the word he tossed
A paper-twist of comfits to her lap,   *405*
And dodged and in a trice was at my back
Nodding from over my shoulder. Then she turned,
Looked our way, smiled the beautiful sad strange smile.
"Is not she fair? 'Tis my new cousin," said he:
"The fellow lurking there i' the black o' the box   *410*
Is Guido, the old scapegrace: she's his wife,
Married three years since: how his Countship sulks!
He has brought little back from Rome beside,
After the bragging, bullying. A fair face,
And—they do say—a pocketful of gold   *415*
When he can worry both her parents dead.
I don't go much there, for the chamber's cold
And the coffee pale. I got a turn at first
Paying my duty: I observed they crouched
—The two old frightened family specters—close   *420*

384–87 **Catullus . . . Ovid** the poet *Catullus* takes liberties with the
usual rules for elision in Latin verse. *Priscian* was a grammarian.
To "break his head" meant to use ungrammatical or impure forms
such as are common in the unclassical Latin of the Church. **Ovid** is
a Latin poet of high elegance.   398 **facchini** porters.

In a corner, each on each like mouse on mouse
I' the cat's cage: ever since, I stay at home.
Hallo, there's Guido, the black, mean and small,
Bends his brows on us—please to bend your own
425 On the shapely nether limbs of Light-skirts there
By way of a diversion! I was a fool
To fling the sweetmeats. Prudence, for God's love!
Tomorrow I'll make my peace, e'en tell some fib,
Try if I can't find means to take you there."

430 That night and next day did the gaze endure,
Burnt to my brain, as sunbeam through shut eyes,
And not once changed the beautiful sad strange smile.
At vespers Conti leaned beside my seat
I' the choir—part said, part sung—*"In ex-cel-sis—*
435 All's to no purpose; I have louted low,
But he saw you staring—*quia sub*—don't incline
To know you nearer: him we would not hold
For Hercules—the man would lick your shoe
If you and certain efficacious friends
440 Managed him warily—but there's the wife:
Spare her, because he beats her, as it is,
She's breaking her heart quite fast enough—*jam tu*—
So, be you rational and make amends
With little Light-skirts yonder—*in secula*
445 *Secu-lo-o-o-o-rum.*° Ah, you rogue! Everyone knows
What great dame she makes jealous: one against one,
Play, and win both!"

                    Sirs, ere the week was out,
I saw and said to myself "Light-skirts hides teeth
Would make a dog sick—the great dame shows spite
450 Should drive a cat mad: 'tis but poor work this—
Counting one's fingers till the sonnet's crowned.
I doubt much if Marino really be
A better bard than Dante after all.
'Tis more amusing to go pace at eve
455 I' the Duomo°—watch the day's last gleam outside

434–45 **In ex-cel-sis . . . Secu-lo-o-o-o-rum** bits of Latin from the
service. 455 **Duomo** cathedral.

Turn, as into a skirt of God's own robe,
Those lancet-windows' jeweled miracle—
Than go eat the Archbishop's ortolans,°
Digest his jokes. Luckily Lent is near:
Who cares to look will find me in my stall   *460*
At the Pieve, constant to this faith at least—
Never to write a canzonet any more."

So, next week, 'twas my patron spoke abrupt,
In altered guise. "Young man, can it be true
That after all your promise of sound fruit,   *465*
You have kept away from Countess young or old
And gone play truant in church all day long?
Are you turning Molinist?" I answered quick:
"Sir, what if I turned Christian? It might be.
The fact is, I am troubled in my mind,   *470*
Beset and pressed hard by some novel thoughts.
This your Arezzo is a limited world;
There's a strange Pope—'tis said, a priest who thinks.
Rome is the port, you say: to Rome I go.
I will live alone, one does so in a crowd,   *475*
And look into my heart a little." "Lent
Ended"—I told friends—"I shall go to Rome."

    One evening I was sitting in a muse
Over the opened "Summa,"° darkened round
By the mid-March twilight, thinking how my life   *480*
Had shaken under me—broke short indeed
And showed the gap 'twixt what is, what should be—
And into what abysm the soul may slip,
Leave aspiration here, achievement there,
Lacking omnipotence to connect extremes—   *485*
Thinking moreover . . . oh, thinking, if you like,
How utterly dissociated was I
A priest and celibate, from the sad strange wife
Of Guido—just as an instance to the point,
Naught more—how I had a whole store of strengths   *490*

---

458 **ortolans** small birds. Table delicacies.   479 **"Summa"** com-
pendium of Christian doctrine.

Eating into my heart, which craved employ,
And she, perhaps, need of a finger's help—
And yet there was no way in the wide world
To stretch out mine and so relieve myself—
495 How when the page o' the "Summa" preached its best,
Her smile kept glowing out of it, as to mock
The silence we could break by no one word—
There came a tap without the chamber-door,
And a whisper; when I bade who tapped speak out.
500 And, in obedience to my summons, last
In glided a masked muffled mystery,
Laid lightly a letter on the opened book,
Then stood with folded arms and foot demure,
Pointing as if to mark the minutes' flight.

505 I took the letter, read to the effect
That she, I lately flung the comfits to,
Had a warm heart to give me in exchange,
And gave it—loved me and confessed it thus,
And bade me render thanks by word of mouth,
510 Going that night to such a side o' the house
Where the small terrace overhangs a street
Blind and deserted, not the street in front:
Her husband being away, the surly patch,
At his villa of Vittiano.

                    "And you?"—I asked:
515 "What may you be?" "Count Guido's kind of maid—
Most of us have two functions in his house.
We all hate him, the lady suffers much,
'Tis just we show compassion, furnish help,
Specially since her choice is fixed so well.
520 What answer may I bring to cheer the sweet
Pompilia?"

                Then I took a pen and wrote
"No more of this! That you are fair, I know:
But other thoughts now occupy my mind.
I should not thus have played the insensible
525 Once on a time. What made you—may one ask—

Marry your hideous husband? 'Twas a fault,
And now you taste the fruit of it. Farewell."

"There!" smiled I as she snatched it and was gone—
"There, let the jealous miscreant—Guido's self,
Whose mean soul grins through this transparent trick— 530
Be baulked so far, defrauded of his aim!
What fund of satisfaction to the knave,
Had I kicked this his messenger downstairs,
Trussed to the middle of her impudence,
And set his heart at ease so! No, indeed! 535
There's the reply which he shall turn and twist
At pleasure, snuff at till his brain grow drunk,
As the bear does when he finds a scented glov
That puzzles him—a hand and yet no hand,
Of other perfume than his own foul paw! 540
Last month, I had doubtless chosen to play the dupe,
Accepted the mock-invitation, kept
The sham appointment, cudgel beneath cloak,
Prepared myself to pull the appointer's self
Out of the window from his hiding-place 545
Behind the gown of this part-messenger
Part-mistress who would personate the wife.
Such had seemed once a jest permissible:
Now I am not i' the mood."

              Back next morn brought
The messenger, a second letter in hand. 550
"You are cruel, Thyrsis, and Myrtilla° moans
Neglected but adores you, makes request
For mercy: why is it you dare not come?
Such virtue is scarce natural to your age.
You must love someone else; I hear you do, 555
The Baron's daughter or the Advocate's wife,
Or both—all's one, would you make me the third—
I take the crumbs from table gratefully
Nor grudge who feasts there. 'Faith, I blush and blaze!
Yet if I break all bounds, there's reason sure. 560

551 **Thyrsis** . . . **Myrtilla** conventional names in pastoral literature.

Are you determinedly bent on Rome?
I am wretched here, a monster tortures me:
Carry me with you! Come and say you will!
Concert this very evening! Do not write!
565 I am ever at the window of my room
Over the terrace, at the *Ave.*° Come!"

I questioned—lifting half the woman's mask
To let her smile loose. "So, you gave my line
To the merry lady?" "She kissed off the wax,
570 And put what paper was not kissed away,
In her bosom to go burn: but merry, no!
She wept all night when evening brought no friend,
Alone, the unkind missive at her breast;
Thus Philomel,° the thorn at her breast too,
575 Sings" . . . "Writes this second letter?" "Even so!
Then she may peep at vespers forth?"—"What risk
Do we run o' the husband?"—"Ah—no risk at all!
He is more stupid even than jealous. Ah—
That was the reason? Why, the man's away!
580 Beside, his bugbear is that friend of yours,
Fat little Canon Conti. He fears him,
How should he dream of you? I told you truth:
He goes to the villa at Vittiano—'tis
The time when Spring-sap rises in the vine—
585 Spends the night there. And then his wife's a child:
Does he think a child outwits him? A mere child:
Yet so full grown, a dish for any duke.
Don't quarrel longer with such cates,° but come!"
I wrote "In vain do you solicit me.
590 I am a priest: and you are wedded wife,
Whatever kind of brute your husband prove.
I have scruples, in short. Yet should you really show
Sign at the window . . . but nay, best be good!
My thoughts are elsewhere," "Take her that!"

                                                     "Again
595 Let the incarnate meanness, cheat and spy,

566 **Ave** Evidently vespers (see 1.576).   574 **Philomel** poetic name
for nightingale.   588 **cates** delicacies.

Mean to the marrow of him, make his heart
His food, anticipate hell's worm once more!
Let him watch shivering at the window—ay,
And let this hybrid, this his light-of-love
And lackey-of-lies—a sage economy—   600
Paid with embracings for the rank brass coin—
Let her report and make him chuckle o'er
The breakdown of my resolution now,
And lour at disappointment in good time!
—So tantalize and so enrage by turns,   605
Until the two fall each on the other like
Two famished spiders, as the coveted fly
That toys long, leaves their net and them at last!"
And so the missives followed thick and fast
For a month, say—I still came at every turn   610
On the soft sly adder, endlong 'neath my tread.
I was met i' the street, made sign to in the church,
A slip was found i' the doorsill, scribbled word
'Twixt page and page o' the prayer book in my place.
A crumpled thing dropped even before my feet,   615
Pushed through the blind, above the terrace-rail,
As I passed, by day, the very window once.
And ever from corners would be peering up
The messenger, with the self-same demand
"Obdurate still, no flesh but adamant?   620
Nothing to cure the wound, assuage the throe
O' the sweetest lamb that ever loved a bear?"
And ever my one answer in one tone—
"Go your ways, temptress! Let a priest read, pray,
Unplagued of vain talk, visions not for him!   625
In the end, you'll have your will and ruin me!"

One day, a variation: thus I read:
"You have gained little by timidity.
My husband has found out my love at length,
Sees cousin Conti was the stalking-horse,   630
And you the game he covered, poor fat soul!
My husband is a formidable foe,
Will stick at nothing to destroy you. Stand
Prepared, or better, run till you reach Rome!

635 I bade you visit me, when the last place
My tyrant would have turned suspicious at,
Or cared to seek you in, was . . . why say, where?
But now all's changed: beside, the season's past
At the villa—wants the master's eye no more.
640 Anyhow, I beseech you, stay away
From the window! He might well be posted there."

I wrote—"You raise my courage, or call up
My curiosity, who am but man.
Tell him he owns the palace, not the street
645 Under—that's his and yours and mine alike.
If it should please me pad the path this eve,
Guido will have two troubles, first to get
Into a rage and then get out again.
Be cautious, though: at the *Ave!*"

                                 You of the Court!
650 When I stood question here and reached this point
O' the narrative—search notes and see and say
If someone did not interpose with smile
And sneer, "And prithee why so confident
That the husband must, of all needs, not the wife,
655 Fabricate thus—what if the lady loved?
What if she wrote the letters?"

                                 Learned Sir,
I told you there's a picture in our church.
Well, if a low-browed verger sidled up
Bringing me, like a blotch, on his prod's point,
660 A transfixed scorpion, let the reptile writhe,
And then said "See a thing that Raphael made—
This venom issued from Madonna's mouth!"
I should reply, "Rather, the soul of you
Has issued from your body, like from like,
By way of the ordure-corner!"

665   But no less,
I tired of the same long black teasing lie
Obtruded thus at every turn; the pest
Was far too near the picture, anyhow:

One does Madonna service, making clowns
Remove their dung-heap from the sacristy.   670
"I will to the window, as he tempts," said I:
"Yes, whom the easy love has failed allure,
This new bait of adventure tempts—thinks he.
Though the imprisoned lady keeps afar,
There will they lie in ambush, heads alert,   675
Kith, kin, and Count mustered to bite my heel.
No mother nor brother viper of the brood
Shall scuttle off without the instructive bruise!"

So I went: crossed street and street: "The next street's
        turn,
I stand beneath the terrace, see, above,   680
The black of the ambush-window. Then, in place
Of hand's throw of soft prelude over lute,
And cough that clears way for the ditty last"—
I began to laugh already—"he will have
'Out of the hole you hide in, on to the front,   685
Count Guido Franceschini, show yourself!
Hear what a man thinks of a thing like you,
And after, take this foulness in your face!' "

The words lay living on my lip, I made
The one-turn more—and there at the window stood,   690
Framed in its black square length, with lamp in hand,
Pompilia; the same great, grave, griefful air
As stands i' the dusk, on altar that I know,
Left alone with one moonbeam in her cell,
Our Lady of all the Sorrows. Ere I knelt—   695
Assured myself that she was flesh and blood—
She had looked one look and vanished.

                            I thought—"Just so:
It was herself, they have set her there to watch—
Stationed to see some wedding-band go by,
On fair pretense that she must bless the bride,   700
Or wait some funeral with friends wind past,
And crave peace for the corpse that claims its due.
She never dreams they used her for a snare,

And now withdraw the bait has served its turn.
705 Well done, the husband, who shall fare the worse!"
And on my lip again was—"Out with thee,
Guido!" When all at once she reappeared;
But, this time, on the terrace overhead,
So close above me, she could almost touch
710 My head if she bent down; and she did bend,
While I stood still as stone, all eye, all ear.

She began—"You have sent me letters, Sir:
I have read none, I can neither read nor write;
But she you gave them to, a woman here,
715 One of the people in whose power I am,
Partly explained their sense, I think, to me
Obliged to listen while she inculcates
That you, a priest, can dare love me, a wife,
Desire to live or die as I shall bid,
720 (She makes me listen if I will or no)
Because you saw my face a single time.
It cannot be she says the thing you mean;
Such wickedness were deadly to us both:
But good true love would help me now so much—
725 I tell myself, you may mean good and true.
You offer me, I seem to understand,
Because I am in poverty and starve,
Much money, where one piece would save my life.
The silver cup upon the altar-cloth
730 Is neither yours to give nor mine to take;
But I might take one bit of bread therefrom,
Since I am starving, and return the rest,
Yet do no harm: this is my very case.
I am in that strait, I may not dare abstain
735 From so much of assistance as would bring
The guilt of theft on neither you nor me;
But no superfluous particle of aid.
I think, if you will let me state my case,
Even had you been so fancy-fevered here,
740 Not your sound self, you must grow healthy now—
Care only to bestow what I can take.
That it is only you in the wide world,

Knowing me nor in thought nor word nor deed,
Who, all unprompted save by your own heart,
Come proffering assistance now—were strange   *745*
But that my whole life is so strange: as strange
It is, my husband whom I have not wronged
Should hate and harm me. For his own soul's sake,
Hinder the harm! But there is something more,
And that the strangest: it has got to be   *750*
Somehow for my sake too, and yet not mine,
—This is a riddle—for some kind of sake
Not any clearer to myself than you,
And yet as certain as that I draw breath—
I would fain live, not die—oh no, not die!   *755*
My case is, I was dwelling happily
At Rome with those dear Comparini, called
Father and mother to me; when at once
I found I had become Count Guido's wife:
Who then, not waiting for a moment, changed   *760*
Into a fury of fire, if once he was
Merely a man: his face threw fire at mine,
He laid a hand on me that burned all peace,
All joy, all hope, and last all fear away,
Dipping the bough of life, so pleasant once,   *765*
In fire which shriveled leaf and bud alike,
Burning not only present life but past,
Which you might think was safe beyond his reach.
He reached it, though, since that beloved pair,
My father once, my mother all those years,   *770*
That loved me so, now say I dreamed a dream
And bid me wake, henceforth no child of theirs,
Never in all the time their child at all.°
Do you understand? I cannot: yet so it is.
Just so I say of you that proffer help: *775*
I cannot understand what prompts your soul,
I simply needs must see that it is so,
Only one strange and wonderful thing more.

772–73 **no child ... at all** Violante claimed to have bought Pompilia
from a prostitute in order to secure for herself and her husband an
inheritance that was contingent on their having a child.

They came here with me, those two dear ones, kept
780 All the old love up, till my husband, till
His people here so tortured them, they fled.
And now, is it because I grow in flesh
And spirit one with him their torturer,
That they, renouncing him, must cast off me?
785 If I were graced by God to have a child,
Could I one day deny God graced me so?
Then, since my husband hates me, I shall break
No law that reigns in this fell house of hate,
By using—letting have effect so much
790 Of hate as hides me from that whole of hate
Would take my life which I want and must have—
Just as I take from your excess of love
Enough to save my life with, all I need.
The Archbishop said to murder me were sin:
795 My leaving Guido were a kind of death
With no sin—more death, he must answer for.
Hear now what death to him and life to you
I wish to pay and owe. Take me to Rome!
You go to Rome, the servant makes me hear.
800 Take me as you would take a dog, I think,
Masterless left for strangers to maltreat:
Take me home like that—leave me in the house
Where the father and the mother are; and soon
They'll come to know and call me by my name,
805 Their child once more, since child I am, for all
They now forget me, which is the worst o' the dream—
And the way to end dreams is to break them, stand,
Walk, go: then help me to stand, walk and go!
The Governor said the strong should help the weak:
810 You know how weak the strongest women are.
How could I find my way there by myself?
I cannot even call out, make them hear—
Just as in dreams: I have tried and proved the fact.
I have told this story and more to good great men,
815 The Archbishop and the Governor: they smiled.
'Stop your mouth, fair one!'—presently they frowned,
'Get you gone, disengage you from our feet!'
I went in my despair to an old priest,

Only a friar, no great man like these two,
But good, the Augustinian, people name 820
Romano—he confessed me two months since:
He fears God, why then needs he fear the world?
And when he questioned how it came about
That I was found in danger of a sin—
Despair of any help from providence— 825
'Since, though your husband outrage you,' said he,
'That is a case too common, the wives die
Or live, but do not sin so deep as this'—
Then I told—what I never will tell you—
How, worse than husband's hate, I had to bear 830
The love—soliciting to shame called love—
Of his brother—the young idle priest i' the house
With only the devil to meet there. 'This is grave—
Yes, we must interfere: I counsel—write
To those who used to be your parents once, 835
Of dangers here, bid them convey you hence!'
'But,' said I, 'when I neither read nor write?'
Then he took pity and promised 'I will write.'
If he did so—why, they are dumb or dead:
Either they give no credit to the tale, 840
Or else, wrapped wholly up in their own joy
Of such escape, they care not who cries, still
I' the clutches. Anyhow, no word arrives.
All such extravagance and dreadfulness
Seems incident to dreaming, cured one way— 845
Wake me! The letter I received this morn,
Said—if the woman spoke your very sense—
'You would die for me:' I can believe it now:
For now the dream gets to involve yourself.
First of all, you seemed wicked and not good, 850
In writing me those letters: you came in
Like a thief upon me. I this morning said
In my extremity, entreat the thief!
Try if he have in him no honest touch!
A thief might save me from a murderer. 855
'Twas a thief said the last kind word to Christ:
Christ took the kindness and forgave the theft:
And so did I prepare what I now say.

But now, that you stand and I see your face,
860 Though you have never uttered word yet—well, I know,
Here too has been dream-work, delusion too,
And that at no time, you with the eyes here,
Ever intended to do wrong by me,
Nor wrote such letters therefore. It is false,
865 And you are true, have been true, will be true.
To Rome then—when is it you take me there?
Each minute lost is mortal. When?—I ask."

I answered "It shall be when it can be.
I will go hence and do your pleasure, find
870 The sure and speedy means of travel, then
Come back and take you to your friends in Rome.
There wants a carriage, money and the rest—
A day's work by tomorrow at this time.
How shall I see you and assure escape?"

875 She replied, "Pass, tomorrow at this hour.
If I am at the open window, well:
If I am absent, drop a handkerchief
And walk by! I shall see from where I watch,
And know that all is done. Return next eve,
880 And next, and so till we can meet and speak!"
"Tomorrow at this hour I pass," said I.
She was withdrawn.

                    Here is another point
I bid you pause at. When I told thus far,
Someone said, subtly, "Here at least was found
885 Your confidence in error—you perceived
The spirit of the letters, in a sort,
Had been the lady's, if the body should be
Supplied by Guido: say, he forged them all!
Here was the unforged fact—she sent for you,
890 Spontaneously elected you to help,
—What men call, loved you: Guido read her mind,
Gave it expression to assure the world
The case was just as he foresaw: he wrote,
She spoke."

Sirs, that first simile serves still—
That falsehood of a scorpion hatched, I say,   *895*
Nowhere i' the world but in Madonna's mouth.
Go on! Suppose, that falsehood foiled, next eve
Pictured Madonna raised her painted hand,
Fixed the face Raphael bent above the Babe,
On my face as I flung me at her feet: *900*
Such miracle vouchsafed and manifest,
Would that prove the first lying tale was true?
Pompilia spoke, and I at once received,
Accepted my own fact, my miracle
Self-authorized and self-explained—she chose   *905*
To summon me and signify her choice.
Afterward—oh! I gave a passing glance
To a certain ugly cloud-shape, goblin-shred
Of hell-smoke hurrying past the splendid moon
Out now to tolerate no darkness more,   *910*
And saw right through the thing that tried to pass
For truth and solid, not an empty lie:
"So, he not only forged the words for her
But words for me, made letters he called mine:
What I sent, he retained, gave these in place,   *915*
All by the mistress-messenger! As I
Recognized her, at potency of truth,
So she, by the crystalline soul, knew me,
Never mistook the signs. Enough of this—
Let the wraith go to nothingness again,   *920*
Here is the orb, have only thought for her!"

"Thought?" nay, Sirs, what shall follow was not
        thought:
I have thought sometimes, and thought long and hard.
I have stood before, gone round a serious thing,
Tasked my whole mind to touch and clasp it close,   *925*
As I stretch forth my arm to touch this bar.
God and man, and what duty I owe both—
I dare to say I have confronted these
In thought: but no such faculty helped here.
I put forth no thought—powerless, all that night   *930*
I paced the city: it was the first spring.

By the invasion I lay passive to,
In rushed new things, the old were rapt away;
Alike abolished—the imprisonment
935 Of the outside air, the inside weight o' the world
That pulled me down. Death meant, to spurn the
    ground,
Soar to the sky—die well and you do that.
The very immolation made the bliss;
Death was the heart of life, and all the harm
940 My folly had crouched to avoid, now proved a veil
Hiding all gain my wisdom strove to grasp:
As if the intense center of the flame
Should turn a heaven to that devoted fly
Which hitherto, sophist alike and sage,
945 Saint Thomas with his sober gray goose-quill,
And sinner Plato by Cephisian reed,°
Would fain, pretending just the insect's good,
Whisk off, drive back, consign to shade again.
Into another state, under new rule
950 I knew myself was passing swift and sure;
Whereof the initiatory pang approached,
Felicitous annoy, as bitter-sweet
As when the virgin-band, the victors chaste,
Feel at the end the earthly garments drop,
955 And rise with something of a rosy shame
Into immortal nakedness: so I
Lay, and let come the proper throe would thrill
Into the ecstasy and outthrob pain.

I' the gray of dawn it was I found myself
960 Facing the pillared front o' the Pieve—mine,
My church: it seemed to say for the first time,
"But am not I the Bride, the mystic love
O' the Lamb, who took thy plighted troth, my priest,
To fold thy warm heart on my heart of stone
965 And freeze thee nor unfasten any more?
This is a fleshly woman—let the free
Bestow their life-blood, thou art pulseless now!"

946 **Cephisian reed** pen made from a reed of the river Cephisus at
Athens.

See! Day by day I had risen and left this church
At the signal waved me by some foolish fan,
With half a curse and half a pitying smile   970
For the monk I stumbled over in my haste,
Prostrate and corpse-like at the altar-foot
Intent on his *corona*:° then the church
Was ready with her quip, if word conduced,
To quicken my pace nor stop for prating—"There!   975
Be thankful you are no such ninny, go
Rather to teach a black-eyed novice cards
Than gabble Latin and protrude that nose
Smoothed to a sheep's through no brains and much
      faith!"
That sort of incentive! Now the church changed tone—   980
Now, when I found out first that life and death
Are means to an end, that passion uses both,
Indisputably mistress of the man
Whose form of worship is self-sacrifice:
Now, from the stone lungs sighed the scrannel voice   985
"Leave that live passion, come be dead with me!"
As if, i' the fabled garden,° I had gone
On great adventure, plucked in ignorance
Hedge-fruit, and feasted to satiety,
Laughing at such high fame for hips and haws,°   990
And scorned the achievement: then come all at once
O' the prize o' the place, the thing of perfect gold,
The apple's self: and, scarce my eye on that,
Was 'ware as well o' the sevenfold dragon's watch.

Sirs, I obeyed. Obedience was too strange—   995
This new thing that had been struck into me
By the look o' the lady—to dare disobey
The first authoritative word. 'Twas God's.
I had been lifted to the level of her,
Could take such sounds into my sense. I said   1000
"We two are cognizant o' the Master now;

973 **corona** rosary.   987 **fabled garden** in the Garden of the Hes-
perides there was a tree bearing a golden apple, guarded by a
dragon. Hercules killed the dragon and took the fruit.   990 **hips
and haws** fruits of rose and hawthorn.

She it is bids me bow the head: how true,
I am a priest! I see the function here;
I thought the other way self-sacrifice:
1005 This is the true, seals up the perfect sum.
I pay it, sit down, silently obey."

So, I went home. Dawn broke, noon broadened, I—
I sat stone-still, let time run over me.
The sun slanted into my room, had reached
1010 The west. I opened book—Aquinas° blazed
With one black name only on the white page.
I looked up, saw the sunset: vespers rang:
"She counts the minutes till I keep my word
And come say all is ready. I am a priest.
1015 Duty to God is duty to her: I think
God, who created her, will save her too
Some new way, by one miracle the more,
Without me. Then, prayer may avail perhaps."
I went to my own place i' the Pieve, read
1020 The office: I was back at home again
Sitting i' the dark. "Could she but know—but know
That, were there good in this distinct from God's,
Really good as it reached her, though procured
By a sin of mine—I should sin: God forgives.
1025 She knows it is no fear withholds me: fear?
Of what? Suspense here is the terrible thing.
If she should, as she counts the minutes, come
On the fantastic notion that I fear
The world now, fear the Archbishop, fear perhaps
1030 Count Guido, he who, having forged the lies,
May wait the work, attend the effect—I fear
The sword of Guido! Let God see to that—
Hating lies, let not her believe a lie!"

Again the morning found me. "I will work,
1035 Tie down my foolish thoughts. Thank God so far!
I have saved her from a scandal, stopped the tongues
Had broken else into a cackle and hiss

1010 **Aquinas** St. Thomas Aquinas, whose *Summa* he had been reading.

Around the noble name. Duty is still
Wisdom: I have been wise." So the day wore.

At evening—"But, achieving victory,   *1040*
I must not blink the priest's peculiar part,
Nor shrink to counsel, comfort: priest and friend—
How do we discontinue to be friends?
I will go minister, advise her seek
Help at the source—above all, not despair: *1045*
There may be other happier help at hand.
I hope it—wherefore then neglect to say?"

There she stood—leaned there, for the second time,
Over the terrace, looked at me, then spoke:
"Why is it you have suffered me to stay   *1050*
Breaking my heart two days more than was need?
Why delay help, your own heart yearns to give?
You are again here, in the selfsame mind,
I see here, steadfast in the face of you—
You grudge to do no one thing that I ask.   *1055*
Why then is nothing done? You know my need.
Still, through God's pity on me, there is time
And one day more: shall I be saved or no?"
I answered—"Lady, waste no thought, no word
Even to forgive me! Care for what I care—   *1060*
Only! Now follow me as I were fate!
Leave this house in the dark tomorrow night,
Just before daybreak:—there's new moon this eve—
It sets, and then begins the solid black.
Descend, proceed to the Torrione, step   *1065*
Over the low dilapidated wall,
Take San Clemente, there's no other gate
Unguarded at the hour: some paces thence
An inn stands; cross to it; I shall be there."

She answered, "If I can but find the way.   *1070*
But I shall find it. Go now!"

                    I did go,
Took rapidly the route myself prescribed,

Stopped at Torrione, climbed the ruined place,
Proved that the gate was practicable, reached
1075 The inn, no eye, despite the dark, could miss,
Knocked there and entered, made the host secure:
"With Caponsacchi it is ask and have;
I know my betters. Are you bound for Rome?
I get swift horse and trusty man," said he.

1080 Then I retraced my steps, was found once more
In my own house for the last time: there lay
The broad pale opened *Summa*. "Shut his book,
There's other showing! 'Twas a Thomas too
Obtained—more favored than his namesake here—
1085 A gift, tied faith fast, foiled the tug of doubt—
Our Lady's girdle; down he saw it drop
As she ascended into Heaven, they say:
He kept that safe and bade all doubt adieu.°
I too have seen a lady and hold a grace."

1090 I know not how the night passed: morning broke;
Presently came my servant. "Sir, this eve—
Do you forget?" I started. "How forget?
What is it you know?" "With due submission, Sir,
This being last Monday in the month but one
1095 And a vigil, since tomorrow is Saint George,°
And feast day, and moreover day for copes,
And Canon Conti now away a month,
And Canon Crispi sour because, forsooth,
You let him sulk in stall and bear the brunt
Of the octave . . . Well, Sir, 'tis important!"

1100   "True!
Hearken, I have to start for Rome this night.
No word, lest Crispi overboil and burst!

1083–88 a **Thomas . . . doubt adieu** Thomas the Apostle, who had
doubted Christ's Resurrection, was said also to have doubted that
the Virgin Mary had been taken up into Heaven. In order to con-
vince him of the fact she threw down the belt of her garment.
1095 **Saint George** Browning altered the date of the flight (April 29)
so it could take place on the Feast of St. George (April 23).

Provide me with a laic dress! Throw dust
I' the Canon's eye, stop his tongue's scandal so!
See there's a sword in case of accident."   *1105*
I knew the knave, the knave knew me.

                                              And thus
Through each familiar hindrance of the day
Did I make steadily for its hour and end—
Felt time's old barrier-growth of right and fit
Give way through all its twines, and let me go.   *1110*
Use and wont recognized the excepted man,
Let speed the special service—and I sped
Till, at the dead between midnight and morn,
There was I at the goal, before the gate,
With a tune in the ears, low leading up to loud,   *1115*
A light in the eyes, faint that would soon be flare,
Ever some spiritual witness new and new
In faster frequence, crowding solitude
To watch the way o' the warfare—till, at last,
When the ecstatic minute must bring birth,   *1120*
Began a whiteness in the distance, waxed
Whiter and whiter, near grew and more near,
Till it was she: there did Pompilia come:
The white I saw shine through her was her soul's,
Certainly, for the body was one black,   *1125*
Black from head down to foot. She did not speak,
Glided into the carriage—so a cloud
Gathers the moon up. "By San Spirito,
To Rome, as if the road burned underneath!
Reach Rome, then hold my head in pledge, I pay   *1130*
The run and the risk to heart's content!" Just that
I said—then, in another tick of time,
Sprang, was beside her, she and I alone.

So it began, our flight thro' dusk to clear,
Through day and night and day again to night   *1135*
Once more, and to last dreadful dawn of all.
Sirs, how should I lie quiet in my grave
Unless you suffer me wring, drop by drop,
My brain dry, make a riddance of the drench
Of minutes with a memory in each,   *1140*

Recorded motion, breath or look of hers,
Which poured forth would present you one pure glass,
Mirror you plain—as God's sea,° glassed in gold,
His saints—the perfect soul Pompilia? Men,
1145 You must know that a man gets drunk with truth
Stagnant inside him! Oh, they've killed her, Sirs!
Can I be calm?

           Calmly! Each incident
Proves, I maintain, that action of the flight
For the true thing it was. The first faint scratch
1150 O' the stone will test its nature, teach its worth
To idiots who name Parian—coprolite.°
After all, I shall give no glare—at best
Only display you certain scattered lights
Lamping the rush and roll of the abyss:
1155 Nothing but here and there a fire-point pricks
Wavelet from wavelet: well!

              For the first hour
We both were silent in the night, I know:
Sometimes I did not see nor understand.
Blackness engulfed me—partial stupor, say—
1160 Then I would break way, breathe through the surprise,
And be aware again, and see who sat
In the dark vest with the white face and hands.
I said to myself—"I have caught it, I conceive
The mind o' the mystery: 'tis the way they wake
1165 And wait, two martyrs somewhere in a tomb
Each by each as their blessing was to die;
Some signal they are promised and expect—
When to arise before the trumpet scares:
So, through the whole course of the world they wait
1170 The last day, but so fearless and so safe!
No otherwise, in safety and not fear,
I lie, because she lies too by my side."
You know this is not love, Sirs—it is faith,

1143 **God's sea** Revelation 4:6–7.   1151 **Parian—coprolite** Parian
marble is of high quality; coprolite is petrified excrement of ancient
reptiles.

The feeling that there's God, he reigns and rules
Out of this low world: that is all; no harm!   1175
At times she drew a soft sigh—music seemed
Always to hover just above her lips,
Not settle—break a silence music too.

In the determined morning, I first found
Her head erect, her face turned full to me,   1180
Her soul intent on mine through two wide eyes.
I answered them. "You are saved hitherto.
We have passed Perugia—gone round by the wood,
Not through, I seem to think—and opposite
I know Assisi; this is holy ground."°   1185
Then she resumed. "How long since we both left
Arezzo?" "Years—and certain hours beside."

It was at . . . ah, but I forget the names!
'Tis a mere post-house and a hovel or two;
I left the carriage and got bread and wine   1190
And brought it her. "Does it detain to eat?"
"They stay perforce, change horses—therefore eat!
We lose no minute: we arrive, be sure!"
This was—I know not where—there's a great hill
Close over, and the stream has lost its bridge,   1195
One fords it. She began—"I have heard say
Of some sick body that my mother knew,
'Twas no good sign when in a limb diseased
All the pain suddenly departs—as if
The guardian angel discontinued pain   1200
Because the hope of cure was gone at last:
The limb will not again exert itself,
It needs be pained no longer: so with me,
—My soul whence all the pain is past at once:
All pain must be to work some good in the end.   1205
True, this I feel now, this may be that good,
Pain was because of—otherwise, I fear!"

She said—a long while later in the day,

1185 **Assisi . . . holy ground** birthplace of St. Francis.

When I had let the silence be—abrupt—
1210 "Have you a mother?" "She died, I was born."
"A sister then?" "No sister." "Who was it—
What woman were you used to serve this way,
Be kind to, till I called you and you came?"
I did not like that word. Soon afterward—
1215 "Tell me, are men unhappy, in some kind
Of mere unhappiness at being men,
As women suffer, being womanish?
Have you, now, some unhappiness, I mean,
Born of what may be man's strength overmuch,
1220 To match the undue susceptibility,
The sense at every pore when hate is close?
It hurts us if a baby hides its face
Or child strikes at us punily, calls names
Or makes a mouth—much more if stranger men
1225 Laugh or frown—just as that were much to bear!
Yet rocks split—and the blow-ball does no more,
Quivers to feathery nothing at a touch;
And strength may have its drawback weakness 'scapes."
Once she asked "What is it that made you smile,
1230 At the great gate with the eagles and the snakes,
Where the company entered, 'tis a long time since?"
"—Forgive—I think you would not understand:
Ah, but you ask me—therefore, it was this.
That was a certain bishop's villa-gate,
1235 I knew it by the eagles—and at once
Remembered this same bishop was just he
People of old were wont to bid me please
If I would catch preferment: so, I smiled
Because an impulse came to me, a whim—
1240 What if I prayed the prelate leave to speak,
Began upon him in his presence-hall
—'What, still at work so gray and obsolete?
Still rocheted and mitered more or less?
Don't you feel all that out of fashion now?
1245 I find out when the day of things is done!' "

At eve we heard the *angelus*: she turned—

"I told you I can neither read nor write.
My life stopped with the playtime; I will learn,
If I begin to live again: but you—
Who are a priest—wherefore do you not read 1250
The service at this hour? Read Gabriel's song,
The lesson, and then read the little prayer
To Raphael, proper for us travelers!"
I did not like that, neither, but I read.

When we stopped at Foligno it was dark. 1255
The people of the post came out with lights:
The driver said, "This time tomorrow, may
Saints only help, relays continue good,
Nor robbers hinder, we arrive at Rome."
I urged, "Why tax your strength a second night? 1260
Trust me, alight here and take brief repose!
We are out of harm's reach, past pursuit: go sleep
If but an hour! I keep watch, guard the while
Here in the doorway." But her whole face changed,
The misery grew again about her mouth, 1265
The eyes burned up from faintness, like the fawn's
Tired to death in the thicket, when she feels
The probing spear o' the huntsman. "Oh, no stay!"
She cried, in the fawn's cry, "On to Rome, on, on—
Unless 'tis you who fear—which cannot be!" 1270

We did go on all night; but at its close
She was troubled, restless, moaned low, talked at
          whiles
To herself, her brow on quiver with the dream:
Once, wide awake, she menaced, at arms' length
Waved away something—"Never again with you! 1275
My soul is mine, my body is my soul's:
You and I are divided ever more
In soul and body: get you gone!" Then I—
"Why, in my whole life I have never prayed!
Oh, if the God, that only can, would help! 1280
Am I his priest with power to cast out fiends?
Let God arise and all his enemies

Be scattered!"° By morn, there was peace, no sigh
Out of the deep sleep.

               When she woke at last,
1285 I answered the first look—"Scarce twelve hours more,
Then, Rome! There probably was no pursuit,
There cannot now be peril: bear up brave!
Just some twelve hours to press through to the prize:
Then, no more of the terrible journey!" "Then,
1290 No more o' the journey: if it might but last!
Always, my life-long, thus to journey still!
It is the interruption that I dread—
With no dread, ever to be here and thus!
Never to see a face nor hear a voice!
1295 Yours is no voice; you speak when you are dumb;
Nor face, I see it in the dark. I want
No face nor voice that change and grow unkind."
That I liked, that was the best thing she said.

In the broad day, I dared entreat, "Descend!"
1300 I told a woman, at the garden-gate
By the post-house, white and pleasant in the sun,
"It is my sister—talk with her apart!
She is married and unhappy, you perceive;
I take her home because her head is hurt;
1305 Comfort her as you women understand!"
So, there I left them by the garden-wall,
Paced the road, then bade put the horses to,
Came back, and there she sat: close to her knee,
A black-eyed child still held the bowl of milk,
1310 Wondered to see how little she could drink,
And in her arms the woman's infant lay.
She smiled at me "How much good this has done!
This is a whole night's rest and how much more!
I can proceed now, though I wish to stay.
1315 How do you call that tree with the thick top
That holds in all its leafy green and gold
The sun now like an immense egg of fire?"

1282–83 **Let God arise . . . scattered!** Psalm 68:1.

(It was a million-leaved mimosa.) "Take
The babe away from me and let me go!"
And in the carriage "Still a day, my friend!   *1320*
And perhaps half a night, the woman fears.
I pray it finish since it cannot last:
There may be more misfortune at the close,
And where will you be? God suffice me then!"
And presently—for there was a roadside-shrine—   *1325*
"When I was taken first to my own church
Lorenzo in Lucina, being a girl,
And bid confess my faults, I interposed
'But teach me what fault to confess and know!'
So, the priest said—'You should bethink yourself: *1330*
Each human being needs must have done wrong!'
Now, be you candid and no priest but friend—
Were I surprised and killed here on the spot,
A runaway from husband and his home,
Do you account it were in sin I died?   *1335*
My husband used to seem to harm me, not . . .
Not on pretense he punished sin of mine,
Nor for sin's sake and lust of cruelty,
But as I heard him bid a farming-man
At the villa take a lamb once to the wood   *1340*
And there ill-treat it, meaning that the wolf
Should hear its cries, and so come, quick be caught,
Enticed to the trap: he practiced thus with me
That so, whatever were his gain thereby,
Others than I might become prey and spoil.   *1345*
Had it been only between our two selves—
His pleasure and my pain—why, pleasure him
By dying, nor such need to make a coil!
But this was worth an effort, that my pain
Should not become a snare, prove pain threefold   *1350*
To other people—strangers—or unborn—
How should I know? I sought release from that—
I think, or else from—dare I say, some cause
Such as is put into a tree, which turns
Away from the north wind with what nest it holds—   *1355*
The woman said that trees so turn: now, friend,
Tell me, because I cannot trust myself!"

You are a man: what have I done amiss?"
You must conceive my answer—I forget—
1360 Taken up wholly with the thought, perhaps,
This time she might have said—might, did not say—
"You are a priest." She said, "my friend."

                                        Day wore,
We passed the places, somehow the calm went,
Again the restless eyes began to rove
1365 In new fear of the foe mine could not see.
She wandered in her mind—addressed me once
"Gaetano!"°—that is not my name: whose name?
I grew alarmed, my head seemed turning too.
I quickened pace with promise now, now threat:
1370 Bade drive and drive, nor any stopping more.
"Too deep i' the thick of the struggle, struggle through!
Then drench her in repose though death's self pour
The plenitude of quiet—help us, God,
Whom the winds carry!"

                            Suddenly I saw
1375 The old tower, and the little white-walled clump
Of buildings and the cypress-tree or two—
"Already Castelnuovo—Rome!" I cried,
"As good as Rome—Rome is the next stage, think!
This is where travelers' hearts are wont to beat.
1380 Say you are saved, sweet lady!" Up she woke.
The sky was fierce with color from the sun .
Setting. She screamed out "No, I must not die!
Take me no farther, I should die: stay here!
I have more life to save than mine!"

                                    She swooned.
1385 We seemed safe: what was it foreboded so?
Out of the coach into the inn I bore
The motionless and breathless pure and pale
Pompilia—bore her through a pitying group
And laid her on a couch, still calm and cured

1367 **Gaetano** the name Pompilia is to give her son.

By deep sleep of all woes at once. The host   *1390*
Was urgent "Let her stay an hour or two!
Leave her to us, all will be right by morn!"
Oh, my foreboding! But I could not choose.

I paced the passage, kept watch all night long.
I listened—not one movement, not one sigh.   *1395*
"Fear not: she sleeps so sound!" they said: but I
Feared, all the same, kept fearing more and more,
Found myself throb with fear from head to foot,
Filled with a sense of such impending woe,
That, at first pause of night, pretense of gray,   *1400*
I made my mind up it was morn.—"Reach Rome,
Lest hell reach her! A dozen miles to make,
Another long breath, and we emerge!" I stood
I' the courtyard, roused the sleepy grooms. "Have out
Carriage and horse, give haste, take gold!" said I.   *1405*
While they made ready in the doubtful morn—
'Twas the last minute—needs must I ascend
And break her sleep; I turned to go.

                        And there
Faced me Count Guido, there posed the mean man
As master—took the field, encamped his rights,   *1410*
Challenged the world: there leered new triumph, there
Scowled the old malice in the visage bad
And black o' the scamp. Soon triumph suppled the
    tongue
A little, malice glued to his dry throat,
And he part howled, part hissed . . . oh, how he kept   *1415*
Well out o' the way, at arm's length and to spare!—
"My salutation to your priestship! What?
Matutinal, busy with book so soon
Of an April day that's damp as tears that now
Deluge Arezzo at its darling's flight?—   *1420*
'Tis unfair, wrongs feminity at large,
To let a single dame monopolize
A heart the whole sex claims, should share alike:
Therefore I overtake you, Canon! Come!
The lady—could you leave her side so soon?   *1425*

You have not yet experienced at her hands
My treatment, you lay down undrugged, I see!
Hence this alertness—hence no death-in-life
Like what held arms fast when she stole from mine.
1430 To be sure, you took the solace and repose
That first night at Foligno!—news abound
O' the road by this time—men regaled me much,
As past them I came halting after you,
Vulcan pursuing Mars,° as poets sing—
1435 Still at the last here pant I, but arrive,
Vulcan—and not without my Cyclops° too,
The Commissary and the unpoisoned arm
O' the Civil Force, should Mars turn mutineer.
Enough of fooling: capture the culprits, friend!
1440 Here is the lover in the smart disguise
With the sword—he is a priest, so mine lies still.
There upstairs hides my wife the runaway,
His leman: the two plotted, poisoned first,
Plundered me after, and eloped thus far
1445 Where now you find them. Do your duty quick!
Arrest and hold him! That's done: now catch her!"
During this speech of that man—well, I stood
Away, as he managed—still, I stood as near
The throat of him—with these two hands, my own—
1450 As now I stand near yours, Sir—one quick spring,
One great good satisfying gripe, and lo!
There had he lain abolished with his lie,
Creation purged o' the miscreate, man redeemed,
A spittle wiped off from the face of God!
1455 I, in some measure, seek a poor excuse
For what I left undone, in just this fact
That my first feeling at the speech I quote
Was—not of what a blasphemy was dared,
Not what a bag of venomed purulence
1460 Was split and noisome—but how splendidly

1434 **Vulcan pursuing Mars** ugly Vulcan was the husband of Venus, goddess of love and beauty, the dashing Mars her lover. 1436 **Cyclops** the one-eyed monsters of the *Odyssey* were sometimes thought of as workmen of Vulcan.

Mirthful, how ludicrous a lie was launched!
Would Molière's self° wish more than hear such man
Call, claim such woman for his own, his wife,
Even though, in due amazement at the boast,
He had stammered, she moreover was divine?   1465
She to be his—were hardly less absurd
Than that he took her name into his mouth,
Licked, and then let it go again, the beast,
Signed with his slaver. Oh, she poisoned him,
Plundered him, and the rest! Well, what I wished   1470
Was, that he would but go on, say once more
So to the world, and get his meed of men,
The fist's reply to the filth. And while I mused,
The minute, oh the misery, was gone!
On either idle hand of me there stood   1475
Really an officer, nor laughed i' the least:
Nay, rendered justice to his reason, laid
Logic to heart, as 'twere submitted them
"Twice two makes four."

                    "And now, catch her!" he cried.
That sobered me. "Let myself lead the way—   1480
Ere you arrest me, who am somebody,
Being, as you hear, a priest and privileged—
To the lady's chamber! I presume you—men
Expert, instructed how to find out truth,
Familiar with the guise of guilt. Detect   1485
Guilt on her face when it meets mine, then judge
Between us and the mad dog howling there!"
Up we all went together, in they broke
O' the chamber late my chapel. There she lay,
Composed as when I laid her, that last eve,   1490
O' the couch, still breathless, motionless, sleep's self,
Wax-white, seraphic, saturate with the sun
O' the morning that now flooded from the front
And filled the window with a light like blood.
"Behold the poisoner, the adulteress,   1495
—And feigning sleep too! Seize, bind!" Guido hissed.

1462 **Molière's self** in Molière's *Don Juan* the libertine claims a nun
as his wife.

She started up, stood erect, face to face
With the husband: back he fell, was buttressed there
By the window all a flame with morning-red,
1500 He the black figure, the opprobrious blur
Against all peace and joy and light and life.
"Away from between me and hell!" she cried:
"Hell for me, no embracing any more!
I am God's, I love God, God—whose knees I clasp,
1505 Whose utterly most just award I take,
But bear no more love-making devils: hence!"
I may have made an effort to reach her side
From where I stood i' the doorway—anyhow
I found the arms, I wanted, pinioned fast,
1510 Was powerless in the clutch to left and right
O' the rabble pouring in, rascality
Enlisted, rampant on the side of hearth,
Home and the husband—pay in prospect too!
They heaped themselves upon me. "Ha!—and him
1515 Also you outrage? Him, too, my sole friend,
Guardian and savior? That I balk you of,
Since—see how God can help at last and worst!"
She sprang at the sword that hung beside him, seized,
Drew, brandished it, the sunrise burned for joy
1520 O' the blade, "Die," cried she, "devil, in God's name!"
Ah, but they all closed round her, twelve to one
—The unmanly men, no woman-mother made,
Spawned somehow! Dead-white and disarmed she lay.
No matter for the sword, her word sufficed
1525 To spike the coward through and through: he shook,
Could only spit between the teeth—"You see?
You hear? Bear witness, then! Write down . . but no—
Carry these criminals to the prison-house,
For first thing! I begin my search meanwhile
1530 After the stolen effects, gold, jewels, plate,
Money and clothes, they robbed me of and fled,
With no few amorous pieces, verse and prose,
I have much reason to expect to find."

When I saw that—no more than the first mad speech,
1535 Made out the speaker mad and a laughing-stock,

So neither did this next device explode
One listener's indignation—that a scribe
Did sit down, set himself to write indeed,
While sundry knaves began to peer and pry
In corner and hole—that Guido, wiping brow   *1540*
And getting him a countenance, was fast
Losing his fear, beginning to strut free
O' the stage of his exploit, snuff here, sniff there—
Then I took truth in, guessed sufficiently
The service for the moment. "What I say,   *1545*
Slight at your peril! We are aliens here,
My adversary and I, called noble both;
I am the nobler, and a name men know.
I could refer our cause to our own Court
In our own country, but prefer appeal   *1550*
To the nearer jurisdiction. Being a priest,
Though in a secular garb—for reasons good
I shall adduce in due time to my peers—
I demand that the Church I serve, decide
Between us, right the slandered lady there.   *1555*
A Tuscan noble, I might claim the Duke:
A priest, I rather choose the Church—bid Rome
Cover the wronged with her inviolate shield."

There was no refusing this: they bore me off,
They bore her off, to separate cells o' the same   *1560*
Ignoble prison, and, separate, thence to Rome.
Pompilia's face, then and thus, looked on me
The last time in this life: not one sight since,
Never another sight to be! And yet
I thought I had saved her. I appealed to Rome: *1565*
It seems I simply sent her to her death.
You tell me she is dying now, or dead;
I cannot bring myself to quite believe
This is a place you torture people in:
What if this your intelligence were just   *1570*
A subtlety, an honest wile to work
On a man at unawares? 'Twere worthy you.
No, Sirs, I cannot have the lady dead!
That erect form, flashing brow, fulgurant eye,

1575 That voice immortal (oh, that voice of hers!)
     That vision in the blood-red daybreak—that
     Leap to life of the pale electric sword
     Angels go armed with—that was not the last
     O' the lady! Come, I see through it, you find—
1580 Know the maneuver! Also herself said
     I had saved her: do you dare say she spoke false?
     Let me see for myself if it be so!
     Though she were dying, a priest might be of use,
     The more when he's a friend too—she called me
1585 Far beyond "friend." Come, let me see her—indeed
     It is my duty, being a priest: I hope
     I stand confessed, established, proved a priest?
     My punishment had motive that, a priest
     I, in a laic garb, a mundane mode,
1590 Did what were harmlessly done otherwise.
     I never touched her with my fingertip
     Except to carry her to the couch, that eve,
     Against my heart, beneath my head, bowed low,
     As we priests carry the paten:° that is why
1595 —To get leave and go see her of your grace—
     I have told you this whole story over again.
     Do I deserve grace? For I might lock lips,
     Laugh at your jurisdiction: what have you
     To do with me in the matter? I suppose
1600 You hardly think I donned a bravo's dress
     To have a hand in the new crime; on the old,
     Judgment's delivered, penalty imposed,
     I was chained fast at Civita hand and foot—
     She had only you to trust to, you and Rome,
1605 Rome and the Church, and no pert meddling priest
     Two days ago, when Guido, with the right,
     Hacked her to pieces. One might well be wroth;
     I have been patient, done my best to help:
     I come from Civita and punishment
1610 As friend of the Court—and for pure friendship's sake
     Have told my tale to the end—nay, not the end—
     For, wait—I'll end—not leave you that excuse!

1594 **paten** plate used in the celebration of the Eucharist. It is
carried in this manner by the subdeacon at High Mass.

When we were parted—shall I go on there?
I was presently brought to Rome—yes, here I stood
Opposite yonder very crucifix—   1615
And there sat you and you, Sirs, quite the same.
I heard charge, and bore question, and told tale
Noted down in the book there—turn and see
If, by one jot or tittle, I vary now!
I' the color the tale takes, there's change perhaps;   1620
'Tis natural, since the sky is different,
Eclipse in the air now; still, the outline stays.
I showed you how it came to be my part
To save the lady. Then your clerk produced
Papers, a pack of stupid and impure   1625
Banalities called letters about love—
Love, indeed—I could teach who styled them so,
Better, I think, though priest and loveless both!
"—How was it that a wife, young, innocent,
And stranger to your person, wrote this page?"—   1630
"—She wrote it when the Holy Father wrote
The bestiality that posts through Rome,
Put in his mouth by Pasquin."° "Nor perhaps
Did you return these answers, verse and prose,
Signed, sealed and sent the lady? There's your hand!"   1635
"—This precious piece of verse, I really judge,
Is meant to copy my own character,
A clumsy mimic; and this other prose,
Not so much even; both rank forgery:
Verse, quotha? Bembo's verse! When Saint John
    wrote   1640
The tract *De Tribus*,° I wrote this to match."
"—How came it, then, the documents were found
At the inn on your departure?"—"I opine,
Because there were no documents to find
In my presence—you must hide before you find.   1645
Who forged them hardly practiced in my view;

1633 **Pasquin** a statue in Rome to which satiric verses, often scur-
rilous or obscene, were fastened.   1640–41 **Bembo's verse . . . De
Tribus** Cardinal Bembo was a celebrated humanist and elegant man
of letters. The "tract *De Tribus*" was referred to as a piece of es-
pecially terrible blasphemy.

Who found them waited till I turned my back."
"—And what of the clandestine visits paid,
Nocturnal passage in and out the house
1650 With its lord absent? 'Tis alleged you climbed . . ."
"—Flew on a broomstick to the man i' the moon!
Who witnessed or will testify this trash?"
"—The trusty servant, Margherita's self,
Even she who brought you letters, you confess,
1655 And, you confess, took letters in reply:
Forget not we have knowledge of the facts!"
"—Sirs, who have knowledge of the facts, defray
The expenditure of wit I waste in vain,
Trying to find out just one fact of all!
1660 She who brought letters from who could not write,
And took back letters to who could not read—
Who was that messenger, of your charity?"
"—Well, so far favors you the circumstance
That this same messenger . . . how shall we say? . . .
1665 *Sub imputatione meretricis*
Laborat°—which makes accusation null:
We waive this woman's: naught makes void the next.
Borsi, called Venerino, he who drove,
O' the first night when you fled away, at length
1670 Deposes to your kissings in the coach,
—Frequent, frenetic . . ." "When deposed he so?"
"After some weeks of sharp imprisonment . . ."
"—Granted by friend the Governor, I engage—"
"—For his participation in your flight!
1675 At length his obduracy melting made
The avowal mentioned . . ." "Was dismissed forthwith
To liberty, poor knave, for recompense.
Sirs, give what credit to the lie you can!
For me, no word in my defense I speak,
And God shall argue for the lady!"

1680   So
Did I stand question, and make answer, still
With the same result of smiling disbelief,

1665–66 **Sub . . . laborat** labors under the imputation of being a
prostitute.

Polite impossibility of faith
In such affected virtue in a priest;
But a showing fair play, an indulgence, even,   1685
To one no worse than others after all—
Who had not brought disgrace to the order, played
Discreetly, ruffled gown nor ripped the cloth
In a bungling game at romps: I have told you, Sirs—
If I pretended simply to be pure   1690
Honest and Christian in the case—absurd!
As well go boast myself above the needs
O' the human nature, careless how meat smells,
Wine tastes—a saint above the smack! But once
Abate my crest, own flaws i' the flesh, agree   1695
To go with the herd, be hog no more nor less,
Why, hogs in common herd have common rights:
I must not be unduly borne upon,
Who just romanced a little, sowed wild oats,
But 'scaped without a scandal, flagrant fault.   1700
My name helped to a mirthful circumstance:
"Joseph would do well to amend his plea:
Undoubtedly—some toying with the wife,
But as for ruffian violence and rape,
Potiphar pressed too much on the other side!°   1705
The intrigue, the elopement, the disguise—well
      charged!
The letters and verse looked hardly like the truth.
Your apprehension was—of guilt enough
To be compatible with innocence,
So, punished best a little and not too much.   1710
Had I struck Guido Franceschini's face,
You had counseled me withdraw for my own sake,
Balk him of bravo-hiring. Friends came round,
Congratulated, "Nobody mistakes!
The pettiness o' the forfeiture defines   1715
The peccadillo: Guido gets his share:
His wife is free of husband and hook-nose,

1702–5 **"Joseph"** . . . **other side** the story of Joseph and Potiphar's
wife is found in Genesis 39. From Browning's point of view, Capon-
sacchi has more in common with St. Joseph, husband of the Virgin
Mary.

The moldy viands and the mother-in-law.
To Civita with you and amuse the time,
1720 Travesty us *De Raptu Helenae!*°
A funny figure must the husband cut
When the wife makes him skip—too ticklish, eh?
Do it in Latin, not the Vulgar, then!
Scazons°—we'll copy and send his Eminence.
1725 Mind—one iambus in the final foot!
He'll rectify it, be your friend for life!"
Oh, Sirs, depend on me for much new light
Thrown on the justice and religion here
By this proceeding, much fresh food for thought!

1730 And I was just set down to study these
In relegation, two short days ago,
Admiring how you read the rules, when, clap,
A thunder comes into my solitude—
I am caught up in a whirlwind and cast here,
1735 Told of a sudden, in this room where so late
You dealt out law adroitly, that those scales,
I meekly bowed to, took my allotment from,
Guido has snatched at, broken in your hands,
Metes to himself the murder of his wife,
1740 Full measure, pressed down, running over now!
Can I assist to an explanation?—Yes,
I rise in your esteem, sagacious Sirs,
Stand up a renderer of reasons, not
The officious priest would personate Saint George
1745 For a mock Princess in undragoned days.
What, the blood startles you? What, after all
The priest who needs must carry sword on thigh
May find imperative use for it? Then, there was
A Princess, was a dragon belching flame,
1750 And should have been a Saint George also? Then,
There might be worse schemes than to break the bonds
At Arezzo, lead her by the little hand,
Till she reached Rome, and let her try to live?
But you were law and gospel—would one please

1720 **'De Raptu Helenae'** a late Greek poem on the rape of **Helen** of Troy. 1724 **Scazons** classical verse form.

Stand back, allow your faculty elbow-room?   *1755*
You blind guides who must needs lead eyes that see!
Fools, alike ignorant of man and God!
What was there here should have perplexed your wit
For a wink of the owl-eyes of you? How miss, then,
What's now forced on you by this flare of fact—   *1760*
As if Saint Peter failed to recognize
Nero as no apostle, John or James,
Till someone burned a martyr, made a torch
O' the blood and fat to show his features by!
Could you fail read this cartulary aright   *1765*
On head and front of Franceschini there,
Large-lettered like hell's masterpiece of print—
That he, from the beginning pricked at heart
By some lust, letch of hate against his wife,
Plotted to plague her into overt sin   *1770*
And shame, would slay Pompilia body and soul,
And save his mean self—miserably caught
I' the quagmire of his own tricks, cheats and lies?
—That himself wrote those papers—from himself
To himself—which, i' the name of me and her,   *1775*
His mistress-messenger gave her and me,
Touching us with such pustules of the soul
That she and I might take the taint, be shown
To the world and shuddered over, speckled so?
—That the agent put her sense into my words,   *1780*
Made substitution of the thing she hoped,
For the thing she had and held, its opposite,
While the husband in the background bit his lips
At each fresh failure of his precious plot?
—That when at the last we did rush each on each,   *1785*
By no chance but because God willed it so—
The spark of truth was struck from out our souls—
Made all of me, descried in the first glance,
Seem fair and honest and permissible love
O' the good and true—as the first glance told me   *1790*
There was no duty patent in the world
Like daring try be good and true myself,
Leaving the shows of things to the Lord of Show
And Prince o' the Power of the Air. Our very flight,

1795 Even to its most ambiguous circumstance,
    Irrefragably proved how futile, false . . .
    Why, men—men and not boys—boys and not babes—
    Babes and not beasts—beasts and not stocks and
        stones!—
    Had the liar's lie been true one pinpoint speck,
1800 Were I the accepted suitor, free o' the place,
    Disposer of the time, to come at a call
    And go at a wink as who should say me nay—
    What need of flight, what were the gain therefrom
    But just damnation, failure or success?
1805 Damnation pure and simple to her the wife
    And me the priest—who bartered private bliss
    For public reprobation, the safe shade
    For the sunshine which men see to pelt me by:
    What other advantage—we who led the days
1810 And nights alone i' the house—was flight to find?
    In our whole journey did we stop an hour,
    Diverge a foot from straight road till we reached
    Or would have reached—but for that fate of ours—
    The father and mother, in the eye of Rome,
1815 The eye of yourselves we made aware of us
    At the first fall of misfortune? And indeed
    You did so far give sanction to our flight,
    Confirm its purpose, as lend helping hand,
    Deliver up Pompilia not to him
1820 She fled, but those the flight was ventured for.
    Why then could you, who stopped short, not go on
    One poor step more, and justify the means,
    Having allowed the end?—not see and say
    "Here's the exceptional conduct that should claim
1825 To be exceptionally judged on rules
    Which, understood, make no exception here"—
    Why play instead into the devil's hands
    By dealing so ambiguously as gave
    Guido the power to intervene like me,
1830 Prove one exception more? I saved his wife
    Against law: against law he slays her now:
    Deal with him!

I have done with being judged.
I stand here guiltless in thought, word and deed,
To the point that I apprise you—in contempt
For all misapprehending ignorance   *1835*
O' the human heart, much more the mind of Christ—
That I assuredly did bow, was blessed
By the revelation of Pompilia. There!
Such is the final fact I fling you, Sirs,
To mouth and mumble and misinterpret: there!   *1840*
"The priest's in love," have it the vulgar way!
Unpriest me, rend the rags o' the vestment, do—
Degrade deep, disenfranchise all you dare—
Remove me from the midst, no longer priest
And fit companion for the like of you—   *1845*
Your gay Abati with the well-turned leg
And rose i' the hat-rim, Canons, cross at neck
And silk mask in the pocket of the gown,
Brisk Bishops with the world's musk still unbrushed
From the rochet; I'll no more of these good things: *1850*
There's a crack somewhere, something that's unsound
I' the rattle!

        For Pompilia—be advised,
Build churches, go pray! You will find me there,
I know, if you come—and you will come, I know.
Why, there's a Judge weeping! Did not I say   *1855*
You were good and true at bottom? You see the
    truth—
I am glad I helped you: she helped me just so.

But for Count Guido—you must counsel there!
I bow my head, bend to the very dust,
Break myself up in shame of faultiness.   *1860*
I had him one whole moment, as I said—
As I remember, as will never out
O' the thoughts of me—I had him in arm's reach
There—as you stand, Sir, now you cease to sit—
I could have killed him ere he killed his wife,   *1865*
And did not: he went off alive and well

And then effected this last feat—through me!
Me—not through you—dismiss that fear! 'Twas you
Hindered me staying here to save her—not
1870 From leaving you and going back to him
And doing service in Arezzo. Come,
Instruct me in procedure! I conceive—
In all due self-abasement might I speak—
How you will deal with Guido: oh, not death!
1875 Death, if it let her life be: otherwise
Not death—your lights will teach you clearer! I
Certainly have an instinct of my own
I' the matter: bear with me and weigh its worth!
Let us go away—leave Guido all alone
1880 Back on the world again that knows him now!
I think he will be found (indulge so far!)
Not to die so much as slide out of life,
Pushed by the general horror and common hate
Low, lower—left o' the very ledge of things,
1885 I seem to see him catch convulsively
One by one at all honest forms of life,
At reason, order, decency and use—
To cramp him and get foothold by at least;
And still they disengage them from his clutch.
1890 "What, you are he, then, had Pompilia once
And so forwent her? Take not up with us!"
And thus I see him slowly and surely edged
Off all the tableland whence life upsprings
Aspiring to be immortality,
1895 As the snake, hatched on hilltop by mischance,
Despite his wriggling, slips, slides, slidders down
Hillside, lies low and prostrate on the smooth
Level of the outer place, lapsed in the vale:
So I lose Guido in the loneliness,
1900 Silence and dusk, till at the doleful end,
At the horizontal line, creation's verge,
From what just is to absolute nothingness—
Whom is it, straining onward still, he meets?
What other man deep further in the fate,
1905 Who, turning at the prize of a footfall
To flatter him and promise fellowship,

Discovers in the act a frightful face—
Judas, made monstrous by much solitude!
The two are at one now! Let them love their love
That bites and claws like hate, or hate their hate   *1910*
That mops and mows and makes as it were love!
There, let them each tear each in devil's-fun,
Or fondle this the other while malice aches—
Both teach, both learn detestability!
Kiss him the kiss, Iscariot! Pay that back,   *1915*
That smatch o' the slaver blistering on your lip,
By the better trick, the insult he spared Christ—
Lure him the lure o' the letters, Aretine!
Lick him o'er slimy-smooth with jelly-filth
O' the verse-and-prose pollution in love's guise!   *1920*
The cockatrice is with the basilisk!°
There let them grapple, denizens o' the dark,
Foes or friends, but indissolubly bound,
In their one spot out of the ken of God
Or care of man, forever and ever more!   *1925*

Why, Sirs, what's this? Why, this is sorry and strange!
Futility, divagation: this from me
Bound to be rational, justify an act
Of sober man!—whereas, being moved so much,
I give you cause to doubt the lady's mind: *1930*
A pretty sarcasm for the world! I fear
You do her wit injustice—all through me!
Like my fate all through—ineffective help!
A poor rash advocate I prove myself.
You might be angry with good cause: but sure   *1935*
At the advocate—only at the undue zeal
That spoils the force of his own plea, I think?
My part was just to tell you how things stand,
State facts and not be flustered at their fume.
But then 'tis a priest speaks: as for love—no!   *1940*
If you let buzz a vulgar fly like that
About your brains, as if I loved, forsooth,
Indeed, Sirs, you do wrong! We had no thought

1921 **cockatrice . . . basilisk!** mythological monsters supposed to
kill beholders with their glance.

Of such infatuation, she and I:
1945 There are many points that prove it: do be just!
I told you—at one little roadside-place
I spent a good half-hour, paced to and fro
The garden; just to leave her free awhile,
I plucked a handful of spring herb and bloom:
1950 I might have sat beside her on the bench
Where the children were: I wish the thing had been,
Indeed: the event could not be worse, you know:
One more half-hour of her saved! She's dead now,
Sirs!
While I was running on at such a rate,
1955 Friends should have plucked me by the sleeve: I went
Too much o' the trivial outside of her face
And the purity that shone there—plain to me,
Not to you, what more natural? Nor am I
Infatuated—oh, I saw, be sure!
1960 Her brow had not the right line, leaned too much,
Painters would say; they like the straight-up Greek:
This seemed bent somewhat with an invisible crown
Of martyr and saint, not such as art approves.
And how the dark orbs dwelt deep underneath,
1965 Looked out of such a sad sweet heaven on me!
The lips, compressed a little, came forward too,
Careful for a whole world of sin and pain.
That was the face, her husband makes his plea,
He sought just to disfigure—no offense
1970 Beyond that! Sirs, let us be rational!
He needs must vindicate his honor—ay,
Yet shirks, the coward, in a clown's disguise,
Away from the scene, endeavors to escape.
Now, had he done so, slain and left no trace
1975 O' the slayer—what were vindicated, pray?
You had found his wife disfigured or a corpse,
For what and by whom? It is too palpable!
Then, here's another point involving law:
I use this argument to show you meant
1980 No calumny against us by that title
O' the sentence—liars try to twist it so:
What penalty it bore, I had to pay

Till further proof should follow of innocence—
Probationis ob defectum°—proof?
How could you get proof without trying us? 1985
You went through the preliminary form,
Stopped there, contrived this sentence to amuse
The adversary. If the title ran
For more than fault imputed and not proved,
That was a simple penman's error, else 1990
A slip i' the phrase—as when we say of you
"Charged with injustice"—which may either be
Or not be—'tis a name that sticks meanwhile.
Another relevant matter: fool that I am!
Not what I wish true, yet a point friends urge: 1995
It is not true—yet, since friends think it helps—
She only tried me when some others failed—
Began with Conti, whom I told you of,
And Guillichini, Guido's kinsfolk both,
And when abandoned by them, not before, 2000
Turned to me. That's conclusive why she turned.
Much good they got by the happy cowardice!
Conti is dead, poisoned a month ago:
Does that much strike you as a sin? Not much,
After the present murder—one mark more 2005
On the Moor's skin—what is black by blacker still?
Conti had come here and told truth. And so
With Guillichini; he's condemned of course
To the galleys, as a friend in this affair,
Tried and condemned for no one thing i' the world, 2010
A fortnight since by who but the Governor?—
The just judge, who refused Pompilia help
At first blush, being her husband's friend, you know.
There are two tales to suit the separate courts,
Arezzo and Rome: he tells you here, we fled 2015
Alone, unhelped—lays stress on the main fault,
The spiritual sin, Rome looks to: but elsewhere
He likes best we should break in, steal, bear off,
Be fit to brand and pillory and flog—
That's the charge goes to the heart of the Governor: 2020

1984 **Probationis ob defectum** through lack of sufficient proof.

If these unpriest me, you and I may yet
Converse, Vincenzo Marzi-Medici!
Oh, Sirs, there are worse men than you, I say!
More easily duped, I mean; this stupid lie,
2025 Its liar never dared propound in Rome,
He gets Arezzo to receive—nay more,
Gets Florence and the Duke to authorize!
This is their Rota's° sentence, their Granduke
Signs and seals! Rome for me henceforward—Rome,
2030 Where better men are—most of all, that man
The Augustinian of the Hospital,
Who writes the letter—he confessed, he says,
Many a dying person, never one
So sweet and true and pure and beautiful.
2035 A good man! Will you make him Pope one day?
Not that he is not good too, this we have—
But old—else he would have his word to speak,
His truth to teach the world: I thirst for truth,
But shall not drink it till I reach the source.

2040 Sirs, I am quiet again. You see, we are
So very pitiable, she and I,
Who had conceivably been otherwise.
Forget distemperature and idle heat!
Apart from truth's sake, what's to move so much?
2045 Pompilia will be presently with God;
I am, on earth, as good as out of it,
A relegated priest; when exile ends,
I mean to do my duty and live long.
She and I are mere strangers now: but priests
2050 Should study passion; how else cure mankind,
Who come for help in passionate extremes?
I do but play with an imagined life
Of who, unfettered by a vow, unblessed
By the higher call—since you will have it so—
2055 Leads it companioned by the woman there.
To live, and see her learn, and learn by her,
Out of the low obscure and petty world—

2028 **Rota** court.

Or only see one purpose and one will
Evolve themselves i' the world, change wrong to right:
To have to do with nothing but the true,   2060
The good, the eternal—and these, not alone
In the main current of the general life,
But small experiences of every day,
Concerns of the particular hearth and home:
To learn not only by a comet's rush   2065
But a rose's birth—not by the grandeur, God—
But the comfort, Christ. All this, how far away!
Mere delectation, meet for a minute's dream!—
Just as a drudging student trims his lamp,
Opens his Plutarch,° puts him in the place   2070
Of Roman, Grecian; draws the patched gown close,
Dreams, "Thus should I fight, save or rule the
      world!"—
Then smilingly, contentedly, awakes
To the old solitary nothingness.
So I, from such communion, pass content . . .   2075

O great, just, good God! Miserable me!

THE POPE

Like to Ahasuerus,° that shrewd prince,
I will begin—as is, these seven years now,
My daily wont—and read a History
(Written by one whose deft right hand was dust
To the last digit, ages ere my birth)   5
Of all my predecessors, Popes of Rome:

2070 **Plutarch** ancient biographer.
1 **Ahasuerus** Esther 6:1.

For though mine ancient early dropped the pen,
Yet others picked it up and wrote it dry,
Since of the making books there is no end.
10 And so I have the papacy complete
From Peter first to Alexander last;
Can question each and take instruction so.
Have I to dare?—I ask, how dared this Pope?
To suffer?—Suchanone, how suffered he?
15 Being about to judge, as now, I seek
How judged once, well or ill, some other Pope;
Study some signal judgment that subsists
To blaze on, or else blot, the page which seals
The sum up of what gain or loss to God
20 Came of His one more Vicar in the world.
So, do I find example, rule of life;
So, square and set in order the next page,
Shall be stretched smooth o'er my own funeral cyst.°

Eight hundred years exact before the year
25 I was made Pope, men made Formosus Pope,
Say Sigebert and other chroniclers.
Ere I confirm or quash the trial here
Of Guido Franceschini and his friends,
Read—How there was a ghastly trial once
30 Of a dead man by a live man, and both, Popes:
Thus—in the antique penman's very phrase.

"Then Stephen, Pope and seventh of the name,
Cried out, in synod as he sat in state,
While choler quivered on his brow and beard,
35 'Come into court, Formosus, thou lost wretch,
That claimedst to be late Pope as even I!'

"And at the word the great door of the church
Flew wide, and in they brought Formosus' self,
The body of him, dead, even as embalmed
40 And buried duly in the Vatican
Eight months before, exhumed thus for the nonce.

23 **funeral cyst** coffin.

They set it, that dead body of a Pope,
Clothed in pontific vesture now again,
Upright on Peter's chair as if alive.

"And Stephen, springing up, cried furiously   45
'Bishop of Porto, wherefore didst presume
'To leave that see and take this Roman see,
Exchange the lesser for the greater see,
—A thing against the canons of the Church?'

"Then one—(a Deacon who, observing forms,   50
Was placed by Stephen to repel the charge,
Be advocate and mouthpiece of the corpse)—
Spoke as he dared, set stammeringly forth
With white lips and dry tongue—as but a youth,
For frightful was the corpse-face to behold—   55
How nowise lacked there precedent for this.

"But when, for his last precedent of all,
Emboldened by the Spirit, out he blurts
'And, Holy Father, didst not thou thyself
Vacate the lesser for the greater see,   60
Half a year since change Arago for Rome?'
'—Ye have the sin's defense now, Synod mine!'
Shrieks Stephen in a beastly froth of rage:
'Judge now betwixt him dead and me alive!
Hath he intruded, or do I pretend?   65
Judge, judge!'—breaks wavelike one whole foam of
          wrath.

"Whereupon they, being friends and followers,
Said 'Ay, thou art Christ's Vicar, and not he!
Away with what is frightful to behold!
This act was uncanonic and a fault.'   70

"Then, swallowed up in rage, Stephen exclaimed
'So, guilty! So, remains I punish guilt!
He is unpoped, and all he did I damn:
The Bishop, that ordained him, I degrade:
Depose to laics those he raised to priests: 75

What they have wrought is mischief nor shall stand,
It is confusion, let it vex no more!
Since I revoke, annul and abrogate
All his decrees in all kinds: they are void!
80 In token whereof and warning to the world,
Strip me yon miscreant of those robes usurped,
And clothe him with vile serge befitting such!
Then hale the carrion to the marketplace:
Let the town-hangman chop from his right hand
85 Those same three fingers which he blessed withal;
Next cut the head off once was crowned forsooth:
And last go fling them, fingers, head and trunk,
To Tiber that my Christian fish may sup!'
—Either because of IXθYΣ which means Fish
90 And very aptly symbolizes Christ,
Or else because the Pope is Fisherman,
And seals with Fisher's-signet.°

                       "Anyway,
So said, so done: himself, to see it done,
Followed the corpse they trailed from street to street
95 Till into Tiber wave they threw the thing.
The people, crowded on the banks to see,
Were loud or mute, wept or laughed, cursed or jeered,
According as the deed addressed their sense;
A scandal verily: and out spake a Jew
100 'Wot ye your Christ had vexed our Herod thus?'

"Now when, Formosus being dead a year,
His judge Pope Stephen tasted death in turn,
Made captive by the mob and strangled straight,
Romanus, his successor for a month,
105 Did make protest Formosus was with God,
Holy, just, true in thought and word and deed.
Next Theodore, who reigned but twenty days,

89-92 IXθYΣ . . . **Fisher's signet** the Greek word for fish is a common symbol of Christ, the letters standing for the first letters, in Greek, of "Jesus Christ, Son of God, Savior." The Pope is a Fisherman because of Jesus' promise to make Peter (considered the first Pope) a "fisher of men" (Matthew 4:19). The Pope's ring is called the Ring of the Fisherman.

Therein convoked a synod, whose decree
Did reinstate, repope the late unpoped,
And do away with Stephen as accursed.   *110*
So that when presently certain fisher-folk
(As if the queasy river could not hold
Its swallowed Jonas, but discharged the meal)
Produced the timely product of their nets,
The mutilated man, Formosus—saved   *115*
From putrefaction by the embalmer's spice,
Or, as some said, by sanctity of flesh—
'Why, lay the body again,' bade Theodore,
'Among his predecessors, in the church
And burial-place of Peter!' which was done.   *120*
'And,' addeth Luitprand, 'many of repute,
Pious and still alive, avouch to me
That, as they bore the body up the aisle,
The saints in imaged row bowed each his head
For welcome to a brother-saint come back.'   *125*
As for Romanus and this Theodore,
These two Popes, through the brief reign granted
     each,
Could but initiate what John came to close
And give the final stamp to: he it was
Ninth of the name (I follow the best guides)   *130*
Who—in full synod at Ravenna held
With Bishops seventy-four, and present too
Eude King of France with his Archbishopry—
Did condemn Stephen, anathematize
The disinterment, and make all blots blank,   *135*
'For,' argueth here Auxilius in a place
De Ordinationibus,° 'precedents
Had been, no lack, before Formosus long,
Of Bishops so transferred from see to see—
Marinus, for example:' read the tract.   *140*

"But, after John, came Sergius, reaffirmed
The right of Stephen, cursed Formosus, nay
Cast out, some say, his corpse a second time.

137 **De Ordinationibus** concerning ordinations.

And here—because the matter went to ground,
145 Fretted by new griefs, other cares of the age—
Here is the last pronouncing of the Church,
Her sentence that subsists unto this day.
Yet constantly opinion hath prevailed
I' the Church, Formosus was a holy man."

150 Which of the judgments was infallible?
Which of my predecessors spoke for God?
And what availed Formosus that this cursed,
That blessed, and then this other cursed again?
"Fear ye not those whose power can kill the body
155 And not the soul," saith Christ, "but rather those
Can cast both soul and body into hell!"

John judged thus in Eight Hundred Ninety-Eight,
Exact eight hundred years ago today
When, sitting in his stead, Vice-gerent here,
160 I must give judgment on my own behoof.
So worked the predecessor: now, my turn!

In God's name! Once more on this earth of God's,
While twilight lasts and time wherein to work,
I take His staff with my uncertain hand,
165 And stay my six and fourscore years, my due
Labor and sorrow, on His judgment-seat,
And forthwith think, speak, act, in place of Him—
The Pope for Christ. Once more appeal is made
From man's assize to mine: I sit and see
170 Another poor weak trembling human wretch
Pushed by his fellows, who pretend the right,
Up to the gulf which, where I gaze, begins
From this world to the next—gives way and way,
Just on the edge over the awful dark:
175 With nothing to arrest him but my feet.
He catches at me with convulsive face,
Cries "Leave to live the natural minute more!"
While hollowly the avengers echo "Leave?
None! So has he exceeded man's due share
180 In man's fit license, wrung by Adam's fall,

To sin and yet not surely die—that we,
All of us sinful, all with need of grace,
All chary of our life—the minute more
Or minute less of grace which saves a soul—
Bound to make common cause with who craves time,   185
—We yet protest against the exorbitance
Of sin in this one sinner, and demand
That his poor sole remaining piece of time
Be plucked from out his clutch: put him to death!
Punish him now! As for the weal or woe   190
Hereafter, God grant mercy! Man be just,
Nor let the felon boast he went scot-free!"
And I am bound, the solitary judge,
To weigh the worth, decide upon the plea,
And either hold a hand out, or withdraw   195
A foot and let the wretch drift to the fall.
Ay, and while thus I dally, dare perchance
Put fancies for a comfort 'twixt this calm
And yonder passion that I have to bear—
As if reprieve were possible for both   200
Prisoner and Pope—how easy were reprieve!
A touch o' the hand-bell here, a hasty word
To those who wait, and wonder they wait long,
I' the passage there, and I should gain the life!—
Yea, though I flatter me with fancy thus,   205
I know it is but nature's craven-trick.
The case is over, judgment at an end,
And all things done now and irrevocable:
A mere dead man is Franceschini here,
Even as Formosus centuries ago.   210
I have worn through this somber wintry day,
With winter in my soul beyond the world's,
Over these dismalest of documents
Which drew night down on me ere eve befell—
Pleadings and counter-pleadings, figure of fact   215
Beside fact's self, these summaries to wit—
How certain three were slain by certain five:
I read here why it was, and how it went,
And how the chief o' the five preferred excuse,
And how law rather chose defense should lie—   220

What argument he urged by wary word
When free to play off wile, start subterfuge,
And what the unguarded groan told, torture's feat
When law grew brutal, outbroke, overbore
225 And glutted hunger on the truth, at last—
No matter for the flesh and blood between.
All's a clear rede° and no more riddle now.
Truth, nowhere, lies yet everywhere in these—
Not absolutely in a portion, yet
230 Evolvible from the whole: evolved at last
Painfully, held tenaciously by me.
Therefore there is not any doubt to clear
When I shall write the brief word presently
And chink the hand-bell, which I pause to do.
235 Irresolute? Not I, more than the mound
With the pine-trees on it yonder! Some surmise,
Perchance, that since man's wit is fallible,
Mine may fail here? Suppose it so—what then?
Say—Guido, I count guilty, there's no babe
240 So guiltless, for I misconceive the man!
What's in the chance should move me from my mind?
If, as I walk in a rough countryside,
Peasants of mine cry "Thou art he can help,
Lord of the land and counted wise to boot:
245 Look at our brother, strangling in his foam,
He fell so where we find him—prove thy worth!"
I may presume, pronounce, "A frenzy-fit,
A falling-sickness or a fever-stroke!
Breathe a vein, copiously let blood at once!"
250 So perishes the patient, and anon
I hear my peasants—"All was error, lord!
Our story, thy prescription: for there crawled
In due time from our hapless brother's breast
The serpent which had stung him: bleeding slew
255 Whom a prompt cordial had restored to health."
What other should I say than "God so willed:
Mankind is ignorant, a man am I:
Call ignorance my sorrow, not my sin!"

227 **rede** story.

So and not otherwise, in after-time,
If some acuter wit, fresh probing, sound   *260*
This multifarious mass of words and deeds
Deeper, and reach through guilt to innocence,
I shall face Guido's ghost nor blench a jot.
"God who set me to judge thee, meted out
So much of judging faculty, no more: *265*
Ask Him if I was slack in use thereof!"
I hold a heavier fault imputable
Inasmuch as I changed a chaplain once,
For no cause—no, if I must bare my heart—
Save that he snuffled somewhat saying mass.   *270*
For I am ware it is the seed of act,
God holds appraising in His hollow palm,
Not act grown great thence on the world below,
Leafage and branchage, vulgar eyes admire.
Therefore I stand on my integrity,   *275*
Nor fear at all: and if I hesitate,
It is because I need to breathe awhile,
Rest, as the human right allows, review
Intent the little seeds of act, my tree—
The thought, which, clothed in deed, I give the world   *280*
At chink of bell and push of arrased door.

O pale departure, dim disgrace of day!
Winter's in wane, his vengeful worst art thou,
To dash the boldness of advancing March!
Thy chill persistent rain has purged our streets   *285*
Of gossipry; pert tongue and idle ear
By this, consort 'neath archway, portico.
But wheresoe'er Rome gathers in the gray,
Two names now snap and flash from mouth to
        mouth—
(Sparks, flint and steel strike) Guido and the Pope.   *290*
By this same hour tomorrow eve—aha,
How do they call him?—the sagacious Swede°
Who finds by figures how the chances prove,
Why one comes rather than another thing,

292 **sagacious Swede** authority on probability theory, not identified.

295 As, say, such dots turn up by throw of dice,
Or, if we dip in Virgil here and there
And prick for such a verse, when such shall point.°
Take this Swede, tell him, hiding name and rank,
Two men are in our city this dull eve;
300 One doomed to death—but hundreds in such plight
Slip aside, clean escape by leave of law
Which leans to mercy in this latter time;
Moreover in the plenitude of life
Is he, with strength of limb and brain adroit,
305 Presumably of service here: beside,
The man is noble, backed by nobler friends:
Nay, they so wish him well, the city's self
Makes common cause with who—house-magistrate,
Patron of hearth and home, domestic lord—
310 But ruled his own, let aliens cavil. Die?
He'll bribe a gaoler or break prison first!
Nay, a sedition may be helpful, give
Hint to the mob to batter wall, burn gate,
And bid the favorite malefactor march.
315 Calculate now these chances of escape! .
"It is not probable, but well may be."
Again, there is another man, weighed now
By twice eight years beyond the seven-times-ten,
Appointed overweight to break our branch.
320 And this man's loaded branch lifts, more than snow,
All the world's cark and care, though a bird's nest
Were a superfluous burden: notably
Hath he been pressed, as if his age were youth,
From today's dawn till now that day departs,
325 Trying one question with true sweat of soul
"Shall the said doomed man fitlier die or live?"
When a straw swallowed in his posset, stool
Stumbled on where his path lies, any puff
That's incident to such a smoking flax,
330 Hurries the natural end and quenches him!
Now calculate, thou sage, the chances here,

296–97 **Virgil . . . point** the practice of opening a volume of Virgil at
random and taking counsel from the passage on which one's finger
lights.

Say, which shall die the sooner, this or that?
"That, possibly, this in all likelihood."
I thought so: yet thou tripp'st, my foreign friend!
No, it will be quite otherwise—today   *335*
Is Guido's last: my term is yet to run.

But say the Swede were right, and I forthwith
Acknowledge a prompt summons and lie dead:
Why, then I stand already in God's face
And hear "Since by its fruit a tree is judged,   *340*
Show me thy fruit, the latest act of thine!
For in the last is summed the first and all—
What thy life last put heart and soul into,
There shall I taste thy product." I must plead
This condemnation of a man today.   *345*

Not so! Expect nor question nor reply
At what we figure as God's judgment-bar!
None of this vile way by the barren words
Which, more than any deed, characterize
Man as made subject to a curse: no speech—   *350*
That still bursts o'er some lie which lurks inside,
As the split skin across the coppery snake,
And most denotes man! since, in all beside,
In hate or lust or guile or unbelief,
Out of some core of truth the excrescence comes,   *355*
And, in the last resort, the man may urge
"So was I made, a weak thing that gave way
To truth, to impulse only strong since true,
And hated, lusted, used guile, forwent faith."
But when man walks the garden of this world   *360*
For his own solace, and, unchecked by law,
Speaks or keeps silence as himself sees fit,
Without the least incumbency to lie,
—Why, can he tell you what a rose is like,
Or how the birds fly, and not slip to false   *365*
Though truth serve better? Man must tell his mate
Of you, me and himself, knowing he lies,
Knowing his fellow knows the same—will think
"He lies, it is the method of a man!"

370 And yet will speak for answer "It is truth"
To him who shall rejoin "Again a lie!"
Therefore these filthy rags of speech, this coil
Of statement, comment, query and response,
Tatters all too contaminate for use,
375 Have no renewing: He, the Truth, is, too,
The Word. We men, in our degree, may know
There, simply, instantaneously, as here
After long time and amid many lies,
Whatever we dare think we know indeed
380 —That I am I, as He is He—what else?
But be man's method for man's life at least!
Wherefore, Antonio Pignatelli, thou
My ancient self, who wast no Pope so long
But studiedst God and man, the many years
385 I' the school, i' the cloister, in the diocese
Domestic, legate-rule in foreign lands—
Thou other force in those old busy days
Than this gray ultimate decrepitude—
Yet sensible of fires that more and more
390 Visit a soul, in passage to the sky,
Left nakeder than when flesh-robe was new—
Thou, not Pope but the mere old man o' the world,
Supposed inquisitive and dispassionate,
Wilt thou, the one whose speech I somewhat trust,
395 Question the after-me, this self now Pope,
Hear his procedure, criticize his work?
Wise in its generation is the world.

This is why Guido is found reprobate.
I see him furnished forth for his career,
400 On starting for the life-chance in our world,
With nearly all we count sufficient help:
Body and mind in balance, a sound frame,
A solid intellect: the wit to seek,
Wisdom to choose, and courage wherewithal
405 To deal in whatsoever circumstance
Should minister to man, make life succeed.
Oh, and much drawback! what were earth without?
Is this our ultimate stage, or starting-place

To try man's foot, if it will creep or climb,
'Mid obstacles in seeming, points that prove   410
Advantage for who vaults from low to high
And makes the stumbling block a stepping-stone?
So, Guido, born with appetite, lacks food:
Is poor, who yet could deftly play-off wealth:
Straitened, whose limbs are restless till at large,   415
He, as he eyes each outlet of the cirque°
And narrow penfold for probation, pines
After the good things just outside its grate,
With less monition, fainter conscience-twitch,
Rarer instinctive qualm at the first feel   420
Of greed unseemly, prompting grasp undue,
Than nature furnishes her main mankind—
Making it harder to do wrong than right
The first time, careful lest the common ear
Break measure, miss the outstep of life's march.   425
Wherein I see a trial fair and fit
For one else too unfairly fenced about,
Set above sin, beyond his fellows here:
Guarded from the arch-tempter all must fight,
By a great birth, traditionary name,   430
Diligent culture, choice companionship,
Above all, conversancy with the faith
Which puts forth for its base of doctrine just
"Man is born nowise to content himself,
But please God." He accepted such a rule,   435
Recognized man's obedience; and the Church,
Which simply is such rule's embodiment,
He clave to, he held on by—nay, indeed,
Near pushed inside of, deep as layman durst,
Professed so much of priesthood as might sue   440
For priest's-exemption where the layman sinned—
Got his arm frocked which, bare, the law would
     bruise.
Hence, at this moment, what's his last resource,
His extreme stay and utmost stretch of hope
But that—convicted of such crime as law   445

416 **cirque** arena.

Wipes not away save with a worldling's blood—
Guido, the three-parts consecrate, may 'scape?
Nay, the portentous brothers of the man
Are veritably priests, protected each
450 May do his murder in the Church's pale,
Abate Paul, Canon Girolamo!
This is the man proves irreligiousest
Of all mankind, religion's parasite!
This may forsooth plead dinned ear, jaded sense,
455 The vice o' the watcher who bides near the bell,
Sleeps sound because the clock is vigilant,
And cares not whether it be shade or shine,
Doling out day and night to all men else!
Why was the choice o' the man to niche himself
460 Perversely 'neath the tower where Time's own tongue
Thus undertakes to sermonize the world?
Why, but because the solemn is safe too,
The belfry proves a fortress of a sort,
Has other uses than to teach the hour:
465 Turns sunscreen, paravent and ombrifuge°
To whoso seeks a shelter in its pale,
—Ay, and attractive to unwary folk
Who gaze at storied portal, statued spire,
And go home with full head but empty purse,
470 Nor dare suspect the sacristan the thief!
Shall Judas—hard upon the donor's heel,
To filch the fragments of the basket—plead
He was too near the preacher's mouth, nor sat
Attent with fifties in a company?°
475 No—closer to promulgated decree,
Clearer the censure of default. Proceed!

I find him bound, then, to begin life well;
Fortified by propitious circumstance,
Great birth, good breeding, with the Church for guide,
480 How lives he? Cased thus in a coat of proof,
Mailed like a man-at-arms, though all the while
A puny starveling—does the breast pant big,

465 **paravent and ombrifuge** shelters from wind and rain. **471–74
donor's heel . . . company** Mark 6:34–44.

The limb swell to the limit, emptiness
Strive to become solidity indeed?
Rather, he shrinks up like the ambiguous fish,°   485
Detaches flesh from shell and outside show,
And steals by moonlight (I have seen the thing)
In and out, now to prey and now to skulk.
Armor he boasts when a wave breaks on beach,
Or bird stoops for the prize: with peril nigh—   490
The man of rank, the much-befriended-man,
The man almost affiliate to the Church,
Such is to deal with, let the world beware!
Does the world recognize, pass prudently?
Do tides abate and seafowl hunt i' the deep?   495
Already is the slug from out its mew,
Ignobly faring with all loose and free,
Sand fly and slush-worm at their garbage-feast,
A naked blotch no better than they all:
Guido has dropped nobility, slipped the Church,   500
Plays trickster if not cutpurse, body and soul
Prostrate among the filthy feeders—faugh!
And when Law takes him by surprise at last,
Catches the foul thing on its carrion-prey,
Behold, he points to shell left high and dry,   505
Pleads "But the case out yonder is myself!"
Nay, it is thou, Law prongs amid thy peers,
Congenial vermin; that was none of thee,
Thine outside—give it to the soldier-crab!

For I find this black mark impinge the man,   510
That he believes in just the vile of life.
Low instinct, base pretension, are these truth?
Then, that aforesaid armor, probity
He figures in, is falsehood scale on scale;
Honor and faith—a lie and a disguise,   515
Probably for all livers in this world,
Certainly for himself! All say good words
To who will hear, all do thereby bad deeds
To who must undergo; so thrive mankind!

485 **ambiguous fish** hermit (or soldier) crab. It lives in abandoned
shells.

520 See this habitual creed exemplified
Most in the last deliberate act; as last,
So, very sum and substance of the soul
Of him that planned and leaves one perfect piece,
The sin brought under jurisdiction now,
525 Even the marriage of the man: this act
I sever from his life as sample, show
For Guido's self, intend to test him by,
As, from a cup filled fairly at the fount,
By the components we decide enough
530 Or to let flow as late, or staunch the source.

He purposes this marriage, I remark,
On no one motive that should prompt thereto—
Farthest, by consequence, from ends alleged
Appropriate to the action; so they were:
535 The best, he knew and feigned, the worst he took.
Not one permissible impulse moves the man,
From the mere liking of the eye and ear,
To the true longing of the heart that loves,
No trace of these: but all to instigate,
540 Is what sinks man past level of the brute
Whose appetite if brutish is a truth.
All is the lust for money: to get gold—
Why, lie, rob, if it must be, murder! Make
Body and soul wring gold out, lured within
545 The clutch of hate by love, the trap's pretense!
What good else get from bodies and from souls?
This got, there were some life to lead thereby,
—What, where or how, appreciate those who tell
How the toad lives: it lives—enough for me!
550 To get this good—with but a groan or so,
Then, silence of the victims—were the feat.
He foresaw, made a picture in his mind—
Of father and mother stunned and echoless
To the blow, as they lie staring at fate's jaws
555 Their folly danced into, till the woe fell;
Edged in a month by strenuous cruelty
From even the poor nook whence they watched the
        wolf

Feast on their heart, the lamb-like child his prey;
Plundered to the last remnant of their wealth,
(What daily pittance pleased the plunderer dole)   560
Hunted forth to go hide head, starve and die,
And leave the pale awestricken wife, past hope
Of help i' the world now, mute and motionless,
His slave, his chattel, to first use, then destroy.
All this, he bent mind how to bring about,   565
Put plain in act and life, as painted plain,
So have success, reach crown of earthly good,
In this particular enterprise of man,
By marriage—undertaken in God's face
With all these lies so opposite God's truth,   570
For end so other than man's end.

                       Thus schemes
Guido, and thus would carry out his scheme:
But when an obstacle first blocks the path,
When he finds none may boast monopoly
Of lies and trick i' the tricking lying world—   575
That sorry timid natures, even this sort
O' the Comparini, want nor trick nor lie
Proper to the kind—that as the gorcrow treats
The bramble-finch so treats the finch the moth,
And the great Guido is minutely matched   580
By this same couple—whether true or false
The revelation of Pompilia's birth,
Which in a moment brings his scheme to naught—
Then, he is piqued, advances yet a stage,
Leaves the low region to the finch and fly,   585
Soars to the zenith whence the fiercer fowl
May dare the inimitable swoop. I see.
He draws now on the curious crime, the fine
Felicity and flower of wickedness;
Determines, by the utmost exercise   590
Of violence, made safe and sure by craft,
To satiate malice, pluck one last arch-pang
From the parents, else would triumph out of reach,
By punishing their child, within reach yet,
Who, by thought, word or deed, could nowise wrong   595

I' the matter that now moves him. So plans he,
Always subordinating (note the point!)
Revenge, the manlier sin, to interest
The meaner—would pluck pang forth, but unclench
600 No gripe in the act, let fall no money-piece.
Hence a plan for so plaguing, body and soul,
His wife, so putting, day by day, hour by hour,
The untried torture to the untouched place,
As must precipitate an end foreseen,
605 Goad her into some plain revolt, most like
Plunge upon patent suicidal shame,
Death to herself, damnation by rebound
To those whose hearts he, holding hers, holds still:
Such plan as, in its bad completeness, shall
610 Ruin the three together and alike,
Yet leave himself in luck and liberty,
No claim renounced, no right a forfeiture,
His person unendangered, his good fame
Without a flaw, his pristine worth intact—
615 While they, with all their claims and rights that cling,
Shall forthwith crumble off him every side,
Scorched into dust, a plaything for the winds.
As when, in our Campagna, there is fired
The nest-like work that overruns a hut;
620 And, as the thatch burns here, there, everywhere,
Even to the ivy and wild vine, that bound
And blessed the home where men were happy once,
There rises gradual, black amid the blaze,
Some grim and unscathed nucleus of the nest—
625 Some old malicious tower, some obscene tomb
They thought a temple in their ignorance,
And clung about and thought to lean upon—
There laughs it o'er their ravage—where are they?
So did his cruelty burn life about,
630 And lay the ruin bare in dreadfulness,
Try the persistency of torment so
Upon the wife, that, at extremity,
Some crisis brought about by fire and flame,
The patient frenzy-stung must needs break loose,
635 Fly anyhow, find refuge anywhere,

Even in the arms of who should front her first,
No monster but a man—while nature shrieked
"Or thus escape, or die!" The spasm arrived,
Not the escape by way of sin—O God,
Who shall pluck sheep Thou holdest, from Thy hand?   640
Therefore she lay resigned to die—so far
The simple cruelty was foiled. Why then,
Craft to the rescue, let craft supplement
Cruelty and show hell a masterpiece!
Hence this consummate lie, this love-intrigue,   645
Unmanly simulation of a sin,
With place and time and circumstance to suit—
These letters false beyond all forgery—
Not just handwriting and mere authorship,
But false to body and soul they figure forth—   650
As though the man had cut out shape and shape
From fancies of that other Aretine,°
To paste below—incorporate the filth
With cherub faces on a missal-page!

Whereby the man so far attains his end   655
That strange temptation is permitted—see!
Pompilia wife, and Caponsacchi priest,
Are brought together as nor priest nor wife
Should stand, and there is passion in the place,
Power in the air for evil as for good,   660
Promptings from heaven and hell, as if the stars
Fought in their courses for a fate to be.
Thus stand the wife and priest, a spectacle,
I doubt not, to unseen assemblage there.
No lamp will mark that window for a shrine,   665
No tablet signalize the terrace, teach
New generations which succeed the old
The pavement of the street is holy ground;
No bard describe in verse how Christ prevailed
And Satan fell like lightning! Why repine?   670
What does the world, told truth, but lie the more?

652 that other Aretine Pietro Aretino, author of ribald and scurrilous works.

A second time the plot is foiled; nor, now,
By corresponding sin for countercheck,
No wile and trick that baffle trick and wile—
675 The play o' the parents! Here the blot is blanched
By God's gift of a purity of soul
That will not take pollution, ermine-like
Armed from dishonor by its own soft snow.
Such was this gift of God who showed for once
680 How He would have the world go white: it seems
As a new attribute were born of each
Champion of truth, the priest and wife I praise—
As a new safeguard sprang up in defense
Of their new noble nature: so a thorn
685 Comes to the aid of and completes the rose—
Courage to wit, no woman's gift nor priest's,
I' the crisis; might leaps vindicating right.
See how the strong aggressor, bad and bold,
With every vantage, preconcerts surprise,
690 Leaps of a sudden at his victim's throat
In a byway—how fares he when face to face
With Caponsacchi? Who fights, who fears now?
There quails Count Guido armed to the chattering
     teeth,
Cowers at the steadfast eye and quiet word
695 O' the Canon of the Pieve! There skulks crime
Behind law called in to back cowardice:
While out of the poor trampled worm the wife,
Springs up a serpent!

                    But anon of these.
Him I judge now—of him proceed to note,
700 Failing the first, a second chance befriends
Guido, gives pause ere punishment arrive.
The law he called, comes, hears, adjudicates,
Nor does amiss i' the main—secludes the wife
From the husband, respites the oppressed one, grants
705 Probation to the oppressor, could he know
The mercy of a minute's fiery purge!
The furnace-coals alike of public scorn,

Private remorse, heaped glowing on his head,
What if—the force and guile, the ore's alloy,
Eliminate, his baser soul refined—   *710*
The lost be saved even yet, so as by fire?
Let him, rebuked, go softly all his days
And, when no graver musings claim their due,
Meditate on a man's immense mistake
Who, fashioned to use feet and walk, deigns crawl—   *715*
Takes the unmanly means—ay, though to ends
Man scarce should make for, would but reach through
          wrong—
May sin, but nowise needs shame manhood so:
Since fowlers hawk, shoot, nay and snare the game,
And yet eschew vile practice, nor find sport   *720*
In torchlight treachery or the luring owl.

But how hunts Guido? Why, the fraudful trap—
Late spurned to ruin by the indignant feet
Of fellows in the chase who loved fair play—
Here he picks up its fragments to the least,   *725*
Lades him and hies to the old lurking-place
Where haply he may patch again, refit
The mischief, file its blunted teeth anew,
Make sure, next time, first snap shall break the bone.
Craft, greed and violence complot revenge: *730*
Craft, for its quota, schemes to bring about
And seize occasion and be safe withal:
Greed craves its act may work both far and near,
Crush the tree, branch and trunk and root, beside.
Whichever twig or leaf arrests a streak   *735*
Of possible sunshine else would coin itself,
And drop down one more gold piece in the path:
Violence stipulates "Advantage proved
And safety sure, be pain the overplus!
Murder with jagged knife! Cut but tear too!   *740*
Foiled oft, starved long, glut malice for amends!"
And what, craft's scheme? scheme sorrowful and
          strange
As though the elements, whom mercy checked,

Had mustered hate for one eruption more,
745 One final deluge to surprise the Ark
Cradled and sleeping on its mountaintop:
Their outbreak-signal—what but the dove's coo,
Back with the olive in her bill for news
Sorrow was over?° 'Tis an infant's birth,
750 Guido's first born, his son and heir, that gives
The occasion: other men cut free their souls
From care in such a case, fly up in thanks
To God, reach, recognize His love for once:
Guido cries "Soul, at last the mire is thine!
755 Lie there in likeness of a money-bag
My babe's birth so pins down past moving now,
That I dare cut adrift the lives I late
Scrupled to touch lest thou escape with them!
These parents and their child my wife—touch one,
760 Lose all! Their rights determined on a head
I could but hate, not harm, since from each hair
Dangled a hope for me: now—chance and change!
No right was in their child but passes plain
To that child's child and through such child to me.
765 I am a father now—come what, come will,
I represent my child; he comes between—
Cuts sudden off the sunshine of this life
From those three: why, the gold is in his curls!
Not with old Pietro's, Violante's head,
770 Not his gray horror, her more hideous black—
Go these, devoted to the knife!"

                              'Tis done:
Wherefore should mind misgive, heart hesitate?
He calls to counsel, fashions certain four
Colorless natures counted clean till now,
773 —Rustic simplicity, uncorrupted youth,
Ignorant virtue! Here's the gold o' the prime
When Saturn° ruled, shall shock our leaden day—
The clown abash the courtier! Mark it, bards!
The courtier tries his hand on clownship here,

745–49 **deluge . . . over** Genesis 8.   777 **Saturn** supreme god during
the Golden Age, when men lived in happy simplicity.

Speaks a word, names a crime, appoints a price—   780
Just breathes on what, suffused with all himself,
Is red-hot henceforth past distinction now
I' the common glow of hell. And thus they break
And blaze on us at Rome, Christ's birthnight-eve!
Oh angels that sang erst "On the earth, peace!   785
To man, good will!"—such peace finds earth today!
After the seventeen hundred years, so man
Wills good to man, so Guido makes complete
His murder! what is it I said?—cuts loose
Three lives that hitherto he suffered cling,   790
Simply because each served to nail secure,
By a corner of the money-bag, his soul—
Therefore, lives sacred till the babe's first breath
O'erweights them in the balance—off they fly!

So is the murder managed, sin conceived   795
To the full: and why not crowned with triumph too?
Why must the sin, conceived thus, bring forth death?
I note how, within hair'sbreadth of escape,
Impunity and the thing supposed success,
Guido is found when the check comes, the change,   800
The monitory touch o' the tether—felt
By few, not marked by many, named by none
At the moment, only recognized aright
I' the fullness of the days, for God's, lest sin
Exceed the service, leap the line: such check—   805
A secret which this life finds hard to keep,
And, often guessed, is never quite revealed—
Needs must trip Guido on a stumbling block
Too vulgar, too absurdly plain i' the path!
Study this single oversight of care,   810
This hebetude° that marred sagacity,
Forgetfulness of all the man best knew—
How any stranger having need to fly,
Needs but to ask and have the means of flight.
Why, the first urchin tells you, to leave Rome,   815
Get horses, you must show the warrant, just
The banal scrap, clerk's scribble, a fair word buys,

811 **hebetude** dullness.

Or foul one, if a ducat sweeten word—
And straight authority will back demand,
820 Give you the pick o' the post-house!—how should he,
Then, resident at Rome for thirty years,
Guido, instruct a stranger! And himself
Forgets just this poor paper scrap, wherewith
Armed, every door he knocks at opens wide
825 To save him: horsed and manned, with such advance
O' the hunt behind, why, 'twere the easy task
Of hours told on the fingers of one hand,
To reach the Tuscan frontier, laugh at-home,
Lighthearted with his fellows of the place—
830 Prepared by that strange shameful judgment, that
Satire upon a sentence just pronounced
By the Rota and confirmed by the Granduke—
Ready in a circle to receive their peer,
Appreciate his good story how, when Rome,
835 The Pope-King and the populace of priests
Made common cause with their confederate
The other priestling who seduced his wife,
He, all unaided, wiped out the affront
With decent bloodshed and could face his friends,
840 Frolic it in the world's eye. Ay, such tale
Missed such applause, and by such oversight!
So, tired and footsore, those blood-flustered five
Went reeling on the road through dark and cold,
The few permissible miles, to sink at length,
845 Wallow and sleep in the first wayside straw,
As the other herd quenched, i' the wash o' the wave,
—Each swine, the devil inside him:° so slept they,
And so were caught and caged—all through one trip,
One touch of fool in Guido the astute!
850 He curses the omission, I surmise,
More than the murder. Why, thou fool and blind,
It is the mercy-stroke that stops thy fate,
Hamstrings and holds thee to thy hurt—but how?
On the edge o' the precipice! One minute more,
855 Thou hadst gone farther and fared worse, my son,

846–47 other herd ... inside him Matthew 8:30–32.

Fathoms down on the flint and fire beneath!
Thy comrades each and all were of one mind,
Thy murder done, to straightway murder thee
In turn, because of promised pay withheld.
So, to the last, greed found itself at odds   860
With craft in thee, and, proving conqueror,
Had sent thee, the same night that crowned thy hope,
Thither where, this same day, I see thee not,
Nor, through God's mercy, need, tomorrow, see.

Such I find Guido, midmost blotch of black   865
Discernible in this group of clustered crimes
Huddling together in the cave they call
Their palace outraged day thus penetrates.
Around him ranged, now close and now remote,
Prominent or obscure to meet the needs   870
O' the mage and master, I detect each shape
Subsidiary i' the scene nor loathed the less,
All alike colored, all descried akin
By one and the same pitchy furnace stirred
At the center: see, they lick the master's hand—   875
This fox-faced horrible priest, this brother-brute
The Abate—why, mere wolfishness looks well,
Guido stands honest in the red o' the flame,
Beside this yellow that would pass for white,
Twice Guido, all craft but no violence,   880
This copier of the mien and gait and garb
Of Peter and Paul, that he may go disguised,
Rob halt and lame, sick folk i' the temple-porch!
Armed with religion, fortified by law,
A man of peace, who trims the midnight lamp   885
And turns the classic page—and all for craft,
All to work harm with, yet incur no scratch!
While Guido brings the struggle to a close,
Paul steps back the due distance, clear o' the trap
He builds and baits. Guido I catch and judge;   890
Paul is past reach in this world and my time:
That is a case reserved. Pass to the next,
The boy of the brood, the young Girolamo
Priest, Canon, and what more? nor wolf nor fox,

895 But hybrid, neither craft nor violence
Wholly, part violence part craft: such cross
Tempts speculation—will both blend one day,
And prove hell's better product? Or subside
And let the simple quality emerge,
900 Go on with Satan's service the old way?
Meanwhile, what promise—what performance too!
For there's a new distinctive touch, I see,
Lust—lacking in the two—hell's own blue tint
That gives a character and marks the man
905 More than a match for yellow and red. Once more,
A case reserved: why should I doubt? Then comes
The gaunt gray nightmare in the furthest smoke,
The hag that gave these three abortions birth,
Unmotherly mother and unwomanly
910 Woman, that near turns motherhood to shame,
Womanliness to loathing: no one word,
No gesture to curb cruelty a whit
More than the she-pard thwarts her playsome whelps
Trying their milk-teeth on the soft o' the throat
915 O' the first fawn, flung, with those beseeching eyes,
Flat in the covert! How should she but couch,
Lick the dry lips, unsheath the blunted claw,
Catch 'twixt her placid eyewinks at what chance
Old bloody half-forgotten dream may flit,
920 Born when herself was novice to the taste,
The while she lets youth take its pleasure. Last,
These God-abandoned wretched lumps of life,
These four companions—countryfolk this time,
Not tainted by the unwholesome civic breath,
925 Much less the curse o' the Court! Mere striplings too,
Fit to do human nature justice still!
Surely when impudence in Guido's shape
Shall propose crime and proffer money's-worth
To these stout tall rough bright-eyed black-haired
    boys,
930 The blood shall bound in answer to each cheek
Before the indignant outcry break from lip!
Are these i' the mood to murder, hardly loosed
From healthy autumn-finish of ploughed glebe,

Grapes in the barrel, work at happy end,
And winter near with rest and Christmas play?　　　935
How greet they Guido with his final task—
(As if he but proposed "One vineyard more
To dig, ere frost come, then relax indeed!")
"Anywhere, anyhow and anywhy,
Murder me some three people, old and young,　　　940
Ye never heard the names of—and be paid
So much!" And the whole four accede at once.
Demur? Do cattle bidden march or halt?
Is it some lingering habit, old fond faith
I' the lord o' the land, instructs them—birthright
　　　badge　　　945
Of feudal tenure claims its slaves again?
Not so at all, thou noble human heart!
All is done purely for the pay—which, earned,
And not forthcoming at the instant, makes
Religion heresy, and the lord o' the land　　　950
Fit subject for a murder in his turn.
The patron with cut throat and rifled purse,
Deposited i' the roadside-ditch, his due,
Naught hinders each good fellow trudging home,
The heavier by a piece or two in poke,　　　955
And so with new zest to the common life,
Mattock and spade, plow-tail and wagon-shaft,
Till some such other piece of luck betide,
Who knows? Since this is a mere start in life,
And none of them exceeds the twentieth year.　　　960
Nay, more i' the background yet? Unnoticed forms
Claim to be classed, subordinately vile?
Complacent lookers-on that laugh—perchance
Shake head as their friend's horseplay grows too rough
With the mere child he manages amiss—　　　965
But would not interfere and make bad worse
For twice the fractious tears and prayers: thou
　　　know'st
Civility better, Marzi-Medici,
Governor for thy kinsman the Granduke!
Fit representative of law, man's lamp　　　970
I' the magistrate's grasp full-flare, no rushlight-end

Sputtering 'twixt thumb and finger of the priest!
Whose answer to the couple's cry for help
Is a threat—whose remedy of Pompilia's wrong,
975 A shrug o' the shoulder, and facetious word
Or wink, traditional with Tuscan wits,
To Guido in the doorway. Laud to law!
The wife is pushed back to the husband, he
Who knows how these home-squabblings persecute
980 People who have the public good to mind,
And work best with a silence in the court!

Ah, but I save my word at least for thee,
Archbishop, who art under, i' the Church,
As I am under God—thou, chosen by both
985 To do the shepherd's office, feed the sheep—
How of this lamb that panted at thy foot
While the wolf pressed on her within crook's reach?
Wast thou the hireling that did turn and flee?
With thee at least anon the little word!

990 Such denizens o' the cave now cluster round
And heat the furnace sevenfold: time indeed
A bolt from heaven should cleave roof and clear
place,
Transfix and show the world, suspiring flame,
The main offender, scar and brand the rest
995 Hurrying, each miscreant to his hole: then flood
And purify the scene with outside day—
Which yet, in the absolutest drench of dark,
Ne'er wants a witness, some stray beauty-beam
To the despair of hell.

First of the first,
1000 Such I pronounce Pompilia, then as now
Perfect in whiteness: stoop thou down, my child,
Give one good moment to the poor old Pope
Heartsick at having all his world to blame—
Let me look at thee in the flesh as erst,
1005 Let me enjoy the old clean linen garb,
Not the new splendid vesture! Armed and crowned,

Would Michael, yonder, be, nor crowned nor armed,
The less pre-eminent angel? Everywhere
I see in the world the intellect of man,
That sword, the energy his subtle spear,   1010
The knowledge which defends him like a shield—
Everywhere; but they make not up, I think,
The marvel of a soul like thine, earth's flower
She holds up to the softened gaze of God!
It was not given Pompilia to know much,   1015
Speak much, to write a book, to move mankind,
Be memorized by who records my time.
Yet if in purity and patience, if
In faith held fast despite the plucking fiend,
Safe like the signet stone with the new name   1020
That saints are known by—if in right returned
For wrong, most pardon for worst injury,
If there be any virtue, any praise—
Then will this woman-child have proved—who
      knows?—
Just the one prize vouchsafed unworthy me,   1025
Seven years a gardener of the untoward ground,
I till—this earth, my sweat and blood manure
All the long day that barrenly grows dusk:
At least one blossom makes me proud at eve
Born 'mid the briers of my enclosure! Still   1030
(Oh, here as elsewhere, nothingness of man!)
Those be the plants, imbedded yonder South
To mellow in the morning, those made fat
By the master's eye, that yield such timid leaf,
Uncertain bud, as product of his pains!   1035
While—see how this mere chance-sown cleft-nursed
      seed
That sprang up by the wayside 'neath the foot
Of the enemy, this breaks all into blaze,
Spreads itself, one wide glory of desire
To incorporate the whole great sun it loves   1040
From the inch-height whence it looks and longs! My
      flower,
My rose, I gather for the breast of God,
This I praise most in thee, where all I praise,

That having been obedient to the end
1045 According to the light allotted, law
Prescribed thy life, still tried, still standing test—
Dutiful to the foolish parents first,
Submissive next to the bad husband—nay,
Tolerant of those meaner miserable
1050 That did his hests, eked out the dole of pain—
Thou, patient thus, couldst rise from law to law,
The old to the new, promoted at one cry
O' the trump of God to the new service, not
To longer bear, but henceforth fight, be found
1055 Sublime in new impatience with the foe!
Endure man and obey God: plant firm foot
On neck of man, tread man into the hell
Meet for him, and obey God all the more!
Oh child that didst despise thy life so much
1060 When it seemed only thine° to keep or lose,
How the fine ear felt fall the first low word
"Value life, and preserve life for My sake!"
Thou didst . . . how shall I say? . . . receive so long
The standing ordinance of God on earth,
1065 What wonder if the novel claim had clashed
With old requirement, seemed to supersede
Too much the customary law? But, brave,
Thou at first prompting of what I call God,
And fools call Nature, didst hear, comprehend,
1070 Accept the obligation laid on thee,
Mother elect, to save the unborn child,
As brute and bird do, reptile and the fly,
Ay and, I nothing doubt, even tree, shrub, plant
And flower o' the field, all in a common pact
1075 To worthily defend the trust of trusts,
Life from the Ever Living:—didst resist—
Anticipate the office that is mine—
And with his own sword stay the upraised arm,
The endeavor of the wicked, and defend
1080 Him who—again in my default—was there
For visible providence: one less true than thou

1060 **only thine** before she knew she was to have a child.

To touch, i' the past, less practiced in the right,
Approved less far in all docility
To all instruction—how had such an one
Made scruple "Is this motion a decree?"   1085
It was authentic to the experienced ear
O' the good and faithful servant. Go past me
And get thy praise—and be not far to seek
Presently when I follow if I may!

And surely not so very much apart   1090
Need I place thee, my warrior-priest—in whom
What if I gain the other rose, the gold,°
We grave to imitate God's miracle,
Greet monarchs with, good rose in its degree?
Irregular noble scapegrace—son the same!   1095
Faulty—and peradventure ours the fault
Who still misteach, mislead, throw hook and line,
Thinking to land leviathan forsooth,
Tame the scaled neck, play with him as a bird,
And bind him for our maidens! Better bear   1100
The King of Pride° go wantoning awhile,
Unplagued by cord in nose and thorn in jaw,
Through deep to deep, followed by all that shine,
Churning the blackness hoary: He who made
The comely terror, He shall make the sword   1105
To match that piece of netherstone his heart,
Ay, nor miss praise thereby; who else shut fire
I' the stone, to leap from mouth at sword's first stroke,
In lamps of love and faith, the chivalry
That dares the right and disregards alike   1110
The yea and nay o' the world? Self-sacrifice—
What if an idol took it? Ask the Church
Why she was wont to turn each Venus here—
Poor Rome perversely lingered round, despite
Instruction, for the sake of purblind love—   1115
Into Madonna's shape, and waste no whit

1092 **the other rose, the gold** golden rose given by the Pope as mark
of distinction.   1098–1101 **leviathan . . . King of Pride** Job 41.

Of aught so rare on earth as gratitude!
All this sweet savor was not ours but thine,
Nard of the rock, a natural wealth we name
1120 Incense, and treasure up as food for saints,
When flung to us—whose function was to give
Not find the costly perfume. Do I smile?
Nay, Caponsacchi, much I find amiss,
Blameworthy, punishable in this freak
1125 Of thine, this youth prolonged, though age was ripe,
This masquerade in sober day, with change
Of motley too—now hypocrite's disguise,
Now fool's-costume: which lie was least like truth,
Which the ungainlier, more discordant garb
1130 With that symmetric soul inside my son,
The churchman's or the worldling's—let him judge,
Our adversary° who enjoys the task!
I rather chronicle the healthy rage—
When the first moan broke from the martyr-maid
1135 At that uncaging of the beasts—made bare
My athlete on the instant, gave such good
Great undisguised leap over post and pale
Right into the mid-cirque, free fighting-place.
There may have been rash stripping—every rag
1140 Went to the winds—infringement manifold
Of laws prescribed pudicity,° I fear,
In this impulsive and prompt self-display!
Ever such tax comes of the foolish youth;
Men mulct the wiser manhood, and suspect
1145 No veritable star swims out of cloud.
Bear thou such imputation, undergo
The penalty I nowise dare relax—
Conventional chastisement and rebuke.
But for the outcome, the brave starry birth
1150 Conciliating earth with all that cloud,
Thank heaven as I do! Ay, such championship
Of God at first blush, such prompt cheery thud
Of glove on ground that answers ringingly
The challenge of the false knight—watch we long

1132 **Our adversary** the devil.   1141 **pudicity** modesty.

And wait we vainly for its gallant like 1155
From those appointed to the service, sworn
His bodyguard with pay and privilege—
White-cinct, because in white walks sanctity,
Red-socked, how else proclaim fine scorn of flesh,
Unchariness of blood when blood faith begs! 1160
Where are the men-at-arms with cross on coat?
Aloof, bewraying their attire: whilst thou
In mask and motley, pledged to dance not fight,
Sprang'st forth the hero! In thought, word and deed,
How throughout all thy warfare thou wast pure, 1165
I find it easy to believe: and if
At any fateful moment of the strange
Adventure, the strong passion of that strait,
Fear and surprise, may have revealed too much—
As when a thundrous midnight, with black air 1170
That burns, raindrops that blister, breaks a spell,
Draws out the excessive virtue of some sheathed
Shut unsuspected flower that hoards and hides
Immensity of sweetness—so, perchance,
Might the surprise and fear release too much 1175
The perfect beauty of the body and soul
Thou savedst in thy passion for God's sake,
He who is Pity. Was the trial sore?
Temptation sharp? Thank God a second time!
Why comes temptation but for man to meet 1180
And master and make crouch beneath his foot,
And so be pedestaled in triumph? Pray
"Lead us into no such temptations, Lord!"
Yea, but, O Thou whose servants are the bold,
Lead such temptations by the head and hair, 1185
Reluctant dragons, up to who dares fight,
That so he may do battle and have praise!
Do I not see the praise?—that while thy mates
Bound to deserve i' the matter, prove at need
Unprofitable through the very pains 1190
We gave to train them well and start them fair—
Are found too stiff, with standing ranked and ranged,
For onset in good earnest, too obtuse
Of ear, through iteration of command,

1195 For catching quick the sense of the real cry—
Thou, whose sword-hand was used to strike the lute,
Whose sentry-station graced some wanton's gate,
Thou didst push forward and show mettle, shame
The laggards, and retrieve the day. Well done!
1200 Be glad thou hast let light into the world
Through that irregular breach o' the boundary—see
The same upon thy path and march assured,
Learning anew the use of soldiership,
Self-abnegation, freedom from all fear,
1205 Loyalty to the life's end! Ruminate,
Deserve the initiatory spasm—once more
Work, be unhappy but bear life, my son!

And troop you, somewhere 'twixt the best and worst,
Where crowd the indifferent product, all too poor
1210 Makeshift, starved samples of humanity!
Father and mother, huddle there and hide!
A gracious eye may find you! Foul and fair,
Sadly mixed natures: self-indulgent—yet
Self-sacrificing too: how the love soars,
1215 How the craft, avarice, vanity and spite
Sink again! So they keep the middle course,
Slide into silly crime at unaware,
Slip back upon the stupid virtue, stay
Nowhere enough for being classed, I hope
1220 And fear. Accept the swift and rueful death,
Taught, somewhat sternlier than is wont, what waits
The ambiguous creature—how the one black tuft
Steadies the aim of the arrow just as well
As the wide faultless white on the bird's breast!
1225 Nay, you were punished in the very part
That looked most pure of speck—'twas honest love
Betrayed you—did love seem most worthy pains,
Challenge such purging, since ordained survive
When all the rest of you was done with? Go!
1230 Never again elude the choice of tints!
White shall not neutralize the black, nor good
Compensate bad in man, absolve him so:
Life's business being just the terrible choice.

So do I see, pronounce on all and some
Grouped for my judgment now—profess no doubt   *1235*
While I pronounce: dark, difficult enough
The human sphere, yet eyes grow sharp by use,
I find the truth, dispart the shine from shade,
As a mere man may, with no special touch
O' the lynx-gift in each ordinary orb: *1240*
Nay, if the popular notion class me right,
One of well-nigh decayed intelligence—
What of that? Through hard labor and good will,
And habitude that gives a blind man sight
At the practiced finger-ends of him, I do   *1245*
Discern, and dare decree in consequence,
Whatever prove the peril of mistake.
Whence, then, this quite new quick cold thrill—
     cloudlike,
This keen dread creeping from a quarter scarce
Suspected in the skies I nightly scan?   *1250*
What slacks the tense nerve, saps the wound-up
     spring
Of the act that should and shall be, sends the mount
And mass o' the whole man's-strength—conglobed so
     late—
Shudderingly into dust, a moment's work?
While I stand firm, go fearless, in this world,   *1255*
For this life recognize and arbitrate,
Touch and let stay, or else remove a thing,
Judge "This is right, this object out of place,"
Candle in hand that helps me and to spare—
What if a voice deride me, "Perk and pry!   *1260*
Brighten each nook with thine intelligence!
Play the good householder, ply man and maid
With tasks prolonged into the midnight, test
Their work and nowise stint of the due wage
Each worthy worker: but with gyves and whip   *1265*
Pay thou misprision° of a single point
Plain to thy happy self who lift'st the light,
Lament'st the darkling—bold to all beneath!

1266 **misprision** mistake.

What if thyself adventure, now the place
1270 Is purged so well? Leave pavement and mount roof,
Look round thee for the light of the upper sky,
The fire which lit thy fire which finds default
In Guido Franceschini to his cost!
What if, above in the domain of light,
1275 Thou miss the accustomed signs, remark eclipse?
Shalt thou still gaze on ground nor lift a lid—
Steady in thy superb prerogative,
Thy inch of inkling—nor once face the doubt
I' the sphere above thee, darkness to be felt?"

1280 Yet my poor spark had for its source, the sun;
Thither I sent the great looks which compel
Light from its fount: all that I do and am
Comes from the truth, or seen or else surmised,
Remembered or divined, as mere man may:
1285 I know just so, nor otherwise. As I know,
I speak—what should I know, then, and how speak
Were there a wild mistake of eye or brain
As to recorded governance above?
If my own breath, only, blew coal alight
1290 I styled celestial and the morning-star?
I, who in this world act resolvedly,
Dispose of men, their bodies and their souls,
As they acknowledge or gainsay the light
I show them—shall I too lack courage?—leave
1295 I, too, the post of me, like those I blame?
Refuse, with kindred inconsistency,
To grapple danger whereby souls grow strong?
I am near the end; but still not at the end;
All to the very end is trial in life:
1300 At this stage is the trial of my soul
Danger to face, or danger to refuse?
Shall I dare try the doubt now, or not dare?

O Thou—as represented here to me
In such conception as my soul allows—
1305 Under Thy measureless, my atom width!—
Man's mind, what is it but a convex glass

Wherein are gathered all the scattered points
Picked out of the immensity of sky,
To reunite there, be our heaven for earth,
Our known unknown,° our God revealed to man?   *1310*
Existent somewhere, somehow, as a whole;
Here, as a whole proportioned to our sense—
There (which is nowhere, speech must babble thus!)
In the absolute immensity, the whole
Appreciable solely by Thyself—   *1315*
Here, by the little mind of man, reduced
To littleness that suits his faculty,
In the degree appreciable too;
Between Thee and ourselves—nay even, again,
Below us, to the extreme of the minute,   *1320*
Appreciable by how many and what diverse
Modes of the life Thou madest be! (why live
Except for love—how love unless they know?)
Each of them, only filling to the edge,
Insect or angel, his just length and breadth,   *1325*
Due facet of reflection—full, no less,
Angel or insect, as Thou framedst things.
I it is who have been appointed here
To represent Thee, in my turn, on earth,
Just as, if new philosophy° know aught,   *1330*
This one earth, out of all the multitude
Of peopled worlds, as stars are now supposed—
Was chosen, and no sun-star of the swarm,
For stage and scene of Thy transcendent act°
Beside which even the creation fades   *1335*
Into a puny exercise of power.
Choice of the world, choice of the thing I am,
Both emanate alike from Thy dread play
Of operation outside this our sphere
Where things are classed and counted small or great— *1340*
Incomprehensibly the choice is Thine!
I therefore bow my head and take Thy place.
There is, beside the works, a tale of Thee

1310 **Our known unknown** cf. Keats's *Endymion*, Bk. II, l. 739.
1330 **new philosophy** "modern science."   1334 **Thy transcendent act**
the Incarnation.

In the world's mouth, which I find credible:
1345 I love it with my heart: unsatisfied,
I try it with my reason, nor discept°
From any point I probe and pronounce sound.
Mind is not matter nor from matter, but
Above—leave matter then, proceed with mind!
1350 Man's be the mind recognized at the height—
Leave the inferior minds and look at man!
Is he the strong, intelligent and good
Up to his own conceivable height? Nowise.
Enough o' the low—soar the conceivable height,
1355 Find cause to match the effect in evidence,
The work i' the world, not man's but God's; leave
      man!
Conjecture of the worker by the work:
Is there strength there?—enough: intelligence?
Ample: but goodness in a like degree?
1360 Not to the human eye in the present state,
An isoscele deficient in the base.
What lacks, then, of perfection fit for God
But just the instance which this tale supplies
Of love without a limit? So is strength,
1365 So is intelligence; let love be so,
Unlimited in its self-sacrifice,
Then is the tale true and God shows complete.
Beyond the tale, I reach into the dark,
Feel what I cannot see, and still faith stands:
1370 I can believe this dread machinery
Of sin and sorrow, would confound me else,
Devised—all pain, at most expenditure
Of pain by Who devised pain—to evolve,
By new machinery in counterpart,
1375 The moral qualities of man—how else?—
To make him love in turn and be beloved,
Creative and self-sacrificing too,
And thus eventually God-like, (ay,
"I have said ye are Gods,"°—shall it be said for
      naught?)

1346 **discept** dissent.   1379 **"I . . . Gods"** John 10:34.

Enable man to wring, from out all pain,   *1380*
All pleasure for a common heritage
To all eternity: this may be surmised,
The other is revealed—whether a fact,
Absolute, abstract, independent truth,
Historic, not reduced to suit man's mind—   *1385*
Or only truth reverberate, changed, made pass
A spectrum into mind, the narrow eye—
The same and not the same, else unconceived—
Though quite conceivable to the next grade
Above it in intelligence—as truth   *1390*
Easy to man were blindness to the beast
By parity of procedure—the same truth
In a new form, but changed in either case:
What matter so intelligence be filled?
To a child, the sea is angry, for it roars: *1395*
Frost bites, else why the tooth-like fret on face?
Man makes acoustics deal with the sea's wrath,
Explains the choppy cheek by chymic law°—
To man and child remains the same effect
On drum of ear and root of nose, change cause   *1400*
Never so thoroughly: so my heart be struck,
What care I—by God's gloved hand or the bare?
Nor do I much perplex me with aught hard,
Dubious in the transmitting of the tale—
No, nor with certain riddles set to solve.   *1405*
This life is training and a passage; pass—
Still, we march over some flat obstacle
We made give way before us; solid truth
In front of it, what motion for the world?
The moral sense grows but by exercise.   *1410*
'Tis even as man grew probatively
Initiated in Godship, set to make
A fairer moral world than this he finds,
Guess now what shall be known hereafter. Deal
Thus with the present problem: as we see,   *1415*
A faultless creature is destroyed, and sin
Has had its way i' the world where God should rule.

1398 **Explains . . . law** man explains how cheeks become chapped by
appealing to chemical laws.

Ay, but for this irrelevant circumstance
Of inquisition after blood, we see
1420 Pompilia lost and Guido saved: how long?
For his whole life: how much is that whole life?
We are not babes, but know the minute's worth,
And feel that life is large and the world small,
So, wait till life have passed from out the world.
1425 Neither does this astonish at the end,
That whereas I can so receive and trust,
Other men, made with hearts and souls the same,
Reject and disbelieve—subordinate
The future to the present—sin, nor fear.
1430 This I refer still to the foremost fact,
Life is probation and the earth no goal
But starting-point of man: compel him strive,
Which means, in man, as good as reach the goal—
Why institute that race, his life, at all?
1435 But this does overwhelm me with surprise,
Touch me to terror—not that faith, the pearl,
Should be let lie by fishers wanting food—
Nor, seen and handled by a certain few
Critical and contemptuous, straight consigned
1440 To shore and shingle for the pebble it proves—
But that, when haply found and known and named
By the residue made rich for evermore,
These—that these favored ones, should in a trice
Turn, and with double zest go dredge for whelks,
1445 Mud-worms that make the savory soup! Enough
O' the disbelievers, see the faithful few!
How do the Christians here deport them, keep
Their robes of white unspotted by the world?
What is this Aretine Archbishop, this
1450 Man under me as I am under God,
This champion of the faith, I armed and decked,
Pushed forward, put upon a pinnacle,
To show the enemy his victor—see!
What's the best fighting when the couple close?
1455 Pompilia cries, "Protect me from the wolf!"
He—"No, thy Guido is rough, heady, strong,
Dangerous to disquiet: let him bide!

He needs some bone to mumble, help amuse
The darkness of his den with: so, the fawn
Which limps up bleeding to my foot and lies,   1460
—Come to me, daughter!—thus I throw him back!"
Have we misjudged here, overarmed our knight,
Given gold and silk where plain hard steel serves best,
Enfeebled whom we sought to fortify,
Made an archbishop and undone a saint?   1465
Well, then, descend these heights, this pride of life,
Sit in the ashes with a barefoot monk
Who long ago stamped out the worldly sparks,
By fasting, watching, stone cell and wire scourge,
—No such indulgence as unknits the strength—   1470
These breed the tight nerve and tough cuticle,
And the world's praise or blame runs rillet-wise
Off the broad back and brawny breast, we know!
He meets the first cold sprinkle of the world,
And shudders to the marrow. "Save this child?   1475
Oh, my superiors, oh, the Archbishop's self!
Who was it dared lay hand upon the ark
His betters saw fall nor put finger forth?°
Great ones could help yet help not: why should small?
I break my promise: let her break her heart!"   1480
These are the Christians not the worldlings, not
The skeptics, who thus battle for the faith!
If foolish virgins disobey and sleep,
What wonder? But, this time, the wise that watch,
Sell lamps and buy lutes, exchange oil for wine,   1485
The mystic Spouse betrays the Bridegroom here.°
To our last resource, then! Since all flesh is weak,
Bind weaknesses together, we get strength:
The individual weighed, found wanting, try
Some institution, honest artifice   1490
Whereby the units grow compact and firm!
Each props the other, and so stand is made
By our embodied cowards that grow brave.
The Monastery called of Convertites,
Meant to help women because these helped Christ—   1495

1477–78 **Who . . . forth?** 2 Samuel 6:6–7.   1483–86 **foolish virgins
. . . Bridegroom here** Matthew 25.

A thing existent only while it acts,
Does as designed, else a nonentity—
For what is an idea unrealized?—
Pompilia is consigned to these for help.
1500 They do help: they are prompt to testify
To her pure life and saintly dying days.
She dies, and lo, who seemed so poor, proves rich.
What does the body that lives through helpfulness
To women for Christ's sake? The kiss turns bite,
1505 The dove's note changes to the crow's cry: judge!
"Seeing that this our Convent claims of right
What goods belong to those we succor, be
The same proved women of dishonest life—
And seeing that this trial made appear
1510 Pompilia was in such predicament—
The Convent hereupon pretends to said
Succession of Pompilia, issues writ,
And takes possession by the Fisc's° advice."
Such is their attestation to the cause
1515 Of Christ, who had one saint at least, they hoped:
But, is a title-deed to filch, a corpse
To slander, and an infant-heir to cheat?
Christ must give up his gains then! They unsay
All the fine speeches—who was saint is whore.
1520 Why, scripture yields no parallel for this!
The soldiers only threw dice for Christ's coat;
We want another legend of the Twelve
Disputing if it was Christ's coat at all,
Claiming as prize the woof of price—for why?
1525 The Master was a thief, purloined the same,
Or paid for it out of the common bag!
Can it be this is end and outcome, all
I take with me to show as stewardship's fruit,
The best yield of the latest time, this year
1530 The seventeen-hundredth since God died for man?
Is such effect proportionate to cause?
And still the terror keeps on the increase
When I perceive . . . how can I blink the fact?

1513 **Fisc** prosecutor.

That the fault, the obduracy to good,
Lies not with the impracticable stuff   *1535*
Whence man is made, his very nature's fault,
As if it were of ice the moon may gild
Not melt, or stone 'twas meant the sun should warm
Not make bear flowers—nor ice nor stone to blame:
But it can melt, that ice, can bloom, that stone,   *1540*
Impassible to rule of day and night!
This terrifies me, thus compelled perceive,
Whatever love and faith we looked should spring
At advent of the authoritative star,
Which yet lie sluggish, curdled at the source—   *1545*
These have leaped forth profusely in old time,
These still respond with promptitude today,
At challenge of—what unacknowledged powers
O' the air, what uncommissioned meteors, warmth
By law, and light by rule should supersede?   *1550*
For see this priest, this Caponsacchi, stung
At the first summons—"Help for honor's sake,
Play the man, pity the oppressed!"—no pause,
How does he lay about him in the midst,
Strike any foe, right wrong at any risk,   *1555*
All blindness, bravery and obedience!—blind?
Ay, as a man would be inside the sun,
Delirious with the plenitude of light
Should interfuse him to the finger-ends—
Let him rush straight, and how shall he go wrong?   *1560*
Where are the Christians in their panoply?
The loins we girt about with truth, the breasts
Righteousness plated round, the shield of faith,
The helmet of salvation, and that sword
O' the Spirit, even the word of God°—where these? *1565*
Slunk into corners! Oh, I hear at once
Hubbub of protestation! "What, we monks
We friars, of such an order, such a rule,
Have not we fought, bled, left our martyr-mark
At every point along the boundary-line   *1570*
'Twixt true and false, religion and the world,

1562-65 **The loins ... of God** Ephesians 6:13-17.

Where this or the other dogma of our Church
Called for defense?" And I, despite myself,
How can I but speak loud what truth speaks low,
1575 "Or better than the best, or nothing serves!
What boots deed, I can cap and cover straight
With such another doughtiness to match,
Done at an instinct of the natural man?"
Immolate body, sacrifice soul too—
1580 Do not these publicans the same? Outstrip!
Or else stop race you boast runs neck and neck,
You with the wings, they with the feet—for shame!
Oh, I remark your diligence and zeal!
Five years long, now, rounds faith into my ears,
1585 "Help thou, or Christendom is done to death!"
Five years since, in the Province of To-kien,
Which is in China as some people know,
Maigrot, my Vicar Apostolic there,
Having a great qualm, issues a decree.
1590 Alack, the converts use as God's name, not
Tien-chu but plain *Tien* or else mere *Shang-ti,*
As Jesuits please to fancy politic,
While, say Dominicans, it calls down fire—
For *Tien* means Heaven, and *Shang-ti,* supreme
  prince,
1595 While *Tien-chu* means the lord of Heaven: all cry,
"There is no business urgent for dispatch
As that thou send a legate, specially
Cardinal Tournon, straight to Pekin, there
To settle and compose the difference!"
1600 So have I seen a potentate all fume
For some infringement of his realm's just right,
Some menace to a mud-built straw-thatched farm
O' the frontier; while inside the mainland lie,
Quite undisputed-for in solitude,
1605 Whole cities plague may waste or famine sap:
What if the sun crumble, the sands encroach,
While he looks on sublimely at his ease?
How does their ruin touch the empire's bound?

And is this little all that was to be?

Where is the gloriously decisive change,   1610
Metamorphosis the immeasurable
Of human clay to divine gold, we looked
Should, in some poor sort, justify its price?
Had an adept of the mere Rosy Cross
Spent his life to consummate the Great Work,°   1615
Would not we start to see the stuff it touched
Yield not a grain more than the vulgar got
By the old smelting-process years ago?
If this were sad to see in just the sage
Who should profess so much, perform no more,   1620
What is it when suspected in that Power
Who undertook to make and made the world,
Devised and did effect man, body and soul,
Ordained salvation for them both, and yet . . .
Well, is the thing we see, salvation?

                                        I   1625
Put no such dreadful question to myself,
Within whose circle of experience burns
The central truth, Power, Wisdom, Goodness—God:
I must outlive a thing ere know it dead:
When I outlive the faith there is a sun,   1630
When I lie, ashes to the very soul—
Someone, not I, must wail above the heap,
"He died in dark whence never morn arose."
While I see day succeed the deepest night—
How can I speak but as I know?—my speech   1635
Must be, throughout the darkness, "It will end:
The light that did burn, will burn!" Clouds obscure—
But for which obscuration all were bright?
Too hastily concluded! Sun-suffused,
A cloud may soothe the eye made blind by blaze— 1640
Better the very clarity of heaven:
The soft streaks are the beautiful and dear.
What but the weakness in a faith supplies
The incentive to humanity, no strength

1614-15 **an adept . . . Great Work** an alchemist of the Rosicrucian
order, who claims to have found the secret of turning base metals
into gold.

1645 Absolute, irresistible, comports?
How can man love but what he yearns to help?
And that which men think weakness within strength,
But angels know for strength and stronger yet—
What were it else but the first things made new,
1650 But repetition of the miracle,
The divine instance of self-sacrifice
That never ends and aye begins for man?
So, never I miss footing in the maze,
No—I have light nor fear the dark at all.

1655 But are mankind not real, who pace outside
My petty circle, world that's measured me?
And when they stumble even as I stand,
Have I a right to stop ear when they cry,
As they were phantoms who took clouds for crags,
Tripped and fell, where man's march might safely
1660   move?
Beside, the cry is other than a ghost's,
When out of the old time there pleads some bard,°
Philosopher, or both, and—whispers not,
But words it boldly. "The inward work and worth
1665 Of any mind, what other mind may judge
Save God who only knows the thing He made,
The veritable service He exacts?
It is the outward product men appraise.
Behold, an engine hoists a tower aloft:
1670 'I looked that it should move the mountain too!'
Or else 'Had just a turret toppled down,
Success enough!'—may say the Machinist
Who knows what less or more result might be:
But we, who see that done we cannot do,
1675 'A feat beyond man's force,' we men must say.
Regard me and that shake I gave the world!
I was born, not so long before Christ's birth
As Christ's birth haply did precede thy day—
But many a watch before the star of dawn:
1680 Therefore I lived—it is thy creed affirms,

1662 **some bard** Euripides.

Pope Innocent, who art to answer me!—
Under conditions, nowise to escape,
Whereby salvation was impossible.
Each impulse to achieve the good and fair,
Each aspiration to the pure and true,   *1685*
Being without a warrant or an aim,
Was just as sterile a felicity
As if the insect, born to spend his life
Soaring his circles, stopped them to describe
(Painfully motionless in the mid-air)   *1690*
Some word of weighty counsel for man's sake,
Some 'Know thyself' or 'Take the golden mean!'
—Forwent his happy dance and the glad ray,
Died half an hour the sooner and was dust.
I, born to perish like the brutes, or worse,   *1695*
Why not live brutishly, obey brutes' law?
But I, of body as of soul complete,
A gymnast at the games, philosopher
I' the schools, who painted, and made music—all
Glories that met upon the tragic stage   *1700*
When the Third Poet's tread surprised the Two°—
Whose lot fell in a land where life was great
And sense went free and beauty lay profuse,
I, untouched by one adverse circumstance,
Adopted virtue as my rule of life,   *1705*
Waived all reward, loved but for loving's sake,
And, what my heart taught me, I taught the world,
And have been teaching now two thousand years.
Witness my work—plays that should please, forsooth!
'They might please, they may displease, they shall
          teach,   *1710*
For truth's sake,' so I said, and did, and do.
Five hundred years ere Paul spoke, Felix° heard—
How much of temperance and righteousness,
Judgment to come, did I find reason for,
Corroborate with my strong style that spared   *1715*
No sin, nor swerved the more from branding brow

1701 **Third Poet . . . the Two** Euripides, the third of the great Greek
dramatists, after Aeschylus and Sophocles. 1712 **Paul . . . Felix**
Acts 24.

Because the sinner was called Zeus and God?
How nearly did I guess at that Paul knew?
How closely come, in what I represent
1720 As duty, to his doctrine yet a blank?
And as that limner not untruly limns
Who draws an object round or square, which square
Or round seems to the unassisted eye,
Though Galileo's tube° display the same
1725 Oval or oblong—so, who controverts
I rendered rightly what proves wrongly wrought
Beside Paul's picture? Mine was true for me.
I saw that there are, first and above all,
The hidden forces, blind necessities,
1730 Named Nature, but the thing's self unconceived:
Then follow—how dependent upon these,
We know not, how imposed above ourselves,
We well know—what I name the gods, a power
Various or one: for great and strong and good
1735 Is there, and little, weak and bad there too,
Wisdom and folly: say, these make no God—
What is it else that rules outside man's self?
A fact then—always, to the naked eye—
And so, the one revealment possible
1740 Of what were unimagined else by man.
Therefore, what gods do, man may criticize,
Applaud, condemn—how should he fear the truth?—
But likewise have in awe because of power,
Venerate for the main munificence,
1745 And give the doubtful deed its due excuse
From the acknowledged creature of a day
To the Eternal and Divine. Thus, bold
Yet self-mistrusting, should man bear himself,
Most assured on what now concerns him most—
1750 The law of his own life, the path he prints—
Which law is virtue and not vice, I say—
And least inquisitive where search least skills,
I' the nature we best give the clouds to keep.
What could I paint beyond a scheme like this

1724 **Galileo's tube** telescope.

Out of the fragmentary truths where light   *1755*
Lay fitful in a tenebrific time?
You have the sunrise now, joins truth to truth,
Shoots life and substance into death and void;
Themselves compose the whole we made before:
The forces and necessity grow God—   *1760*
The beings so contrarious that seemed gods,
Prove just His operation manifold
And multiform, translated, as must be,
Into intelligible shape so far
As suits our sense and sets us free to feel.   *1765*
What if I let a child think, childhood-long,
That lightning, I would have him spare his eye,
Is a real arrow shot at naked orb?
The man knows more, but shuts his lids the same:
Lightning's cause comprehends nor man nor child.   *1770*
Why then, my scheme, your better knowledge broke,
Presently readjusts itself, the small
Proportioned largelier, parts and whole named new:
So much, no more two thousand years have done!
Pope, dost thou dare pretend to punish me,   *1775*
For not descrying sunshine at midnight,
Me who crept all-fours, found my way so far—
While thou rewardest teachers of the truth,
Who miss the plain way in the blaze of noon—
Though just a word from that strong style of mine, *1780*
Grasped honestly in hand as guiding-staff,
Had pricked them a sure path across the bog,
That mire of cowardice and slush of lies
Wherein I find them wallow in wide day!"
How should I answer this Euripides?   *1785*
Paul—'tis a legend—answered Seneca,°
But that was in the day-spring; noon is now:
We have got too familiar with the light.
Shall I wish back once more that thrill of dawn?
When the whole truth-touched man burned up, one
      fire?   *1790*
—Assured the trial, fiery, fierce, but fleet,

1786 **Seneca** Roman philosopher.

Would, from his little heap of ashes, lend
Wings to that conflagration of the world
Which Christ awaits ere He makes all things new:
1795 So should the frail become the perfect, rapt
From glory of pain to glory of joy; and so,
Even in the end—the act renouncing earth,
Lands, houses, husbands, wives and children here—
Begin that other act which finds all, lost,
1800 Regained, in this time even, a hundredfold,
And, in the next time, feels the finite love
Blent and embalmed with the eternal life.
So does the sun ghastlily seem to sink
In those north parts, lean all but out of life,
1805 Desist a dread mere breathing-stop, then slow
Reassert day, begin the endless rise.
Was this too easy for our after-stage?
Was such a lighting-up of faith, in life,
Only allowed initiate, set man's step
1810 In the true way by help of the great glow?
A way wherein it is ordained he walk,
Bearing to see the light from heaven still more
And more encroached on by the light of earth,
Tentatives earth puts forth to rival heaven,
1815 Earthly incitements that mankind serve God
For man's sole sake, not God's and therefore man's.
Till at last, who distinguishes the sun
From a mere Druid fire on a far mount?
More praise to him who with his subtle prism
1820 Shall decompose both beams and name the true.
In such sense, who is last proves first indeed
For how could saints and martyrs fail see truth
Streak the night's blackness? Who is faithful now?
Who untwists heaven's white from the yellow flare
O' the world's gross torch, without night's foil that
1825   helped
Produce the Christian act so possible
When in the way stood Nero's cross and stake—
So hard now when the world smiles "Right and wise!
Faith points the politic, the thrifty way,
1830 Will make who plods it in the end returns

Beyond mere fool's-sport and improvidence.
We fools dance through the cornfield of this life,
Pluck ears to left and right and swallow raw,
—Nay, tread, at pleasure, a sheaf underfoot,
To get the better at some poppy-flower—   *1835*
Well aware we shall have so much less wheat
In the eventual harvest: you meantime
Waste not a spike—the richlier will you reap!
What then? There will be always garnered meal
Sufficient for our comfortable loaf,   *1840*
While you enjoy the undiminished sack!"
Is it not this ignoble confidence,
Cowardly hardihood, that dulls and damps,
Makes the old heroism impossible?

Unless . . . what whispers me of times to come?   *1845*
What if it be the mission of that age
My death will usher into life, to shake
This torpor of assurance from our creed,
Reintroduce the doubt discarded, bring
That formidable danger back, we drove   *1850*
Long ago to the distance and the dark?
No wild beast now prowls round the infant camp:
We have built wall and sleep in city safe:
But if some earthquake try the towers that laugh
To think they once saw lions rule outside,   *1855*
And man stand out again, pale, resolute,
Prepared to die—which means, alive at last?
As we broke up that old faith of the world,
Have we, next age, to break up this the new—
Faith, in the thing, grown faith in the report—   *1860*
Whence need to bravely disbelieve report
Through increased faith i' the thing reports belie?
Must we deny—do they, these Molinists,
At peril of their body and their soul—
Recognized truths, obedient to some truth   *1865*
Unrecognized yet, but perceptible?—
Correct the portrait by the living face,
Man's God, by God's God in the mind of man?
Then, for the few that rise to the new height,

1870 The many that must sink to the old depth,
The multitude found fall away! A few,
E'en ere new law speak clear, may keep the old,
Preserve the Christian level, call good good
And evil evil (even though razed and blank
1875 The old titles), helped by custom, habitude,
And all else they mistake for finer sense
O' the fact that reason warrants—as before,
They hope perhaps, fear not impossibly.
At least some one Pompilia left the world
1880 Will say "I know the right place by foot's feel,
I took it and tread firm there; wherefore change?"
But what a multitude will surely fall
Quite through the crumbling truth, late subjacent,
Sink to the next discoverable base,
1885 Rest upon human nature, settle there
On what is firm, the lust and pride of life!
A mass of men, whose very souls even now
Seem to need recreating—so they slink
Worm-like into the mud, light now lays bare—
1890 Whose future we dispose of with shut eyes
And whisper—"They are grafted, barren twigs,
Into the living stock of Christ: may bear
One day, till when they lie deathlike, not dead"—
Those who with all the aid of Christ succumb,
1895 How, without Christ, shall they, unaided, sink?
Whither but to this gulf before my eyes?
Do not we end, the century and I?
The impatient antimasque treads close on kibe
O' the very masque's self it will mock°—on me,
1900 Last lingering personage, the impatient mime
Pushes already—will I block the way?
Will my slow trail of garments ne'er leave space
For pantaloon, sock,° plume and castanet?
Here comes the first experimentalist
1905 In the new order of things—he plays a priest;
Does he take inspiration from the Church,

1898–99 **antimasque . . . mock** grotesque interlude between acts of
a masque. *Kibe* is here used loosely for heel.   1903 **sock** boot worn
by comic actor.

Directly make her rule his law of life?
Not he: his own mere impulse guides the man—
Happily sometimes, since ourselves allow
He has danced, in gaiety of heart, i' the main   *1910*
The right step through the maze we bade him foot.
But if his heart had prompted him break loose
And mar the measure? Why, we must submit,
And thank the chance that brought him safe so far.
Will he repeat the prodigy? Perhaps.   *1915*
Can he teach others how to quit themselves,
Show why this step was right while that were wrong?
How should he? "Ask your hearts as I asked mine,
And get discreetly through the morrice° too;
If your hearts misdirect you—quit the stage,   *1920*
And make amends—be there amends to make!"
Such is, for the Augustin that was once,
This Canon Caponsacchi we see now.
"But my heart answers to another tune,"
Puts in the Abate, second in the suite,   *1925*
"I have my taste too, and tread no such step!
You choose the glorious life, and may, for me!
I like the lowest of life's appetites—
So you judge—but the very truth of joy
To my own apprehension which decides.   *1930*
Call me knave and you get yourself called fool!
I live for greed, ambition, lust, revenge;
Attain these ends by force, guile: hypocrite,
Today, perchance tomorrow recognized
The rational man, the type of common sense."   *1935*
There's Loyola° adapted to our time!
Under such guidance Guido plays his part,
He also influencing in the due turn
These last clods where I track intelligence
By any glimmer, these four at his beck   *1940*
Ready to murder any, and, at their own,
As ready to murder him—such make the world!
And, first effect of the new cause of things,
There they lie also duly—the old pair

1919 **morrice** morris dance. 1936 **Loyola** St. Ignatius Loyola,
founder of the Society of Jesus.

1945 Of the weak head and not so wicked heart,
With the one Christian mother, wife and girl,
—Which three gifts seem to make an angel up—
The world's first foot o' the dance is on their heads!
Still, I stand here, not off the stage though close
1950 On the exit: and my last act, as my first,
I owe the scene, and Him who armed me thus
With Paul's sword as with Peter's key. I smite
With my whole strength once more, ere end my part,
Ending, so far as man may, this offense.
1955 And when I raise my arm, who plucks my sleeve?
Who stops me in the righteous function—foe
Or friend? Oh, still as ever, friends are they
Who, in the interest of outraged truth
Deprecate such rough handling of a lie!
1960 The facts being proved and incontestable,
What is the last word I must listen to?
Perchance—"Spare yet a term this barren stock
We pray thee dig about and dung and dress
Till he repent and bring forth fruit even yet!"
1965 Perchance—"So poor and swift a punishment
Shall throw him out of life with all that sin:
Let mercy rather pile up pain on pain
Till the flesh expiate what the soul pays else!"
Nowise! Remonstrants on each side commence
1970 Instructing, there's a new tribunal now
Higher than God's—the educated man's!
Nice sense of honor in the human breast
Supersedes here the old coarse oracle—
Confirming none the less a point or so
1975 Wherein blind predecessors worked aright
By rule of thumb: as when Christ said—when, where?
Enough, I find it pleaded in a place—
"All other wrongs done, patiently I take:
But touch my honor and the case is changed!
1980 I feel the due resentment—*nemini
Honorem trado°* is my quick retort."

1980–81 **nemini . . . trado** I will not give my honor to another.
The Pope is echoing the misuse of a biblical text by the defense
attorney.

Right of Him, just as if pronounced today!
Still, should the old authority be mute
Or doubtful or in speaking clash with new,
The younger takes permission to decide.   1985
At last we have the instinct of the world
Ruling its household without tutelage:
And while the two laws, human and divine,
Have busied finger with this tangled case,
In pushes the brisk junior, cuts the knot,   1990
Pronounces for acquittal. How it trips
Silverly o'er the tongue! "Remit the death!
Forgive . . . well, in the old way, if thou please,
Decency and the relics of routine
Respected—let the Count go free as air!   1995
Since he may plead a priest's immunity—
The minor orders help enough for that,
With Farinacci's° license—who decides
That the mere implication of such man,
So privileged, in any cause, before   2000
Whatever Court except the Spiritual,
Straight quashes law-procedure—quash it, then!
Remains a pretty loophole of escape
Moreover, that, beside the patent fact
O' the law's allowance, there's involved the weal   2005
O' the Popedom: a son's privilege at stake,
Thou wilt pretend the Church's interest,
Ignore all finer reasons to forgive!
But herein lies the crowning cogency—
(Let thy friends teach thee while thou tellest beads)   2010
That in this case the spirit of culture speaks,
Civilization is imperative.
To her shall we remand all delicate points
Henceforth, nor take irregular advice
O' the sly, as heretofore: she used to hint   2015
Remonstrances, when law was out of sorts
Because a saucy tongue was put to rest,
An eye that roved was cured of arrogance:
But why be forced to mumble under breath

1998 **Farinacci** legal authority.

2020 What soon shall be acknowledged as plain fact,
Outspoken, say, in thy successor's time?
Methinks we see the golden age return!
Civilization and the Emperor
Succeed to Christianity and Pope.
2025 One Emperor then, as one Pope now: meanwhile,
Anticipate a little! We tell thee 'Take
Guido's life, sapped society shall crash,
Whereof the main prop was, is, and shall be
—Supremacy of husband over wife!'
2030 Does the man rule i' the house, and may his mate
Because of any plea dispute the same?
Oh, pleas of all sorts shall abound, be sure,
One but allowed validity—for, harsh
And savage, for, inept and silly-sooth,
2035 For, this and that, will the ingenious sex
Demonstrate the best master e'er graced slave:
And there's but one short way to end the coil—
Acknowledge right and reason steadily
I' the man and master: then the wife submits
2040 To plain truth broadly stated. Does the time
Advise we shift—a pillar? nay, a stake
Out of its place i' the social tenement?
One touch may send a shudder through the heap
And bring it toppling on our children's heads!
2045 Moreover, if ours breed a qualm in thee,
Give thine own better feeling play for once!
Thou, whose own life winks o'er the socket-edge,
Wouldst thou it went out in such ugly snuff
As dooming sons dead, e'en though justice prompt?
2050 Why, on a certain feast, Barabbas'° self
Was set free, not to cloud the general cheer:
Neither shalt thou pollute thy Sabbath close!
Mercy is safe and graceful. How one hears
The howl begin, scarce the three little taps
2055 O' the silver mallet silent on thy brow°—
'His last act was to sacrifice a Count
And thereby screen a scandal of the Church!

2050 **Barabbas** Matthew 27.   2054–55 **three little taps . . . on thy
brow** ceremony ascertaining that the Pope is dead.

Guido condemned, the Canon justified
Of course—delinquents of his cloth go free!'
And so the Luthers chuckle, Calvins scowl,   2060
So thy hand helps Molinos to the chair
Whence he may hold forth till doom's day on just
These *petit-maître*° priestlings—in thè choir
Sanctus et Benedictus,° with a brush
Of soft guitar-strings that obey the thumb,   2065
Touched by the bedside, for accompaniment!
Does this give umbrage to a husband? Death
To the fool, and to the priest impunity!
But no impunity to any friend
So simply over-loyal as these four   2070
Who made religion of their patron's cause,
Believed in him and did his bidding straight,
Asked not one question but laid down the lives
This Pope took—all four lives together make
Just his own length of days—so, dead they lie,   2075
As these were times when loyalty's a drug,
And zeal in a subordinate too cheap
And common to be saved when we spend life!
Come, 'tis too much good breath we waste in words:
The pardon, Holy Father! Spare grimace,   2080
Shrugs and reluctance! Are not we the world,
Art not thou Priam? Let soft culture plead
Hecuba-like, '*non tali*' (Virgil serves)
'*Auxilio*'° and the rest! Enough, it works!
The Pope relaxes, and the Prince is loth,   2085
The father's bowels yearn, the man's will bends,
Reply is apt. Our tears on tremble, hearts
Big with a benediction, wait the word
Shall circulate through the city in a trice,
Set every window flaring, give each man   2090
O' the mob his torch to wave for gratitude.
Pronounce then, for our breath and patience fail!"

2063 **petit-maître** fop, dandy. 2064 **Sanctus et Benedictus** holy and
blessed. Sanctus and Benedictus are parts of the Latin Mass.
2083–84 '**non tali . . . Auxilio**' as Troy is falling, Hecuba tells her
aged husband, King Priam, who is arming himself, that the situation
does not call for such aid as his. *Aeneid* II. 521–22.

I will, Sirs: but a voice other than yours
Quickens my spirit. *"Quis pro Domino?"*
2095 "Who is upon the Lord's side?" asked the Count.
I, who write—
                "On receipt of this command,
Acquaint Count Guido and his fellows four
They die tomorrow: could it be tonight,
The better, but the work to do, takes time.
2100 Set with all diligence a scaffold up,
Not in the customary place, by Bridge
Saint Angelo, where die the common sort;
But since the man is noble, and his peers
By predilection haunt the People's Square,
2105 There let him be beheaded in the midst,
And his companions hanged on either side:
So shall the quality see, fear and learn.
All which work takes time: till tomorrow, then,
Let there be prayer incessant for the five!"

2110 For the main criminal I have no hope
Except in such a suddenness of fate.
I stood at Naples once, a night so dark
I could have scarce conjectured there was earth
Anywhere, sky or sea or world at all:
2115 But the night's black was burst through by a blaze—
Thunder struck blow on blow, earth groaned and
          bore,
Through her whole length of mountain visible:
There lay the city thick and plain with spires,
And, like a ghost disshrouded, white the sea.
2120 So may the truth be flashed out by one blow,
And Guido see, one instant, and be saved.
Else I avert my face, nor follow him
Into that sad obscure sequestered state
Where God unmakes but to remake the soul
2125 He else made first in vain; which must not be.
Enough, for I may die this very night
And how should I dare die, this man let live?

Carry this forthwith to the Governor!

GUIDO

YOU are the Cardinal Acciaiuoli, and you,
Abate Panciatichi—two good Tuscan names:
Acciaiuoli—ah, your ancestor it was
Built the huge battlemented convent-block
Over the little forky flashing Greve   5
That takes the quick turn at the foot o' the hill
Just as one first sees Florence: oh those days!
'Tis Ema, though, the other rivulet,
The one-arched brown brick bridge yawns over—yes,
Gallop and go five minutes, and you gain   10
The Roman Gate from where the Ema's bridged:
Kingfishers fly there: how I see the bend
O'erturreted by Certosa which he built,
That Seneschal (we styled him) of your House!
I do adjure you, help me, Sirs! My blood   15
Comes from as far a source: ought it to end
This way, by leakage through their scaffold-planks
Into Rome's sink where her red refuse runs?
Sirs, I beseech you by blood-sympathy,
If there be any vile experiment   20
In the air—if this your visit simply prove,
When all's done, just a well-intentioned trick
That tries for truth truer than truth itself,
By startling up a man, ere break of day,
To tell him he must die at sunset—pshaw!   25
That man's a Franceschini; feel his pulse,
Laugh at your folly, and let's all go sleep!
You have my last word—innocent am I
As Innocent my Pope and murderer,
Innocent as a babe, as Mary's own,   30
As Mary's self—I said, say and repeat—

And why, then, should I die twelve hours hence? I—
Whom, not twelve hours ago, the jailer bade
Turn to my straw-truss, settle and sleep sound
35 That I might wake the sooner, promptlier pay
His due of meat-and-drink-indulgence, cross
His palm with fee of the good-hand, beside,
As gallants use who go at large again!
For why? All honest Rome approved my part;
40 Whoever owned wife, sister, daughter—nay,
Mistress—had any shadow of any right
That looks like right, and, all the more resolved,
Held it with tooth and nail—these manly men
Approved! I being for Rome, Rome was for me.
45 Then, there's the point reserved, the subterfuge
My lawyers held by, kept for last resource,
Firm should all else—the impossible fancy!—fail,
And sneaking burgess-spirit° win the day.
The knaves! One plea at least would hold—they
laughed— ·
50 One grappling-iron scratch the bottom-rock
Even should the middle mud let anchor go!
I hooked my cause on to the Clergy's—plea
Which, even if law tipped off my hat and plume,
Revealed my priestly tonsure, saved me so.
55 The Pope moreover, this old Innocent,
Being so meek and mild and merciful,
So fond o' the poor and so fatigued of earth,
So . . . fifty thousand devils in deepest hell!
Why must he cure us of our strange conceit
60 Of the angel in man's likeness, that we loved
And looked should help us at a pinch? He help?
He pardon? Here's his mind and message—death!
Thank the good Pope! Now, is he good in this,
Never mind, Christian—no such stuff's extant—
65 But will my death do credit to his reign,
Show he both lived and let live, so was good?
Cannot I live if he but like? "The law!"
Why, just the law gives him the very chance,

48 **burgess-spirit** middle class point of view.

The precise leave to let my life alone,
Which the archangelic soul of him (he says)   70
Yearns after! Here they drop it in his palm,
My lawyers, capital o' the cursed kind—
Drop life to take and hold and keep: but no!
He sighs, shakes head, refuses to shut hand,
Motions away the gift they bid him grasp,   75
And of the coyness comes—that off I run
And down I go, he best knows whither! mind,
He knows, who sets me rolling all the same!
Disinterested Vicar of our Lord,
This way he abrogates and disallows,   80
Nullifies and ignores—reverts in fine
To the good and right, in detriment of me!
Talk away! Will you have the naked truth?
He's sick of his life's supper—swallowed lies:
So, hobbling bedward, needs must ease his maw   85
Just where I sit o' the doorsill. Sir Abate,
Can you do nothing? Friends, we used to frisk:
What of this sudden slash in a friend's face,
This cut across our good companionship
That showed its front so gay when both were young?   90
Were not we put into a beaten path,
Bid pace the world, we nobles born and bred,
We body of friends with each his scutcheon full
Of old achievement and impunity—
Taking the laugh of morn and Sol's salute   95
As forth we fared, pricked on to breathe our steeds
And take equestrian sport over the green
Under the blue, across the crop—what care?
If we went prancing up hill and down dale,
In and out of the level and the straight,   100
By the bit of pleasant byway, where was harm?
Still Sol salutes me and the morning laughs:
I see my grandsire's hoof-prints—point the spot
Where he drew rein, slipped saddle, and stabbed
      knave
For daring throw gibe—much less, stone—from pale: 105
Then back, and on, and up with the cavalcade.
Just so wend we, now canter, now converse,

Till, 'mid the jauncing° pride and jaunty port,
Something of a sudden jerks at somebody—
110 A dagger is out, a flashing cut and thrust,
Because I play some prank my grandsire played,
And here I sprawl: where is the company? Gone!
A trot and a trample! only I lie trapped,
Writhe in a certain novel springe just set
By the good old Pope: I'm first prize. Warn me?
115   Why?
Apprise me that the law o' the game is changed?
Enough that I'm a warning, as I writhe,
To all and each my fellows of the file,
And make law plain henceforward past mistake,
120 "For such a prank, death is the penalty!"
Pope the Five Hundredth (what do I know or care?)
Deputes your Eminency and Abateship
To announce that, twelve hours from this time, he
    needs
I just essay upon my body and soul
125 The virtue of his brand-new engine, prove
Represser of the pranksome! I'm the first!
Thanks. Do you know what teeth you mean to try
The sharpness of, on this soft neck and throat?
I know it—I have seen and hate it—ay,
130 As you shall, while I tell you! Let me talk,
Or leave me, at your pleasure! talk I must:
What is your visit but my lure to talk?
Nay, you have something to disclose?—a smile,
At end of the forced sternness, means to mock
135 The heartbeats here? I call your two hearts stone!
Is your charge to stay with me till I die?
Be tacit as your bench, then! Use your ears,
I use my tongue: how glibly yours will run
At pleasant supper-time . . . God's curse! . . . tonight
140 When all the guests jump up, begin so brisk
"Welcome, his Eminence who shrived the wretch!
Now we shall have the Abate's story!"

108 **jauncing** prancing

Life!

How I could spill this overplus of mine
Among those hoar-haired, shrunk-shanked odds and
    ends
Of body and soul old age is chewing dry!   *145*
Those windlestraws that stare while purblind death
Mows here, mows there, makes hay of juicy me,
And misses just the bunch of withered weed
Would brighten hell and streak its smoke with flame!
How the life I could shed yet never shrink,   *150*
Would drench their stalks with sap like grass in May!
Is it not terrible, I entreat you, Sirs?—
With manifold and plenitudinous life,
Prompt at death's menace to give blow for threat,
Answer his "Be thou not!" by "Thus I am!"—   *155*
Terrible so to be alive yet die?

How I live, how I see! so—how I speak!
Lucidity of soul unlocks the lips:
I never had the words at will before.
How I see all my folly at a glance!   *160*
"A man requires a woman and a wife":
There was my folly; I believed the saw.
I knew that just myself concerned myself,
Yet needs must look for what I seemed to lack,
In a woman—why, the woman's in the man!   *165*
Fools we are, how we learn things when too late!
Overmuch life turns round my woman-side:
The male and female in me, mixed before,
Settle of a sudden: I'm my wife outright
In this unmanly appetite for truth,   *170*
This careless courage as to consequence,
This instantaneous sight through things and through,
This voluble rhetoric, if you please—'tis she!
Here you have that Pompilia whom I slew,
Also the folly for which I slew her!

Fool!   *175*

And, fool-like, what is it I wander from?
What did I say of your sharp iron tooth?

Ah—that I know the hateful thing! this way.
I chanced to stroll forth, many a good year gone,
180 One warm spring eve in Rome, and unaware
Looking, mayhap, to count what stars were out,
Came on your fine ax in a frame, that falls
And so cuts off a man's head underneath,
Mannaia°—thus we made acquaintance first:
185 Out of the way, in a by-part o' the town,
At the Mouth-of-Truth° o' the riverside, you know:
One goes by the Capitol: and wherefore coy,
Retiring out of crowded noisy Rome?
Because a very little time ago
190 It had done service, chopped off head from trunk
Belonging to a fellow whose poor house
The thing must make a point to stand before—
Felice Whatsoever-was-the-name
Who stabled buffaloes and so gained bread,
195 (Our clowns unyoke them in the ground hard by)
And, after use of much improper speech,
Had struck at Duke Some-title-or-other's face,
Because he kidnaped, carried away and kept
Felice's sister who would sit and sing
200 I' the filthy doorway while she plaited fringe
To deck the brutes with—on their gear it goes—
The good girl with the velvet in her voice.
So did the Duke, so did Felice, so
Did Justice, intervening with her ax.
205 There the man-mutilating engine stood
At ease, both gay and grim, like a Swiss guard
Off duty—purified itself as well,
Getting dry, sweet and proper for next week—
And doing incidental good, 'twas hoped,
210 To the rough lesson-lacking populace
Who now and then, forsooth, must right their wrongs!
There stood the twelve-foot-square of scaffold, railed
Considerately round to elbow-height,
For fear an officer should tumble thence

184 **Mannaia** guillotine. 186 **Mouth-of-Truth.** marble mask of a
Triton with an open mouth said to bite off the hands of perjurers.

And sprain his ankle and be lame a month   215
Through starting when the ax fell and head too!
Railed likewise were the steps whereby 'twas reached.
All of it painted red: red, in the midst,
Ran up two narrow tall beams barred across,
Since from the summit, some twelve feet to reach,   220
The iron plate with the sharp shearing edge
Had slammed, jerked, shot, slid—I shall soon find
    which!—
And so lay quiet, fast in its fit place,
The wooden half-moon collar, now eclipsed
By the blade which blocked its curvature: apart,   225
The other half—the under half-moon board
Which, helped by this, completes a neck's embrace—
Joined to a sort of desk that wheels aside
Out of the way when done with—down you kneel,
In you're pushed, over you the other drops,   230
Tight you're clipped, whiz, there's the blade cleaves
    its best,
Out trundles body, down flops head on floor,
And where's your soul gone? That, too, I shall find!
This kneeling-place was red, red, never fear!
But only slimy-like with paint, not blood,   235
For why? a decent pitcher stood at hand,
A broad dish to hold sawdust, and a broom
By some unnamed utensil—scraper-rake—
Each with a conscious air of duty done.
Underneath, loungers—boys and some few men—   240
Discoursed this platter, named the other tool,
Just as, when grooms tie up and dress a steed,
Boys lounge and look on, and elucubrate
What the round brush is used for, what the square—
So was explained—to me the skill-less then—   245
The manner of the grooming for next world
Undergone by Felice What's-his-name.
There's no such lovely month in Rome as May—
May's crescent is no half-moon of red plank,
And came now tilting o'er the wave i' the west,   250
One greenish-golden sea, right 'twixt those bars
Of the engine—I began acquaintance with,

Understood, hated, hurried from before,
To have it out of sight and cleanse my soul!
255 Here it is all again, conserved for use:
Twelve hours hence, I may know more, not hate
    worse.

That young May-moon-month! Devils of the deep!
Was not a Pope then Pope as much as now?
Used not he chirrup o'er the Merry Tales,
260 Chuckle—his nephew so exact the wag
To play a jealous cullion° such a trick
As wins the wife i' the pleasant story! Well?
Why do things change? Wherefore is Rome un-
    Romed?
I tell you, ere Felice's corpse was cold,
265 The Duke, that night, threw wide his palace-doors,
Received the compliments o' the quality
For justice done him—bowed and smirked his best,
And in return passed round a pretty thing,
A portrait of Felice's sister's self,
270 Florid old rogue Albano's masterpiece,
As—better than virginity in rags—
Bouncing Europa on the back o' the bull°:
They laughed and took their road the safelier home.
Ah, but times change, there's quite another Pope,
275 I do the Duke's deed, take Felice's place,
And, being no Felice, lout and clout,
Stomach but ill the phrase "I lose my head!"
How euphemistic! Lose what? Lose your ring.
Your snuffbox, tablets, kerchief!—but, your head?
280 I learned the process at an early age;
'Twas useful knowledge, in those same old days,
To know the way a head is set on neck.
My fencing-master urged "Would you excel?
Rest not content with mere bold give-and-guard,
285 Nor pink the antagonist somehow-anyhow!
See me dissect a little, and know your game!
Only anatomy makes a thrust the thing."

261 **cullion** rascal.   272 **Europa . . . bull** Zeus took the form of a
bull to carry off the maiden Europa.

Oh Cardinal, those lithe live necks of ours!
Here go the vertebrae, here's *Atlas,* here
Axis, and here the symphyses stop short,   290
So wisely and well—as, o'er a corpse, we cant—
And here's the silver cord which . . . what's our word?
Depends from the gold bowl,° which loosed (not
      "lost")
Lets us from Heaven to hell—one chop, we're loose!
"And not much pain i' the process," quoth a sage: 295
Who told him? Not Felice's ghost, I think!
Such "losing" is scarce Mother Nature's mode.
She fain would have cord ease itself away,
Worn to a thread by threescore years and ten,
Snap while we slumber: that seems bearable.   300
I'm told one clot of blood extravasate
Ends one as certainly as Roland's sword—
One drop of lymph suffused proves Oliver's° mace—
Intruding, either of the pleasant pair,
On the arachnoid tunic of my brain.   305
That's Nature's way of loosing cord!—but Art,
How of Art's process with the engine here,
When bowl and cord alike are crushed across,
Bored between, bruised through? Why, if Fagon's self,
The French Court's pride, that famed practitioner,   310
Would pass his cold pale lightning of a knife,
Pistoja-ware, adroit 'twixt joint and joint,
With just a "See how facile, gentlefolk!"—
The thing were not so bad to bear! Brute force
Cuts as he comes, breaks in, breaks on, breaks out   315
O' the hard and soft of you: is that the same?
A lithe snake thrids the hedge, makes throb no leaf:
A heavy ox sets chest to brier and branch,
Bursts somehow through, and leaves one hideous hole
Behind him!

      And why, why must this needs be?   320
Oh, if men were but good! They are not good,
Nowise like Peter: people called him rough,

292–93 **silver cord . . . bowl** Ecclesiastes 12:6.   302–3 **Roland . . .**
Oliver heroes of romance.

But if, as I left Rome, I spoke the Saint,
—"*Petrus, quo vadis?*"°—doubtless, I should hear,
325 "To free the prisoner and forgive his fault!
I plucked the absolute dead from God's own bar,
And raised up Dorcas°—why not rescue thee?"
What would cost one such nullifying word?
If Innocent succeeds to Peter's place,
330 Let him think Peter's thought, speak Peter's speech!
I say, he is bound to it: friends, how say you?
Concede I be all one bloodguiltiness
And mystery of murder in the flesh,
Why should that fact keep the Pope's mouth shut
      fast?
335 He execrates my crime—good!—sees hell yawn
One inch from the red plank's end which I press—
Nothing is better! What's the consequence?
How should a Pope proceed that knows his cue?
Why, leave me linger out my minute here,
Since close on death comes judgment and comes
340   doom,
Not crib at dawn its pittance from a sheep
Destined ere dewfall to be butcher's-meat!
Think, Sirs, if I have done you any harm,
And you require the natural revenge,
345 Suppose, and so intend to poison me,
—Just as you take and slip into my draft
The paperful of powder that clears scores,
You notice on my brow a certain blue:
How you both overset the wine at once!
350 How you both smile! "Our enemy has the plague!
Twelve hours hence he'll be scraping his bones bare
Of that intolerable flesh, and die,
Frenzied with pain: no need for poison here!
Step aside and enjoy the spectacle!"
355 Tender for souls are you, Pope Innocent!

---

324 **"Petrus, quo vadis?"** When Peter was fleeing from Rome he met
Jesus and asked him "Domine, quo vadis?" (Where are you going,
Lord?). When Jesus replied that he had come to be crucified again,
Peter returned to the city and was martyred. 327 **Dorcas** Acts
9:36–41.

Christ's maxim is—one soul outweighs the world:
Respite me, save a soul, then, curse the world!
"No," venerable sire, I hear you smirk,
"No: for Christ's gospel changes names, not things,
Renews the obsolete, does nothing more! 360
Our fire-new gospel is re-tinkered law,
Our mercy, justice—Jove's rechristened God—
Nay, whereas, in the popular conceit,
'Tis pity that old harsh Law somehow limps,
Lingers on earth, although Law's day be done, 365
Else would benignant Gospel interpose,
Not furtively as now, but bold and frank
O'erflutter us with healing in her wings,
Law being harshness, Gospel only love—
We tell the people, on the contrary, 370
Gospel takes up the rod which Law lets fall;
Mercy is vigilant when justice sleeps!
Does Law permit a taste of Gospel-grace?
The secular arm allow the spiritual power
To act for once?—no compliment so fine 375
As that our Gospel handsomely turn harsh,
Thrust victim back on Law the nice and coy!"
Yes, you do say so, else you would forgive
Me whom Law does not touch but tosses you!
Don't think to put on the professional face! 380
You know what I know: casuists as you are,
Each nerve must creep, each hair start, sting and
    stand,
At such illogical inconsequence!
Dear my friends, do but see! A murder's tried,
There are two parties to the cause: I'm one, 385
—Defend myself, as somebody must do:
I have the best o' the battle: that's a fact,
Simple fact—fancies find no place just now.
What though half Rome condemned me? Half ap-
    proved:
And, none disputes, the luck is mine at last, 390
All Rome, i' the main, acquitting me: whereon,
What has the Pope to ask but "How finds Law?"
"I find," replies Law, "I have erred this while:

Guilty or guiltless, Guido proves a priest,
395 No layman: he is therefore yours, not mine:
I bound him: loose him, you whose will is Christ's!"
And now what does this Vicar of our Lord,
Shepherd o' the flock—one of whose charge bleats
     sore
For crook's help from the quag wherein it drowns?
400 Law suffers him employ the crumpled end:
His pleasure is to turn staff, use the point,
And thrust the shuddering sheep, he calls a wolf,
Back and back, down and down to where hell gapes!
"Guiltless," cries Law—"Guilty" corrects the Pope!
"Guilty," for the whim's sake! "Guilty," he somehow
405   thinks,
And anyhow says: 'tis truth; he dares not lie!

Others should do the lying. That's the cause
Brings you both here: I ought in decency
Confess to you that I deserve my fate,
410 Am guilty, as the Pope thinks—ay, to the end,
Keep up the jest, lie on, lie ever, lie
I' the latest gasp of me! What reason, Sirs?
Because tomorrow will succeed today
For you, though not for me: and if I stick
415 Still to the truth, declare with my last breath,
I die an innocent and murdered man—
Why, there's the tongue of Rome will wag apace
This time tomorrow: don't I hear the talk!
"So, to the last he proved impenitent?
420 Pagans have said as much of martyred saints!
Law demurred, washed her hands of the whole case.
Prince Somebody said this, Duke Something, that,
Doubtless the man's dead, dead enough, don't fear!
But, hang it, what if there have been a spice,
425 A touch of . . . eh? You see, the Pope's so old,
Some of us add, obtuse: age never slips
The chance of shoving youth to face death first!"
And so on. Therefore to suppress such talk
You two come here, entreat I tell you lies,
430 And end, the edifying way. I end,

Telling the truth! Your self-styled shepherd thieves!
A thief—and how thieves hate the wolves we know:
Damage to theft, damage to thrift, all's one!
The red hand is sworn foe of the black jaw.
That's only natural, that's right enough: 435
But why the wolf should compliment the thief
With shepherd's title, bark out life in thanks,
And, spiteless, lick the prong that spits him—eh,
Cardinal? My Abate, scarcely thus!
There, let my sheepskin-garb, a curse on't, go—   440
Leave my teeth free if I must show my shag!
Repent? What good shall follow? If I pass
Twelve hours repenting, will that fact hold fast
The thirteenth at the horrid dozen's end?
If I fall forthwith at your feet, gnash, tear,   445
Foam, rave, to give your story the due grace,
Will that assist the engine halfway back
Into its hiding-house?—boards, shaking now,
Bone against bone, like some old skeleton bat
That wants, at winter's end, to wake and prey!   450
Will howling put the specter back to sleep?
Ah, but I misconceive your object, Sirs!
Since I want new life like the creature—life,
Being done with here, begins i' the world away:
I shall next have "Come, mortals, and be judged!"   455
There's but a minute betwixt this and then:
So, quick, be sorry since it saves my soul!
Sirs, truth shall save it, since no lies assist!
Hear the truth, you, whatever you style yourselves,
Civilization and society!   460
Come, one good grapple, I with all the world!
Dying in cold blood is the desperate thing;
The angry heart explodes, bears off in blaze
The indignant soul, and I'm combustion-ripe.
Why, you intend to do your worst with me!   465
That's in your eyes! You dare no more than death,
And mean no less. I must make up my mind.
So Pietro—when I chased him here and there,
Morsel by morsel cut away the life
I loathed—cried for just respite to confess   470

And save his soul: much respite did I grant!
Why grant me respite who deserve my doom?
Me—who engaged to play a prize,° fight you,
Knowing your arms, and foil you, trick for trick,
475 At rapier-fence, your match and, maybe, more.
I knew that if I chose sin certain sins,
Solace my lusts out of the regular way
Prescribed me, I should find you in the path,
Have to try skill with a redoubted foe;
480 You would lunge, I would parry, and make end.
At last, occasion of a murder comes:
We cross blades, I, for all my brag, break guard,
And in goes the cold iron at my breast,
Out at my back, and end is made of me.
485 You stand confessed the adroiter swordsman—ay,
But on your triumph you increase, it seems,
Want more of me than lying flat on face:
I ought to raise my ruined head, allege
Not simply I pushed worse blade o' the pair,
490 But my antagonist dispensed with steel!
There was no passage of arms, you looked me low,
With brow and eye abolished cut and thrust
Nor used the vulgar weapon! This chance scratch,
This incidental hurt, this sort of hole
495 I' the heart of me? I stumbled, got it so!
Fell on my own sword as a bungler may!
Yourself proscribe such heathen tools, and trust
To the naked virtue: it was virtue stood
Unarmed and awed me—on my brow there burned
500 Crime out so plainly intolerably red,
That I was fain to cry—"Down to the dust
With me, and bury there brow, brand and all!"
Law had essayed the adventure—but what's Law?
Morality exposed the Gorgon shield!°
505 Morality and Religion conquer me.
If Law sufficed would you come here, entreat
I supplement law, and confess forsooth?

473 **play a prize** play and win.   504 **Gorgon shield** Athene bore on
her shield the head of the Gorgon, whose glance turned the beholder
to stone.

Did not the trial show things plain enough?
"Ah, but a word of the man's very self
Would somehow put the keystone in its place   510
And crown the arch!" Then take the word you want!

I say that, long ago, when things began,
All the world made agreement, such and such
Were pleasure-giving profit-bearing acts,
But henceforth extralegal, nor to be: 515
You must not kill the man whose death would please
And profit you, unless his life stop yours
Plainly, and need so be put aside:
Get the thing by a public course, by law,
Only no private bloodshed as of old!   520
All of us, for the good of everyone,
Renounced such license and conformed to law:
Who breaks law, breaks pact therefore, helps himself
To pleasure and profit over and above the due,
And must pay forfeit—pain beyond his share: 525
For, pleasure being the sole good in the world,
Anyone's pleasure turns to someone's pain,
So, law must watch for everyone—say we,
Who call things wicked that give too much joy,
And nickname mere reprisal, envy makes,
Punishment: quite right! thus the world goes round. 530
I, being well aware such pact there was,
I, in my time who found advantage come
Of law's observance and crime's penalty—
Who, but for wholesome fear law bred in friends,   535
Had doubtless given example long ago,
Furnished forth some friend's pleasure with my pain,
And, by my death, pieced out his scanty life—
I could not, for that foolish life of me,
Help risking law's infringement—I broke bond,   540
And needs must pay price—wherefore, here's my
     head,
Flung with a flourish! But, repentance too?
But pure and simple sorrow for law's breach
Rather than blunderer's-ineptitude?
Cardinal, no! Abate, scarcely thus!   545

'Tis the fault, not that I dared try a fall
With Law and straightway am found undermost,
But that I failed to see, above man's law,
God's precept you, the Christians, recognize?
550 Colly my cow! Don't fidget, Cardinal!
Abate, cross your breast and count your beads
And exorcize the devil, for here he stands
And stiffens in the bristly nape of neck,
Daring you drive him hence! You, Christians both?
555 I say, if ever was such faith at all
Born in the world, by your community
Suffered to live its little tick of time,
'Tis dead of age, now, ludicrously dead;
Honor its ashes, if you be discreet,
560 In epitaph only! For, concede its death,
Allow extinction, you may boast unchecked
What feats the thing did in a crazy land
At a fabulous epoch—treat your faith, that way,
Just as you treat your relics: "Here's a shred
565 Of saintly flesh, a scrap of blessed bone,
Raised King Cophetua, who was dead, to life
In Mesopotamy twelve centuries since,
Such was its virtue!"—twangs the Sacristan,
Holding the shrine-box up, with hands like feet
570 Because of gout in every finger joint:
Does he bethink him to reduce one knob,
Allay one twinge by touching what he vaunts?
I think he half uncrooks fist to catch fee,
But, for the grace, the quality of cure—
575 Cophetua was the man put that to proof!
Not otherwise, your faith is shrined and shown
And shamed at once: you banter while you bow!
Do you dispute this? Come, a monster-laugh,
A madman's laugh, allowed his Carnival
580 Later ten days than when all Rome, but he,
Laughed at the candle-contest:° mine's alight,
'Tis just it sputter till the puff o' the Pope
End it tomorrow and the world turn ash.

581 **candle-contest** game of blowing out each others' candles on the last night of Carnival.

Come, thus I wave a wand and bring to pass
In a moment, in the twinkle of an eye,   *585*
What but that—feigning everywhere grows fact,
Professors turn possessors, realize
The faith they play with as a fancy now,
And bid it operate, have full effect
On every circumstance of life, today,   *590*
In Rome—faith's flow set free at fountainhead!
Now, you'll own, at this present, when I speak,
Before I work the wonder, there's no man
Woman or child in Rome, faith's fountainhead,
But might, if each were minded, realize   *595*
Conversely unbelief, faith's opposite—
Set it to work on life unflinchingly,
Yet give no symptom of an outward change:
Why should things change because men disbelieve
What's incompatible, in the whited tomb,   *600*
With bones and rottenness one inch below?
What saintly act is done in Rome today
But might be prompted by the devil—"is"
I say not—"has been, and again may be—"
I do say, full i' the face o' the crucifix   *605*
You try to stop my mouth with! Off with it!
Look in your own heart, if your soul have eyes!
You shall see reason why, though faith were fled,
Unbelief still might work the wires and move
Man, the machine, to play a faithful part.   *610*
Preside your college, Cardinal, in your cape,
Or—having got above his head, grown Pope—
Abate, gird your loins and wash my feet!°
Do you suppose I am at loss at all
Why you crook, why you cringe, why fast or feast? *615*
Praise, blame, sit, stand, lie or go!—all of it,
In each of you, purest unbelief may prompt,
And wit explain to who has eyes to see.
But, lo, I wave wand, made the false the true!
Here's Rome believes in Christianity!   *620*
What an explosion, how the fragments fly

613 **gird . . . feet** John 13:4–14.

Of what was surface, mask and make-believe!
Begin now—look at this Pope's-halberdier
In wasp-like black and yellow foolery!°
625 He, doing duty at the corridor,
Wakes from a muse and stands convinced of sin!
Down he flings halbert, leaps the passage-length,
Pushes into the presence, pantingly
Submits the extreme peril of the case
630 To the Pope's self—whom in the world beside?—
And the Pope breaks talk with ambassador,
Bids aside bishop, wills the whole world wait
Till he secure that prize, outweighs the world,
A soul, relieve the sentry of his qualm!
635 His Altitude the Referendary—
Robed right, and ready for the usher's word
To pay devoir—is, of all times, just then
'Ware of a masterstroke of argument
Will cut the spinal cord . . . ugh, ugh! . . . I mean,
640 Paralyse Molinism for evermore!
Straight he leaves lobby, trundles, two and two,
Down steps to reach home, write, if but a word
Shall end the impudence: he leaves who likes
Go pacify the Pope: there's Christ to serve!
645 How otherwise would men display their zeal?
If the same sentry had the least surmise
A powder-barrel 'neath the pavement lay
In neighborhood with what might prove a match,
Meant to blow sky-high Pope and presence both—
650 Would he not break through courtiers, rank and file,
Bundle up, bear off and save body so,
The Pope, no matter for his priceless soul?
There's no fool's-freak here, naught to soundly
    swinge,
Only a man in earnest, you'll so praise
655 And pay and prate about, that earth shall ring!
Had thought possessed the Referendary
His jewel-case at home was left ajar,
What would be wrong in running, robes awry,

623–24 **look . . . foolery** the Swiss Guard, whose costume was designed by Michelangelo.

To be beforehand with the pilferer?
What talk then of indecent haste? Which means,   *660*
That both these, each in his degree, would do
Just that—for a comparative nothing's sake,
And thereby gain approval and reward—
Which, done for what Christ says is worth the world,
Procures the doer curses, cuffs and kicks.   *665*
I call such difference 'twixt act and act,
Sheer lunacy unless your truth on lip
Be recognized a lie in heart of you!
How do you all act, promptly or in doubt,
When there's a guest poisoned at supper-time   *670*
And he sits chatting on with spot on cheek?
"Pluck him by the skirt, and round him in the ears,
Have at him by the beard, warn anyhow!"
Good, and this other friend that's cheat and thief
And dissolute—go stop the devil's feast,   *675*
Withdraw him from the imminent hellfire!
Why, for your life, you dare not tell your friend
"You lie, and I admonish you for Christ!"
Who yet dare seek that same man at the Mass
To warn him—on his knees, and tinkle° near—   *680*
He left a cask atilt, a tap unturned,
The Trebbian running: what a grateful jump
Out of the Church rewards your vigilance!
Perform that selfsame service just a thought
More maladroitly—since a bishop sits   *685*
At function!—and he budges not, bites lip—
"You see my case: how can I quit my post?
He has an eye to any such default.
See to it, neighbor, I beseech your love!"
He and you know the relative worth of things,   *690*
What is permissible or inopportune.
Contort your brows! You know I speak the truth:
Gold is called gold, and dross called dross, i' the
     Book:
Gold you let lie and dross pick up and prize!
—Despite your muster of some fifty monks   *695*

680 **tinkle** of the mass bell.

And nuns a-maundering here and mumping there,
Who could, and on occasion would, spurn dross,
Clutch gold, and prove their faith a fact so far—
I grant you! Fifty times the number squeak
700 And gibber in the madhouse—firm of faith,
This fellow, that his nose supports the moon;
The other, that his straw hat crowns him Pope:
Does that prove all the world outside insane?
Do fifty miracle-mongers match the mob
705 That acts on the frank faithless principle,
Born-baptized-and-bred Christian-atheists, each
With just as much a right to judge as you—
As many senses in his soul, and nerves
I' neck of him as I—whom, soul and sense,
710 Neck and nerve, you abolish presently—
I being the unit in creation now
Who pay the Maker, in this speech of mine,
A creature's duty, spend my last of breath
In bearing witness, even by my worst fault,
715 To the creature's obligation, absolute,
Perpetual: my worst fault protests, "The faith
Claims all of me: I would give all she claims,
But for a spice of doubt: the risk's too rash:
Double or quits, I play, but, all or naught,
720 Exceeds my courage: therefore, I descend
To the next faith with no dubiety—
Faith in the present life, made last as long
And prove as full of pleasure as may hap,
Whatever pain it cause the world." I'm wrong?
725 I've had my life, whate'er I lose: I'm right?
I've got the single good there was to gain.
Entire faith, or else complete unbelief!
Aught between has my loathing and contempt,
Mine and God's also, doubtless: ask yourself,
730 Cardinal, where and how you like a man!
Why, either with your feet upon his head,
Confessed your caudatory,° or, at large,
The stranger in the crowd who caps to you

732 **caudatory** train-bearer.

But keeps his distance—why should he presume?
You want no hanger-on and dropper-off,   735
Now yours, and now not yours but quite his own,
According as the sky looks black or bright.
Just so I capped to and kept off from faith—
You promised trudge behind through fair and foul,
Yet leave i' the lurch at the first spit of rain.   740
Who holds to faith whenever rain begins?
What does the father when his son lies dead,
The merchant when his money-bags take wing,
The politician whom a rival ousts?
No case but has its conduct, faith prescribes: 745
Where's the obedience that shall edify?
Why, they laugh frankly in the face of faith
And take the natural course—this rends his hair
Because his child is taken to God's breast,
That gnashes teeth and raves at loss of trash   750
Which rust corrupts and thieves break through and
    steal,
And this, enabled to inherit earth
Through meekness, curses till your blood runs cold!
Down they all drop to my low level, rest
Heart upon dungy earth that's warm and soft,   755
And let who please attempt the altitudes.
Each playing prodigal son of heavenly sire,
Turning his nose up at the fatted calf,
Fain to fill belly with the husks, we swine
Did eat by born depravity of taste!   760

Enough of the hypocrites. But you, Sirs, you—
Who never budged from litter where I lay,
And buried snout i' the draff-box while I fed,
Cried amen to my creed's one article—
"Get pleasure, 'scape pain—give your preference   765
To the immediate good, for time is brief,
And death ends good and ill and everything!
What's got is gained, what's gained soon is gained
    twice,
And—inasmuch as faith gains most—feign faith!"
So did we brother-like pass word about: 770

—You, now—like bloody drunkards but half-drunk,
Who fool men yet perceive men find them fools—
Vexed that a titter gains the gravest mouth—
O' the sudden you must needs reintroduce
775 Solemnity, straight sober undue mirth
By a blow dealt me your boon companion here
Who, using the old license, dreamed of harm
No more than snow in harvest: yet it falls!
You check the merriment effectually
780 By pushing your abrupt machine i' the midst,
Making me Rome's example: blood for wine!
The general good needs that you chop and change!
I may dislike the hocus-pocus—Rome,
The laughter-loving people, won't they stare
785 Chap-fallen!—while serious natures sermonize
"The magistrate, he beareth not the sword
In vain; who sins may taste its edge, we see!"
Why my sin, drunkards? Where have I abused
Liberty, scandalized you all so much?
790 Who called me, who crooked finger till I came,
Fool that I was, to join companionship?
I knew my own mind, meant to live my life,
Elude your envy, or else make a stand,
Take my own part and sell you my life dear.
795 But it was "Fie! No prejudice in the world
To the proper manly instinct! Cast your lot
Into our lap, one genius ruled our births,
We'll compass joy by concert; take with us
The regular irregular way i' the wood;
800 You'll miss no game through riding breast by breast,
In this preserve, the Church's park and pale,
Rather than outside where the world lies waste!"
Come, if you said not that, did you say this?
Give plain and terrible warning, "Live, enjoy?
805 Such life begins in death and ends in hell!
Dare you bid us assist your sins, us priests
Who hurry sin and sinners from the earth?
No such delight for us, why then for you?
Leave earth, seek Heaven or find its opposite!"
810 Had you so warned me, not in lying words

But veritable deeds with tongues of flame,
That had been fair, that might have struck a man,
Silenced the squabble between soul and sense,
Compelled him to make mind up, take one course
Or the other, peradventure!—wrong or right,   *815*
Foolish or wise, you would have been at least
Sincere, no question—forced me choose, indulge
Or else renounce my instincts, still play wolf
Or find my way submissive to your fold,
Be red-crossed on my fleece, one sheep the more.   *820*
But you as good as bade me wear sheep's wool
Over wolf's skin, suck blood and hide the noise
By mimicry of something like a bleat—
Whence it comes that because, despite my care,
Because I smack my tongue too loud for once,   *825*
Drop baaing, here's the village up in arms!
Have at the wolf's throat, you who hate the breed!
Oh, were it only open yet to choose—
One little time more—whether I'd be free
Your foe, or subsidized your friend forsooth!   *830*
Should not you get a growl through the white fangs
In answer to your beckoning! Cardinal,
Abate, managers o' the multitude,
I'd turn your gloved hands to account, be sure!
You should manipulate the coarse rough mob: *835*
'Tis you I'd deal directly with, not them—
Using your fears: why touch the thing myself
When I could see you hunt, and then cry "Shares!
Quarter the carcase or we quarrel; come,
Here's the world ready to see justice done!"   *840*
Oh, it had been a desperate game, but game
Wherein the winner's chance were worth the pains!
We'd try conclusions!—at the worst, what worse
Than this Mannaia-machine, each minute's talk
Helps push an inch the nearer me? Fool, fool!   *845*

You understand me and forgive, sweet Sirs?
I blame you, tear my hair and tell my woe—
All's but a flourish, figure of rhetoric!
One must try each expedient to save life.

850 One makes fools look foolisher fifty-fold
By putting in their place men wise like you,
To take the full force of an argument
Would buffet their stolidity in vain.
If you should feel aggrieved by the mere wind
855 O' the blow that means to miss you and maul them,
That's my success! Is it not folly, now,
To say with folk, "A plausible defense—
We see through notwithstanding, and reject?"
Reject the plausible they do, these fools,
860 Who never even make pretense to show
One point beyond its plausibility
In favor of the best belief they hold!
"Saint Somebody-or-other raised the dead":
Did he? How do you come to know as much?
865 "Know it, what need? The story's plausible,
Avouched for by a martyrologist,
And why should good men sup on cheese and leeks
On such a saint's day, if there were no saint?"
I praise the wisdom of these fools, and straight
870 Tell them my story—"plausible, but false!"
False, to be sure! What else can story be
That runs—a young wife tired of an old spouse,
Found a priest whom she fled away with—both
Took their full pleasure in the two-days' flight,
875 Which a gray-headed grayer-hearted pair,
(Whose best boast was, their life had been a lie)
Helped for the love they bore all liars. Oh,
Here incredulity begins! Indeed?
Allow then, were no one point strictly true,
880 There's that i' the tale might seem like truth at least
To the unlucky husband—jaundiced patch—
Jealousy maddens people, why not him?
Say, he was maddened, so forgivable!
Humanity pleads that though the wife were true,
885 The priest true, and the pair of liars true,
They might seem false to one man in the world!
A thousand gnats make up a serpent's sting,
And many sly soft stimulants to wrath

Compose a formidable wrong at last
That gets called easily by some one name   890
Not applicable to the single parts,
And so draws down a general revenge,
Excessive if you take crime, fault by fault.
Jealousy! I have known a score of plays,
Were listened to and laughed at in my time   895
As like the everyday-life on all sides,
Wherein the husband, mad as a March hare,
Suspected all the world contrived his shame.
What did the wife? The wife kissed both eyes blind,
Explained away ambiguous circumstance,   900
And while she held him captive by the hand,
Crowned his head—you know what's the mockery—
By half her body behind the curtain. That's
Nature now! That's the subject of a piece
I saw in Vallombrosa Convent, made   905
Expressly to teach men what marriage was!
But say "Just so did I misapprehend,
Imagine she deceived me to my face,"
And that's pretense too easily seen through!
All those eyes of all husbands in all plays,   910
At stare like one expanded peacock-tail,
Are laughed at for pretending to be keen
While horn-blind: but the moment I step forth—
Oh, I must needs o' the sudden prove a lynx
And look the heart, that stone-wall, through and
        through!   915
Such an eye, God's may be—not yours nor mine.

Yes, presently . . . what hour is fleeting now?
When you cut earth away from under me,
I shall be left alone with, pushed beneath
Some such an apparitional dread orb   920
As the eye of God, since such an eye there glares:
I fancy it go filling up the void
Above my mote-self it devours, or what
Proves—wrath, immensity wreaks on nothingness.
Just how I felt once, couching through the dark,   925

Hard by Vittiano; young I was, and gay,
And wanting to trap fieldfares:° first a spark
Tipped a bent, as a mere dew-globule might
Any stiff grass-stalk on the meadow—this
930   Grew fiercer, flamed out full, and proved the sun.
What do I want with proverbs, precepts here?
Away with man! What shall I say to God?
This, if I find the tongue and keep the mind—
"Do Thou wipe out the being of me, and smear
935   This soul from off Thy white of things, I blot!
I am one huge and sheer mistake—whose fault?
Not mine at least, who did not make myself!"
Someone declares my wife excused me so!
Perhaps she knew what argument to use.
940   Grind your teeth, Cardinal: Abate, writhe!
What else am I to cry out in my rage,
Unable to repent one particle
O' the past? Oh, how I wish some cold wise man
Would dig beneath the surface which you scrape,
945   Deal with the depths, pronounce on my desert
Groundedly! I want simple sober sense,
That asks, before it finishes with a dog,
Who taught the dog that trick you hang him for?
You both persist to call that act a crime,
950   Which sense would call . . . yes, I maintain it, Sirs, . . .
A blunder! At the worst, I stood in doubt
On crossroad, took one path of many paths:
It leads to the red thing, we all see now,
But nobody saw at first: one primrose-patch
955   In bank, one singing-bird in bush, the less,
Had warned me from such wayfare: let me prove!
Put me back to the crossroad, start afresh!
Advise me when I take the first false step!
Give me my wife: how should I use my wife,
960   Love her or hate her? Prompt my action now!
There she is, there she stands alive and pale,
The thirteen-years' old child, with milk for blood,
Pompilia Comparini, as at first,

927 **fieldfares** thrushes.

Which first is only four brief years ago!
I stand too in the little ground-floor room 965
O' the father's house at Via Vittoria: see!
Her so-called mother—one arm round the waist
O' the child to keep her from the toys, let fall
At wonder I can live yet look so grim—
Ushers her in, with deprecating wave 970
Of the other—and she fronts me loose at last,
Held only by the mother's fingertip.
Struck dumb—for she was white enough before!—
She eyes me with those frightened balls of black,
As heifer—the old simile comes pat— 975
Eyes tremblingly the altar and the priest.
The amazed look, all one insuppressive prayer—
Might she but breathe, set free as heretofore,
Have this cup leave her lips unblistered, bear
Any cross anywhither anyhow, 980
So but alone, so but apart from me!
You are touched? So am I, quite otherwise,
If 'tis with pity. I resent my wrong,
Being a man: I only show man's soul
Through man's flesh: she sees mine, it strikes her
    thus! 985
Is that attractive? To a youth perhaps—
Calf-creature, one-part boy to three-parts girl,
To whom it is a flattering novelty
That he, men use to motion from their path,
Can thus impose, thus terrify in turn 990
A chit whose terror shall be changed apace
To bliss unbearable when grace and glow,
Prowess and pride descend the throne and touch
Esther in all that pretty tremble,° cured
By the dove o' the scepter! But myself am old, 995
O' the wane at least, in all things: what do you say
To her who frankly thus confirms my doubt?
I am past the prime, I scare the woman-world,
Done-with that way: you like this piece of news?
A little saucy rosebud minx can strike 1000

Death-damp into the breast of doughty king
Though 'twere French Louis—soul I understand—
Saying, by gesture of repugnance, just
"Sire, you are regal, puissant and so forth,
1005 But—young you have been, are not, nor will be!"
In vain the mother nods, winks, bustles up,
"Count, girls incline to mature worth like you!
As for Pompilia, what's flesh, fish, or fowl
To one who apprehends no difference,
1010 And would accept you even were you old
As you are . . . youngish by her father's side?
Trim but your beard a little, thin your bush
Of eyebrow; and for presence, portliness,
And decent gravity, you beat a boy!"
1015 Deceive yourself one minute, if you may,
In presence of the child that so loves age,
Whose neck writhes, cords itself against your kiss,
Whose hand you wring stark, rigid with despair!
Well, I resent this; I am young in soul,
1020 Nor old in body—thews and sinews here—
Though the vile surface be not smooth as once—
Far beyond that first wheelwork which went wrong
Through the untempered iron ere 'twas proof:
I am the wrought man worth ten times the crude,
1025 Would woman see what this declines to see,
Declines to say "I see"—the officious word
That makes the thing, pricks on the soul to shoot
New fire into the half-used cinder, flesh!
Therefore 'tis she begins with wronging me,
1030 Who cannot but begin with hating her.
Our marriage follows: there she stands again!
Why do I laugh? Why, in the very gripe
O' the jaws of death's gigantic skull, do I
Grin back his grin, make sport of my own pangs?
1035 Why from each clashing of his molars, ground
To make the devil bread from out my grist,
Leaps out a spark of mirth, a hellish toy?
Take notice we are lovers in a church,
Waiting the sacrament to make us one
1040 And happy! Just as bid, she bears herself,

Comes and kneels, rises, speaks, is silent—goes:
So have I brought my horse, by word and blow,
To stand stock-still and front the fire he dreads.
How can I other than remember this,
Resent the very obedience? Gain thereby?   1045
Yes, I do gain my end and have my will—
Thanks to whom? When the mother speaks the word,
She obeys it—even to enduring me!
There had been compensation in revolt—
Revolt's to quell: but martyrdom rehearsed,   1050
But predetermined saintship for the sake
O' the mother?—"Go!" thought I, "we meet again!"
Pass the next weeks of dumb contented death,
She lives—wakes up, installed in house and home,
Is mine, mine all day-long, all night-long mine.   1055
Good folk begin at me with open mouth
"Now, at least, reconcile the child to life!
Study and make her love . . . that is, endure
The . . . hem! the . . . all of you though somewhat
        old,
Till it amount to something, in her eye,   1060
As good as love, better a thousand times—
Since nature helps the woman in such strait,
Makes passiveness her pleasure: failing which,
What if you give up boy-and-girl-fools'-play
And go on to wise friendship all at once?   1065
Those boys and girls kiss themselves cold, you know,
Toy themselves tired and slink aside full soon
To friendship, as they name satiety:
Thither go you and wait their coming!" Thanks,
Considerate advisers—but, fair play!   1070
Had you and I, friends, started fair at first
We, keeping fair, might reach it, neck by neck,
This blessed goal, whenever fate so please:
But why am I to miss the daisied mile
The course begins with, why obtain the dust   1075
Of the end precisely at the starting-point?
Why quaff life's cup blown free of all the beads,
The bright red froth wherein our beard should steep
Before our mouth essay the black o' the wine?

1080 Foolish, the love-fit? Let me prove it such
Like you, before like you I puff things clear!
"The best's to come, no rapture but content!
Not love's first glory but a sober glow,
Not a spontaneous outburst in pure boon,
1085 So much as, gained by patience, care and toil,
Proper appreciation and esteem!"
Go preach that to your nephews, not to me
Who, tired i' the midway of my life, would stop
And take my first refreshment, pluck a rose:
1090 What's this coarse woolly hip, worn smooth of leaf,
You counsel I go plant in garden-plot,
Water with tears, manure with sweat and blood,
In confidence the seed shall germinate
And, for its very best, some far-off day,
1095 Grow big, and blow me out a dog-rose bell?
Why must your nephews begin breathing spice
O' the hundred-petaled Provence prodigy?°
Nay, more and worse—would such my root bear
        rose—
Prove really flower and favorite, not the kind
That's queen, but those three leaves that make one
1100   cup
And hold the hedge-bird's breakfast—then indeed
The prize though poor would pay the care and toil!
Respect we Nature that makes least as most,
Marvelous in the minim! But this bud,
1105 Bit through and burned black by the tempter's tooth,
This bloom whose best grace was the slug outside
And the wasp inside its bosom—call you "rose"?
Claim no immunity from a weed's fate
For the horrible present! What you call my wife
1110 I call a nullity in female shape,
Vapid disgust, soon to be pungent plague,
When mixed with, made confusion and a curse
By two abominable nondescripts,
That father and that mother: think you see
1115 The dreadful bronze our boast, we Aretines,

1097 **hundred-petaled Provence prodigy** "prize rose."

The Etruscan monster, the three-headed thing,
Bellerophon's foe! How name you the whole beast?
You choose to name the body from one head,
That of the simple kid which droops the eye,
Hangs the neck and dies tenderly enough: 1120
I rather see the grizzly lion belch
Flame out i' the midst, the serpent writhe her rings,
Grafted into the common stock for tail,
And name the brute, Chimera° which I slew!
How was there ever more to be—(concede 1125
My wife's insipid harmless nullity)—
Dissociation from that pair of plagues—
That mother with her cunning and her cant—
The eyes with first their twinkle of conceit,
Then, dropped to earth in mock-demureness—now, 1130
The smile self-satisfied from ear to ear,
Now, the prim pursed-up mouth's protruded lips,
With deferential duck, slow swing of head,
Tempting the sudden fist of man too much—
That owl-like screw of lid and rock of ruff! 1135
As for the father—Cardinal, you know,
The kind of idiot!—such are rife in Rome,
But they wear velvet commonly; good fools,
At the end of life, to furnish forth young folk
Who grin and bear with imbecility: 1140
Since the stalled ass, the joker, sheds from jaw
Corn, in the joke, for those who laugh or starve.
But what say we to the same solemn beast
Wagging his ears and wishful of our pat,
When turned, with holes in hide and bones laid bare, 1145
To forage for himself i' the waste o' the world,
Sir Dignity i' the dumps? Pat him? We drub
Self-knowledge, rather, into frowzy pate,
Teach Pietro to get trappings or go hang!
Fancy this quondam oracle in vogue 1150
At Via Vittoria, this personified

1115–24 **dreadful bronze . . . Chimera** ancient Etruscan statue of the
monster Chimera, a lion in front, kid in the middle, and serpent
behind, named incongruously for its middle part.

Authority when time was—Pantaloon°
Flaunting his tomfool tawdry just the same
As if Ash Wednesday were mid-Carnival!
1155 That's the extreme and unforgivable
Of sins, as I account such. Have you stooped
For your own ends to bestialize yourself
By flattery of a fellow of this stamp?
The ends obtained or else shown out of reach,
1160 He goes on, takes the flattery for pure truth—
"You love, and honor me, of course: what next?"
What, but the trifle of the stabbing, friend?—
Which taught you how one worships when the shrine
Has lost the relic that we bent before.
1165 Angry! And how could I be otherwise?
'Tis plain: this pair of old pretentious fools
Meant to fool me: it happens, I fooled them.
Why could not these who sought to buy and sell
Me—when they found themselves were bought and
    sold,
1170 Make up their mind to the proved rule of right,
Be chattel and not chapman° any more?
Miscalculation has its consequence;
But when the shepherd crooks a sheep-like thing
And meaning to get wool, dislodges fleece
1175 And finds the veritable wolf beneath,
(How that staunch image serves at every turn!)
Does he, by way of being politic,
Pluck the first whisker grimly visible?
Or rather grow in a trice all gratitude,
1180 Protest this sort-of-what-one-might-name sheep
Beats the old other curly-coated kind,
And shall share board and bed, if so it deign,
With its discoverer, like a royal ram?
Ay, thus, with chattering teeth and knocking knees,
1185 Would wisdom treat the adventure! these, forsooth,
Tried whisker-plucking, and so found what trap
The whisker kept perdue,° two rows of teeth—

1152 **Pantaloon** clownish old man in comedy. 1171 **Be chattel and
not chapman** be goods and not merchant. 1187 **perdue** concealed.

Sharp, as too late the prying fingers felt.
What would you have? The fools transgress, the fools
Forthwith receive appropriate punishment: *1190*
They first insult me, I return the blow!
There follows noise enough: four hubbub months,
Now hue and cry, now whimpering and wail—
A perfect goose-yard cackle of complaint
Because I do not gild the geese their oats— *1195*
I have enough of noise, ope wicket wide,
Sweep out the couple to go whine elsewhere,
Frightened a little, hurt in no respect,
And am just taking thought to breathe again,
Taste the sweet sudden silence all about, *1200*
When, there they raise it, the old noise I know,
At Rome i' the distance! "What, begun once more?
Whine on, wail ever, 'tis the loser's right!"
But eh, what sort of voice grows on the wind?
Triumph it sounds and no complaint at all! *1205*
And triumph it is. My boast was premature:
The creatures, I turned forth, clapped wing and crew
Fighting-cock-fashion—they had filched a pearl
From dung-heap, and might boast with cause enough!
I was defrauded of all bargained for: *1210*
You know, the Pope knows, not a soul but knows
My dowry was derision, my gain—muck,
My wife (the Church declared my flesh and blood)
The nameless bastard of a common whore:
My old name turned henceforth to . . . shall I say *1215*
"He that received the ordure in his face?"
And they who planned this wrong, performed this
        wrong,
And then revealed this wrong to the wide world,
Rounded myself in the ears with my own wrong—
Why, these were (note hell's lucky malice, now!) *1220*
These were just they who, they alone, could act
And publish and proclaim their infamy,
Secure that men would in a breath believe
Compassionate and pardon them—for why?
They plainly were too stupid to invent, *1225*
Too simple to distinguish wrong from right—

Inconscious agents they, the silly-sooth,
Of heaven's retributive justice on the strong
Proud cunning violent oppressor—me!
1230 Follow them to their fate and help your best,
You Rome, Arezzo, foes called friends of me,
They gave the good long laugh to, at my cost!
Defray your share o' the cost, since you partook
The entertainment! Do!—assured the while,
1235 That not one stab, I dealt to right and left,
But went the deeper for a fancy—this—
That each might do me twofold service, find
A friend's face at the bottom of each wound,
And scratch its smirk a little!

Panciatichi!
1240 There's a report at Florence—is it true?—
That when your relative the Cardinal
Built, only the other day, that barrack-bulk,
The palace in Via Larga, someone picked
From out the street a saucy quip enough
1245 That fell there from its day's flight through the town,
About the flat front and the windows wide
And bulging heap of cornice—hitched the joke
Into a sonnet, signed his name thereto,
And forthwith pinned on post the pleasantry:
1250 For which he's at the galleys, rowing now
Up to his waist in water—just because
Panciatic and *lymphatic* rhymed so pat!
I hope, Sir, those who passed this joke on me
Were not unduly punished? What say you,
1255 Prince of the Church, my patron? Nay, indeed,
I shall not dare insult your wits so much
As think this problem difficult to solve.
This Pietro and Violante then, I say,
These two ambiguous insects, changing name
1260 And nature with the season's warmth or chill—
Now, groveled, grubbing toiling moiling ants,
A very synonym of thrift and peace—
Anon, with lusty June to prick their heart,
Soared i' the air, winged flies for more offense,

Circled me, buzzed me deaf and stung me blind,   *1265*
And stunk me dead with fetor° in the face
Until I stopped the nuisance: there's my crime!
Pity I did not suffer them subside
Into some further shape and final form
Of execrable life? My masters, no!   *1270*
I, by one blow, wisely cut short at once
Them and their transformations of disgust,
In the snug little villa out of hand.
"Grant me confession, give bare time for that!"—
Shouted the sinner till his mouth was stopped.   *1275*
His life confessed!—that was enough for me,
Who came to see that he did penance. 'S death!
Here's a coil raised, a pother and for what?
Because strength, being provoked by weakness, fought
And conquered—the world never heard the like!   *1280*
Pah, how I spend my breath on them, as if
'Twas their fate troubled me, too hard to range
Among the right and fit and proper things!

Ay, but Pompilia—I await your word—
She, unimpeached of crime, unimplicate   *1285*
In folly, one of alien blood to these
I punish, why extend my claim, exact
Her portion of the penalty? Yes, friends,
I go too fast: the orator's at fault:
Yes, ere I lay her, with your leave, by them   *1290*
As she was laid at San Lorenzo late,
I ought to step back, lead you by degrees,
Recounting at each step some fresh offense,
Up to the red bed—never fear, I will!
Gaze at her, where I place her, to begin,   *1295*
Confound me with her gentleness and worth!
The horrible pair have fled and left her now,
She has her husband for her sole concern:
His wife, the woman fashioned for his help,
Flesh of his flesh, bone of his bone, the bride   *1300*
To groom as is the Church and Spouse to Christ:

1266 **fetor** stench, "foulness."

There she stands in his presence: "Thy desire
Shall be to the husband, o'er thee shall he rule!"
—"Pompilia, who declare that you love God,
1305 You know who said that: then, desire my love,
Yield me contentment and be ruled aright!"
She sits up, she lies down, she comes and goes,
Kneels at the couch-side, overleans the sill
O' the window, cold and pale and mute as stone,
1310 Strong as stone also. "Well, are they not fled?
Am I not left, am I not one for all?
Speak a word, drop a tear, detach a glance,
Bless me or curse me of your own accord!
Is it the ceiling only wants your soul,
1315 Is worth your eyes?" And then the eyes descend,
And do look at me. Is it at the meal?
"Speak!" she obeys, "Be silent!" she obeys,
Counting the minutes till I cry "Depart,"
As brood-bird when you saunter past her eggs.
1320 Departs she? just the same through door and wall
I see the same stone strength of white despair.
And all this will be never otherwise!
Before, the parents' presence lent her life:
She could play off her sex's armory,
1325 Entreat, reproach, be female to my male,
Try all the shrieking doubles of the hare,
Go clamor to the Commissary,° bid
The Archbishop hold my hands and stop my tongue,
And yield fair sport so: but the tactics change,
1330 The hare stands stock-still to enrage the hound!
Since that day when she learned she was no child
Of those she thought her parents—that their trick
Had tricked me whom she thought sole trickster late—
Why, I suppose she said within herself
1335 "Then, no more struggle for my parents' sake!
And, for my own sake, why needs struggle be?"
But is there no third party to the pact?
What of her husband's relish or dislike

1327 **Commissary** "Governor" of Arezzo.

For this new game of giving up the game,
This worst offense of not offending more?   *1340*
I'll not believe but instinct wrought in this,
Set her on to conceive and execute
The preferable plague: how sure they probe—
These jades, the sensitivest soft of man!
The long black hair was wound now in a wisp,   *1345*
Crowned sorrow better than the wild web late:
No more soiled dress, 'tis trimness triumphs now,
For how should malice go with negligence?
The frayed silk looked the fresher for her spite!
There was an end to springing out of bed,   *1350*
Praying me, with face buried on my feet,
Be hindered of my pastime—so an end
To my rejoinder, "What, on the ground at last?
Vanquished in fight, a supplicant for life?
What if I raise you? 'Ware the casting down   *1355*
When next you fight me!" Then, she lay there, mine:
Now, mine she is if I please wring her neck—
A moment of disquiet, working eyes,
Protruding tongue, a long sigh, then no more—
As if one killed the horse one could not ride!   *1360*
Had I enjoined "Cut off the hair!"—why, snap
The scissors, and at once a yard or so
Had fluttered in black serpents to the floor:
But till I did enjoin it, how she combs,
Uncurls and draws out to the complete length,   *1365*
Plaits, places the insulting rope on head
To be an eyesore past dishevelment!
Is all done? Then sit still again and stare!
I advise—no one think to bear that look
Of steady wrong, endured as steadily   *1370*
—Through what sustainment of deluding hope?
Who is the friend i' the background that notes all?
Who may come presently and close accounts?
This self-possession to the uttermost,
How does it differ in aught, save degree,   *1375*
From the terrible patience of God?
                              "All which just means,
She did not love you!" Again the word is launched

And the fact fronts me! What, you try the wards°
With the true key and the dead lock flies ope?
1380 No, it sticks fast and leaves you fumbling still!
You have some fifty servants, Cardinal—
Which of them loves you? Which subordinate
But makes parade of such officiousness
That—if there's no love prompts it—love, the sham,
1385 Does twice the service done by love, the true?
God bless us liars, where's one touch of truth
In what we tell the world, or world tells us,
Of how we love each other? All the same,
We calculate on word and deed, nor err—
1390 Bid such a man do such a loving act,
Sure of effect and negligent of cause,
Just as we bid a horse, with cluck of tongue,
Stretch his legs arch-wise, crouch his saddled back
To foot-reach of the stirrup—all for love,
1395 And some for memory of the smart of switch
On the inside of the foreleg—what care we?
Yet where's the bond obliges horse to man
Like that which binds fast wife to husband? God
Laid down the law: gave man the brawny arm
1400 And ball of fist—woman the beardless cheek
And proper place to suffer in the side:
Since it is he can strike, let her obey!
Can she feel no love? Let her show the more,
Sham the worse, damn herself praiseworthily!
1405 Who's that soprano, Rome went mad about
Last week while I lay rotting in my straw?
The very jailer gossiped in his praise—
How—dressed up like Armida, though a man;
And painted to look pretty, though a fright—
1410 He still made love so that the ladies swooned,
Being a eunuch. "Ah, Rinaldo mine!
But to breathe by thee while Jove slays us both!"
All the poor bloodless creature never felt,
Si, do, re, mi, fa, squeak and squall—for what?
1415 Two gold zecchines the evening. Here's my slave,

1378 wards "fit" of a lock.

Whose body and soul depend upon my nod,
Can't falter out the first note in the scale
For her life! Why blame me if I take the life?
All women cannot give men love, forsooth!
No, nor all pullets lay the henwife eggs—   *1420*
Whereat she bids them remedy the fault,
Brood on a chalk-ball: soon the nest is stocked—
Otherwise, to the plucking and the spit!
This wife of mine was of another mood—
Would not begin the lie that ends with truth,   *1425*
Nor feign the love that brings real love about:
Wherefore I judged, sentenced and punished her.
But why particularize, defend the deed?
Say that I hated her for no one cause
Beyond my pleasure so to do—what then?   *1430*
Just on as much incitement acts the world,
All of you! Look and like! You favor one,
Browbeat another, leave alone a third—
Why should you master natural caprice?
Pure nature! Try: plant elm by ash in file;   *1435*
Both unexceptionable trees enough,
They ought to overlean each other, pair
At top, and arch across the avenue
The whole path to the pleasaunce: do they so—
Or loathe, lie off abhorrent each from each?   *1440*
Lay the fault. elsewhere: since we must have faults,
Mine shall have been—seeing there's ill in the end
Come of my course—that I fare somehow worse
For the way I took: my fault . . . as God's my judge,
I see not where my fault lies, that's the truth!   *1445*
I ought . . . oh, ought in my own interest
Have let the whole adventure go untried,
This chance by marriage: or else, trying it,
Ought to have turned it to account, some one
O' the hundred otherwises? Ay, my friend,   *1450*
Easy to say, easy to do: step right
Now you've stepped left and stumbled on the thing,
—The red thing! Doubt I any more than you
That practice makes man perfect? Give again
The chance—same marriage and no other wife,   *1455*

Be sure I'll edify you! That's because
I'm practiced, grown fit guide for Guido's self.
You proffered guidance—I know, none so well—
You laid down law and rolled decorum out,
1460 From pulpit-corner on the gospel-side°—
Wanted to make your great experience mine,
Save me the personal search and pains so: thanks!
Take your word on life's use? When I take his—
The muzzled ox that treadeth out the corn,
1465 Gone blind in padding round and round one path—
As to the taste of green grass in the field!
What do you know o' the world that's trodden flat
And salted sterile with your daily dung,
Leavened into a lump of loathsomeness?
1470 Take your opinion of the modes of life,
The aims of life, life's triumph or defeat,
How to feel, how to scheme, and how to do
Or else leave undone? You preached long and loud
On high-days, "Take our doctrine upon trust!
1475 Into the mill-house with you! Grind our corn,
Relish our chaff, and let the green grass grow!"
I tried chaff, found I famished on such fare,
So made this mad rush at the mill-house-door,
Buried my head up to the ears in dew,
1480 Browsed on the best: for which you brain me, Sirs!
Be it so. I conceived of life that way,
And still declare—life, without absolute use
Of the actual sweet therein, is death, not life.
Give me—pay down—not promise, which is air—
1485 Something that's out of life and better still,
Make sure reward, make certain punishment,
Entice me, scare me—I'll forgo this life;
Otherwise, no!—the less that words, mere wind,
Would cheat me of some minutes while they plague,
1490 Balk fullness of revenge here—blame yourselves
For this eruption of the pent-up soul
You prisoned first and played with afterward!
"Deny myself" meant simply pleasure you,

1460 **gospel-side** left (where the gospel is read).

The sacred and superior, save the mark!
You—whose stupidity and insolence 1495
I must defer to, soothe at every turn—
Whose swine-like snuffling greed and grunting lust
I had to wink at or help gratify—
While the same passions—dared they perk in me,
Me, the immeasurably marked, by God, 1500
Master of the whole world of such as you—
I, boast such passions? 'Twas "Suppress them straight!
Or stay, we'll pick and choose before destroy.
Here's wrath in you, a serviceable sword—
Beat it into a ploughshare! What's this long 1505
Lance-like ambition? Forge a pruning hook,
May be of service when our vines grow tall!
But—sword use swordwise, spear thrust out as spear?
Anathema! Suppression is the word!"
My nature, when the outrage was too gross, 1510
Widened itself an outlet over-wide
By way of answer, sought its own relief
With more of fire and brimstone than you wished.
All your own doing: preachers, blame yourselves!

'Tis I preach while the hourglass runs and runs! 1515
God keep me patient! All I say just means—
My wife proved, whether by her fault or mine—
That's immaterial—a true stumbling block
I' the way of me her husband. I but plied
The hatchet yourselves use to clear a path, 1520
Was politic, played the game you warrant wins,
Plucked at law's robe a-rustle through the courts,
Bowed down to kiss divinity's buckled shoe
Cushioned i' the church: efforts all wide the aim!
Procedures to no purpose! Then flashed truth. 1525
The letter kills, the spirit keeps alive
In law and gospel: there be nods and winks
Instruct a wise man to assist himself
In certain matters, nor seek aid at all.
"Ask money of me"—quoth the clownish saw°— 1530

1530 **clownish saw** rustic saying.

"And take my purse! But—speaking with respect—
Need you a solace for the troubled nose?
Let everybody wipe his own himself!"
Sirs, tell me free and fair! Had things gone well
1535 At the wayside inn: had I surprised asleep
The runaways, as was so probable,
And pinned them each to other partridge-wise,
Through back and breast to breast and back, then bade
Bystanders witness if the spit, my sword,
1540 Were loaded with unlawful game for once—
Would you have interposed to damp the glow
Applauding me on every husband's cheek?
Would you have checked the cry "A judgment, see!
A warning, note! Be henceforth chaste, ye wives,
1545 Nor stray beyond your proper precinct, priests!"
If you had, then your house against itself
Divides, nor stands your kingdom any more.
Oh why, why was it not ordained just so?
Why fell not things out so nor otherwise?
1550 Ask that particular devil whose task it is
To trip the all-but-at perfection—slur
The line o' the painter just where paint leaves off
And life begins—put ice into the ode
O' the poet while he cries "Next stanza—fire!"
1555 Inscribe all human effort with one word,
Artistry's haunting curse, the Incomplete!
Being incomplete, my act escaped success.
Easy to blame now! Every fool can swear
To hole in net that held and slipped the fish.
1560 But, treat my act with fair unjaundiced eye,
What was there wanting to a masterpiece
Except the luck that lies beyond a man?
My way with the woman, now proved grossly wrong,
Just missed of being gravely grandly right
1565 And making mouths laugh on the other side.
Do, for the poor obstructed artist's sake,
Go with him over that spoiled work once more!
Take only its first flower, the ended act
Now in the dusty pod, dry and defunct!

I march to the villa, and my men with me, 1570
That evening, and we reach the door and stand.
I say . . . no, it shoots through me lightning-like
While I pause, breathe, my hand upon the latch,
"Let me forebode! Thus far, too much success:
I want the natural failure—find it where? 1575
Which thread will have to break and leave a loop
I' the meshy combination, my brain's loom
Wove this long while, and now next minute tests?
Of three that are to catch, two should go free,
One must: all three surprised—impossible! 1580
Beside, I seek three and may chance on six—
This neighbor, t'other gossip—the babe's birth
Brings such to fireside, and folks give them wine—
'Tis late: but when I break in presently
One will be found outlingering the rest 1585
For promise of a posset—one whose shout
Would raise the dead down in the catacombs,
Much more the city-watch that goes its round.
When did I ever turn adroitly up
To sun some brick embedded in the soil, 1590
And with one blow crush all three scorpions there?
Or Pietro or Violante shambles off—
It cannot be but I surprise my wife—
If only she is stopped and stamped on, good!
That shall suffice: more is improbable. 1595
Now I may knock!" And this once for my sake
The impossible was effected: I called king,
Queen and knave in a sequence, and cards came,
All three, three only! So, I had my way,
Did my deed: so, unbrokenly lay bare 1600
Each taenia° that had sucked me dry of juice,
At last outside me, not an inch of ring
Left now to writhe about and root itself
I' the heart all powerless for revenge! Henceforth
I might thrive: these were drawn and dead and
    damned. 1605
Oh Cardinal, the deep long sigh you heave

1601 **taenia** tapeworm.

When the load's off you, ringing as it runs
All the way down the serpent-stair to hell!
No doubt the fine delirium flustered me,
1610 Turned my brain with the influx of success
As if the sole need now were to wave wand
And find doors fly wide—wish and have my will—
The rest o' the scheme would care for itself: escape
Easy enough were that, and poor beside!
1615 It all but proved so—ought to quite have proved,
Since, half the chances had sufficed, set free
Anyone, with his senses at command,
From thrice the danger of my flight. But, drunk,
Redundantly triumphant—some reverse
1620 Was sure to follow! There's no other way
Accounts for such prompt perfect failure then
And there on the instant. Any day o' the week,
A ducat slid discreetly into palm
O' the mute postmaster, while you whisper him—
1625 How you the Count and certain four your knaves,
Have just been mauling who was malapert,
Suspect the kindred may prove troublesome,
Therefore, want horses in a hurry—that
And nothing more secures you any day
1630 The pick o' the stable! Yet I try the trick,
Double the bribe, call myself Duke for Count,
And say the dead man only was a Jew,
And for my pains find I am dealing just
With the one scrupulous fellow in all Rome—
1635 Just this immaculate official stares,
Sees I want hat on head and sword in sheath,
Am splashed with other sort of wet than wine,
Shrugs shoulder, puts my hand by, gold and all,
Stands on the strictness of the rule o' the road!
1640 "Where's the permission?" Where's the wretched rag
With the due seal and sign of Rome's Police,
To be had for asking, half-an-hour ago?
"Gone? Get another, or no horses hence!"
He dares not stop me, we five glare too grim,
1645 But hinders—hacks and hamstrings sure enough,
Gives me some twenty miles of miry road

More to march in the middle of that night
Whereof the rough beginning taxed the strength
O' the youngsters, much more mine, both soul and
    flesh,
Who had to think as well as act: dead beat,   1650
We gave in ere we reached the boundary
And safe spot out of this irrational Rome—
Where, on dismounting from our steeds next day,
We had snapped our fingers at you, safe and sound,
Tuscans once more in blessed Tuscany,   1655
Where laws make wise allowance, understand
Civilized life and do its champions right!
Witness the sentence of the Rota there,
Arezzo uttered, the Granduke confirmed,
One week before I acted on its hint—   1660
Giving friend Guillichini, for his love,
The galleys, and my wife your saint, Rome's saint—
Rome manufactures saints enough to know—
Seclusion at the Stinche° for her life.
All this, that all but was, might all have been,   1665
Yet was not! balked by just a scrupulous knave
Whose palm was horn through handling horses' hoofs
And could not close upon my proffered gold!
What say you to the spite of fortune? Well,
The worst's in store: thus hindered, haled this way   1670
To Rome again by hangdogs, whom find I
Here, still to fight with, but my pale frail wife?
—Riddled with wounds by one not like to waste
The blows he dealt—knowing anatomy—
(I think I told you) bound to pick and choose   1675
The vital parts! 'Twas learning all in vain!
She too must shimmer through the gloom o' the grave,
Come and confront me—not at judgment-seat
Where I could twist her soul, as erst her flesh,
And turn her truth into a lie—but there,   1680
O' the deathbed, with God's hand between us both,
Striking me dumb, and helping her to speak,
Tell her own story her own way, and turn

1664 **Stinche** prison.

My plausibility to nothingness!
1685 Four whole days did Pompilia keep alive,
With the best surgery of Rome agape
At the miracle—this cut, the other slash,
And yet the life refusing to dislodge,
Four whole extravagant impossible days,
1690 Till she had time to finish and persuade
Every man, every woman, every child
In Rome, of what she would: the selfsame she
Who, but a year ago, had wrung her hands,
Reddened her eyes and beat her breasts, rehearsed
1695 The whole game at Arezzo, nor availed
Thereby to move one heart or raise one hand!
When destiny intends you cards like these,
What good of skill and preconcerted play?
Had she been found dead, as I left her dead,
1700 I should have told a tale brooked no reply:
You scarcely will suppose me found at fault
With that advantage! "What brings me to Rome?
Necessity to claim and take my wife:
Better, to claim and take my new born babe—
1705 Strong in paternity a fortnight old,
When 'tis at strongest: warily I work,
Knowing the machinations of my foe;
I have companionship and use the night:
I seek my wife and child—I find—no child
1710 But wife, in the embraces of that priest
Who caused her to elope from me. These two,
Backed by the pander-pair who watch the while,
Spring on me like so many tiger-cats,
Glad of the chance to end the intruder. I—
1715 What should I do but stand on my defense,
Strike right, strike left, strike thick and threefold, slay,
Not all—because the coward priest escapes.
Last, I escape, in fear of evil tongues,
And having had my taste of Roman law."
1720 What's disputable, refutable here?—
Save by just this one ghost-thing half on earth,
Half out of it—as if she held God's hand

While she leaned back and looked her last at me,
Forgiving me (here monks begin to weep)
Oh, from her very soul, commending mine   *1725*
To heavenly mercies which are infinite—
While fixing fast my head beneath your knife!
'Tis fate not fortune. All is of a piece!
When was it chance informed me of my youths?
My rustic four o' the family, soft swains,   *1730*
What sweet surprise had they in store for me,
Those of my very household—what did Law
Twist with her rack-and-cord-contrivance late
From out their bones and marrow? What but this—
Had no one of these several stumbling blocks   *1735*
Stopped me, they yet were cherishing a scheme,
All of their honest country homespun wit,
To quietly next day at crow of cock
Cut my own throat too, for their own behoof,
Seeing I had forgot to clear accounts   *1740*
O' the instant, nowise slackened speed for that—
And somehow never might find memory,
Once safe back in Arezzo, where things change,
And a court-lord needs mind no country lout.
Well, being the arch-offender, I die last—   *1745*
May, ere my head falls, have my eyesight free,
Nor miss them dangling high on either hand,
Like scarecrows in a hemp-field, for their pains!

And then my trial—'tis my trial that bites
Like a corrosive, so the cards are packed,   *1750*
Dice loaded, and my life-stake tricked away!
Look at my lawyers, lacked they grace of law,
Latin or logic? Were not they fools to the height,
Fools to the depth, fools to the level between,
O' the foolishness set to decide the case?   *1755*
They feign, they flatter; nowise does it skill,
Everything goes against me: deal each judge
His dole of flattery and feigning—why,
He turns and tries and snuffs and savors it,
As some old fly the sugar-grain, your gift;   *1760*

Then eyes your thumb and finger, brushes clean
The absurd old head of him, and whisks away,
Leaving your thumb and finger dirty. Faugh!

And finally, after this long-drawn range
1765 Of affront and failure, failure and affront—
This path, 'twixt crosses leading to a skull,°
Paced by me barefoot, bloodied by my palms
From the entry to the end—there's light at length,
A cranny of escape: appeal may be
1770 To the old man, to the father, to the Pope,
For a little life—from one whose life is spent,
A little pity—from pity's source and seat,
A little indulgence to rank, privilege,
From one who is the thing personified,
1775 Rank, privilege, indulgence, grown beyond
Earth's bearing, even, ask Jansenius° else!
Still the same answer, still no other tune
From the cicala perched at the treetop
Than crickets noisy round the root: 'tis "Die!"
1780 Bids Law—"Be damned!" adds Gospel—nay,
No word so frank—'tis rather, "Save yourself!"
The Pope subjoins—"Confess and be absolved!
So shall my credit countervail your shame,
And the world see I have not lost the knack
1785 Of trying all the spirits: yours, my son,
Wants but a fiery washing to emerge
In clarity! Come, cleanse you, ease the ache
Of these old bones, refresh our bowels, boy!"
Do I mistake your mission from the Pope?
1790 Then, bear his Holiness the mind of me!
I do get strength from being thrust to wall,
Successively wrenched from pillar and from post
By this tenacious hate of fortune, hate
Of all things in, under, and above earth.
1795 Warfare, begun this mean unmanly mode,
Does best to end so—gives earth spectacle
Of a brave fighter who succumbs to odds

1766 **path . . . skull** ascent of Golgotha. 1776 **Jansenius Catholic**
puritan reformer, condemned by the Church.

That turn defeat to victory. Stab, I fold
My mantle round me! Rome approves my act:
Applauds the blow which costs me life but keeps   *1800*
My honor spotless: Rome would praise no more
Had I fallen, say, some fifteen years ago,
Helping Vienna when our Aretines
Flocked to Duke Charles and fought Turk Mustafa;
Nor would you two be trembling o'er my corpse   *1805*
With all this exquisite solicitude.
Why is it that I make such suit to live?
The popular sympathy that's round me now
Would break like bubble that o'er-domes a fly:
Solid enough while he lies quiet there,   *1810*
But let him want the air and ply the wing,
Why, it breaks and bespatters him, what else?
Cardinal, if the Pope had pardoned me,
And I walked out of prison through the crowd,
It would not be your arm I should dare press!   *1815*
Then, if I got safe to my place again,
How sad and sapless were the years to come!
I go my old ways and find things grown gray;
You priests leer at me, old friends look askance,
The mob's in love, I'll wager, to a man,   *1820*
With my poor young good beauteous murdered wife:
For hearts require instruction how to beat,
And eyes, on warrant of the story, wax
Wanton at portraiture in white and black
Of dead Pompilia gracing ballad-sheet,   *1825*
Which eyes, lived she unmurdered and unsung,
Would never turn though she paced street as bare
As the mad penitent ladies do in France.
My brothers quietly would edge me out
Of use and management of things called mine;   *1830*
Do I command? "You stretched command before!"
Show anger? "Anger little helped you once!"
Advise? "How managed you affairs of old?"
My very mother, all the while they gird,
Turns eye up, gives confirmatory groan;   *1835*
For unsuccess, explain it how you will,
Disqualifies you, makes you doubt yourself,

—Much more, is found decisive by your friends.
Beside, am I not fifty years of age?
1840 What new leap would a life take, checked like mine
I' the spring at outset? Where's my second chance?
Ay, but the babe . . . I had forgot my son,
My heir! Now for a burst of gratitude!
There's some appropriate service to intone,
1845 Some *gaudeamus*° and thanksgiving-psalm!
Old, I renew my youth in him, and poor
Possess a treasure—is not that the phrase?
Only I must wait patient twenty years—
Nourishing all the while, as father ought,
1850 The excrescence with my daily blood of life.
Does it respond to hope, such sacrifice—
Grows the wen plump while I myself grow lean?
Why, here's my son and heir in evidence,
Who stronger, wiser, handsomer than I
1855 By fifty years, relieves me of each load—
Tames my hot horse, carries my heavy gun,
Courts my coy mistress—has his apt advice
On house-economy, expenditure,
And what not. All which good gifts and great growth
1860 Because of my decline, he brings to bear
On Guido, but half apprehensive how
He cumbers earth, crosses the brisk young Count,
Who civilly would thrust him from the scene.
Contrariwise, does the blood-offering fail?
1865 There's an ineptitude, one blank the more
Added to earth in semblance of my child?
Then, this has been a costly piece of work,
My life exchanged for his!—why he, not I,
Enjoy the world, if no more grace accrue?
1870 Dwarf me, what giant have you made of him?
I do not dread the disobedient son:
I know how to suppress rebellion there,
Being not quite the fool my father was.
But grant the medium measure of a man,
1875 The usual compromise 'twixt fool and sage,

1845 **gaudeamus** let us rejoice.

—You know—the tolerably-obstinate,
The not-so-much-perverse but you may train,
The true son-servant that, when parent bids
"Go work, son, in my vineyard!" makes reply
"I go, Sir!"—Why, what profit in your son   *1880*
Beyond the drudges you might subsidize,
Have the same work from, at a paul the head?
Look at those four young precious olive-plants
Reared at Vittiano—not on flesh and blood,
These twenty years, but black bread and sour wine! *1885*
I bade them put forth tender branch, hook, hold,
And hurt three enemies I had in Rome:
They did my hest as unreluctantly,
At promise of a dollar, as a son
Adjured by mumping memories of the past.   *1890*
No, nothing repays youth expended so—
Youth, I say, who am young still: grant but leave
To live my life out, to the last I'd live
And die conceding age no right of youth!
It is the will runs the renewing nerve   *1895*
Through flaccid flesh that faints before the time.
Therefore no sort of use for son have I—
Sick, not of life's feast but of steps to climb
To the house where life prepares her feast—of means
To the end: for make the end attainable   *1900*
Without the means—my relish were like yours.
A man may have an appetite enough
For a whole dish of robins ready cooked,
And yet lack courage to face sleet, pad snow,
And snare sufficiently for supper.

                               Thus   *1905*
The time's arrived when, ancient Roman-like,
I am bound to fall on my own sword: why not
Say—Tuscan-like, more ancient, better still?
Will you hear truth can do no harm nor good?
I think I never was at any time   *1910*
A Christian, as you nickname all the world,
Me among others: truce to nonsense now!
Name me, a primitive religionist—

As should the aboriginary be
1915 I boast myself, Etruscan, Aretine,
One sprung—your frigid Virgil's fieriest word—
From fauns and nymphs, trunks and the heart of oak,
With—for a visible divinity—
The portent of a Jove Aegiochus
1920 Descried 'mid clouds, lightning and thunder, couched
On topmost crag of your Capitoline:
'Tis in the Seventh Aeneid—wat, the Eighth?°
Right—thanks, Abate—though the Christian's dumb,
The Latinist's vivacious in you yet!
1925 I know my grandsire had our tapestry
Marked with the motto, 'neath a certain shield,
Whereto his grandson presently will give gules°
To vary azure. First we fight for faiths,
But get to shake hands at the last of all:
1930 Mine's your faith too—in Jove Aegiochus!
Nor do Greek gods, that serve as supplement,
Jar with the simpler scheme, if understood.
We want such intermediary race
To make communication possible;
1935 The real thing were too lofty, we too low,
Midway hang these: we feel their use so plain
In linking height to depth, that we doff hat
And put no question nor pry narrowly
Into the nature hid behind the names.
1940 We grudge no rite the fancy may demand;
But never, more than needs, invent, refine,
Improve upon requirement, idly wise
Beyond the letter, teaching gods their trade,
Which is to teach us: we'll obey when taught.
1945 Why should we do our duty past the need?
When the sky darkens, Jove is wroth—say prayer!
When the sun shines and Jove is glad—sing psalm!
But wherefore pass prescription and devise
Blood-offering for sweat-service, lend the rod
1950 A pungency through pickle of our own?
Learned Abate—no one teaches you

1916–22**Virgil . . . Eighth** *Aeneid* VIII 314–15; 351–54.   1927 **gules**
red (in heraldry).

What Venus means and who's Apollo here!
I spare you, Cardinal—but, though you wince,
You know me, I know you, and both know that!
So, if Apollo bids us fast, we fast: *1955*
But where does Venus order we stop sense
When Master Pietro rhymes a pleasantry?
Give alms prescribed on Friday: but, hold hand
Because your foe lies prostrate—where's the word
Explicit in the book debars revenge?   *1960*
The rationale of your scheme is just
"Pay toll here, there pursue your pleasure free!"
So do you turn to use the medium-powers,
Mars and Minerva, Bacchus and the rest,
And so are saved propitiating—whom?   *1965*
What all-good, all-wise and all-potent Jove
Vexed by the very sins in man, himself
Made life's necessity when man he made?
Irrational bunglers! So, the living truth
Revealed to strike Pan dead, ducks low at last,   *1970*
Prays leave to hold its own and live good days
Provided it go masque grotesquely, called
Christian not Pagan. Oh, you purged the sky
Of all gods save the One, the great and good,
Clapped hands and triumphed! But the change came
     fast: *1975*
The inexorable need in man for life—
(Life, you may mulct and minish to a grain
Out of the lump, so that the grain but live)
Laughed at your substituting death for life,
And bade you do your worst: which worst was done *1980*
In just that age styled primitive and pure
When Saint this, Saint that, dutifully starved,
Froze, fought with beasts, was beaten and abused
And finally ridded of his flesh by fire:
He kept life-long unspotted from the world!   *1985*
Next age, how goes the game, what mortal gives
His life and emulates Saint that, Saint this?
Men mutter, make excuse or mutiny,
In fine are minded all to leave the new,
Stick to the old—enjoy old liberty,   *1990*

No prejudice in enjoyment, if you please,
To the new profession: sin o' the sly, henceforth!
The law stands though the letter kills: what then?
The spirit saves as unmistakably.
1995 Omniscience sees, Omnipotence could stop,
Omnibenevolence pardons: it must be,
Frown law its fiercest, there's a wink somewhere!

Such was the logic in this head of mine:
I, like the rest, wrote "poison" on my bread,
2000 But broke and ate:—said "Those that use the sword
Shall perish by the same"; then stabbed my foe.
I stand on solid earth, not empty air:
Dislodge me, let your Pope's crook hale me hence!
Not he, nor you! And I so pity both,
2005 I'll make the true charge you want wit to make:
"Count Guido, who reveal our mystery,
And trace all issues to the love of life,
We having life to love and guard, like you,
Why did you put us upon self-defense?
2010 You well knew what prompt password would appease
The sentry's ire when folk infringed his bounds,
And yet kept mouth shut: do you wonder then
If, in mere decency, he shot you dead?
He can't have people play such pranks as yours
2015 Beneath his nose at noonday: you disdained
To give him an excuse before the world
By crying 'I break rule to save our camp!'
Under the old rule, such offense were death;
And you had heard the Pontifex° pronounce
2020 'Since you slay foe and violate the form,
Slaying turns murder, which were sacrifice
Had you, while, say, law-suiting foe to death,
But raised an altar to the Unknown God
Or else the Genius of the Vatican.'
2025 Why then this pother?—all because the Pope,
Doing his duty, cried 'A foreigner,
You scandalize the natives: here at Rome

2019 **Pontifex** high priest of Rome (title taken over by the pope).

Romano vivitur more:° wise men, here,
Put the Church forward and efface themselves.
The fit defense had been—you stamped on wheat,   *2030*
Intending all the time to trample tares—
Were fain extirpate, then, the heretic,
You now find, in your haste was slain a fool:
Nor Pietro, nor Violante, nor your wife
Meant to breed up your babe a Molinist!   *2035*
Whence you are duly contrite. Not one word
Of all this wisdom did you urge: which slip
Death must atone for.' "
                              So, let death atone!
So ends mistake, so end mistakers!—end
Perhaps to recommence—how should I know?   *2040*
Only, be sure, no punishment, no pain
Childish, preposterous, impossible,
But some such fate as Ovid could foresee—
Byblis in fluvium, let the weak soul end
In water, *sed Lycaon in lupum,* but   *2045*
The strong become a wolf for evermore!°
Change that Pompilia to a puny stream
Fit to reflect the daisies on its bank!
Let me turn wolf, be whole, and sate, for once—
Wallow in what is now a wolfishness   *2050*
Coerced too much by the humanity
That's half of me as well! Grow out of man,
Glut the wolf-nature—what remains but grow
Into the man again, be man indeed
And all man? Do I ring the changes right?   *2055*
Deformed, transformed, reformed, informed, con-
        formed!
The honest instinct, pent and crossed through life,
Let surge by death into a visible flow
Of rapture: as the strangled thread of flame
Painfully winds, annoying and annoyed,   *2060*
Malignant and maligned, through stone and ore,
Till earth exclude the stranger: vented once,

2028 **Romano vivitur more** do as the Romans do.   2043–46 **Ovid
. . . evermore** stories in the *Metamorphoses*. The delicate Byblis was
turned into a fountain, the fierce Lycaon into a wolf.

It finds full play, is recognized atop
Some mountain as no such abnormal birth,
2065 Fire for the mount, not streamlet for the vale!
Ay, of the water was that wife of mine—
Be it for good, be it for ill, no run
O' the red thread through that insignificance!
Again, how she is at me with those eyes!
2070 Away with the empty stare! Be holy still,
And stupid ever! Occupy your patch
Of private snow that's somewhere in what world
May now be growing icy round your head,
And aguish at your footprint—freeze not me,
2075 Dare follow not another step I take,
Not with so much as those detested eyes,
No, though they follow but to pray me pause
On the incline, earth's edge that's next to hell!
None of your abnegation of revenge!
2080 Fly at me frank, tug while I tear again!
There's God, go tell Him, testify your worst!
Not she! There was no touch in her of hate:
And it would prove her hell, if I reached mine!
To know I suffered, would still sadden her,
2085 Do what the angels might to make amends!
Therefore there's either no such place as hell,
Or thence shall I be thrust forth, for her sake,
And thereby undergo three hells, not one—
I who, with outlet for escape to Heaven,
2090 Would tarry if such flight allowed my foe
To raise his head, relieved of that firm foot
Had pinned him to the fiery pavement else!
So am I made, "who did not make myself":
(How dared she rob my own lip of the word?)
2095 Beware me in what other world may be!—
Pompilia, who have brought me to this pass!
All I know here, will I say there, and go
Beyond the saying with the deed. Some use
There cannot but be for a mood like mine,
2100 Implacable, persistent in revenge.
She maundered "All is over and at end:
I go my own road, go you where God will!

Forgive you? I forget you!" There's the saint
That takes your taste, you other kind of men!
How you had loved her! Guido wanted skill   *2105*
To value such a woman at her worth!
Properly the instructed criticize
"What's here, you simpleton have tossed to take
Its chance i' the gutter? This a daub, indeed?
Why, 'tis a Raphael that you kicked to rags!"   *2110*
Perhaps so: some prefer the pure design:
Give me my gorge of color, glut of gold
In a glory round the Virgin made for me!
Titian's the man, not Monk Angelico
Who traces you some timid chalky ghost   *2115*
That turns the church into a charnel: ay,
Just such a pencil might depict my wife!
She—since she, also, would not change herself—
Why could not she come in some heart-shaped cloud,
Rainbowed about with riches, royalty   *2120*
Rimming her round, as round the tintless lawn°
Guardingly runs the selvage° cloth of gold?
I would have left the faint fine gauze untouched,
Needle-worked over with its lily and rose,
Let her bleach unmolested in the midst,   *2125*
Chill that selected solitary spot
Of quietude she pleased to think was life.
Purity, pallor grace the lawn no doubt
When there's the costly bordure to unthread
And make again an ingot: but what's grace   *2130*
When you want meat and drink and clothes and fire?
A tale comes to my mind that's apposite—
Possibly true, probably false, a truth
Such as all truths we live by, Cardinal!
'Tis said, a certain ancestor of mine   *2135*
Followed—whoever was the potentate,
To Paynimrie, and in some battle, broke
Through more than due allowance of the foe,
And, risking much his own life, saved the lord's.
Battered and bruised, the Emperor scrambles up,   *2140*

2121 **lawn** fine linen (used for bishop's sleeves). 2122 **selvage** edging.

Rubs his eyes and looks round and sees my sire,
Picks a furze-sprig from out his hauberk-joint,
(Token how near the ground went majesty)
And says "Take this, and if thou get safe home,
2145 Plant the same in thy garden-ground to grow:
Run thence an hour in a straight line, and stop:
Describe a circle round (for central point)
The furze aforesaid, reaching every way
The length of that hour's run: I give it thee—
2150 The central point, to build a castle there,
The space circumjacent, for fit demesne,
The whole to be thy children's heritage—
Whom, for thy sake, bid thou wear furze on cap!"
Those are my arms: we turned the furze a tree
2155 To show more, and the greyhound tied thereto,
Straining to start, means swift and greedy both;
He stands upon a triple mount of gold—
By Jove, then, he's escaping from true gold
And trying to arrive at empty air!
2160 Aha! the fancy never crossed my mind!
My father used to tell me, and subjoin
"As for the castle, that took wings and flew:
The broad lands—why, to traverse them today
Scarce tasks my gouty feet, and in my prime
2165 I doubt not I could stand and spit so far:
But for the furze, boy, fear no lack of that,
So long as fortune leaves one field to grub!
Wherefore, hurra for furze and loyalty!"
What may I mean, where may the lesson lurk?
2170 "Do not bestow on man, by way of gift,
Furze without land for framework—vaunt no grace
Of purity, no furze-sprig of a wife,
To me, i' the thick of battle for my bread,
Without some better dowry—gold will do!"
2175 No better gift than sordid muck? Yes, Sirs!
Many more gifts much better. Give them me!
O those Olimpias bold, those Biancas brave,
That brought a husband power worth Ormuz' wealth!
Cried "Thou being mine, why, what but thine am I?
2180 Be thou to me law, right, wrong, heaven and hell!

Let us blend souls, blent, thou in me, to bid
Two bodies work one pleasure! What are these
Called king, priest, father, mother, stranger, friend?
They fret thee or they frustrate? Give the word—
Be certain they shall frustrate nothing more!   *2185*
And who is this young florid foolishness
That holds thy fortune in his pigmy clutch,
—Being a prince and potency, forsooth!—
He hesitates to let the trifle go?
Let me but seal up eye, sing ear to sleep   *2190*
Sounder than Samson—pounce thou on the prize
Shall slip from off my breast, and down couchside,
And on to floor, and far as my lord's feet—
Where he stands in the shadow with the knife,
Waiting to see what Delilah dares do!   *2195*
Is the youth fair? What is a man to me
Who am thy call-bird?° Twist his neck—my dupe's—
Then take the breast shall turn a breast indeed!"
Such women are there; and they marry whom?
Why, when a man has gone and hanged himself   *2200*
Because of what he calls a wicked wife—
See, if the very turpitude bemoaned
Prove not mere excellence the fool ignores!
His monster is perfection—Circe,° sent
Straight from the sun, with wand the idiot blames   *2205*
As not an honest distaff to spin wool!
O thou Lucrezia,° is it long to wait
Yonder where all the gloom is in a glow
With thy suspected presence?—virgin yet,
Virtuous again, in face of what's to teach—   *2210*
Sin unimagined, unimaginable—
I come to claim my bride—thy Borgia's self
Not half the burning bridegroom I shall be!
Cardinal, take away your crucifix!
Abate, leave my lips alone—they bite!   *2215*
Vainly you try to change what should not change,
And shall not. I have bared, you bathe my heart—

2197 **call-bird** decoy.   2204 **Circe** daughter of the sun-god, sorceress
and temptress of the *Odyssey*.   2207 **Lucrezia** sister and, it was
said, the lover of *Cesare Borgia*.

It grows the stonier for your saving dew!
You steep the substance, you would lubricate,
2220 In waters that but touch to petrify!

You too are petrifactions of a kind:
Move not a muscle that shows mercy. Rave
Another twelve hours, every word were waste!
I thought you would not slay impenitence,
2225 But teased, from men you slew, contrition first—
I thought you had a conscience. Cardinal,
You know I am wronged!—wronged, say, and
    wronged, maintain.
Was this strict inquisition made for blood
When first you showed us scarlet on your back,
2230 Called to the College? Your straightforward way
To your legitimate end—I think it passed
Over a scantling of heads brained, hearts broke,
Lives trodden into dust! How otherwise?
Such was the way o' the world, and so you walked.
2235 Does memory haunt your pillow? Not a whit.
God wills you never pace your garden-path,
One appetizing hour ere dinner-time,
But your intrusion there treads out of life
A universe of happy innocent things:
2240 Feel you remorse about that damsel-fly
Which buzzed so near your mouth and flapped your
    face?
You blotted it from being at a blow:
It was a fly, you were a man, and more,
Lord of created things, so took your course.
2245 Manliness, mind—these are things fit to save,
Fit to brush fly from: why, because I take
My course, must needs the Pope kill me?—kill you!
You! for this instrument, he throws away,
Is strong to serve a master, and were yours
2250 To have and hold and get much good from out!
The Pope who dooms me needs must die next year;
I'll tell you how the chances are supposed
For his successor: first the Chamberlain,
Old San Cesario—Colloredo, next—

Then, one, two, three, four, I refuse to name;   2255
After these, comes Altieri; then come you—
Seventh on the list you come, unless . . . ha, ha,
How can a dead hand give a friend a lift?
Are you the person to despise the help
O' the head shall drop in pannier presently?   2260
So a child seesaws on or kicks away
The fulcrum-stone that's all the sage requires
To fit his lever to and move the world.
Cardinal, I adjure you in God's name,
Save my life, fall at the Pope's feet, set forth   2265
Things your own fashion, not in words like these
Made for a sense like yours who apprehend!
Translate into the Court-conventional
"Count Guido must not die, is innocent!
Fair, be assured! But what an he were foul,   2270
Blood-drenched and murder-crusted head to foot?
Spare one whose death insults the Emperor,
Nay, outrages the Louis you so love!
He has friends who will avenge him; enemies
Who will hate God now with impunity,   2275
Missing the old coercive: would you send
A soul straight to perdition, dying frank
An atheist?" Go and say this, for God's sake!
—Why, you don't think I hope you'll say one word?
Neither shall I persuade you from your stand   2280
Nor you persuade me from my station: take
Your crucifix away, I tell you twice!

Come, I am tired of silence! Pause enough!
You have prayed: I have gone inside my soul
And shut its door behind me: 'tis your torch   2285
Makes the place dark: the darkness let alone
Grows tolerable twilight: one may grope
And get to guess at length and breadth and depth.
What is this fact I feel persuaded of—
This something like a foothold in the sea,   2290
Although Saint Peter's bark scuds, billow-borne,
Leaves me to founder where it flung me first?
Spite of your splashing, I am high and dry!

God takes his own part in each thing He made;
2295 Made for a reason, He conserves his work,
Gives each its proper instinct of defense.
My lamblike wife could neither bark nor bite,
She bleated, bleated, till for pity pure
The village roused up, ran with pole and prong
2300 To the rescue, and behold the wolf's at bay!
Shall he try bleating?—or take turn or two,
Since the wolf owns some kinship with the fox,
And, failing to escape the foe by craft,
Give up attempt, die fighting quietly?
2305 The last bad blow that strikes fire in at eye
And on to brain, and so out, life and all,
How can it but be cheated of a pang
If, fighting quietly, the jaws enjoy
One re-embrace in mid backbone they break,
2310 After their weary work through the foe's flesh?
That's the wolf-nature. Don't mistake my trope!
A Cardinal so qualmish? Eminence,
My fight is figurative, blows i' the air,
Brain-war with powers and principalities,
2315 Spirit-bravado, no real fisticuffs!
I shall not presently, when the knock comes,
Cling to this bench nor claw the hangman's face,
No, trust me! I conceive worse lots than mine.
Whether it be, the old contagious fit
2320 And plague o' the prison have surprised me too,
The appropriate drunkenness of the death-hour
Crept on my sense, kind work o' the wine and
    myrrh°—
I know not—I begin to taste my strength,
Careless, gay even. What's the worth of life?
2325 The Pope's dead now, my murderous old man,
For Tozzi told me so: and you, forsooth—
Why, you don't think, Abate, do your best,
You'll live a year more with that hacking cough
And blotch of crimson where the cheek's a pit?
2330 Tozzi has got you also down in book!

2322 **wine and myrrh** Mark 15:23. Given to deaden pain.

Cardinal, only seventh of seventy near,
Is not one called Albano in the lot?
Go eat your heart, you'll never be a Pope!
Inform me, is it true you left your love,
A Pucci, for promotion in the church?   *2335*
She's more than in the church—in the churchyard!
Plautilla Pucci, your affianced bride,
Has dust now in the eyes that held the love—
And Martinez, suppose they make you Pope,
Stops that with *veto*°—so, enjoy yourself!   *2340*
I see you all reel to the rock, you waves—
Some forthright, some describe a sinuous track,
Some, crested brilliantly, with heads above,
Some in a strangled swirl sunk who knows how,
But all bound whither the main-current sets,   *2345*
Rockward, an end in foam for all of you!
What if I be o'ertaken, pushed to the front
By all you crowding smoother souls behind,
And reach, a minute sooner than was meant,
The boundary whereon I break to mist?   *2350*
Go to! the smoothest safest of you all,
Most perfect and compact wave in my train,
Spite of the blue tranquillity above,
Spite of the breadth before of lapsing peace
Where broods the halcyon and the fish leaps free,   *2355*
Will presently begin to feel the prick
At lazy heart, the push at torpid brain,
Will rock vertiginously in turn, and reel,
And, emulative, rush to death like me.
Later or sooner by a minute then,   *2360*
So much for the untimeliness of death!
And, as regards the manner that offends,
The rude and rough, I count the same for gain.
Be the act harsh and quick! Undoubtedly
The soul's condensed and, twice itself, expands   *2365*
To burst through life, by alternation due,
Into the other state whate'er it prove.
You never know what life means till you die:

2339–40 **Martinez . . . veto** minister of the emperor, who had veto
power over papal elections.

Even throughout life, 'tis death that makes life live,
2370 Gives it whatever the significance.
For see, on your own ground and argument,
Suppose life had no death to fear, how find
A possibility of nobleness
In man, prevented daring any more?
2375 What's love, what's faith without a worst to dread?
Lackluster jewelry! but faith and love
With death behind them bidding do or die—
Put such a foil at back, the sparkle's born!
From out myself how the strange colors come!
2380 Is there a new rule in another world?
Be sure I shall resign myself: as here
I recognized no law I could not see,
There, what I see, I shall acknowledge too:
On earth I never took the Pope for God,
2385 In Heaven I shall scarce take God for the Pope.
Unmanned, remanned: I hold it probable—
With something changeless at the heart of me
To know me by, some nucleus that's myself:
Accretions did it wrong? Away with them—
You soon shall see the use of fire!

2390   Till when,
All that was, is; and must forever be.
Nor is it in me to unhate my hates—
I use up my last strength to strike once more
Old Pietro in the wine-house-gossip-face,
2395 To trample underfoot the whine and wile
Of beast Violante—and I grow one gorge
To loathingly reject Pompilia's pale
Poison my hasty hunger took for food.
A strong tree wants no wreaths about its trunk,
2400 No cloying cups, no sickly sweet of scent,
But sustenance at root, a bucketful.
How else lived that Athenian who died so,
Drinking hot bull's blood, fit for men like me?
I lived and died a man, and take man's chance,
2405 Honest and bold: right will be done to such.

Who are these you have let descend my stair?
Ha, their accursed psalm! Lights at the sill!
Is it "Open" they dare bid you? Treachery!
Sirs, have I spoken one word all this while
Out of the world of words I had to say?   *2410*
Not one word! All was folly—I laughed and mocked!
Sirs, my first true word, all truth and no lie,
Is—save me notwithstanding! Life is all!
I was just stark mad—let the madman live
Pressed by as many chains as you please pile!   *2415*
Don't open! Hold me from them! I am yours,
I am° the Granduke's—no, I am the Pope's!
Abate—Cardinal—Christ—Maria—God, . . .
Pompilia, will you let them murder me?

2417 **am** in jurisdiction.

from *FIFINE AT THE FAIR*

(1872)

AMPHIBIAN°

I

THE fancy I had today,
    Fancy which turned a fear!
I swam far out in the bay,
    Since waves laughed warm and clear.

II

I lay and looked at the sun,   5
    The noon-sun looked at me:
Between us two, no one
    Live creature, that I could see.

III

Yes! There came floating by
    Me, who lay floating too.   10
Such a strange butterfly!
    Creature as dear as new:

Amphibian prologue to *Fifine at the Fair*.

417

IV

Because the membraned wings
So wonderful, so wide,
So sun-suffused, were things
Like soul and naught beside.

V

A handbreadth over head!
All of the sea my own,
It owned the sky instead;
Both of us were alone.

VI

I never shall join its flight,
For, naught buoys flesh in air.
If it touch the sea—good night!
Death sure and swift waits there.

VII

Can the insect feel the better
For watching the uncouth play
Of limbs that slip the fetter,
Pretend as they were not clay?

VIII

Undoubtedly I rejoice
That the air comports so well
With a creature which had the choice
Of the land once. Who can tell?

IX

What if a certain soul
Which early slipped its sheath,

And has for its home the whole
   Of Heaven, thus look beneath,

X

Thus watch one who, in the world,
   Both lives and likes life's way,
Nor wishes the wings unfurled
   That sleep in the worm, they say?   40

XI

But sometimes when the weather
   Is blue, and warm waves tempt
To free oneself of tether,
   And try a life exempt

XII

From worldly noise and dust,   45
   In the sphere which overbrims
With passion and thought—why, just
   Unable to fly, one swims!

XIII

By passion and thought upborne,
   One smiles to oneself—"They fare   50
Scarce better, they need not scorn
   Our sea, who live in the air!"

XIV

Emancipate through passion
   And thought, with sea for sky,
We substitute, in a fashion,   55
   For Heaven—poetry:

XV

Which sea, to all intent,
  Gives flesh such noon-disport
As a finer element
  Affords the spirit-sort.

XVI

Whatever they are, we seem:
  Imagine the thing they know;
All deeds they do, we dream;
  Can Heaven be else but so?

XVII

And meantime, yonder streak
  Meets the horizon's verge;
That is the land, to seek
  If we tire or dread the surge:

XVIII

Land the solid and safe—
  To welcome again (confess!)
When, high and dry, we chafe
  The body, and don the dress.

XIX

Does she look, pity, wonder
  At one who mimics flight,
Swims—Heaven above, sea under,
  Yet always earth in sight?

from ARISTOPHANES' APOLOGY

(1875)

THAMURIS MARCHING°

THAMURIS marching—lyre and song of Thrace—
(Perpend the first, the worst of woes that were
Allotted lyre and song, ye poet-race!)

Thamuris from Oichalia, feasted there   5
By kingly Eurutos of late, now bound
For Dorion at the uprise broad and bare

Of Mount Pangaios (ore with earth enwound
Glittered beneath his footstep)—marching gay
And glad, Thessalia through, came, robed and crowned,

From triumph on to triumph, mid a ray   10
Of early morn—came, saw and knew the spot
Assigned him for his worst of woes, that day.

Thamuris Marching interlude in a long poem, *Aristophanes' Apology*
(ll. 104–80 of conclusion, here renumbered). Thamyris was a mu-
sician of Thrace who challenged the muses to a song contest. When
he was defeated, the muses punished him with blindness and by de-
priving him of song.

Balura—happier while its name was not°—
Met him, but nowise menaced; slipped aside,
15 Obsequious river to pursue its lot

Of solacing the valley—say, some wide
Thick busy human cluster, house and home,
Embanked for peace, or thrift that thanks the tide.

Thamuris, marching, laughed "Each flake of foam"
20 (As sparklingly the ripple raced him by)
"Mocks slower clouds adrift in the blue dome!"

For Autumn was the season; red the sky
Held morn's conclusive signet of the sun
To break the mists up, bid them blaze and die.

25 Morn had the mastery as, one by one
All pomps produced themselves along the tract
From earth's far ending to near Heaven begun.

Was there a ravaged tree? it laughed compact
With gold, a leaf-ball crisp, high-brandished now,
30 Tempting to onset frost which late attacked.

Was there a wizened shrub, a starveling bough,
A fleecy thistle filched from by the wind,
A weed, Pan's trampling hoof would disallow?

Each, with a glory and a rapture twined
35 About it, joined the rush of air and light
And force: the world was of one joyous mind.

Say not the birds flew! they forebore their right—
Swam, reveling onward in the roll of things.
Say not the beasts' mirth bounded! that was flight—

40 How could the creatures leap, no lift of wings?

13 **Balura . . . not** according to legend the river Balyra took its
name from the fact that it was there the blinded Thamyris threw
away (*ballein* in Greek) his lyre.

Such earth's community of purpose, such
The ease of earth's fulfilled imaginings—

So did the near and far appear to touch
I' the moment's transport—that an interchange
Of function, far with near, seemed scarce too much;   *45*

And had the rooted plant aspired to range
With the snake's license, while the insect yearned
To glow fixed as the flower, it were not strange—

No more than if the fluttery treetop turned
To actual music, sang itself aloft;   *50*
Or if the wind, impassioned chantress, earned

The right to soar embodied in some soft
Fine form all fit for cloud-companionship,
And, blissful, once touch beauty chased so oft.

Thamuris, marching, let no fancy slip   *55*
Born of the fiery transport; lyre and song
Were his, to smite with hand and launch from lip—

Peerless recorded, since the list grew long
Of poets (saith Homeros) free to stand
Pedestaled mid the Muses' temple-throng,   *60*

A statued service, laureled, lyre in hand,
(Ay, for we see them)—Thamuris of Thrace
Predominating foremost of the band.

Therefore the morn-ray that enriched his face,
If it gave lambent chill, took flame again   *65*
From flush of pride; he saw, he knew the place.

What wind arrived with all the rhythms from plain,
Hill, dale, and that rough wildwood interspersed?
Compounding these to one consummate strain,

It reached him, music; but his own outburst   *70*

Of victory concluded the account,
And that grew song which was mere music erst.

"Be my Parnassos, thou Pangaian mount!
And turn thee, river, nameless hitherto!
75   Famed shalt thou vie with famed Pieria's fount!°

"Here I await the end of this ado:
Which wins—Earth's poet or the Heavenly Muse." . . .

75 **Pieria's fount** haunt of the Muses.

from PACCHIAROTTO AND HOW HE WORKED IN DIS-TEMPER; WITH OTHER POEMS

(1876)

NATURAL MAGIC

I

ALL I can say is—I saw it!
The room was as bare as your hand.
I locked in the swarth little lady—I swear,
From the head to the foot of her—well, quite as bare!
"No Nautch° shall cheat me," said I, "taking my stand   *5*
At this bolt which I draw!" And this bolt—I with-
   draw it,
And there laughs the lady, not bare, but embowered
With—who knows what verdure, o'erfruited, o'er-
   flowered?
   Impossible! Only—I saw it!

II

   All I can sing is—I feel it!   *10*
This life was as blank as that room;

5 **Nautch** here seems to mean something like gypsy.

425

I let you pass in here. Precaution, indeed?
Walls, ceiling and floor—not a chance for a weed!
Wide opens the entrance: where's cold now, where's
 gloom?
15 No May to sow seed here, no June to reveal it,
Behold you enshrined in these blooms of your bring-
 ing,
These fruits of your bearing—nay, birds of your
 winging!
 A fairy tale! Only—I feel it!

MAGICAL NATURE

I

FLOWER—I never fancied, jewel—I profess you!
 Bright I see and soft I feel the outside of a flower.
Save but glow inside and—jewel, I should guess you,
 Dim to sight and rough to touch: the glory is the
 dower.

II

5 You, forsooth, a flower? Nay, my love, a jewel—
 Jewel at no mercy of a moment in your prime!
Time may fray the flower-face: kind be time or cruel,
 Jewel, from each facet, flash your laugh at time!

NUMPHOLEPTOS°

STILL you stand, still you listen, still you smile!
Still melts your moonbeam through me, white awhile,
Softening, sweetening, till sweet and soft
Increase so round this heart of mine, that oft
I could believe your moonbeam-smile has passed   5
The pallid limit, lies, transformed at last
To sunlight and salvation—warms the soul
It sweetens, softens! Would you pass that goal,
Gain love's birth at the limit's happier verge,
And, where an iridescence lurks, but urge   10
The hesitating pallor on to prime
Of dawn!—true blood-streaked, sun-warmth, action-
        time,
By heart-pulse ripened to a ruddy glow
Of gold above my clay—I scarce should know
From gold's self, thus suffused! For gold means love.   15
What means the sad slow silver smile above
My clay but pity, pardon?—at the best,
But acquiescence that I take my rest,
Contented to be clay, while in your Heaven
The sun reserves love for the Spirit-Seven   20
Companioning God's throne they lamp before,°
—Leaves earth a mute waste only wandered o'er
By that pale soft sweet disempassioned moon
Which smiles me slow forgiveness! Such the boon
I beg? Nay, dear, submit to this—just this   25
Supreme endeavor! As my lips now kiss
Your feet, my arms convulse your shrouding robe,
My eyes, acquainted with the dust, dare probe
Your eyes above for—what, if born, would blind
Mine with redundant bliss, as flash may find   30

Numpholeptos one captured by a nymph.   **20–21 Spirit-Seven** ...
before Revelation 4:5.

The inert nerve, sting awake the palsied limb,
Bid with life's ecstasy sense overbrim
And suck back death in the resurging joy—
Love, the love whole and sole without alloy!

35 Vainly! The promise withers! I employ
Lips, arms, eyes, pray the prayer which finds the
        word,
Make the appeal which must be felt, not heard,
And none the more is changed your calm regard:
Rather, its sweet and soft grow harsh and hard—
40 Forbearance, then repulsion, then disdain.
Avert the rest! I rise, see!—make, again
Once more, the old departure for some track
Untried yet through a world which brings me back
Ever thus fruitlessly to find your feet,
45 To fix your eyes, to pray the soft and sweet
Which smile there—take from his new pilgrimage
Your outcast, once your inmate, and assuage
With love—not placid pardon now—his thirst
For a mere drop from out the ocean erst
50 He drank at! Well, the quest shall be renewed.
Fear nothing! Though I linger, unembued
With any drop, my lips thus close. I go!
So did I leave you, I have found you so,
And doubtlessly, if fated to return,
55 So shall my pleading persevere and earn
Pardon—not love—in that same smile, I learn,
And lose the meaning of, to learn once more,
Vainly!

            What fairy track do I explore?
What magic hall return to, like the gem
60 Centuply-angled o'er a diadem?
You dwell there, hearted; from your midmost home
Rays forth—through that fantastic world I roam
Ever—from center to circumference,
Shaft upon colored shaft: this crimsons thence,
65 That purples out its precinct through the waste.
Surely I had your sanction when I faced,

Fared forth upon that untried yellow ray
Whence I retrack my steps? They end today
Where they began—before your feet, beneath
Your eyes, your smile: the blade is shut in sheath, 70
Fire quenched in flint; irradiation, late
Triumphant through the distance, finds its fate,
Merged in your blank pure soul, alike the source
And tomb of that prismatic glow: divorce
Absolute, all-conclusive! Forth I fared, 75
Treading the lambent flamelet: little cared
If now its flickering took the topaz tint,
If now my dull-caked path gave sulphury hint
Of subterranean rage—no stay nor stint
To yellow, since you sanctioned that I bathe, 80
Burnish me, soul and body, swim and swathe
In yellow license. Here I reek suffused
With crocus, saffron, orange, as I used
With scarlet, purple, every dye o' the bow
Born of the storm-cloud. As before, you show 85
Scarce recognition, no approval, some
Mistrust, more wonder at a man become
Monstrous in garb, nay—flesh disguised as well,
Through his adventure. Whatsoe'er befell,
I followed, whereso'er it wound, that vein 90
You authorized should leave your whiteness, stain
Earth's somber stretch beyond your midmost place
Of vantage—trode that tint whereof the trace
On garb and flesh repel you! Yes, I plead
Your own permission—your command, indeed, 95
That who would worthily retain the love
Must share the knowledge shrined those eyes above,
Go boldly on adventure, break through bounds
O' the quintessential whiteness that surrounds
Your feet, obtain experience of each tinge 100
That bickers forth to broaden out, impinge
Plainer his foot its pathway all distinct
From every other. Ah, the wonder, linked
With fear, as exploration manifests
What agency it was first tipped the crests 105
Of unnamed wildflower, soon protruding grew

Portentous mid the sands, as when his hue
Betrays him and the burrowing snake gleams through;
Till, last . . . but why parade more shame and pain?
110 Are not the proofs upon me? Here again
I pass into your presence, I receive
Your smile of pity, pardon, and I leave . . .
No, not this last of times I leave you, mute,
Submitted to my penance, so my foot
115 May yet again adventure, tread, from source
To issue, one more ray of rays which course
Each other, at your bidding, from the sphere
Silver and sweet, their birthplace, down that drear
Dark of the world—you promise shall return
120 Your pilgrim jeweled as with drops o' the urn
The rainbow paints from, and no smatch° at all
Of ghastliness at edge of some cloud-pall
Heaven cowers before, as earth awaits the fall
O' the bolt and flash of doom. Who trusts your word
125 Tries the adventure: and returns—absurd
As frightful—in that sulphur-steeped disguise
Mocking the priestly cloth-of-gold, sole prize
The arch-heretic was wont to bear away
Until he reached the burning. No, I say:
130 No fresh adventure! No more seeking love
At end of toil, and finding, calm above
My passion, the old statuesque regard,
The sad petrific smile!

          O you—less hard
And hateful than mistaken and obtuse
135 Unreason of a she-intelligence!
You very woman with the pert pretense
To match the male achievement! Like enough!
Ay, you were easy victors, did the rough
Straightway efface itself to smooth, the gruff
140 Grind down and grow a whisper—did man's truth
Subdue, for sake of chivalry and ruth,

121 **smatch** smack, touch or suggestion of something.

Its rapier-edge to suit the bulrush-spear
Womanly falsehood fights with! O that ear
All fact pricks rudely, that thrice-superfine
Feminity of sense, with right divine   *145*
To waive all process, take result stain-free
From out the very muck wherein . . .

                                        Ah me!
The true slave's querulous outbreak! All the rest
Be resignation! Forth at your behest
I fare. Who knows but this—the crimson-quest—   *150*
May deepen to a sunrise, not decay
To that cold sad sweet smile?—which I obey.

ST. MARTIN'S SUMMER°

I

No protesting, dearest!
   Hardly kisses even!
      Don't we both know how it ends?
How the greenest leaf turns serest:
   Bluest outbreak—blankest heaven,   *5*
      Lovers—friends?

II

You would build a mansion,
   I would weave a bower

St. Martin's Summer "Indian Summer."

—Want the heart for enterprise.
10   Walls admit of no expansion:
      Trellis-work may haply flower
      Twice the size.

III

What makes glad Life's Winter?
New buds, old blooms after.
15   Sad the sighing "How suspect
Beams would ere mid-Autumn splinter,
    Rooftree scarce support a rafter,
      Walls lie wrecked?"

IV

You are young, my princess!
20   I am hardly older:
      Yet—I steal a glance behind.
Dare I tell you what convinces
    Timid me that you, if bolder,
      Bold—are blind?

V

25 Where we plan our dwelling
    Glooms a graveyard surely!
      Headstone, footstone moss may drape—
Name, date, violets hide from spelling—
    But, though corpses rot obscurely,
30   Ghosts escape.

VI

Ghosts! O breathing Beauty,
   Give my frank word pardon!
      What if I—somehow, somewhere—
Pledged my soul to endless duty
35   Many a time and oft? Be hard on
      Love—laid there?

VII

Nay, blame grief that's fickle,
  Time that proves a traitor,
    Chance, change, all that purpose warps—
Death who spares to thrust the sickle *40*
  Laid Love low, through flowers which later
    Shroud the corpse!

VIII

And you, my winsome lady,
  Whisper with like frankness!
    Lies nothing buried long ago? *45*
Are yon—which shimmer mid the shady
  Where moss and violet run to rankness—
    Tombs or no?

IX

Who taxes you with murder?
  My hands are clean—or nearly! *50*
    Love being mortal needs must pass.
Repentance? Nothing were absurder.
  Enough: we felt Love's loss severely;
    Though now—alas!

X

Love's corpse lies quiet therefore, *55*
  Only Love's ghost plays truant,
    And warns us have in wholesome awe
Durable mansionry; that's wherefore
  I weave but trellis-work, pursuant
    —Life, to law. *60*

XI

The solid, not the fragile,
  Tempts rain and hail and thunder.

If bower stand firm at Autumn's close,
Beyond my hope—why, boughs were agile;
65   If bower fall flat, we scarce need wonder
Wreathing—rose!

XII

So, truce to the protesting,
So, muffled be the kisses!
For, would we but avow the truth,
70   Sober is genuine joy. No jesting!
Ask else Penelope, Ulysses—
Old in youth!

XIII

For why should ghosts feel angered?
Let all their interference
75   Be faint march-music in the air!
"Up! Join the rear of us the vanguard!
Up, lovers, dead to all appearance,
Laggard pair!"

XIV

The while you clasp me closer,
80   The while I press you deeper,
As safe we chuckle—under breath,
Yet all the slier, the jocoser—
"So, life can boast its day, like leap year,
Stolen from death!"

XV

85   Ah me—the sudden terror!
Hence quick—avaunt, avoid me,
You cheat, the ghostly flesh-disguised!
Nay, all the ghosts in one! Strange error!
So, 'twas Death's self that clipped and coyed me,
90   Loved—and lied!

XVI

Ay, dead loves are the potent!
　Like any cloud they used you,
　　Mere semblance you, but substance they!
Build we no mansion, weave we no tent!
　Mere flesh—their spirit interfused you!　　　*95*
　　Hence, I say!

XVII

All theirs, none yours the glamor!
　Theirs each low word that won me,
　　Soft look that found me Love's, and left
What else but you—the tears and clamor　　　*100*
　That's all your very own! Undone me—
　　Ghost-bereft!

from *JOCOSERIA*

(1883)

WANTING IS—WHAT?

WANTING is—what?
Summer redundant,
Blueness abundant,
—Where is the blot?
Beamy the world, yet a blank all the same,   5
—Framework which waits for a picture to frame:
What of the leafage, what of the flower?
Roses embowering with naught they embower!
Come then, complete incompletion, O comer,
Pant through the blueness, perfect the summer!   10
Breathe but one breath
Rose-beauty above,
And all that was death
Grows life, grows love,
Grows love!   15

from *FERISHTAH'S FANCIES*

(1884)

NOT WITH MY SOUL, LOVE!

Not with my Soul, Love!—bid no Soul like mine
  Lap thee around nor leave the poor Sense room!
Soul—travel-worn, toil-weary—would confine
  Along the Soul, Soul's gains from glow and gloom,
Captures from soarings high and divings deep.   *5*
Spoil-laden Soul, how should such memories sleep?
Take Sense, too—let me love entire and whole—
    Not with my Soul!

Eyes shall meet eyes and find no eyes between,
  Lips feed on lips, no other lips to fear!   *10*
No past, no future—so thine arms but screen
  The present from surprise! not there, 'tis here—
Not then, 'tis now:—back, memories that intrude!
Make, Love, the universe our solitude,
And, over all the rest, oblivion roll—   *15*
    Sense quenching Soul!

EPILOGUE TO *FERISHTAH'S FANCIES*

OH, Love—no, Love! All the noise below, Love,
    Groanings all and moanings—none of Life I lose!
All of Life's a cry just of weariness and woe, Love—
    "Hear at least, thou happy one!" How can I, Love,
        but choose?

5 Only, when I do hear, sudden circle round me
    —Much as when the moon's might frees a space
        from cloud—
Iridescent splendors: gloom—would else confound
    me—
    Barriered off and banished far—bright-edged the
        blackest shroud!

Thronging through the cloud-rift, whose are they, the
    faces
    Faint revealed yet sure divined, the famous ones of
10   old?
"What"—they smile—"our names, our deeds so soon
    erases
    Time upon his tablet where Life's glory lies en-
        rolled?

"Was it for mere fool's-play, make-believe and mum-
    ming,
    So we battled it like men, not boylike sulked or
        whined?
Each of us heard clang God's 'Come!' and each was
15   coming?
    Soldiers all, to forward-face, not sneaks to lag be-
        hind!

"How of the field's fortune? That concerned our
    Leader!
  Led, we struck our stroke nor cared for doings left
    and right:
Each as on his sole head, failer or succeeder,
  Lay the blame or lit the praise: no care for cow-
    ards: fight!"   20

Then the cloud-rift broadens, spanning earth that's
    under
  Wide our world displays its worth, man's strife and
    strife's success:
All the good and beauty, wonder crowning wonder,
  Till my heart and soul applaud perfection, nothing
    less.

Only, at heart's utmost joy and triumph, terror   25
  Sudden turns the blood to ice: a chill wind disen-
    charms
All the late enchantment! What if all be error—
  If the halo irised round my head were, Love, thine
    arms?

from PARLEYINGS WITH CERTAIN PEOPLE OF IMPORTANCE IN THEIR DAY

(1887)

APOLLO AND THE FATES°

Apollo. [*From above.*] FLAME at my footfall, Parnas-
    sus! Apollo,
  Breaking ablaze on thy topmost peak,
Burns thence, down to the depths—dread hollow—
Haunt of the Dire Ones. Haste! They wreak
Wrath on Admetus whose respite I seek.   *5*

The Fates. [*Below. Darkness.*] Dragonwise couched in
    the womb of our Mother,
  Coiled at thy nourishing heart's core, Night!
Dominant Dreads, we, one by the other,
  Deal to each mortal his dole of light
On earth—the upper, the glad, the bright.   *10*

Clotho. Even so: thus from my loaded spindle

Apollo and the Fates prologue to the volume in which it appears.
In an introductory note Browning cites the passage in the Homeric
Hymn to Hermes that says that the Fates will speak truth when fed
honey. References (omitted here) to Aeschylus' *Eumenides* and
Euripides' *Alcestis* refer to Apollo's success in saving the life of
Admetus by getting the Fates drunk.

Plucking a pinch of the fleece, lo, "Birth"
Brays from my bronze lip: life I kindle:
Look, 'tis a man! go, measure on earth
15   The minute thy portion, whatever its worth!

Lachesis. Woe-purfled, weal-pranked°—if it speed, if
    it linger—
Life's substance and show are determined by me,
Who, meting out, mixing with sure thumb and
    finger,
Lead life the due length: is all smoothness and
    glee,
20   All tangle and grief? Take the lot, my decree!

Atropos. —Which I make an end of: the smooth as
    the tangled
My shears cut asunder: each snap shrieks "One
    more
Mortal makes sport for us Moirai who dangled
The puppet grotesquely till earth's solid floor
Proved film he fell through, lost in Naught as be-
25   fore."

Clotho. I spin thee a thread. Live, Admetus! Produce
    him!

Lachesis. Go—brave, wise, good, happy; Now checker
    the thread!
He is slaved for, yet loved by a god. I unloose him
A goddess-sent plague. He has conquered, is
    wed,°
Men crown him, he stands at the height—

Atropos.   He is . . .

30 *Apollo.* [*Entering: Light.*]   "Dead?"
Nay, swart spinsters! So I surprise you
Making and marring the fortunes of Man?
Huddling—no marvel, your enemy eyes you—

---

16 **Woe-purfled, weal-pranked** adorned with grief or prosperity.
28–29 **slaved for . . . wed** Apollo had served Admetus as herdsman
as a punishment from Zeus. Artemis plagued Admetus with serpents
when he neglected his offering to her on his wedding day.

Head by head batlike, blots under the ban
Of daylight earth's blessing since time began! 35

The Fates. Back to thy blessed earth, prying Apollo!
Shaft upon shaft transpierce with thy beams
Earth to the center—spare but this hollow
Hewn out of Night's heart, where our mystery seems
Mewed° from day's malice: wake earth from her dreams! 40

Apollo. Crones, 'tis your dusk selves I startle from slumber:
Day's god deposes you—queens Night-crowned!
—Plying your trade in a world ye encumber,
Fashioning Man's web of life—spun, wound,
Left the length ye allot till a clip strews the ground! 45

Behold I bid truce to your doleful amusement—
Annulled by a sunbeam!

The Fates.   Boy, are not we peers?

Apollo. You with the spindle grant birth: whose inducement
But yours—with the niggardly digits—endears
To mankind chance and change, good and evil?
Your shears . . . 50

Atropos. Ay, mine end the conflict: so much is no fable.
We spin, draw to length, cut asunder: what then?
So it was, and so is, and so shall be: art able
To alter life's law for ephemeral men?

Apollo. Nor able nor willing. To threescore and ten 55

Extend but the years of Admetus! Disaster
O'ertook me, and, banished by Zeus, I became
A servant to one who forbore me though master:
True lovers were we. Discontinue your game,

40 **mewed** sheltered.

Let him live whom I loved, then hate on, all the
60   same!

The Fates. And what if we granted—law-flouter, use-
trampler—
His life at the suit of an upstart? Judge, thou—
Of joy were it fuller, of span because ampler?
For love's sake, not hate's, end Admetus—ay,
now—
65   Not a gray hair on head, nor a wrinkle on brow!

For, boy, 'tis illusion: from thee comes a glimmer
Transforming to beauty life blank at the best.
Withdraw—and how looks life at worst, when to
shimmer
Succeeds the sure shade, and Man's lot frowns—
confessed
Mere blackness chance-brightened? Whereof shall
70   attest

The truth this same mortal, the darling thou stylest,
Whom love would advantage—eke out, day by
day,
A life which 'tis solely thyself reconcilest
Thy friend to endure—life with hope: take away
Hope's gleam from Admetus, he spurns it. For,
75   say—

What's infancy? Ignorance, idleness, mischief:
Youth ripens to arrogance, foolishness, greed:
Age—impotence, churlishness, rancor: call *this*
chief
Of boons for thy loved one? Much rather bid
speed
80   Our function, let live whom thou hatest indeed!

Persuade thee, bright boy-thing! Our eld be instruc-
tive!

Apollo. And certes youth owns the experience of age.

Ye hold then, grave seniors, my beams are produc-
tive
  —They solely—of good that's mere semblance,
engage
Man's eye—gilding evil, Man's true heritage?   85

The Fates. So, even so! From without—at due dis-
tance
  If viewed—set a-sparkle, reflecting thy rays—
Life mimics the sun: but withdraw such assistance,
  The counterfeit goes, the reality stays—
An ice-ball disguised as a fire-orb.

Apollo.   What craze   90

Possesses the fool then whose fancy conceits him
  As happy?

The Fates.   Man happy?

Apollo.   If otherwise—solve
This doubt which besets me! What friend ever
  greets him
  Except with "Live long as the seasons revolve,"
Not "Death to thee straightway"? Your doctrines
  absolve   95
Such hailing from hatred: yet Man should know
  best.
  He talks it, and glibly, as life were a load
Man fain would be rid off: when put to the test,
  He whines "Let it lie, leave me trudging the road
That is rugged so far, but methinks . . ."

The Fates.   Ay, 'tis owed   100

To that glamor of thine, he bethinks him "Once
  past
  The stony, some patch, nay, a smoothness of
  sward
Awaits my tired foot: life turns easy at last"—
  Thy largess so lures him, he looks for reward
Of the labor and sorrow.

105 *Apollo.*   It seems, then—debarred

Of illusion—(I needs must acknowledge the plea)
  Man desponds and despairs. Yet—still further to
    draw
Due profit from counsel—suppose there should be
  Some power in himself, some compensative law
By virtue of which, independently . . .

110 *The Fates.*   Faugh!

Strength hid in the weakling!
                        What bowl-shape hast there,
  Thus laughingly proffered? A gift to our shrine?
Thanks—worsted in argument! Not so? Declare
  Its purpose!

Apollo.   I proffer earth's product, not mine.
115 Taste, try, and approve Man's invention of—WINE!

The Fates. We feeding suck honeycombs.

Apollo.   Sustenance meager!
Such fare breeds the fumes that show all things
    amiss.
Quaff wine—how the spirits rise nimble and eager,
  Unscale the dim eyes! To Man's cup grant one
    kiss
120 Of your lip, then allow—no enchantment like this!

Clotho. Unhook wings, unhood brows! Dost hearken?

Lachesis.   I listen:
  I see—smell the food these fond mortals prefer
    To our feast, the bee's bounty!

Atropos.   The thing leaps! But—glisten
  Its best, I withstand it—unless all concur
In adventure so novel.

Apollo.   Ye drink?
125 *The Fates.*   We demur.

Apollo. Sweet Trine, be indulgent nor scout the con-
        trivance
    Of Man—Bacchus°-prompted! The juice, I up-
        hold,
  Illuminates gloom without sunny connivance,
    Turns fear into hope and makes cowardice
        bold—
  Touching all that is leadlike in life turns it gold!   *130*

The Fates. Faith foolish as false!

Apollo.   But essay it, soft sisters!
    Then mock as ye may. Lift the chalice to lip!
    Good: thou next—and thou! Seems the web, to
        you twisters
    Of life's yarn, so worthless?

Clotho.   Who guessed that one sip
    Would impart such a lightness of limb?

Lachesis.   I could skip   *135*

  In a trice from the pied to the plain in my woof!
    What parts each from either? A hair's breadth,
        no inch.
  Once learn the right method of stepping aloof,
    Though on black next foot falls, firm I fix it, nor
        flinch,
    —Such my trust white succeeds!

Atropos.   One could live—at a pinch!   *140*

Apollo. What beldames? Earth's yield, by Man's skill,
        can effect
    Such a cure of sick sense that ye spy the relation
  Of evil to good? But drink deeper, correct
    Blear sight more convincingly still! Take your
        station
  Beside me, drain dregs! Now for edification!   *145*

127 **Bacchus** god of wine.

Whose gift have ye gulped? Thank not me but my
     brother,
     Blithe Bacchus, our youngest of godships. 'Twas
     he
Found all boons to all men, by one god or other
Already conceded, so judged there must be
150   New guerdon to grace the new advent, you see!

Else how would a claim to Man's homage arise?
     The plan lay arranged of his mixed woe and
     weal,
So disposed—such Zeus' will—with design to make
     wise
     The witless—that false things were mingled with
     real,
Good with bad: such the lot whereto law set the
155   seal.

Now, human of instinct—since Semele's son,
     Yet minded divinely—since fathered by Zeus,
With naught Bacchus tampered, undid not things
     done,
     Owned wisdom anterior, would spare wont and
     use,
160   Yet change—without shock to old rule—introduce.

Regard how your cavern from crag-tip to base
     Frowns sheer, height and depth adamantine,°
     one death!
I rouse with a beam the whole rampart, displace
     No splinter—yet see how my flambeau,° beneath
And above, bids this gem wink, that crystal un-
165   sheath!

Withdraw beam—disclosure once more Night for-
     bids you
     Of spangle and sparkle—Day's chance-gift, sur-
     mised

---

162 **adamantine** impenetrable.   164 **flambeau** torch.

Rock's permanent birthright: my potency rids you
  No longer of darkness, yet light—recognized—
Proves darkness a mask: day lives on though dis-
    guised.   *170*

If Bacchus by wine's aid avail so to fluster
  Your sense, that life's fact grows from adverse
    and thwart
To helpful and kindly by means of a cluster—
  Mere hand-squeeze, earth's nature sublimed by
    Man's art—
Shall Bacchus claim thanks wherein Zeus has no
    part?   *175*

Zeus—wisdom anterior? No, maids, be admonished!
  If morn's touch at base worked such wonders,
    much more
Had noontide in absolute glory astonished
  Your den, filled atop to o'erflowing. I pour
No such mad confusion. 'Tis Man's to explore   *180*

Up and down, inch by inch, with the taper his rea-
    son:
  No torch, it suffices—held deftly and straight.
Eyes, purblind at first, feel their way in due season,
  Accept good with bad, till unseemly debate
Turns concord—despair, acquiescence in fate.   *185*

Who works this but Zeus? Are not instinct and im-
    pulse,
  Not concept and incept his work through Man's
    soul
On Man's sense? Just as wine ere it reach brain
    must brim pulse,
  Zeus' flash stings the mind that speeds body to
    goal,
Bids pause at no part but press on, reach the whole. *190*

For petty and poor is the part ye envisage

When—(quaff away, cummers°!)—ye view, last
   and first,
As evil Man's earthly existence. Come! *Is* age,
   Is infancy—manhood—so uninterspersed
With good—some faint sprinkle?

195 *Clotho.*   I'd speak if I durst.

Apollo. Drafts dregward loose tongue-tie.

Lachesis.   I'd see, did no web
Set eyes somehow winking.

Apollo.   Drains-deep lies their purge
—True collyrium!°

Atropos.   Words, surging at high tide, soon ebb
From starved ears.

Apollo. Drink but down to the source, they resurge.
   Join hands! Yours and yours too! A dance or a
200   dirge?

Chorus. Quashed be our quarrel! Sourly and smilingly,
   Bare and gowned, bleached limbs and browned,
Drive we a dance, three and one, reconcilingly,
   Thanks to the cup where dissension is drowned,
205 Defeat proves triumphant and slavery crowned.

Infancy? What if the rose-streak of morning
   Pale and depart in a passion of tears?
Once to have hoped is no matter for scorning!
   Love once—e'en love's disappointment endears!
210 A minute's success pays the failure of years.

Manhood—the actual? Nay, praise the potential!
   (Bound upon bound, foot it around!)
What *is?* No, what *may* be—sing! that's Man's
   essential!
   (Ramp, tramp, stamp and compound
215 Fancy with fact—the lost secret is found!)

---

192 **cummers** "gossips" (women friends). 198 **collyrium** medicine
for the eyes.

Age? Why, fear ends there: the contest concluded,
   Man *did* live his life, *did* escape from the fray:
Not scratchless but unscathed, he somehow eluded
Each blow fortune dealt him, and conquers today:
Tomorrow—new chance and fresh strength—might
   we say?   220

Laud then Man's life—no defeat but a triumph!
        [*Explosion from the earth's center.*]

Clotho. Ha, loose hands!

Lachesis.   I reel in a swound.

Atropos. Horror yawns under me, while from on high
   —humph!
   Lightnings astound, thunders resound,
   Vault-roof reverberates, groans the ground!   225
                         [*Silence.*]

Apollo. I acknowledge.

The Fates. Hence, trickster! Straight sobered are we!
   The portent assures 'twas our tongue spoke the
   truth,
   Not thine. While the vapor encompassed us three
   We conceived and bore knowledge—a bantling
   uncouth,
   Old brains shudder back from: so—take it, rash
   youth!   230

Lick the lump into shape till a cry comes!

Apollo.   I hear.

The Fates. Dumb music, dead eloquence! Say it, or
   sing!
   What was quickened in us and thee also?

Apollo.   I fear.

The Fates. Half female, half male—go, ambiguous
   thing!
   While we speak—perchance sputter—pick up what
   we fling!   235

Known yet ignored, nor divined nor unguessed,
  Such is Man's law of life. Do we strive to declare
What is ill, what is good in our spinning? Worst,
    best,
    Change hues of a sudden: now here and now
      there
240   Flits the sign which decides: all about yet nowhere.

'Tis willed so—that Man's life be lived, first to last,
  Up and down, through and through—not in
    portions, forsooth,
To pick and to choose from. Our shuttles fly fast,
  Weave living, not life sole and whole: as age—
    youth,
245   So death completes living, shows life in its truth.

Man learningly lives: till death helps him—no lore!
  It is doom and must be. Dost submit?

Apollo.   I assent—
  Concede but Admetus! So much if no more
  Of my prayer grant as peace-pledge! Be gracious
    though, blent,
  Good and ill, love and hate streak your life-gift!

250 *The Fates.*   Content!

Such boon we accord in due measure. Life's term
  We lengthen should any be moved for love's sake
To forego life's fulfillment, renounce in the germ
  Fruit mature—bliss or woe—either infinite. Take
255   Or leave thy friend's lot: on his head be the stake!

Apollo. On mine, grizzly gammers! Admetus, I know
    thee!
  Thou prizest the right these unwittingly give
  Thy subjects to rush, pay obedience they owe thee!
  Importunate one with another they strive
260   For the glory to die that their king may survive.

Friends rush: and who first in all Pherae appears
 But thy father to serve as thy substitute?

Clotho.   Bah!

Apollo. Ye wince? Then his mother, well-stricken in
 years,
Advances her claim——or his wife——

Lachesis.   Tra-la-la!

Apollo. But he spurns the exchange, rather dies!°

Atropos.   Ha, ha, ha! 265
       [*Apollo ascends. Darkness.*]

258–65 **Thy subjects . . . dies** but only his wife is willing and he
accepts her offer.

from ASOLANDO

(1889)

PROLOGUE

"THE Poet's age is sad: for why?
  In youth, the natural world could show
No common object but his eye
  At once involved with alien glow—
His own soul's iris-bow.°   5

"And now a flower is just a flower:
  Man, bird, beast are but beast, bird, man—
Simply themselves, uncinct by dower
  Of dyes which, when life's day began,
Round each in glory ran."   10

Friend, did you need an optic glass,
  Which were your choice? A lens to drape
In ruby, emerald, chrysopras,
  Each object—or reveal its shape
Clear outlined, past escape,   15

The naked very thing?—so clear
  That, when you had the chance to gaze,

---

5 **iris-bow** rainbow. Cf. the "visionary gleam" of Wordsworth's Intimations Ode.

You found its inmost self appear
   Through outer seeming—truth ablaze,
20 Not falsehood's fancy-haze?

How many a year, my Asolo,°
   Since—one step just from sea to land—
I found you, loved yet feared you so—
   For natural objects seemed to stand
25 Palpably fire-clothed! No—

No mastery of mine o'er these!
   Terror with beauty, like the Bush
Burning but unconsumed.° Bend knees,
   Drop eyes to earthward! Language? Tush!
30 Silence 'tis awe decrees.

And now? The lambent flame is—where?
   Lost from the naked world: earth, sky,
Hill, vale, tree, flower—Italia's rare
   O'er-running beauty crowds the eye—
35 But flame? The Bush is bare.

Hill, vale, tree, flower—they stand distinct,
   Nature to know and name. What then?
A Voice spoke thence which straight unlinked
   Fancy from fact: see, all's in ken:
40 Has once my eyelid winked?

No, for the purged ear apprehends
   Earth's import, not the eye late dazed:
The Voice said "Call my works thy friends!
   At Nature dost thou shrink amazed?
45 God is it who transcends."

21 **Asolo** city in northern Italy   27–28 **the Bush . . . unconsumed**
Exodus 3:2.

FLUTE MUSIC, WITH AN ACCOMPANIMENT

He. Ah, the bird-like fluting
    Through the ash-tops yonder—
Bullfinch-bubblings, soft sounds suiting
    What sweet thoughts, I wonder?
Fine-pearled notes that surely   *5*
    Gather, dewdrop-fashion,
Deep-down in some heart which purely
    Secretes globuled passion—
Passion insuppressive—
    Such is piped, for certain;   *10*
Love, no doubt, nay, love excessive
    'Tis, your ash-tops curtain.

Would your ash-tops open
    We might spy the player—
Seek and find some sense which no pen   *15*
    Yet from singer, sayer,
Ever has extracted:
    Never, to my knowledge,
Yet has pedantry enacted
    That, in Cupid's College,   *20*
Just this variation
    Of the old old yearning
Should by plain speech have salvation,
    Yield new men new learning.

"Love!" but what love, nicely   *25*
    New from old disparted,
Would the player teach precisely?
    First of all, he started
In my brain Assurance—
    Trust—entire Contentment—   *30*
Passion proved by much endurance;

Then came—not resentment,
No, but simply Sorrow:
What was seen had vanished:
35 Yesterday so blue! Tomorrow
Blank, all sunshine banished.

Hark! 'Tis Hope resurges,
Struggling through obstruction—
Forces a poor smile which verges
40   On Joy's introduction.
Now, perhaps, mere Musing:
"Holds earth such a wonder?
Fairy-mortal, soul-sense-fusing
Past thought's power to sunder!"
45 What? calm Acquiescence?
"Daisied turf gives room to
Trefoil, plucked once in her presence—
Growing by her tomb too!"

She. All's your fancy-spinning!
50   Here's the fact: a neighbor
Never-ending, still beginning,
Recreates his labor:
Deep o'er desk he drudges,
Adds, divides, subtracts and
55 Multiplies, until he judges
Noonday-hour's exact sand
Shows the hourglass emptied:
Then comes lawful leisure,
Minutes rare from toil exempted,
60   Fit to spend in pleasure.

Out then with—what treatise?
Youth's Complete Instructor-
How to play the Flute. Quid petis?°
Follow Youth's conductor
65 On and on, through *Easy,*
Up to *Harder, Hardest*

63 **Quid petis?** what do you want?

Flute-piece, till thou, flautist wheezy,
  Possibly discardest
Tootlings hoarse and husky,
  Mayst expend with courage   70
Breath—on tunes once bright now dusky—
  Meant to cool thy porridge.

That's an air of Tulou's
  He maltreats persistent,
Till as lief I'd hear some Zulu's   75
  Bone-piped bag, breath-distent,
Madden native dances.
  I'm the man's familiar:
Unexpectedness enhances
  What your ear's auxiliar   80
—Fancy—finds suggestive.
  Listen! That's *legato*
Rightly played, his fingers restive
  Touch as if *staccato.*°

He. Ah, you trick-betrayer!   85
  Telling tales, unwise one?
So the secret of the player
  Was—he could surprise one
Well-nigh into trusting
  Here was a musician   90
Skilled consummately, yet lusting
  Through no vile ambition
After making captive
  All the world—rewarded
Amply by one stranger's rapture,   95
  Common praise discarded.

So, without assistance
  Such as music rightly
Needs and claims—defying distance,
  Overleaping lightly   100

82–84 **legato . . . staccato** musical terms referring to pasages played, respectively, without a break between notes and with a pronounced break.

Obstacles which hinder—
He, for my approval,
All the same and all the kinder
Made mine what might move all
105   Earth to kneel adoring:
Took—while he piped Gounod's
Bit of passionate imploring—
Me for Juliet:° who knows?

No! as you explain things,
110   All's mere repetition,
Practice-pother: of all vain things
Why waste pooh or pish on
Toilsome effort—never
Ending, still beginning—
115   After what should pay endeavor
—Right-performance? winning
Weariness from you who,
Ready to admire some
Owl's fresh hooting—Tu-whit, tu-who—
120   Find stale thrush-songs tiresome.

She. Songs, Spring thought perfection,
Summer criticizes:
What in May escaped detection,
August, past surprises,
125   Notes, and names each blunder.
You, the just-initiate,
Praise to heart's content (what wonder?)
Tootings I hear vitiate
Romeo's serenading—
130   I who, times full twenty,
Turned to ice—no ash-tops aiding—
At his *caldamente.*°

So, 'twas distance altered
Sharps to flats? The missing
135   Bar when syncopation faltered

106–8 **Gounod's ... Juliet** Charles Gounod's opera based on Shakespeare's play. 132 **caldamente** with warmth (musical term).

(You thought—paused for kissing!)
Ash-tops too felonious
    Intercepted? Rather
Say—they well-nigh made euphonious
    Discord, helped to gather   *140*
Phrase, by phrase, turn patches
    Into simulated
Unity which botching matches—
    Scraps redintegrated.

He. Sweet, are you suggestive   *145*
    Of an old suspicion
Which has always found me restive
    To its admonition
When it ventured whisper
    "Fool, the strifes and struggles   *150*
Of your trembler—blusher—lisper
    Were so many juggles,
Tricks tried—oh, so often!—
    Which once more do duty,
Find again a heart to soften,   *155*
    Soul to snare with beauty."

Birth-blush of the briar-rose,
    Mist-bloom of the hedge-sloe,
Someone gains the prize: admire rose
    Would he, when noon's wedge—slow—   *160*
Sure, has pushed, expanded
    Rathe pink to raw redness?
Would he covet sloe when sanded
    By road-dust to deadness?
So—restore their value!   *165*
    Ply a water-sprinkle!
Then guess sloe is fingered, shall you?
    Find in rose a wrinkle?

Here what played Aquarius?°
    Distance—ash-tops aiding,   *170*

169 **Aquarius** constellation "water carrier," associated with rainy
weather.

Reconciled scraps else contrarious,
  Brightened stuff fast fading.
Distance—call your shyness:
  Was the fair one peevish?
175 Coyness softened out of slyness.
  Was she cunning, thievish,
All-but-proved impostor?
  Bear but one day's exile,
Ugly traits were wholly lost or
180   Screened by fancies flexile—

Ash-tops these, you take me?
  Fancies' interference
Changed . . .
          But since I sleep, don't wake me!
  What if all's appearance?
185 Is not outside seeming
  Real as substance inside?
Both are facts, so leave me dreaming:
  If who loses wins I'd
Ever lose—conjecture,
190   From one phrase trilled deftly,
All the piece. So, end your lecture
  Let who lied be left lie!